The Last Goodbye

JOHN FRATANGELO

PAGE PUBLISHING, INC.
Conneaut Lake, PA

First originally published by Page Publishing 2020

Cover illustration by Karen Mazzoline

ISBN 978-1-64628-139-8 (pbk)
ISBN 978-1-64628-140-4 (digital)

Printed in the United States of America

LEGACY

What you are about to read in this book is my story. There are hundreds of thousands of you men and women who each have a story to be told. I urge all of you to tell it. Your children and grandchildren need and deserve to know. Some of you may not think so, but your family and friends truly want to hear your story and you need to tell them. Do not leave this world keeping them in the dark, wondering and wishing that you would have shared your legacy with them. Think about it.

ACKNOWLEDGEMENTS

I would like to give a special and everlasting thanks to all the medics, comrades, doctors, nurses, aides, and priests who devotedly took part in the saving of my life and the healing of my physical and mental wounds. For this I am eternally grateful. You will never be forgotten. May God bless you all, wherever you may be.

I would also like to thank my wonderful wife and children for pushing me to finish this book. If it weren't for them, my story would have never been told.

PREFACE

This book is not intended as an autobiography. The author simply relates his personal experiences to tell of what an individual encounters for two years in the military service. He wishes to make aware to those who have never served in the military of how a man feels and what he thinks during his stay in service; of how combat is the hardest job in the world and of its physical and mental strains and its long-lasting effects on men and women; to show the horror and hazards of war, not only actual combat but also the everyday struggles with disease, insects, thirst and hunger, and climate changes and how a man regresses from society to becoming one step above being an animal.

He chose to use the actual names of the men he knew throughout his time spent in the service. He feels that they deserve to be remembered and spoken of; for they were not like movie stars, famous politicians, or historians; rather, they were the multitude of unknowns who gave their all and whatever it took so that all back home could have a land to continue to roam free and have the opportunity to live in the greatest country in the world.

He wishes to dedicate this book to all those men and women who served in the armed forces, particularly to those who fought and endured in the jungles of Vietnam and to those who gave their lives, especially Tony, his cousin.

"So those who can remember will remember."

"Tony, this one's for you."

INTRODUCTION

The drive from my home in the Bronx to the cemetery did not take too long, and I would make the trip as often as I could. A strange feeling always came over me as I drove through the iron gates of Saint Raymond's Cemetery and up the narrow roadways that separated the many sections of burial grounds. I felt as if I were entering a private world, one of peace and serenity—a world that seemed to not want to be interrupted by the boisterous disturbances caused by the living. I knew I was on hallowed grounds that deserved the uttermost respect, so I turned off the radio of my car. As I passed by all the headstones, I couldn't help but think that all these people who once roamed the earth did all the things that I do and that this was only a tiny morsel of the dead throughout the world. When I drove passed the large mausoleums, I knew I was getting close to my destination. At the road's end, I encircled a small island of flowers, which allowed one to drive around and back out.

I stopped my car halfway around the circle and reached over and grabbed hold of the Christmas wreath that I had purchased before entering the cemetery, along with a piece of twine. I got out of my car and slowly walked the fifty-foot concrete pathway that led to a large wall that was home to those who once were and who had chosen this site as their final resting place.

The huge monument that stood towering before me was sectioned off by rows of square marble slabs, each containing the names and dates of those it held within. I stood before the one slab that held my cousin and best friend, Tony. It was at eye level, so I was able to reach it easily and place the wreath on the tiny stainless-steel cross that separated his first and last name. I secured it with the piece of rope then stood back and stared solemnly as I placed my right hand to my mouth, kissed the tips of my fingers, reached out, and ever so gently made the sign of the cross on the silver-coated lettering that spelled out his name and the dates of his birth and death: "Anthony Rutigliano 1947–1967."

The slab at Tony's right side held the remains of John Rotonelli, another who had met a similar and premature death in a far and distant land. The two had been friends during life and now lay side by side as eternal companions.

The chill autumn wind that whistled around the corner of the structure caused my eyes to tear up and blurred my vision. I continued to gaze at the wreath, hoping that it would bring Tony comfort and warmth and a reminder of all the wonderful Christmases we had spent together. As I continued to gaze through the opening of the wreath at Tony's name, I was mesmerized as one is when one stares into the flames of a fire; but what stood out mostly and pierced my heart deeply were the three words under his name and John's. Words that reminded all those who read them of a tragic event, a drama that, for myself and half a million other men and women, would burn in our memories forever: "DIED IN VIETNAM."

CHAPTER I

THE PREMONITION

It was Thanksgiving Day back in November of 1965. We spent the holiday at Tony's house on 187th Street and Valentine Avenue in the Bronx. It was the first time we celebrated any holiday away from my house; but that didn't matter, we were still together as always. I couldn't imagine any holiday without Tony. We had just finished eating a typical Italian dinner. If you could think of it, it was there on the table to eat. By the time dessert was served, it was a must to lean back in your seat, suck in your stomach, and undo your belt buckle.

After dinner, Tony and I decided to go for a ride. We had both turned eighteen that year: Tony on February 17 and me on September 1. We got our driver's licenses. He had bought a light-blue 1963 Pontiac Lemans that past summer of which he was so proud and happy to have. He truly earned it. He was the firstborn; and at the age of just thirteen, to help his parents pay their bills and raise his two brothers and three sisters, he had gotten a job at the marketplace on Arthur Avenue as a delivery boy using a bicycle that had a large basket attached to its handlebars to hold the groceries. Soon afterward, he worked as a butcher at Petrillo's Meat Market on 187 Street by Third Avenue, known as the Little Italy section of the Bronx. He gave his mother most of his salary and saved the rest so he'd be able to buy a car someday. Tony was a terrific human being, a quiet and gentle soul who seldom cursed or got angry.

We cruised down Webster Avenue and throughout the neighborhood and headed toward Fordham Road. It being Thanksgiving, the streets were quiet and desolate; there was hardly any traffic and not many pedestrians, especially girls, of which we were mainly looking for. We talked and listened to the radio, which seemed to broadcast nothing but news, mainly about Vietnam. We couldn't help but to speak about Nam, for we both knew that we were probably destined to be there very soon. I took it lightly, the thought of where we might soon be, but then I took most anything lightly.

Tony, however, had a different perception of what the near future had in store for us; and when I asked him what he felt like doing, he answered with a remark that, till this day, remains fresh in my mind. He said, "Let's go home, Johnny. I have a feeling that this is going to be the last Thanksgiving we'll be spending with our families."

I answered him by saying, "Okay, Tony, if that's what you want, let's go home." It was not only the words he spoke which live on in me but also the way he said them. It was as if he had a premonition and a vision of what lay ahead of him, and I heard it in his tone. There was a foretelling sadness in his words. From then on, Tony was never the same. Whenever we got together, his mind seemed to be constantly preoccupied.

The months went by, and the fighting in Vietnam grew worse. Tony turned nineteen in February of 1966, and in September of that year (when I turned nineteen), he received his draft notice, which had in it a single subway token and said that he was to report to the Army induction center down on White Hall Street in Manhattan two weeks from the date of the letter. This was not good news at all. I knew that I was next, but Tony was six months older than me; so I figured that I had that much more time before I received my one-way ticket. Some of us cousins figured that before Tony was to leave, we would get together and have a few drinks; we set it up for the following Saturday night. We went to a small cozy club in Throggs Neck in the Bronx. It was dark inside the place, and we sat at the bar and talked while we drank. Tony was very quiet. I could see his reflection in the mirror and watched him stare into it the entire night. He barely spoke at all. He just played with his car keys in his hand and sat silently in deep thought.

The night before his departure, I attended his farewell party. It was at his home, and it was not a happy time for any of us. Tony went into his room and stayed alone for quite some time. When he came out, I could see his eyes were red and bloodshot.

At the party's end, the final farewells began. I watched with tears in my eyes as each of his siblings, one by one, went to hold him; then all the others did the same. It was a very touching moment. I waited for the last person to say goodbye then walked over to Tony and shook his hand. Our eyes met momentarily, then we wrapped our arms around each other and tightly embraced. It was the last time that I would see Tony…or was it?

The time frame between Tony's letter and mine was not as I anticipated. I came home from work one day in late October to find my notice waiting to greet me, token and all. I, too, had been drafted into the United States Army and had to report to White Hall Street on November 16, right on my mother's birthday and just eleven days before Thanksgiving. Tony's words from the year before flashed through my head.

I had been working for a very good friend of mine's father, Joe Trongone. He was a large man, weighed 360 pounds, was about six foot two, and was a very funny guy. He had an oil-burner business. I started working for him right after I graduated high school in 1965. It was only the two of us. I was well schooled in mechanical skills due to the fact that Tony and I built things from junk we'd find in the neighborhood lots when we were kids. But Joe taught me so much in that short period that helped my skills in plumbing, carpentry, electrical, and masonry. His son Joe and I grew up together and went to the same elementary school, P. S.78. He played the guitar and was very good at it. I was a drummer, and we played in a band together. We played pro by the time we were thirteen and had to be driven to our gigs by our parents. I started playing the drums at the age of four and played all through elementary school, John Phillip Sousa Junior

High School, and De Witt Clinton High School—all located in the Bronx. I performed in all the stage and musical shows held in all the schools.

I remember when I was four years old. We were living in the southeast section of the Bronx on Bronx River Avenue between Westchester Avenue and 174th Street in a two-story, four-family apartment building. I was sitting on the front stoop with my friend Richie Tessara, who was two years older than me. He had a red-and-blue metal drum that we were beating on. A teenager named Pete, who lived in our building stopped and listened to me play a march on the drum. He told me to wait there, and he entered the apartment. He came back out in a few minutes, and he had a pair of fat wooden drumsticks in his hand. He gave them to me and told me to keep them. He said that I was very good and to keep on playing. I guess I wisely took his advice.

I got my first car when I turned eighteen. It was a 1957 Buick Special for which I paid fifteen dollars. Joe, my boss, told me to take the rest of the time off before I had to leave for the Army. "Spend all the time you can with your family and girlfriend," he said.

My girl, Marilyn (whom I had met back in March at a club we played at called the Airways located in City Island), was five foot seven and quite pretty with long dark-brown hair reaching to her waist. She had round brown eyes and sported a set of 40 Ds. She turned heads wherever we went. I spent every possible minute with her. I even drove her to her job in Midtown Manhattan and picked her up every day.

I never had much of a social life. Practicing the drums daily and rehearsing with the band once a week then playing on weekends plus school work took up most of my time. Aside from all that, I had been a bodybuilder since I was thirteen and worked out three hours a day. To make socializing even harder, De Witt Clinton was an all-boys school with over six thousand guys attending split sessions. On the ride home, the bus would pass by Evander Childs High School, which was coed and the school Joe attended. I would gaze out of the window and drool with my tongue hanging down to the floor at the sight of all the beauties walking by. Let's face it, when you're a teen-ager, your hormones are jetting sky high; and three years of looking at male mugs could make you nuts. And now I was about to enter the Army for two years, which was embodied by all men; so when I met Marilyn, I wanted to hold on to her.

I had another good friend named Armando Rizzo. He was known as Junior. He lived on the same street as me but one block up. He was eight years my senior, and we became very close friends. He was very instrumental to me meeting Marilyn. One Saturday night back in March of 1966, I had just finished a heavy three-hour work-out at home alone. I never liked going to gyms—too much bullshit. I took my workouts very seriously. No matter where I was, when three o'clock rolled around, I stopped whatever I was doing and went home to train. I decided to go and visit Junior. He was always part of an older crowd, so we were never very close friends. I would see him walking by, and it was just a wave of hello or "How yah doin'?" He was Italian, and in his prime, he was slender and athletic. He was a heartthrob for my sister's generation. He loved playing baseball and was very good at it. He almost went pro, but he had gained a lot of weight. He wasn't what you would call fat. I guess plump would be a better word. He was an only child and mostly stayed cooped up in his house. Except for my friendship, he basically shut out all others. His idea of a good time was watching TV and drinking beer, quite a far cry from his yesteryears.

Junior's life changed drastically because of a girl. Her name was Pat. She lived just a few houses down from him. He was crazy about her. They had been dating for years and never left each other's side. She was a very pretty girl, of what I remember of her. I'd see them many times walking around the neighborhood, always hand in hand and very happy. But her family decided to move to California. Junior's heart was torn in two. He just gave up on life, never put a baseball mitt on again. Didn't even work. He sat home day after day and wasted away drinking and gaining weight. He even started smoking. His highlight in life, whenever he left his safe haven, was to visit me or hang out in the bar on Gun Hill Road across from my house. He began to have heart trouble and was on medication along with antidepressants. He was advised by his doctor to stop the drinking and smoking and to become more active; therefore, his knowing me was a good thing. I never drank excessively or smoked at all. I was always into health and exercise. He started to train with me and began to feel much better.

When I got to his house that Saturday evening, he was alone. His parents had gone to a wedding. I asked him if he wanted to go out. "No," he answered, "my folks are out, so I'd better stay home."

"Junior," I said, "come on, man. You're twenty-six years old. Let's go. Go and get changed, and we'll head to Fordham."

He finally agreed and started to walk up the steps from his living room. He suddenly stopped halfway up the staircase and headed back down and said, "Nah, I'd better not."

"Will you stop fuckin' around and go and get ready?" I yelled at him.

"All right," he retorted and proceeded back up the stairs.

After his lollygagging getting ready, which took forever, we finally left; but before we departed, Junior had to look out of his rear window that faced the driveway behind his house to sneak a peek at his Cadillac parked just below his kitchen window. He said, "Look, there's my baby with just a thin layer of dust on it. You have to keep it a little dirty so that people will think that you're in the mob." We drove in my car to Fordham. There was a bar on Webster Avenue that he knew, so we stopped in there. It was dead, so we had one drink and left. We headed out to City Island to the Airways, a club that my band played at occasionally. We sat at a table and scoped out the place. It was very crowded. I spotted Marilyn dancing with a blond girl. I turned to Junior and nodded to see what he thought about Marilyn. He told me to go for it. I walked over and cut in. She was wearing a tight pink outfit. Her hair was teased up high with the rest of it in a long ponytail that reached to the middle of her back. She looked good. We danced the next dance to a song sung by Frank Sinatra and his daughter Nancy, "Strangers in the Night." It seemed so appropriate. Junior looked over and gave me the thumbs-up. Marilyn and her girlfriend Dianne joined us at our table.

A couple of my cousins happened to be there: Freddy and Patty Fusco. They lived right nearby in City Island along with eight other brothers and two sisters. Freddy pulled me aside and tried to warn me about Marilyn. He told me that they knew of her and that she'd been around the block a few times and to be careful and not to get serious with her and that she was nothing but a good piece of ass. I thanked him for the input, but I wanted to find out for myself. I knew that people had a tendency to say things about others without having proof or out of just plain jealousy. She seemed nice enough to me, and I wanted to give her the benefit of the doubt. I wasn't looking to get serious with her. I was just out to have a good time; besides, I had a crush on a girl that lived three houses down from me. Her name was Sandra. She had moved into the neighborhood a year earlier and was two years younger than me. When you're a teenager, a couple of years makes a big difference. I really liked her a lot. She was young and real sexy and had a great body. There wasn't anything I wouldn't do for her. I'd drive her to school and pick her up in the afternoon or take her anywhere that she wanted to go. She had a boyfriend, but I didn't care. We made out a bunch of times.

One night my cousin Tony and I went to Arthur Murray's dance studio located on Fordham Road, near the Grand Concourse. My band played there on separate occasions. The place was jam-packed with younger teenagers. Sandra was there; and when she saw me, she came running into my arms, screaming out my name, "Johnny!" Man, did that feel good—to have the girl you cared so much about wrap her arms around you. "Come on," I said, "We'll take you home." Tony drove; and Sandra and I sat in the back seat, making out. That was a great night.

That Easter, I bought Sandra a live rabbit and put it in an Easter basket along with all sorts of goodies. Her face lit up when she unwrapped the purple cellophane and saw a live bunny staring up and wiggling its nose. She said, "I'll name him Johnny." To say the least, I had to build a rabbit coop to house her new pet. I don't think

Rocky, her father, was happy about the little critter; but he liked me, so he was willing to deal with it. He just told me that the bunny was cute but he was tired of finding little rabbit pellets of shit all around the house. Rocky owned a candy store on Crotona Avenue and 187th Street. Sandra's older sister Carol and younger brother Frank would go along with Sandra and stay there most of the day. I always waited anxiously for her to come home, which, many times, was very late at night. I was relieved when I knew she was home safe and sound. I knew she liked me and the way I looked from all the years of weight training; and when she named her rabbit after me instead of her boyfriend, George, I felt very special. I thought she was the girl for me and waited for her to get older.

Jr. and I drove Marilyn and Dianne home, and I got Marilyn's phone number. I continued to date her. She seemed more mature than Sandra, more like a woman instead of a girl. There's a big difference between the two. She was one and a half years older than me. She had just turned twenty-one on March 17, Saint Patrick's Day. We dated steadily, and the rest was history.

After I dropped Junior off, I went home on cloud nine due to the happy events the evening had brought my way. I lay in bed thinking about the girl I had just met, but my thoughts were mainly on Tony and how he was doing. He had been sent to Fort Gordon, Georgia, for his basic training. We had been through so many childhood adventures together. For you to understand, I'd have to go back to where it all began.

During WWII, the prime minister of Italy, Benito Mussolini, initiated a baby boom in his country. My mother's mother, Laura, gave birth to twenty-one children. They lived on a farm in Bari, Italy. She was given a trip to Rome by Mussolini himself for having so many kids. To look at her, you would never think it possible. She stood under five feet tall and was pudgy. She told me that she never cut her hair. It was worn tied in a bun; and when she let it out to brush it, it touched the floor. She was such a sweetheart. I only remember a little about my grandfather, Frank. I was four, and I recall he had a wooden leg. It was noticeable when he sat down because I was able to see part of it showing above his sock. Once, I saw the whole leg, leaning against the corner of the wall, with the straps hanging down. He would kid with me and grab me by the neck with his wooden cane whenever I walked passed him. He also showed me how to make Indian tepees out of a deck of cards. The two of them had been living in America.

Five of their children died as infants, under two years of age. Of those that lived longer, there were nine boys and seven girls. However, believe it or not, there were three Mikes and three Steves. When one Mike died, the next born male was renamed Mike. It happened three times. Ditto with the Steves.

On Halloween Day in 1952, my parents bought a house on Bouck Avenue, off Gun Hill Road, in the northeast section of the Bronx. My mother, Sophie (who was the eldest of the girls), wanted to bring the rest of her family to America. She and my father paid for their visas and passageway. Having the house gave us the room to put them up temporarily until they all got on their feet.

Tony and his family came from Italy when he was six years old via ocean liner across the Atlantic in the summer of 1953. His mother, Catherine, was one of my mother's sisters; and his father, Frank (whom we called Chi Chi), had six children: Tony, Teresa, Franky, Laura, Joey, and Anna. From that day forward in July, Tony and I were inseparable.

Along with them came another one of my mother's sisters, Tina, and her husband, Pete, whom we called Petrooch. They had seven children: Tony, Teresa, Franky, Laura, Pasquale, Jacky, and John, who we referred to as Joowhan.

Another of the sisters, Angelina, and her husband, Ralph (known to us as Yooch), came with their two kids: Tony and Franky. Yooch would entertain us by playing Italian melodies on his accordion. My father would accompany him on his guitar. We really had great times. With all the laughter and noise, we never had one complaint from any neighbors.

One other sister, Anna, stayed in Italy with her husband and their three kids to take care of the farm and are still there. My mother's two youngest sisters, Mary and Antoniette, came to the United States with their parents and lived with them in an apartment on 157th Street and Courtland Avenue. They were teenagers.

I hope you are getting all this. Now, one of my mother's brothers, Patsy (no nickname), went to Italy to marry the wife of his deceased brother Mike, who died in his late twenties. Her name was Lonnina, and she had a daughter with Mike named Laura. Patsy brought them to America; and they later had three more children of their own: Clara, Fran, and Paul. An interesting fact about my uncle Patsy and well worth mentioning is that he fought in the Italian Army in WWII and was captured by the Germans and remained a prisoner of war for twenty-two months, which was the cause of him walking with a limp for the rest of his life. They hadn't heard anything from him all those months, so they all thought he was dead. When he was finally freed and went home, my grandmother fainted when he showed up at the front door of their farmhouse.

Jack, whom we called Mimi, was single at that time. He came to our country a short time later and joined the clan. He later met his wife Teresa and had three sons, Frank, Rocco and John. My mother's oldest brother, John (who was nicknamed Turk) was married to Fanny. They had four children: Lauretta, Franky, Mella, and Lucien. They lived on Webster Avenue.

When they all got here, one family stayed in our basement, another was in the living room, and another on the top floor. It was quite crowded. We even had to use the furniture drawers as beds for the toddlers to sleep in. It wasn't a large house. It had three bedrooms on the upper floor with one bathroom and a small kitchen, which, till this day, I don't know how my mother managed to cook for all those people. The open area in the basement was used for a bedroom. It had a sink, a stove, and a washing machine. There was a tiny bathroom with a shower stall but no washbasin. It had a small backyard that was big enough for all of us to enjoy for parties, BBQs, and song and dance. It may have been overpopulated, but we all got along so well. No one ever argued. Everyone chipped in to help. Those of us who were old enough to attend school went to P. S. 78. They only spoke Italian but were eager to learn English. All said and done, I would give anything to have those days back again.

It wasn't long before they moved into their own apartments. My father, John, also known by all as Johnny Legs was a crane operator and worked in Bronx Iron and Metals, a scrap-iron yard in Hunts Point down in the South Bronx. It was there where he got Chi Chi and Mimi a job as yardmen. Petrooch worked as a laborer for a concrete company. Yooch got a job in a beauty supply factory. My mother's two younger sisters, Mary, married her first cousin, John Fusco, and had four children, Maria, Lauretta, Angela, and John. Antonietta married John Attanasio and had three girls, Emily, Lisa, and Lauretta.

One by one, they all moved out on their own. They got apartments near to one another on Webster Avenue. I guess you can now see why it was necessary for us to have nicknames for everybody. Oh! By the way, they called me Johnny Boy.

Our house always had relatives staying with us or visiting. Of my father's siblings, only two of his sisters had children. Mary married Al Davis, and they had five children, Nora, Joseph, John, Timothy, and Susan. Grace married Frank Cafaro and had two children, Albert and Mary. Isabella married Nicholas Siciliano; Madeline married Nicholas Spicciati, and Joe who was a renown radio disc jockey in Sumter South Carolina married Joyce. He went by the name Joe Anthony and would send me boxes of 45 RPM demo records. John, Timothy, and Susan lived with us one entire summer because their mother had to work. Albert often stayed over with Tony and Joowan. We were all the same age. Like I said, "They were great times."

Tony would make sure to come over and visit me every weekend, every holiday, and for the entire summer vacations. He'd ride the bus to and from his place. I'd wait by the window and watch for his shopping bag that held his clothes peer from around the door of the bus when he got off. I didn't have a brother, so his being there was like having one. We did everything together—whether it was going to a movie, going on hikes, climbing trees, reading comic books, or just talking. We were inseparable. He used to enjoy listening to me play the drums and coming to watch my baseball games. One day, when we were twelve years old, we were walking to the baseball field; and I told Tony that my third time up at bat, I would hit a home run for him over the center field fence. When I went to bat the third time, I turned and looked at Tony to remind him of my prediction. He watched attentively as the opposing pitcher named Keith threw me a fastball. I clocked it, sending it sailing over the center field wall. I crossed home plate and saw Tony smiling from ear to ear. He never forgot that day and neither did I.

Going back even further in time, Tony and I were always wandering the neighborhood together, looking for adventures. We enjoyed romping through the lots and finding wood or old baby carriages that were thrown away and dumped in the neighborhood lots. We'd gather the materials that we'd collect and bring them to my house and tear them down to make use of whatever we could and use them for building things. We'd go to the hardware store and buy a pound of nails. Back then, they sold the nails loose, by the pound. Then we'd get busy making a wagon or a scooter.

To build a wagon, we'd take a two-by-four piece of wood to use for the chassis and then two more short pieces to use for the front and rear cross sections. We used a handsaw to cut the wood to the sizes that we needed. We'd drill a hole in the front one and a hole in the front of the chassis then insert a bolt with nuts and washers to join them together. The rear crosspiece and rear end of the chassis were nailed together solid. Then we'd drill two more holes in the front crosspiece, one hole on each end, then get a piece of rope and put the ends of the rope through the holes; we'd tie a double knot on each end so the rope wouldn't come through the drilled hole. We'd then take the two axles with the wheels attached and nail the axles to the bottoms of the two crosspieces by driving the nails into the bottom of the two-by-four chassis and bending them over the axle rod. We had to use many nails to do this so the axles would stay in place. The final touch was to get an empty wooden crate and nail it to the chassis to act as a seat. The rope attached to the front crossbar that now was able to swivel was used to steer the wagon. We'd put our feet onto the swivel board to help turn the wagon along with the rope. The brakes were our feet, like in the *Flintstones*.

The scooters were built similarly by using a two-by-four for the base. We'd use a roller skate that we took apart so we could use one half for the front and the other half for the rear. We'd use a bunch of nails to fasten them to the bottom of the running board in the same fashion as the wagon. Then we'd get a wooden crate and nail it to the front of the running board and nail two small pieces of wood on the top of the crate at a forty-five-degree angle to use as handles. We learned how to build things all on our own. We were never shown what to do or how to do anything. These were only a fraction of the things we used to do.

One of our favorite pastimes was when my cousin Tommy De Pirro came over, which was every Saturday. We'd go out, rain or shine, and bat rocks into the lot for hours. Aside from playing ball all day—whether it was baseball, softball, football, basketball, handball, or stickball—we'd do crazy things. We'd find old car tires that were thrown in the lots and roll them down the street and let them go into the oncoming traffic on Gun Hill Road, which was a busy roadway. We'd put our hands up to our foreheads and squint our eyes and wait to see if an oncoming car would hit the tire or vice versa.

Better yet was our frequent rock fights. We'd choose up sides and throw rocks at each other. The gliders were the more dangerous ones. You'd never be sure what direction they would curve. You had to stay alert or else. It's no wonder why we had great reflexes. I only recall two mishaps. One was when my cousin Mella got hit in the forehead with a rock. She bled a lot. My other cousin, Tony Laverro, was hit in the eye with a piece of carpet when shot from a homemade zip gun. To this day, he still has a discolored eye and loss of vision. No one ever said anything. We just did our thing all day and every day. If we got hurt, we'd simply wash up and put a Band-Aid on the cut and get right back out there. Then there was chip the top, flipping and tossing of baseball cards, flying our homemade kites, and so many other street games.

Tony and I loved to set off fireworks on the Fourth of July. We'd save up and buy as many fireworks as we could. One day, when we were eleven, as usual, a bunch of the cousins were over to celebrate the Fourth. We'd light up our punks, which were twelve-inch pieces of skinny-like sticks we'd buy in the candy store. They'd stay lit for hours and caused many burn marks on our arms or cheeks of our faces by us accidentally getting too close to someone holding one. If we didn't have punks, we'd cut eight-inch pieces of clothesline rope and flare out the ends and light them; and they would stay lit all night long. These two methods beat lighting a match every time you wanted to set off a firecracker or M-80, also known as an ash can. They had the fuse in their center, and we'd flare out the tips of the fuses to make it easier to light. These were powerful, much more so than a standard firecracker. We'd put an M-80 under an empty five-gallon bucket and light it. The bucket would go up at least fifteen feet into the air. Sometimes we'd light firecrackers and toss them. One of my cousins twisted the fuses of three firecrackers together and lit them. He quickly tossed them in my direction, and believe it or not, they landed into my right front pants pocket. I grabbed my pants with two hands and squeezed. There wasn't anything I could do but hold on tightly and wait for the explosion. I heard *pop-pop-pop*. I knew I got burned, so I went into the house to check out the damage. I just had a couple of burn blisters. It was no big deal. That's the way it was growing up in the streets. Hell, we even had to learn about the birds and the bees from one of Mike Cotter's three older brothers. Our fathers never gave us that man-to-man talk. I'll never forget the day when we all found out how a baby was really made. We thought it was disgusting. A man putting his thing into a girl's thing. "No way," we all shouted out. Little did we know then.

One of my friends, whose name was Walter Buryk and who was two years older than us, lived two houses down from me. We were very close. We'd take turns sleeping over each other's house from time to time. His sister Rosemarie was good friends with my sister. He also was learning to play the trumpet, so he and I would get other musicians together and try and start a band. His father played the piano and would sing at the church masses every Sunday. His mother Louise was very athletic and would take the time to play soft ball with us as often as possible. He joined the cadets and we kids would all get together and Walter would act as the drill sergeant and show us all the movements he was taught. We'd use toy rifles to do the military maneuvers. We got pretty damn good at it for eight- year-old kids. It sort of prepared us for the real thing when we got older. We were never at a loss for things to do from sunup to sundown. They truly were great times. Walter ended up joining the Air Force as soon as he graduated high school.

Tony was with me all through my puppy love days when I had my first girlfriend named Carol Ann Paulmeno. I liked her all during elementary school. She was the first girl I ever kissed. It was at my nine-year-old birthday party, and she and her mother were over for the party. I grabbed Carol Ann and bent her over backward and smacked one right on her lips, just like in the movies. Our mothers both laughed at that one. The following week, in school, I asked her out on our first date for Saturday. She said, "I'll have to ask my parents first." The next day, in school, she told me that it was okay to go with me. Before I went to get her that Saturday morning, my mother gave me two dollars, and I put the money in my Davy Crockett wallet. At that time, there were all sorts of paraphernalia based on the Walt Disney movie *The Ballad of Davy Crockett*. Coonskin hats, lunch boxes, bubblegum cards—you name it, and it was available.

Tony came with me, and we walked up the block to pick her up. She lived behind the church. I was going to take her to the candy store. On the way to the shop, Tony said, "John, I'll go home so you can be alone with her."

I told him, "Okay, I'll see you later." He gave me a wink and a smile. I knew what he was insinuating.

Carol Ann was somewhat of a tomboy and a very pretty Italian girl. She was wearing a nice blue dress. We sat on the red stools, the kind that spin, and we each ordered a chocolate egg cream. They were made by filling a glass halfway with milk and then squirting a large amount of chocolate syrup, hopefully three squirts into the glass, and then adding seltzer from the fountain while stirring with a spoon as it was poured into the glass. This caused the drink to end up with a white foam and usually overflowed so the soda jerk would take the back of the spoon and scrape it off. It was a great drink. When I went to pay the bill, I was embarrassed to have Carol Ann see my Davy Crocket wallet. I turned to the side, so she wouldn't see me taking the money out of it. I put the wallet back into my pocket and then paid the bill. It was kind of a grown-up feeling being out on my first date. I walked her home and gave her a little kiss; then I went back to my house to tell Tony all about it.

Carol Ann and I went our separate ways when we went to different junior high schools. I only saw her on different occasions throughout the following years such as at the bazaars and the CYO dances that my band played at when I was sixteen. As I was playing, I'd see her come into the dance room and feel good knowing she was there watching me play. After all, she was my first love, and I never lost feelings for her. One time, I got so excited that she was there that while I was doing a drum solo and kind of showing off, my seat slid right off the platform and I fell backward. Now that was embarrassing.

The last time I saw her was the night my nephew Jon was born on September 22, 1965. I was eighteen and driving home and saw her standing at the bus stop on White Plains and Gun Hill Road. I asked her if she wanted a lift home. She said yes. She still lived in the same place. I asked her for her phone number, which she gave to me. When I got home, I called her. I told her that my sister just gave birth to my second nephew, and I asked her if she wanted to go with me to see them in the hospital. She told me that she would like to but that she didn't think her parents would like the idea because her boyfriend was in the Navy and was overseas. And because they were getting engaged, it wouldn't go over too well. I told her that I understood and wished her all the luck in the world. I still wonder what turn of events in my life would have happened if she had gone with me that night.

The day for my entering the Army was getting closer. Marilyn and I had been dating for eight months now. According to the news broadcasts, more and more guys were dying every day in Vietnam. We thought it best for us to get married, just in case I didn't come home. We got engaged, which didn't go over to well with my parents and my sister. They didn't think that I knew Marilyn well enough and wanted me to wait until I got out of the service. I kept on bugging them until they finally consented. They paid for the ring, which was a one-and-a-half karat pear-shaped diamond and cost $1,500. They figured that by the time I got out in two years, I would change my mind.

Before I left, I wanted to make sure that I paid a visit to my other grandparents. My mother's mother lived with us, and her father died when I was four years old. My father's parents were very special to me, and I could not leave without seeing them. As a small boy, I would visit them every week. I'd walk the two miles to their building on Magenta Street and walk up the four flights of steps that led to their apartment. They were always happy to see me. I would take my seat in the corner by the window and listen to their wonderful stories and wise and experienced words.

I'd watch my grandmother feel her way across the tabletop and counter to the refrigerator to get out the milk and chocolate syrup and a piece of chocolate cake. Then she would reach up into the cabinet for a glass. She was amazing. She'd pour the milk into the glass until it touched her finger, add the syrup, cut a piece of cake, place it in a dish, mix the glass of milk, and give it to me. You would never know that she was blind. She had an eye disease known as retinitis pigmentosa.

They always had something for me: a gift of some sort or money. It was a special and unforgettable time of my life, but those were the wonderful yesteryears. I was grown now and couldn't see them as often as I would like.

Marilyn and I drove to their place. When we got there, my grandfather, Joseph, opened the door to let us in. He was a quiet and gentle man in his seventies. He still worked as a security guard for a trucking company in the lower Bronx. He always dressed in a suit and tie and was loved dearly by all who knew him. He even did the shopping for my grandmother. Her name was Rose.

Our stay was short. We sat and chatted for a while, and when it was time to leave, my grandmother stood up and I held her in my arms. She began to cry as her hands ever so gently felt their way across my face, trying to capture my features. As her fingertips touched my eyes, my ears, my nose, and my mouth, she said with tears running down her cheeks, "Oh, Johnny, my dear grandson, I wish I could see you just once. All these years and I don't even know what you look like." I had all to do to keep my composure. I hugged her tighter. She held me as if she didn't want to let go. I released one arm from around her and placed it over my grandfather's shoulder. His eyes were full of tears. He held a handkerchief in his hands and kept wiping his bloodshot eyes. It was a very emotionally heartbreaking moment, and I had no way of knowing then that I would never see my grandfather again.

We left their apartment, and halfway down the stairway, my emotions let loose. "Why did she have to say that?" I said to Marilyn and cried like a baby, burying my head in her shoulder.

November 15 rolled by, and it was my turn for a farewell gathering. It was one party that Tony and I couldn't spend together. He was well into his basic training at Fort Gordon.

The house was full of friends and relatives. I wasn't in much of a mood to be around people. My stomach was in knots, so I went up to my room, and in the dark, I laid down on my bed. I knew now the torment and lonely feeling that Tony felt the night of his party and why he needed to be by himself. Just knowing that I would be going away the next morning and not being able to do anything about it sucked big-time. I'd never been away from home before. I didn't know what to expect.

As I laid there, so many thoughts ran through my mind. I knew I would miss Marilyn and wouldn't see her for a long time. How I would miss being home. I wondered if I would ever see my family and friends again. I thought back two months earlier when my friend Andy tried to talk me into going to Bronx Community College. "Come on, John," he had said, "if we don't go to school, we'll end up in Nam." Against my better judgment, I finally agreed to go with him to the registration seminar. I kept telling Andy how much I hated school and that I had enough of it. For the hell of it, I went anyway. We sat in the auditorium and were handed a bunch of papers. We listened to a speaker for about a half an hour telling us all about Bronx Community College. He went on a break to give us time to fill out the forms. When he stepped down from the podium, I walked out. "This ain't for me," I said to myself. I told Andy that I would wait for him outside. I would just take my chances with the Army.

Well, Andy got out of the draft by enrolling in college, and there I was pondering over the situation that I might have been able to avoid. I kept thinking of Andy and how he tried to talk me into going back to school and all the other crazy ways he spoke about on how to get out of the draft. He was the singer in our band and lived up the street from me. He was a real funny guy. He could make anyone laugh. We'd be talking on my stoop for hours into the evening, and when we decided to call it a night, I'd say, "Come on, Andy, I'll walk you home." We'd walk the one block to his house; and when we'd get there, he would say, "Okay, come on, I'll walk you home." The topper was one day when he came over to work out with me, he grabbed the barbell and started to do dead lifts. He reached an upright position and stood still. Then he told me to add more weight on to the bar. So I did. I visualized his face as it turned red and his long chin stuck out and his teeth clenched tightly. His eyes bulged, and his jaw went through all sorts of contortions. His arms looked like they were touching the floor. He squinted and strained and then started to bounce up and down, still holding on to the barbell. I looked at him and asked, "What the hell are you doing?"

He answered, "They won't draft me if I have a hernia." I just shook my head and laughed. I guess that funny memory helped to put me in a better mood. I was able to go back downstairs and be more sociable. The crowd started to thin out, and by midnight, everyone had left. It had been a long day, and although I was tired, I didn't go to sleep. I didn't want to. I figured the time would go by slower if I stayed awake. I didn't want the night to end. I began to hate the Army for disrupting my life.

CHAPTER II

THE INDUCTION CENTER

The sun slowly turned the darkness into daylight, and there was a knock on the front door. It was Marilyn, and shortly after, Junior came. He was going to drive us to Manhattan.

My sister, Rose, stayed overnight, and she was sitting on the steps that led up to our bedrooms. She was crying. My father had to leave for work. His was a quick goodbye. He shook my hand and gave me a hug. He whispered in my ear to be careful and stay alert. I know he was fighting back the tears. He knew what it was like to leave home and go off to war. He had been in the Marines during WWII and fought over in Guam and Iwo Jima. When I was a kid, I used to watch *Captain Kangaroo* before going to school. He told me he knew the captain and Mr. Green Jeans, Captain Kangaroo's sidekick on the show. They were both over at Iwo.

I kissed my sister goodbye then walked over to my mother. She was beside herself. I held her and tried to hold back my tears and fought to smile through them and said, "Some birthday gift for you, Ma." I kissed her goodbye. Damn, the past couple of months had been nothing but tears, heartaches, and goodbyes. When I walked outside, my next-door neighbor and good friend Mike Cotter was there to see me off. He told me that he would take Marilyn and my mother to the airport later and to phone him with the information. That was good. I'd get to see them one more time.

Before I go any further, I'd like to tell you of a humorous story about Mike Cotter. One of the thousands of games we used to play when we were kids was a game we called "Hot Beans". To play this we took turns to hide a stick somewhere in the lot. The stick was shown to all of us, so we were all able to identify it. We turned our backs while the stick was being hidden. When the stick was found, the one who found it would pick it up and holler, "Hot beans" and then proceed to whack the others with it until they ran to a designated safe area. One day it was Mike's turn to hide the stick. When he yelled ready, we all turned and began searching for it. The sneaky trick was to locate the stick and then play dumb until the others got close. When they did, the person finding it would commence the whacking. Well, anyway, this one day, after Mike hid it, I spotted it and I sneakily hovered close by and waited for everyone to get near me for the stick whacking. When I thought the time was right, I quickly picked it up with my right hand and hollered "Hot Beans" and started to chase the closest victim. But Mike, being the prankster that he was, had dipped the end of the stick in dog shit and I got it all over my hand. Naturally he laughed his ass off, and although it was at my expense, I had to admit it was one hell of a gag. He got me good on that one. Now back to the drive to White Hall Street.

The three of us got into the car. Junior drove while me and Marilyn sat in the back seat. We hardly spoke. She just laid her head on my shoulder and cried the entire trip. We reached Lower Manhattan, and Junior pulled the car right up to the front steps of the building. "Well," I said, "I guess this is it." I gave Marilyn a long kiss and whispered, "Goodbye." I shook Junior's hand and thanked him, grabbed my overnight bag, got out of the car, walked up the wide and high concrete steps that led to the huge doors, and made my way into the building.

It was chaotic. There were guys everywhere. I spotted a friend of mine whom I had gone to elementary school with from the first to the sixth grade. His name was Joe Reul. It was a strange and uncomfortable atmosphere, and being together was a comfort for the both of us. We were in for a long, long day. They put us through one grueling test after another. It began with written exams then blood tests, x-rays, urine samples, and a meeting with a psychiatrist. The most ridiculous segment of the day were the examinations for a hernia and hemorrhoids. My God, what a joke. To perform these two classics, they lined us up in a straight line in the middle of a room wearing only underpants. The place reeked with a horrible, stuffy perspirant odor. For the hernia test, a doctor stood before us and stuck two fingers under our testicles and told us to cough three times. For the hemorrhoids, we were to drop our undies and place our hands on the cheeks of our butts. The examiner, who stood at one end of the line, followed it by saying, "Bend forward and spread your cheeks wide." He then walked rapidly down the line and gave a quick glance at each of our butts. We could have had bleeding piles, and the bastard would never have spotted them.

There were many things overlooked. Uncle Sam wanted every-one he could get his hands on. Unless you had a rich uncle, had a politician for a father, had a sound written medical excuse, were a homosexual, were missing a body part, or were just downright insane, you had no chance of being classified 4F (unqualified for military service).

By now, more of us became acquainted. Joe and I met some guys from our neighborhood, most of whom I had not known. We formed a New York bond and stayed together. Their names were Charles D'addario, Al Cohen, Jerry Borrelli, Paul Going, Bob Di Gregorio, Little Tony Fiore, and Joe Midgette, and also Bob Paulmeno, who was Carol Ann's cousin. I had known Joe Midgette from Sousa Junior High and De Witt Clinton High School. We were in the same homeroom class in Clinton. Little Tony was not from our area. He stemmed from Long Island.

All the testing finally came to an end, and all the new recruits were seated in a room. After listening to a patriotic speech, we were told to stand, face the American flag, and raise our right hand. We repeated the oath of faithfulness to our country, and thus, we were sworn in as soldiers of the United States Army. We now belonged to Uncle Sam, to do with as he pleased.

As if the day wasn't long enough already, it was only late afternoon and it was just beginning. We were told to get ready to board on buses that would take us to Kennedy Airport where we would hop on a Delta airliner to fly us to Columbia, South Carolina. I got to a phone and called home. Marilyn answered, and I related the schedule to her and to tell Mike to hurry because there wasn't much time. The trip to JFK from the Bronx wasn't that far, but at that time of day, the traffic was murder. I knew that they would be cutting it close.

It was still daylight when we left the building. The buses were lined up and ready to go. Their motors were idling, and the smell of the exhaust filled the air. One by one we stepped up and into them. After shuffling our way down the narrow aisle that separated the rows of leather seats, our newly formed gang sat close by one another. The bus pulled out and went via the back roads rather than the highway and started its journey to the terminal of the awaiting airplane. I peered out of the window and watched as the people went about their everyday business. Shoppers were going in and out of stores. Women were wheeling their baby carriages, and kids were riding their bikes. I watched as the life I knew whizzed by me and wondered what kind of life it was that we were about to enter.

The people that I had been looking at seemed to be so free and oblivious to anything around them. I saw them glance up at the bus and wondered if they gave any thought of who we were or where we were going or if they even gave a shit. I wasn't free anymore like all of them. I couldn't reach up and pull the cord that would ring the bell that singled to the bus driver that I wanted to get off at the next stop. I was no longer a civilian. I was a soldier now and property of the US government. For the next two years, I could not be my own man. Reality was beginning to set in, and I didn't like it.

The noise-filled bus continued its way, and before long, we were entering Kennedy Airport. The driver pulled up to the terminal, and we disembarked from the bus. I looked around, hoping to see Marilyn and Mike, but they weren't there. I lagged, walking slowly behind, hoping that they would show up. Time ran out, and I had to follow the line. We walked up a tunnel that led to the doorway of the plane. I had never flown before. This was my first close-up view of an aircraft. The sound of its engines was awesome. I made my way to the rear and scooted into a window seat. It was an old habit of mine to ride in the back of a bus or train and sit by a window.

The plane started to taxi toward the runway. At one point, the side of the plane that I was at faced the terminal. I stared out of the porthole and strained my eyes to see if I could spot Marilyn and Mike. I thought I saw them standing behind a large glass window, but it was too far and the plane was moving, which made it that much harder to recognize anyone. I was very downhearted in not being able to see them. Although the plane was filled with guys, for the first time, I felt alone. It was so quiet, so I guess they all had that same lonely feeling.

It was getting dark, and just before takeoff, the lights inside the plane flicked on and a bell tolled. A voice introducing itself as the captain welcomed us to Delta Airlines. He instructed us to fasten our seat belts, that we'd be flying at an altitude of thirty-two thousand feet, that the flight would take two-and-a-half hours, and to enjoy the ride.

The plane started to move faster. I looked down and watched the ground speeding by. The engines grew louder, and it went even faster. In a wink of an eye and with a weird feeling in my stomach, the ground was suddenly far below us; and in seconds, the plane soared high in the sky. It was a clear night. I was amazed at the sights far below and how I could see the lights of one city beyond another and how the stars seemed so much closer. *This is incredible,* I thought to myself. Realizing that home was behind us now, I settled back in my seat, closed my eyes, and drifted off to sleep.

The sound of a bell brought me out of my twilight nap. The captain announced that we were about to land in Columbia, South Carolina, and to fasten our seat belts. For the first time ever, I got to see what a runway looked like from the air at night. A never-ending row of blue lights lit up the landing strip. The lights got closer, and the ground seemed to come up and hit us. The sound of the engines suddenly changed drastically as the plane touched down and slowed to a halt. It taxied its way to the terminal, and we got off.

When we left the terminal, we were told to get on vehicles that looked like green buses that were waiting to take us somewhere. It was very dark. They slowly made their way across bumpy roads. We couldn't see anything except the reflection of the headlights silhouetting off the trees and bushes, lighting up just enough of the narrow dirt passageways that led into the wilderness.

The ride took about forty-five minutes. They finally stopped in the middle of nowhere. We unloaded and walked a short distance until we found ourselves standing in front of a row of Army barracks. They told us to form into lines and to listen up. One guy, I guess he was the head sergeant, called us to attention and explained the dos and don'ts. He ended his welcoming speech by telling us that we'd be going inside to fill out forms.

They made us stand out there for hours. I'll never forget the effect the chilled night air had on our bodies. We trembled and shook uncontrollably from being so damn cold. None of us were dressed properly to handle that nighttime low temperature. My head was flinching as I turned to Charley, standing to my right. My lips vibrated with the words "Man, this is fucken bullshit."

He replied, "These fucken cocksuckers." His lips were also quivering as he spoke.

At last, a young blond-headed fellow emerged from the warmth of the building we stood in front of. He was one nasty son of a bitch. He made sure that he let us know about the stripe he boldly displayed on his sleeves and yelled, "I'm a private first class, and you will listen to what I tell you!" We all looked at each other and smiled as if to say, "Get a load of this dickhead."

The next words that exploded from this dork's mouth were "Before we get started, I want anyone who is carrying a weapon of any kind to come up and dispose of it now and drop it in this bucket. And I better not find any of you holding out!" So one by one, we slowly made our way toward him. He was sitting. We walked up a couple of steps and began to commence disposing of all our weapons into the five-gallon pail that was by his feet. When I got to him, I peered down into the pail and saw that it was half full of mostly pocketknives. I reached into my left front pocket and pulled out a small knife. I tossed it in. Then I reached into my right front pocket and pulled out a larger knife and threw that in. Gomer (I tagged him as Gomer) looked up at me with a puzzled expression, and as he did, I reached into my right rear pocket and pulled out a utility knife and tossed that into the pail. Only one word, slowly, came out of his pale dumbfounded face: "Shit."

It was about 3:00 AM when we were finally allowed into the building. The heat felt great. Inside there were rows of seats lined up for us. Charley and Joe sat to my right while Al, Little Tony, and Midgette sat to my left. We were happy to get out of the cold night air. They handed us forms to fill out. One of the questions was, If we were wounded, would we want our families to know? All of us agreed that we'd check the box indicating no. We figured if we were only wounded, why cause them to worry? On the top of the forms, next to our names, was a number that started with the letters US followed by eight digits. Being that we all sat side by side, our numbers were in sequence. This number was our service serial number, which was to be like our social security number, and would stay with us for the rest of our lives. It took about an hour to finish filling out the forms.

From there, we went into the next building where they issued us bedding. We were assigned bunks, but before turning in, I needed to use the bathroom, now commonly known (in Army talk) as the latrine. Everyone else also had to go. Inside the latrine there were a row of urinals, but something was different. Something didn't look right. The toilets were right out in the open. There were no dividers or doors separating the commodes. Then I saw two guys drop their drawers and go to the bathroom. "What the hell?" I said to Joe. "Man, I don't think so." I knew that there was no way that I could get used to that. It didn't seem to bother Joe. He just walked over, pulled down his pants, sat down, and did his business. "See yah later," I said, and went to bed. I got to sleep around 4:30 AM. This long-ass day had finally come to an end.

No sooner had we closed our eyes when we heard a loud voice screaming for us to get up. It was our newfound friend, Gomer. He raced down the row of beds, yelling at the top of his lungs, "Get your sorry asses up and outside on the double and into line formation." After two days of no sleep and your eyes close at last and drift off into a deep slumber, a sudden awakening can find you disoriented. My eyes opened long before they wanted to, and I uttered, "What the fuck?" Then realizing where I was, I hopped out of bed, threw on my clothes, and joined my buddies outside.

Gomer, with his green pleated pants and shirt and spit-shined Army boots, stood there mouthing off, talking down on us as if he were a general. Once again, he referred to his stripe and his being a private first class. Hell, we didn't even know what an E-1 was. We came to find out that his one stripe was only one step above us, and it only meant that he had finished his eight weeks of basic training and eight weeks of AIT (advanced infantry training). All those who graduate are automatically promoted to PFC (private first class). When Gomer finished dictating to us, he told us to get some chow and be back in formation by 7:30 AM sharp and not one minute later. We went to what was called the mess hall, got in line, waited our turn to grab a tray, picked out some silverware and a dish and cup, and were then served our first Army meal.

While we were eating our breakfast, I looked around and saw that there were lots of guys with shaved heads. "Oh shit," I said, loud enough for the others to hear.

"What's up?" Joe asked.

"Look around, man," I retorted. "First of all, there're no chicks anywhere, and look at all those bald heads." They all gazed around the room. All of us had a full head of hair, except Joe Midgette. It didn't seem to faze him at all. Being black, he was used to not having any hair on his scalp.

Getting used to not having any females around would not be too difficult for me. I was used to it with the three years I spent in an all-boys school. But not being able to slick my hair back and pull down my pompadour was something I didn't want to think about.

We all looked at one another in disgust, knowing that we were soon to be without our hair. I looked at Midgette; he looked back at me with his one crossed eye and a "welcome to my world" smile. I stared up at his head, visualizing my scalp looking like his, and all I could utter was "Damn."

After breakfast, we formed in line by the barracks and were taken to a building beyond the mess hall. It was there that we were to get our GI haircut. They sent us in groups of three. Me, Joe, and Charley went in together. I sat in the chair and glared up at Joe. The barber standing over him held the electric razor in his hand and raised his arm. Joe cringed his shoulders, squinted his eyes, and rolled back his lips over his teeth in anticipation of the buzzing clippers touching his head. A few swift motions of the barber's arms, and in a flash, all of Joe's hair was gone. And just as fast was Charley's and mine. We waited outside and floated our hands across our scalps, feeling the stubs. We watched as, one by one, guys emerged from the building like a herd of sheep: in the front door with a full head of hair and out the rear door as bald as can be. Everyone looked so different. Amazing how a shaved head changes one's appearance.

They were rushing us through, trying to get us ready to ship out as soon as possible. We were marched over to another building, and as usual, we stood in a line. We made our way past a group of guys that handed us a duffel bag; fatigues (pants, shirt, and hat); underwear; socks; and a belt, all of which were green. The final item was a pair of black Army boots. Before we left, they handed out our dog tags: two metal plates on a chain to be worn around our necks throughout our military service. Engraved into the tags were our name, serial number, and blood type:

> John Fratangelo
> US 52756716
> Blood Type AB

After all the handouts, we lined up. Our duffel bags were filled with all our new attire. We held them up, in front of us, and they ran us double-time back to our barracks. Everywhere we went was double-time. Get there fast and then stand in line. "Hurry up and wait" was what we called it.

There was a mirror hanging on a wall in the barracks. I gazed into it and got the first look at myself without hair. *God,* I thought, *would you look at this.* I did not like the way I looked. It reminded me of the time when I was thirteen years old. My hair was long and greased back like a typical teenager. The part I took great pride in was the long bushy front that I pulled down over my forehead. My father went with me to the local barbershop to get our haircut. It had the red-and-white striped pole outside its door. I'd been going there since I was a small boy. A fellow named Nick—along with his brother, Joe, and father, Tony—owned the place. But what I remember most about the place was Jerry, who was born with Down Syndrome. It was hard to tell how old he was, but I would guess he was in his late thirties. He would shine the customer's shoes and run errands. He was sort of a fixture throughout the neighborhood. Everyone knew him. I always had a hard time understanding what he was saying, but the barbers seemed to know.

When it was our turn, my father went first, and I sat and watched Jerry shine shoes as usual; and as always, both the barbers and the customers were kidding with him and making fun of him in an innocent way, but not making it too obvious. They'd poke fun at the way he dressed. He wore suspenders that held his pants up high above his sneakers, displaying a view of his white socks and choking his crotch. They asked him where he shopped for his clothes or teased him about his girlfriend that he boasted of. It seemed like they were hurting his feelings, but Jerry was used to it. The teasing was a part of a daily routine that had gone on for years. Besides, Jerry wasn't stupid. He'd take it all in and laugh with them or perhaps, secretly, at them. He probably laughed all the way to the bank. He always swallowed up his tips in the palm of his hand and, miserly like, put it into an empty cigar box. He would look around to make sure no one was spying on him, and then he proceeded to admire his daily earnings. I always felt so sorry for him.

"Next!" shouted Nick after he finished with my father's haircut. I sat in the old-fashioned barber chair. And as he did many times before, Nick stepped on a pedal and adjusted the seat to the right height and asked me how I wanted my hair to be cut while he wrapped a black-and-white striped sheet around my neck and clipped it tight. I told him that I just wanted a trim. He started to cut; and when he got to the front of my hair, he grabbed it in his hand and turned to my father and asked, "What do you want me to do with this?"

My dad said to me, "Why do you need all that hair in front of your eyes?" Before I could say anything, he told Nick, "Cut it off!" I hated my father that day, and today I hated the Army.

CHAPTER III

TANK HILL

We had some time to kill before going to our training areas, so I grabbed a pencil and piece of paper and strolled out of the barracks and sat, leaning against the building wall. I was writing a letter to Marilyn when I was disturbed by a loud voice. It was Gomer, once again showing off his authority by demanding something of one of the new recruits that had recently arrived. I understood about having rank and giving orders, but this guy was going overboard. He really needed to have his teeth knocked down his throat. I figured it was best to ignore the clown and continued writing my letter. Charley walked over, shaking his head. He looked down on me and said, "Hey, Goom, I'd like to see our friend come over and talk to you like that." (Charley called me Goom, short for *goombare*, which, in Italian, means "friend.")

Looking up, I said, "He's nothing but a bully. They only pick on someone they think won't fight back." Charley wanted to know what I was doing. I told him I'd been thinking about home and that I missed my girl.

He said, "Yeah, me too."

Just then, some sergeant walked over to Gomer. He must have been listening and had enough of his arrogance. He reamed Gomer a new asshole right in front of everybody. Gomer turned red and just stood there like a wooden pencil with a hat on. Didn't open his mouth. Gomer finally got his. Payback's a bitch.

We stayed at the reception center for three days. We went through aptitude tests, more physical examinations, orientation meetings, a classification interview, and more inoculations. We were also fitted for our dress uniforms, and our personal files were started.

During those three days, I still had a hard time getting used to the layout of the bathroom toilets. I would wait until late at night to relieve myself, when the chances of others being in there were slim.

The time came for us to leave the induction center. We all grabbed our gear and hopped on buses. The buses traveled on dirt roads that were surrounded by trees, bushes, and fields. There were no signs of life at all, only wilderness. As we neared the training center, we traveled on paved roads. Many buildings appeared, and throughout we could see groups of soldiers marching in unison while holding rifles on their shoulders. Others were running in strict form, singing while keeping in perfect rhythm. They looked very impressive. It was about two o'clock in the afternoon when the buses dropped us off at an area in Fort Jackson known as Tank Hill. It was given that name because of a large water tank that stood like a monument high on a hill, overlooking the training areas.

The bright sun blinded our eyes when we got off the bus. A voice shouted, "Place your duffel bags on the ground by the road and get into formation." We lined up on a dirt-covered area that was in front of a row of Army barracks. There were drill sergeants all around wearing "Smokey the Bear" hats, which were held tightly to their heads with a strap that stretched under their chins. The brim of their hats shadowed their faces, making them look more intimidating. They had serious, stern looks on their faces and spoke with sharp-toned voices. Most of them had Southern accents. Their green fatigues were neatly pressed, and their black boots were polished to a gleaming finish with the laces pulled tightly to hold the cuffs of their pants, which were neatly folded and tucked inside their boots. The stripes on the sleeves of their arms showed that they'd been in the Army for quite some time, and their actions made us aware that this was the real deal and that they meant business.

One of them stood on a platform and yelled, "Atten hut!" We all stood tall with our hands down by our sides and were as quiet as could be. He introduced himself as Sergeant Edwards. He told us that the area that we were standing on and the buildings behind him, including the mess hall, were known as the company area and that under no circumstances were we allowed out of that area unless we were training. A barracks was to be assigned to each of us and would be our home for the next eight weeks. We were to be broken into groups of twenty men, forming five platoons. The five platoons made up a company of one hundred men. Each platoon had to assemble in front of their barracks every morning at five o'clock sharp for reveille, also known as roll call, and at seven o'clock sharp in the evening for retreat.

The sergeant went on to tell us, "You will speak only when spoken to. You will do only what you are told to do. You will answer 'Yes, sergeant' or 'No, sergeant.' Is that understood?"

"Yes, sergeant!" we shouted.

"I can't hear you," he blurted out.

Again, we hollered at the top of our lungs, "YES, SERGEANT!"

Then he said, "For the next eight weeks, your sorry asses are mine. You will march until your feet fall off. You will drill until your arms fall off. You will train until you drop, and you will hate my guts. And I don't give a shit. There is a war going on. Most of you will be going to Vietnam. Some of you won't come home. The more you pay attention and learn, the better your chances of living. You are all here for one thing and one thing only: TO LEARN TO KILL. Do you understand me?"

"YES, SERGEANT."

"What are you here for?"

"To KILL?"

"What?" he asked again.

"TO KILL," we answered, as loud as we could.

Next, he shouted out, "Now, spread out for PT [physical training]." We were lined up in rows of ten and ten deep. "Now, let's see what you pussies are made of," he shouted. This son of a bitch then started to blurt out orders.

"On your stomachs!" So we dropped down on our bellies.

"On your backs!" We quickly, with an upward jerk of our bodies, rolled over on our backs.

"On your feet!" So we leaped up to a standing position.

"Run in place!" he commanded. So we started jogging at a fast pace.

"Faster," he shouted, "and get those knees higher." We kept running in place, trying to lift our legs as high as we could. Then he started all over again. "On your stomachs." "On your backs." "On your feet." That dirty bastard did that for a good twenty minutes, and to make it harder, he mixed up his pattern of commands until our heads were spinning. Some guys were able to keep up with this torture while others were completely confused and fell behind. "At ease" finally flowed from his lips. Catching my breath, I looked around. Some guys were sprawled out on the ground. Some could barely stand on their feet while others were throwing up.

It seemed like he would never stop. I was really glad that I had worked out all those years. I was able to endure that test without too much of a problem. Even though I was in really good shape, I was still exhausted. I bent forward and put my hands on my knees to catch my breath. This fellow right in front of me started to wobble. He suddenly passed out and fell backward into my arms. I laid him down and stayed with him. He came to in just a few seconds and seemed to be fine. He looked around in a daze, as if he didn't know where he was or what had happened. One of the other drill sergeants came over to him and glared down at him and said, "Get up, you goddamn pussy, before I kick your sorry ass all over the place." That poor kid stood up and was trembling. That sergeant showed him no compassion at all. He put his face right up to that kid's face and yelled, "You ever drop on a drill again, boy, and I'll stomp on your head."

I stood there and felt so sorry for that young fellow. He was more embarrassed and humiliated than hurt. I wasn't accustomed to seeing people mocked and ridiculed. I had always been raised to be friendly and kind to others and render my aid whenever it was needed; but this display of show-and-tell made me realize that I was in a different world now and life wasn't going to be the same anymore.

They eased up on us for the rest of the day. They assigned us to a barracks. And each platoon had its own drill sergeant and a corporal. Me, Charley, Joe Reul, Al Cohen, Joe Midgette, Little Tony, and Paul Going stayed together. Our DI (drill instructor) was Sergeant Angle, and our corporal's name was Burke. However, Joe Reul and Paul were assigned to Sergeant Edwards and Corporal Massey.

Me and Joe Ruel in Basic Training. Fort Jackson South Carolina.

Sergeant Angle was of average height, kind of slender, and in his midthirties and seemed to be more subdued than most of the other DIs. Corporal Burke was of average height and build and in his midtwenties. Both were sort of on the quiet side. They only said what needed to be said.

Corporal Burke took us into the barracks and assigned us our bunks. We were on the second floor. I had a top bunk, located on the left side of the room and about midway down the aisle. Little Tony was underneath me while the others were on the right side of the room. Against the wall were our stand-up lockers and footlockers made of wood and green in color. Our names were placed on them. The upright lockers were used to hold our boots, dress uniforms, and fatigues, neatly hung. The footlockers contained underwear, socks, bathroom accessories, and miscellaneous items, such as shoe polish and snacks and reading and writing materials. Everyone's lockers had to be arranged in the same and proper order.

The bedding was folded neatly on our bare mattresses. They took us through the process of making our beds, step-by-step. It had to be done a certain way. The sheets had to be folded and tucked tightly according to their specifications. The blanket, too, had to be folded evenly and pulled tightly and tucked under the mattress; and if a quarter was dropped onto the bed and didn't bounce off the green blanket, the bed was torn apart and had to be done over and over until it passed the "bouncing quarter" test.

The same went for the lockers. If there was one item out of place or a speck of dust anywhere, the lockers were emptied onto the floor. "There is a right way, a wrong way, and the Army way" was drilled into our heads; and from then on, until we got the hell out, the Army way was the only way.

Corporal Burke's room was on the second floor while the sergeant's room was on the ground floor. Burke pointed to a paper hung on a wall adjacent to his quarters. The paper had written on it all the details each of us was assigned for each day, from cleaning the barracks or the latrine to KP (kitchen patrol).

The cleaning of the barracks consisted of dusting, wiping, and sweeping. The floors had to be mopped; and when they dried, they had to be polished and buffed with a large electrically operated buffing machine, which was kept in a corner closet with all the other cleaning materials. The black linoleum floors had to be shiny enough to see ourselves in.

In the latrine, the commodes, urinals, floors, and shower stalls had to be scrubbed clean; and the chrome had to be polished to a gleaming shine. There were cases of spinal meningitis, so cleanliness was of top priority. I was grateful for one thing: at least the commodes in these bathrooms had dividers between them.

After Corporal Burke had explained all these duties to us, he told us that lights-out was at nine o'clock sharp and reveille was at 5:00 AM. Then he ended by saying, "I suggest you all turn in. Nights are short here." Before turning in, some of us decided to take a shower. This was another aspect of the Army that took getting used to. There was only one other time in my life that I had taken a gang shower, and that was when I was in elementary school to prepare for a swimming lesson. I was older now, and being nude in front of a bunch of other grown men was uncomfortable.

After Corporal Burke left, and I was lying in my bunk and knowing that the holidays were just around the corner, I thought of last Christmas and the special tree me and Tony decorated together. I was always very big on celebrating and decorating for Christmas. I would buy a Christmas tree from eight to sixteen feet high and get it home and cut the needed eight feet to fit in our living room; then take the other left over section and put it up on the second floor of our house in my mother's bedroom which was located above the living room, so the tree would appear to come right through the floor. The reason for such tall trees was I wanted the top of my tree at the ceiling in the living room to be wide and after it was decorated, the hanging tinsel would make it look like a decorated fountain. That last year's Christmas of 1965, my boss Joe and I were on our way home from a job we were doing in Harlem. When we got close to home, we spotted a Christmas tree lot and we stopped to look. I saw what I told Joe was "my tree". It stood out all by itself, as full as could be. I bought it and after the lot attendant roped it tightly, we tied it on the roof of our truck. I had made an iron stand out of a piece of eight-inch pipe and a twenty-inch piece of diamond plate cut round. I drilled and tapped the pipe to accommodate four 3/8th eyebolts and then I had one of my cousins weld the pipe to the stand. It was heavy enough to counterweight the size of any tree. I set the tree up in front of the window. When I got it up into the stand and secured it with the four eye bolts, I attempted to cut the ropes that held it tightly together. The living room was twelve feet wide. I cut the rope and the tree sprang open and the branches leaned on the walls. It was exactly like the movie with Chevy Chase, "Christmas Vacation". Whoever made that movie, must have grown up knowing me. I phoned Tony to come over that weekend to help me decorate it. It turned out to be quite a sight. We had people knocking on the door, after spotting the tree through the window to ask if they could come in, to see it.

That year was a great Christmas, a great tree and a great memory. It was also Mine and Tony's final Christmas together.

Corporal Burke was right, five o'clock did come fast. We had no sooner closed our eyes when we were woken up by Sergeant Angle rapidly walking down the aisle shouting, "Get up, get up, get up, get up!" We only had minutes to get on our fatigues, throw our boots on, fling our packs on our shoulders, and rush down the stairs and out the doors to line up in formation for roll call. It was cold and still very dark. To recognize someone, you'd have to walk right up to him. The sound of shuffling and scampering by the other platoons was heard, followed by the sergeants giving the order to fall in. They called our names, and we replied, "Here," when each name was called. Then each squad leader called out, "All present and accounted for." The order of "Atten hut" was given. We stood at attention while, off in the distance, a bugle sounded reveille ("Taps"). Then there was a quick rundown of the day ahead, and the order "Fall out" followed. Another day had begun.

We were now able to go back into the barracks to wash up and piss before going to chow. Everything we did was done after waiting in a line. They had a way of curbing our appetites. Just before entering the mess hall, five of us at a time had to lift and cradle a thirty-foot telephone pole in our arms and bend forward at the waist and back up repeatedly. One of the DIs would go to each man and place his hand between the pole and our biceps to make sure each was holding his share of the weight. If not, that guy had to stay and do it all over again with the next crew. When he was satisfied with the performance, he would tell us to stop. From there we had to jump up and grab a chinning bar and do at least ten chin-ups. Believe me, you did not feel like eating after that. And this routine was done before every meal.

Each morning we had to line up in the training area in formation for PT. Sergeant Edwards was always the instructor. He stood on a platform. We stood at attention awaiting his instructions. If anyone flinched, he was told to drop on the ground and give twenty push-ups. We had to remove our shirts. It was mostly calisthenics and running in place. This was done before our day of training began. Some of the training was done in classrooms, learning theory and combat strategy, which consisted of map reading, how to recognize objects at night, identifying different types of weapons, and so much more. I would say that 90 percent of basic training was focused on marching and rifle drilling. This was to get us to operate as one and to give us discipline.

The day came for us to receive our rifles. The M14 was the weapon we were issued. We were excited about this for most of us never fired a weapon before. They were kept in the weapons' pool a few miles away. Everywhere we went, we ran in cadence and always took the long way. Cadence was a form of jogging while the platoon sergeant running alongside would sing out phrases and we'd respond.

Sergeant Angle	Troops
"All the way."	"All the way."
"All the way."	"All the way."
"Sound off."	"One, two."
"Sound off."	"Three, four."
"Bring it on down."	"One, two, three, four."
"One, two,"	"Three, four."
"Hup, two, three, four, your left."	
"Your left, your left, right, left."	

We began to enjoy these runs for it was cold and the maneuvers warmed us up. These Army drills had become second nature to us by now. Even those who fell out that first day were able to endure. Immediately after PT, we'd start running for miles. At some point during a run, we'd look up to the top of a hill that was ahead and think we'd never make it; but we'd reach down deep beyond the point of pain, beyond our second wind, and beyond physical tolerance, and we'd make it and still be able to go on and on.

We received our rifles, and they soon became our third arm. We learned how to take them apart piece by piece and reassemble them. Wherever we went, they came with us. We'd run with them stretched out in front of us or held high above our heads until our shoulders cried for mercy. We drilled for hours every day, performing maneuvers in unison. Left face, right face, about-face was done until we did it as one unit. The rifle, we were told, was our best friend; and if we took care of it, it would someday take care of us. We became more and more conditioned with each passing day, both physically and mentally.

Throughout the training areas, there were signs and pictures of our adversaries halfway across the world, the Vietcong. Written on these signs was the word *kill*. Dummies resembling the VC were used in bayonet practice. We were told to scream as we thrusted our bayonets, which were clipped into our M14 rifles, into the dummies or knocked the heads off with the butts of our rifles. They drilled us until we enjoyed shouting the word "KILL," until we couldn't wait for it to be real.

To some, the Army and everything it stood for was wrong, so they refused to participate in any of the training. They were called conscientious objectors (COs for short). Our company had two of them: Guy and John, both from New York. It took a lot of guts for these guys to refrain from what we were sent there to do. The abuse that the officers and DIs put them through was unbelievable. They were mocked and scorned, treated like animals, and were constantly reminded of being cowards.

One day Guy was forced to stand at attention while we underwent our training. He stood in that position throughout lunch and well into the afternoon. I turned periodically to look at him. His body was swaying slightly. Suddenly, as we were still drilling, I heard a thump from behind me. Guy had grown so weary that he had passed out and fallen flat on his face. No one was permitted to go over and help him. Whether or not he was faking remained a mystery; but before the eight weeks of basic were over, both he and John were discharged. All of us from New York were very close, so they came to me and told me of the news. They were quite happy. They didn't have to be shamed anymore. They were let out on an undesirable discharge.

Now, training became interesting. It was time to fire our weapons. We were taken to the firing range. There were strict rules to follow. This was the real deal, and we were using live ammunition; so there was zero tolerance. It was done step-by-step while under close observation. It turns out that there was more to it than just loading and pulling the trigger. The M14 was a magazine-fed, automatic, semiautomatic rifle. It could be fired in bursts or by single-shot action by merely flicking a switch located on the side, above the trigger. It used a 7.62mm-caliber bullet. The magazine or clip held up to twenty rounds of ammo.

Before shooting at designated targets, we had to zero in our rifles. This meant setting the sights for complete accuracy. We were given three rounds of ammo to fire at a target, with a bull's-eye drawn on it. Once we were all in a prone position, the DI calling the shots would yell out, "Lock and load three rounds of ammo!" We'd load the three bullets into our clips and fasten them onto the rifle and make sure the gun was in semiautomatic to fire one shot at a time. Then he'd yell, "Ready on the left, ready on the right, ready on the firing line, fire." The guns were taken off safety, and we'd empty the three rounds into the target and then removed our magazines from the weapon. Then, before we budged, we had to wait for the "all clear" signal, which was done verbally by one of the instructors.

Once this was done, we went to the targets and took notice of where the group of three rounds were located. The rifles had adjustment dials located near the sight. So if a group of shots were fired too low or too high or off to either side, adjustments were possible by turning the dial one notch at a time. This was repeated until the three rounds hit the bull's-eye in a tight group. When this was accomplished, the rifle was "zeroed in."

When the rifles were zeroed in, we followed the same procedure to shoot at a silhouette target resembling a man. We were given extra ammo for this exercise. These targets were electronically operated to present a more realistic and difficult quarry. We fired until we were ordered to cease firing. We removed our magazines and proceeded to hand in the clip and whatever ammo we had leftover. It was absolutely forbidden for anyone to conceal and smuggle out even a single round of ammo. The consequences forced very harsh disciplinary action. At the turn-in point, the weapons were inspected for assurance of them being unloaded.

We looked forward for each sunset for we knew that another day was ending, and it brought us that much closer to the end of basic training. Being a trainee was no picnic. We were considered the lowest and had no rights or privileges. We were lucky to get a weekend pass, which was given only to those who stayed out of trouble.

To help break up the boredom, Joe Reul, Charley, Little Tony, and I would sneak out at night and go to the PX (post exchange) building where we were able to call home or buy something to eat. I must have spent one hundred dollars on Milky Way candy bars during those eight weeks. I kept one in every pocket. I liked chocolate very much, and everyone knew it. We missed our girls, and getting to a phone was important to all of us. It was great to hear Marilyn's voice.

This phone conversation between me and Marilyn was not like usual. She wanted to get married. I told her that we promised my parents that we would wait until I got out. But she kept forcing the issue and insisting that we do. She wanted me to talk to my parents and explain to them how much we wanted this to happen. I told her that I would call them. She knew that I was coming home for two weeks' leave at Christmas and said that would be the perfect time for us to get married. I hung up and was hesitant on making that call. I knew they weren't too fond of Marilyn, especially my sister. She couldn't stand the thought of me tying the knot with her. Christmas was only a few weeks away; and if this were to take place, I'd have to hurry and make the arrangements.

I called them and told them our plans. They were not pleased at all. I finally convinced them by emphasizing the fact that I would most likely be going to Vietnam and I would like to have a wife and a child to carry on my name in the advent I didn't make it back. I guess they saw my logic and reluctantly agreed. I called Marilyn right back and told her the good news. She was overjoyed with emotion. We set the date for December 24, Christmas Eve.

I made sure that I got all the phone numbers of my friends and that I would call them to give them the time and place. I really wanted them all to be there. They congratulated me and assured me that they would show up.

The days were passing by. Charley and I would go for walks at night, and he'd sing songs. He had a nice singing voice. I liked hearing him sing the oldies. One of the songs he'd sing fit the situation to a tee: "You're a thousand miles away." Charley lived on the same street as me in the Bronx but up a few blocks. Ironically, I never saw him before. We became very close friends. He was kind of short and well-built and could run very fast and had been on his school's track team.

In the evenings, after everyone would be settling in after a hard day of training, Little Tony and I would get a half-assed workout in by going into the latrine and doing push-ups and chin-ups on the crossbar between the stalls. He looked up to me as a big brother. Little Tony was a gymnast. He was only five feet, seven inches tall and well-built. He was soft-spoken and very quiet and shy and was the only guy I'd ever seen who could do a one-arm chin-up with the other arm behind his back and do it strictly. My one arm chin-ups were performed with my other hand grabbing my wrist.

One night, I was doing my workout. Little Tony had gone to the phone located by the company training area a few blocks away. I finished and was sitting on my bunk. I heard the door slam below, followed by rapid, heavy footsteps running up the stairs. It was just before lights-out. My bunk was close by the stairway, and I curiously waited to see who it was. It was Little Tony. He had his hands clasped over his mouth and nose. "Tony, what's wrong?" I asked. His eyes glanced up at me, quickly, above his hands; and without answering me, he ran into the latrine. I'd thought that I'd seen blood flowing through his fingers, so without hesitation, I followed him. He was bent over the sink, and blood was all over his face and shirt. "What happened, Tony?" I blurted out. While he was wiping the blood, Tony told me that as he was talking on the phone, he felt a tap on his shoulder, and when he turned, some creep punched him in the nose.

"What?" I shouted, hardly believing my ears. "That son of a bitch. What did he look like?"

Tony said, "I don't know. It was dark, and it happened so fast. But he was a black guy." With that, I lost no time and started to take off. I heard Little Tony say, "Get him for me, Johnny." Charley had seen me as I was leaving and that I was pissed. "Hey, Goom, what's the matter?"

"Somebody hit Little Tony." I ran to the phone booth, but by the time I got there, the bastard was gone. There was no one in sight. When I turned around and started back, I saw Charley; and the entire platoon was with him. We never did find out who did it, but it showed me one thing that made me feel good. We were ready to back one another up, and although we did not reap his revenge, I'm sure that Little Tony must have felt good too.

Thanksgiving Day rolled around, and we were given the day off. We attended mass service, which was not unusual. It seemed that a soldier felt comfort in practicing his faith; so we went to church every Sunday morning. A special holiday dinner was prepared for everyone at the mess hall, turkey and all. As we were eating, my mind drifted off, and my thoughts returned to the year before and to the words uttered by my cousin Tony. We were both far from home and not spending Thanksgiving together with our families, just as he had predicted. *Where would we be next year?* I thought to myself. Was there something to what Tony said about never being with our loved ones again?

The fourth week of basic training was ending, which meant that the Christmas holidays were just around the corner. We were getting ready to go home for our two-week furlough and counting the minutes until we were aboard the bus, on our way. The trip would take about thirteen hours. I was going home, single and free, but returning married with a wife by my side.

Marilyn and I had to rush to get blood tests and make the arrangements with her parish priest. I made all the calls to my buddies and to my cousin Tony, whom, naturally, I asked to be my best man. There was a blizzard on Christmas Eve that almost put a halt to the wedding. It was so bad that the city transportation was shut down. On my way to the church, I had to get out of my car and push it a few times. My aunts and uncles had to walk the one-mile journey, knee-deep in snow, from their apartments on Webster Avenue. I think even God was trying to tell me something. Charley, Al, Bob, and Joe were there, decked out in their Army dress uniforms. I was wearing mine too. Junior couldn't get there, and Little Tony was unable to make the drive in from the island. My deepest regret was that my cousin Tony was not there by my side. The night before, he had called me and told me that he had to refuse my offer to be my best man. He very much wanted to be it but said that he knew my family was not happy about the marriage and didn't want to go against their wishes. He asked me to not hold it against him. I could hear in his voice that it was killing him to do this. I was deeply hurt and disappointed, but I told him that I understood.

As a last-minute replacement, I asked my next-door neighbor Mike Cotter if he would do me the favor and take Tony's place, which he consented. So because of the terrible weather conditions, only a handful of people were able to show up. An event that was supposed to be a happy one was far from it.

Standing at the altar, I scoped around and saw all the mopey faces; and while all others were standing, my sister,

Me and Mike Cotter as my best man at my wedding.

Rose, was sitting, holding a tissue in her hands, staring into space, and crying. Marilyn's sister, Donna, asked my sister, why she was sitting and crying. My sister told her, "I am not at my brother's wedding. I am at his funeral." I peered at my mother and father and saw the downhearted expressions on their faces. In my mind, I was wrestling with the thought, *Am I doing the right thing?* I turned back to face the priest, who was halfway through his recitation. I wondered, *Do I answer "I do" or "I do not?"* But when he asked, I said, "I do," and it was done. After the ceremony, we went back to Marilyn's place on 197th Street and Decatur Avenue to celebrate. Only my parents, Marilyn's immediate family, and my Army buddies showed up. That was all.

We took in about seven hundred dollars cash, so the day after Christmas, we had to buy tires for our car. We were getting ready to head back to Fort Jackson. There was still a shit pile of snow everywhere. We met up with Joe Reul and his wife, Pat; and the four of us drove down in separate cars. It was a Thursday, so we figured we would get back by Friday and have the weekend to look for a place to stay. We had four weeks of basic training left. We were gambling on getting lucky and staying at Fort Jackson for AIT. One other thing, we also knew that a trainee was not supposed to have his wife with him during training.

We had a setback on the way down to South Carolina. I became ill with the flu and ran a high temperature. And to make matters worse, Joe's wife, Pat, got homesick and wanted to turn around and go back to New York. She was really being one big pain in the ass. He finally convinced her to continue on, and we stayed at a motel in Maryland. I went to a local doctor and got a prescription for medication to help bring the fever down. We got the meds filled at a pharmacy and went back to the room. At one point, I didn't know where I was or who was with me. I slept well the rest of the day and through the night. The drugs must have done the trick because by morning, I felt much better; and we were soon on our way.

We reached South Carolina at about 3:00 PM on Saturday and started to look for a place to live. We ended up in a trailer park and rented a two-bedroom trailer for $95 a month. Since Joe and I were each making $95 per month, we figured that combined, we'd be able to handle whatever all the costs amounted to.

Sunday evening came, and it was time for me and Joe to get back to the fort. We were all settled in, and Joe left before me. Pat drove him. I waited for the last possible minute to leave; after all, we were sort of on our honeymoon. Naturally, we took advantage of the alone time and made the best of it. We spoke about having a baby as soon as possible because of the situation and figured if she had a child to take care of, it would keep her busy and help to pass the time. After a nice long session of sex, she drove me to the fort and dropped me off at my company area. We kissed goodbye, and she assured me that she would know how to get home.

As I approached the barracks in the dark, I saw Charley standing by the door. I was happy to see him, but something was wrong. He did not greet me in the way he normally would. His voice was withdrawn and he said, "Hi, Goom." I feared what he was about to tell me. It was as if I sensed what his next words would be. Before I could say anything, he spoke. "Goom"—he paused momentarily—"Little Tony isn't coming back." I stood silent and numb as Charley, with tear-filled eyes, went on to explain what had happened. "He was killed in an automobile accident during the Christmas leave. He can't be with us anymore." I remained in shock at the sad news. His words reached down into the pit of my stomach like a bolt of lightning.

We both downheartedly walked up the stairs and sat on my footlocker, which faced Little Tony's bed. I asked Charley if he knew the details. He said, "All I was told was that he was in the car with a few of his friends. The car skidded on the parkway, lost control, and crashed." I sat with my elbows on my knees, chewing on my teeth as I listened. I gazed at my lost friend's bunk and expected to see him sitting there looking back at us. My anger erupted, and I slammed my fist down onto the locker. "Dammit. Why Tony? He never did anything to anyone." It was unusually quiet in the barracks that night, and I just couldn't believe Little Tony was dead. I'd lost a good friend, and I missed him already.

Morning came, and the bugle sounded reveille. The names were called, but this time, Little Tony wasn't in formation to answer. It was almost as if he had never been there and the damn Army could have cared less. This lack of compassion made my hate for the Army grow even more.

The days passed by, and we were getting used to Army life. We got to the stage of being able to get weekend passes. However, I wouldn't wait for Friday to come around. I'd call Marilyn and then sneak out of the company area and have her meet me with the car at a rendezvous spot that we had established. I had to cover all the bases, so if I had to take part in some detail or do KP (kitchen patrol), Charley would take my place. At night, when it was my turn for guard duty and the man previously on guard duty came to wake me up, Charley would be sleeping in my bunk and get up and do it for me. He was what you would call a true friend. If he had something to do, one of the other guys would stand in. Marilyn would drive me back early the next morning before roll call. It being dark, I would go unnoticed and be able to slip back into line without anyone knowing the difference. To show my appreciation, I would bring them back beer and food.

One afternoon, I was summoned by Sergeant Edwards, who was Joe's DI. Joe was with him; and when I approached them standing by the PT area, Joe said, "Hey, John, we got a problem."

"What's up?" I asked.

"Our wives. They had a fight, and Pat has a black eye." The two women had gotten jobs as waitresses at a diner and, apparently, didn't agree on certain things. Joe said, "I'm going to take Pat back home. They just can't get along."

"How ironic," I said. "Here we are, forty men in one room, and we get along fantastically. Yet just two women under the same roof can't."

Sergeant Edwards said, "Now you can see why we are against men bringing their wives down with them. I'd advise you to send your wife back home also." By this time, Sergeant Angle had joined us, and he insisted that we send them home. They were pretty cool about the situation and didn't ground us for breaking the rules and kept it under their hats.

Joe drove Pat home the next weekend. He was given a three-day pass and made the eight-hundred-mile trip back to New York. He returned by bus on Sunday. I ignored their advice and kept Marilyn down there with me. It was harder financially, but that's the way we wanted it. I kept up my routine of sneaking off the fort regularly during the week. If we didn't get into any trouble and were granted our weekend passes, Charley and a couple of the guys would come over and stay in the trailer since we now had the extra bedroom. We'd wake up on Saturday and Sunday, and Marilyn would make us bacon and eggs. It was great. It gave us a touch of the life we'd left behind.

The training in the days that followed grew more intense. Now that our marching and spit shine was perfected, it was time to get down to more tactical training.

One morning, we were told to bring our M17 gas masks with us on maneuvers. They ran us to a large clearing surrounded by a wooded area. We stood in formation, made up of twenty rows of men, five in each row. Unexpectedly, while we were standing at attention, we heard a popping sound followed by a hissing noise. Then one of the sergeants yelled, "GAS!" Instinctively, I drew in a deep breath and held it. But in doing so, I took in a slight amount of the poison gas. Within seconds, it became impossible to even attempt another breath. My ears felt as if they were going to burst. My eyes were burning as if soap was being poured into them. Tears were running down my face. I began to foam at the mouth. Saliva ran down my chin. My throat felt like it was on fire. I grabbed my stomach to aid in stopping from vomiting. My nostrils burned. All this from just one short breath of biologically contaminated air. I kept my composure and held my ground. We had been taught to stay put and get our gas masks on as fast as we could and stay the course to be able to fight against an enemy attack. If we panicked and ran, we would be killed either by the chemicals or by the enemy. I tried desperately not to panic and immediately grabbed my mask, which was in a case strapped over my shoulders. I dared not take another breath. Man, I couldn't get that mask on fast enough. After getting it on and strapped tightly over my entire face, I blew what little air I had left in my lungs out through the breathers of the mask to clear them of any contamination. I just stood there, experiencing all the tortures caused by that damn chemical. *Shit, when the hell is this going to stop?* was the thought flowing through my brain. I remained patient and waited. Suddenly, the filters started to work. The agonizing symptoms slowly diminished. I gained my composure and senses. When my eyes cleared enough for me to keep them open long enough to see, I noticed that Charley, who had been standing right beside me, was gone. I waited, not daring to take off that lifesaving piece of equipment. Then I heard a voice shout out, "ALL CLEAR!" I drew in another deep breath and removed the mask ever so slowly. When I looked around, half the battalion was gone. Guys had taken off like jackrabbits. Charley was walking toward me, and I yelled out, "Hey, Charley, what happened to you, man?"

He smiled and said, "I couldn't get the fuckin' mask on, so I ran for the hills."

It was the most horrific thing I had ever experienced. God, I hoped that I would never have to come across that in combat. How could anybody be expected to fight the enemy under those conditions? You had no peripheral vision. Although it was over for today, this was not to be our last encounter with CBR (chemical, biological, radiological agents).

To practice hand-to-hand combat, we formed into circles of ten men. The tactics were simple. They told us to holler "Hah!" with each movement. It was a joke, and I doubt very much that anyone would put them to use in a realistic situation. I knew I wouldn't. One would do so much better by just using his basic knowledge of street fighting. Speed and force were of the uttermost importance. In a close encounter with the enemy, where it is do or die, anything goes.

In the pugil stick training, the entire platoon formed a large circle. Two men were chosen to enter the center. Each combatant was given a helmet and crotch protection and a pugil stick. The sticks were nothing more than a padded piece of rounded wood with two large and bulky pads on each end. This was supposed to simulate a rifle and bayonet. If not anything else, it gave us a chance to relieve our frustrations for instead of tactical movements of parry left or parry right, it became (more or less) a free-for-all. It resembled a pillow fight: knock each other silly without getting hurt.

Our second encounter with CBR was next on the agenda. We were marched into the woods until we came to what appeared to be an abandoned shack. It was about twelve square feet. One of the DIs was already inside preparing a surprise for us. We were instructed to put on our gas masks and enter the shack ten men at a time. The first group went in, and those that were to follow waited anxiously to see what was going to happen. In a matter of minutes, ten men came bursting through the door. Thy flung their masks on the ground. Some were throwing up; others were gasping for air and coughing.

Our group entered the shack. It was dark inside. We formed around a table in the center of the room. On the table, a candle was burning inside a glass container. This was the only means of illumination. There were no windows. We could see the gas rising from its enclosure. We knew what the exercise consisted of and what had to be done. When the DI gave the signal, we were to take in a deep breath and remove our masks. Then, one by one, we were to recite loudly our name, rank, and serial number. And we couldn't leave until we had all completed the task. The glass container was lifted, and the signal was given to begin. We all removed our masks. Each of us shouted as fast, as loud, and as clear as we could, awaiting the man before him to finish so the next guy could take his turn. Our lungs were bursting in anticipation for the tenth man to finish. The farther down the line it went, the more jumbled the wording became. We exploded out of the shed in desperation for fresh air, as those before us had done. I'll tell you what, you do not ever want to experience biological chemicals.

We gathered in formation and doubled-timed back to the company area. Close by the area were the red-brick buildings that we'd passed many times. It was rumored that those taking their AIT there were assured of going to Nam.

There were only a few more facets of basic training left, and one of them was learning first aid. It was highly important for us to know this, for one day, it might help to save the life of an injured friend. They showed us how to make and apply a splint on a broken bone, how to apply a tourniquet to stop the bleeding, and how to make a stretcher out of pieces of wood or branches and a shirt; they stressed the fact that we would have to make best use of what was at hand and to place a wounded man on the side of his injury. The throwing of a live grenade was next. We entered a barricade, one at a time, along with a supervisor. The grenade was placed in the palm of the trainee's throwing hand. The spring-loaded handle was held firmly compressed against the body of the grenade. The pin holding the handle to the explosive was then pulled while the handle was still held tightly. This action made it possible for the handle to be released from the grenade once it was tossed. It was not thrown like one would fling a baseball or a rock; rather, it was heaved with a stiff-arm motion, like the action of a catapult. Once it was tossed, the handle would fall free form the grenade, which, in turn, ignited a ten-second fuse. The pin needed a vigorous tug to be pulled free, not like in the movies when someone would pull it out with his teeth. It could be replaced back through the hole in the handle and the apparatus attached to the crown of the grenade (in the event it wasn't necessary to use) as long as the handle was still being held intact and in its original position.

After I tossed my grenade, the instructor and I ducked down behind the barricade. A grenade was small but powerful and extremely dangerous, filled with compressed BBs; and once blown, it sent hundreds of tiny projectiles in all directions. It was a deadly piece of armor and had to be treated with the utmost respect.

We were taught to throw it three different ways. One was to pull the pin and throw. This allowed the full ten seconds before ignition. The second way was to pull the pin, release the handle, and count five seconds before throwing it. This would cause the grenade to explode in the air, creating an air burst. Personally, I would have not liked to have used it in this way. I was not comfortable with the idea of holding a live grenade in my hand for five seconds. The third was to not toss it but to roll it. We practiced rolling a grenade into a simulated bunker. It was amazing how accurate a grenade could reach its target in this manner.

With less than two weeks to go, we were scheduled to go on our bivouac. This was a three day-and-night campout. It was supposed to simulate a real combat situation completely away from any form of civilization. We took along our packs, mess kits, ponchos, shovels, air mattresses, rifles, and miscellaneous materials, such as wooden pegs and cords to aid in building our hooches.

It was during bivouac that we experienced K rations for the first time. The rations came in small boxes, labeled and neatly packed. Inside was a dinner in a can and also a dessert in a can. There were chocolate or cookies wrapped in tinfoil. The kit contained sugar, salt and pepper, coffee, a tea bag, cocoa, toilet paper, and a tiny can opener known as a P-38.

We were divided into groups of three and assigned areas to pitch our tents. Charley, Joe Reul, and I were together. We used air mattresses for beds, which were inflated by the air produced from our lungs. It was cold, and there was snow on the ground. To keep warm in between maneuvers, we hung out in a large green canvas tent that had in it barrels of wood set on fire. One of the details was "fire watch," where guys would take turns making sure the fire stayed lit by adding logs to it.

At night we took turns on guard duty. We used an infrared scope to aid our vision in the dark. These scopes could be attached to either binoculars or on a rifle. When put on a rifle, it was called a sniper scope. They gave a greenish-tinted vision when one looked through them.

For the three days, we patrolled, slept in the same clothes, and ate rations and food prepared out in the field using our mess kits. We marched over rough terrain for miles, carrying full pack and gear and our rifles. All the previous instructions and training came to a climax here.

After bivouac was over and before the end of the seventh week, we embarked on another realistic phase of being a combat soldier: the night-infiltration course. This was one hundred yards of barbed wire and barriers, along with machine-gun fire and explosive charges. Flares were shot high to illuminate the makeshift nighttime battle-field. They fired automatic weapons over our heads, so keeping low and staying on the move was essential. We crawled through dirt and water and over hills and under barbed wire with our packs on our backs and our rifles held across our arms. It was a grueling and exhausting experience.

As I was on my back, worming my way under the barbed wire, the palm of my right hand was pricked by one of its rusty prongs. It was bleeding, but there wasn't much that I was able to do. I just continued forward.

The following day, we loaded on the deuce-and-a-halfs and were driven back to Tank Hill. It's kind of strange riding on the back of these trucks. Normally, when you rode in a vehicle, you looked at the road coming toward you; but riding in the rear, the road was mov-ing away from you. These two-and-one-half ton trucks were covered with a green canvas that was opened in the back. They held twenty men. And the ride was quite bumpy but were so welcomed by all just to not have to walk or run.

That afternoon, after we showered and refreshed ourselves and ate lunch, we were marched over to the large auditorium where we often watched a film. We always welcomed the chance to get out of the cold and sit and relax; and with the lights being out, it gave us an opportunity to catch a few z's.

This film was about the different military units stationed in Nam. We knew about most of them. The main combat outfits men-tioned in the movie were the 101st Airborne Division, the Twenty-Fifth Armored Division, the Ninth Infantry Division, and the First Cavalry Division; the one mentioned last and stressed upon more than the others was the First Infantry Division, also known as the Big Red One or the Bloody One. This was said to be the cream of the crop of the Army. It was its proudest division, and the film made sure to highlight this fact. As they described each unit, they displayed each insignia patch that was worn on the left arm of all its members. I wondered which one I'd be wearing.

The eighth and final week of basic training had come at last. Before graduation, we had to take the PCPT (physical combat proficiency test), which summed up all the conditioning and skills that we all acquired. I lay in my bunk the night before and thought of many of the past weeks' events that had taken place: that first day of the physical endurance trial and the way our CO (commanding officer) Lt. Gawtarop walked up to me and asked if I was a swimmer; the workouts Little Tony and I would do together; the way Joe Reul, Al Cohen, and Charley would sit on my back—one on my upper back, one in the middle of my back, and one on the back of my legs—to help me get in a strength routine by doing ten reps of push-ups with their combined weight; my wedding; all the times I snuck off the fort and, thanks to Charley, never got caught; going with Marilyn to the Italian House where we'd go out to eat; and so many other good, as well as bad, memories. It was a bitch, but it gave me memories that I knew would live on in me for the rest of my life.

The PCPT consisted of five trials: the low crawl; the grenade toss; the horizontal bars; the run, dodge, and jump; and the mile run. Each event counted for one hundred points. A perfect score was five hundred points. I was concerned about my right palm. It had become infected from the barbed wire. It had formed a large blister and was very sore with the slightest touch. I went into the latrine and took a razor blade and lanced it. A mixture of blood and pus came gushing out. It was instantly relieved from the pain. I wrapped a bandage around it, and that was that.

The following morning, prior to being marched over to the testing area, we underwent our daily PT. Sergeant Edwards took to the platform as usual. After our warm-up exercises, while our blood was flowing, he'd yell out, "What are we here for?"

And with our fists clenched high above our heads, we'd shout back, "To KILL!"

"What?" he'd reply.

"To KILL!" we'd scream back at the top of our lungs.

"I still can't hear you," he'd say, as if it wasn't loud enough for him.

So to get his approval, we'd have to bust a gut to repeat, **"To KILL."**

There we were, only nineteen years old and shouting the word "KILL" like we were bloodthirsty and couldn't wait to do it for real to soothe our hunger. What happened to the lifelong lesson of the Golden Rule to do unto others as you would have them do unto you? We were taught to hate our enemies and to have no mercy.

The time to put up or shut up came. We were divided into groups. My first trial was the low crawl. This maneuver resembled a lizard's crawl, low to the ground. It was sixty feet to the turning point and sixty feet back to the finish line. It had to be done in twenty-one seconds or less to score one hundred points. I watched as the guys ahead of me went. I don't like to laugh or make fun of anyone; but I must admit, some of the performances were quite comical. Some just couldn't get the knack of it; they'd stop and get up on their hands and knees and then collapse and try to continue. Others would hold their butts high in the air, looking more like a struggling turtle instead of a lizard, while some would just stop from exhaustion and lie there like slugs. The memory of Little Tony and me doing this popped into my head. We had the fastest time in the battalion. We were like lightning; we always finished in a dead heat at sixteen seconds flat. When my turn came, I laid down in the prone position and readjusted the bandage on my hand and hoped it wouldn't hinder my performance. I got the signal to go and darted out, never giving my sore hand a second thought. I finished in sixteen seconds and scored one hundred points on the event.

I knew I'd have no trouble on the horizontal bars as long as the bandage on my hand didn't hinder my grasping the bars. Little Tony and I were the fastest in this event also. When told to go, I leaped up to the first bar and let my momentum carry me to the next one, which was the third bar in from the starting one. It was permitted to grab every other bar to aid in completing it sooner. When I approached the last one, I reversed my hand so my body would automatically spin around, thus facing in the right direction for the return, which saved time. I finished in fifteen seconds and scored one hundred points.

While I was waiting my turn for the grenade toss, Sergeant Edwards (who seemed, for some reason, to take a personal interest in my performance) came over and knelt beside me and said, "I want to see a five-hundred-point score from you." I thought that was nice of him; he was Joe Reul's DI, not mine. He stayed and watched me, and I rolled all three of the grenades into the half-moon-shaped target made from some rocks and got my one hundred points. Sergeant Edwards tapped me on my shoulder and, with a satisfied smile on his face, walked away. "So far so good," I said to myself.

Now it was the run, dodge, and jump. The running part of the test was the part that I wasn't so confident about. I think all the years of weight lifting had slowed my running down. It consisted of moving around and between obstacles, dodging barricades, and leaping over trenches. I waited anxiously as I watched others go before me. Some made it within the required twenty-one seconds, and some did not. I stayed close to the barriers to save time. After all the running and dodging, I started back and poured it on. I leaped over the final trench and crossed the finish line in twenty-two seconds, just one damn second shy of the perfect score. I scored eighty-five points. I was disappointed but not surprised.

The climax of the day was the mile run. I knew this would be my biggest challenge. Charley and I ran side by side. Since he had track experience, he set the pace. The track was one quarter of a mile around; therefore, we had to lap it four times. We did fine for the first two laps, but we began to tire during the third—I more so than Charley. By the fourth lap, my lungs were hurting. I saw one fellow stop and throw up. In the final stretch, I turned to Charley and told him to go on and finish under the six-minute deadline. He went on to do so and ended up heaving his guts up. With one hundred feet left to go, I gave it all I could with a daring last-minute attempt. My legs carried me over the finish line in six minutes and twenty seconds, giving me a score of eighty points. I got a combined total of 465 points. Not the highest score but. with all due respect, not too bad. This fairly high score probably assured me of a seat on a plane to Nam, but I didn't care. I wanted that perfect score.

The big day came toward the end of January. It being winter, we wore our dress uniforms instead of khakis. We were issued our first medal, which we proudly displayed above our left breast pocket. It was the one we earned at the rifle range. The medal had three different classifications: marksman, sharp shooter, and expert. The medals were identical; only the insignia under it stated which of the three had been earned. Mine read "Sharp Shooter."

The stands were filled. Marilyn was the only one of my family or friends there to watch the ceremony. We were all decked out and looking good. We put on a show of marching in cadence and rifle drilling. We were flawless and very proud of ourselves. We surely looked like a different group than when we first started eight weeks earlier.

After all the congratulation speeches were over and done with, we were handed our orders to where we'd be going for AIT. As I suspected all along, I was going to the red-brick buildings. Only two other fellows from our platoon were also going there: Joe Midgette and Billy. I didn't know Billy prior to basic training. He was married and wanted to bring his wife down. He knew about me and Marilyn and figured he'd do the same. The rest of the guys were getting split up and going to different forts throughout the country. It was a sad day for all of us. We had become so close, and I was going to miss them deeply, especially Charley. Once again, I had to say goodbye to good friends. The one good thing about it was that I didn't have to pack up and move and Marilyn and I would be able to stay together.

Marilyn wanted to move out of the trailer and into another apartment. She told me that she was afraid to stay alone and didn't trust the landlord. She said that when he came in to check the heater, he made advances toward her. He was an elderly man and didn't appear to be the type of person to do so or risk his business. I took her word for it and told her that we would look for another place. I thought back to three weeks prior. My father had taken a trip to visit us because he had no way to contact us and my mother was worried.

He had the address, so he met with the owner and was told that the owner had seen strange men go into the trailer at night while I was at the base. My father stayed with his brother Joe, who lived in Sumter, South Carolina, and wasn't too far from the fort. We met up when I had a weekend pass. He took me aside and told me what the landlord related to him. I was in denial and didn't want to believe it. Now with this bombshell that Marilyn had dropped on me, I began to wonder about her.

I had a week off before reporting to the fort for AIT. We looked in the newspaper for an apartment. We checked into one that sounded nice. It was a five-apartment complex that were attached to one another about half a mile off the main road in the woods. Some of them were still under construction. They were one-story high and made with brick in a U-shaped format. They were also furnished. The one we were interested in was on one of the two corners. It was rounded with a bay window looking into the dining area and kitchen. It had one large bedroom with a bathroom. From the front door, you were able to see all three rooms. Rent was $120 per month. The owner's name was Jesse, and he was there showing the place to us. We took it with no hesitation and moved in.

CHAPTER IV

AIT

I reported to my new company area the following Monday. Standing at the entrance of the red-brick building and not seeing any familiar faces brought that lonely feeling back again. I guess all the guys, wherever they went, were feeling the same way. I heard my name being called. It was Joe Midgette and Billy. They were a welcome sight.

Billy told me that he was staying in a hotel with his wife, Paula. She had taken a bus down the past weekend. They were looking for somewhere to stay. I told him about the place where we were staying and that other apartments were available. I phoned Jesse and told him about my friend's situation. He told me that he would show it to Bill's wife but it wouldn't be available for a few days. We arranged for our wives to meet, and I told Billy that Paula could stay with Marilyn until their place was ready.

Meanwhile, back at our training facility, Midgette and I stayed together in the same room and platoon. Billy was assigned to a different room and group. There were twelve guys in my facility: nine, including Midgette, were black, and counting me, there were three white guys. The rest were strangers. As I was placing my belongings in my locker, a fellow approached me and asked my name.

"John. What's yours?"

"Eddie." This was the start of a great friendship.

Eddie was from Brooklyn, New York. He was about my height and stocky. His hair was receding and seemed to be kind of shy. His last name was Husband. He had taken his basic at Fort Gordon, Georgia; so everything here was totally strange to him. He puffed on a cigarette and told me how much he missed his girl, Kathy, whom he intended on getting engaged to very soon. I explained to him that it wasn't too bad for me and that I had my wife down here with me. "Yeah, but how do you get to see her?" he asked.

I told him, "Oh, they're ways. I used to see her just about every night during basic, and believe me, I'll find a way to see her just as much during AIT."

Aside from the two of us, the room was empty. Another fellow walked in. He was Caucasian, small, and slender. He and Eddie had already met. His name was Herbie, also from New York. Some of the other roommates slowly came in one by one. We all introduced ourselves. One guy's name was Inge. He became our squad leader. Another was Price, whose bunk was above mine. Brown, who was only eighteen, bunked with Midgette. Pierce bunked with Inge. I don't remember the other four names. We all got along great.

It was time to get back to training, and that's exactly what we did. We knew where we were going, and they worked us hard. We ran many miles every day, even if it meant running around in circles in a parking lot. No matter where they ran us, it was always done in rhythm and song:

> GI beans and GI ham,
> Gee, we're going to Vietnam
> Sound off—one-two
> Sound off—three-four
> Bring it on down,
> One-two-three-four—one-two—three-four.

Everywhere we went, we ran. It had gotten so that once we reached our second wind, we could go all day. It even became inspiring when we clapped our hands in beat and yelled out simultaneously as our left foot stomped the ground. When they discovered that I was a drummer, they asked me to beat on a large bass drum in rhythm with our marching.

AIT taught us more of the fundamentals of the Army as far as weapons and strategy were concerned. We received our MOS (military operational status). It was 11H, which pertained to the 106mm recoilless rifle used for antitank purposes. Why they called it a rifle was beyond me. It was far from it and we also trained with the 90 MM recoilless rifle, which had a similar action to that of a bazooka and could be carried into combat. Most of our training was concentrated on these two weapons.

The 106mm was an interesting weapon. It was mounted on a jeep and resembled a large cannon. Its barrel was about eight feet in length, and the cannisters were two feet long. Located and attached to its rear was the breechblock, which was the loading mechanism. The 106 was operated by a two-man team: a gunner and a loader. The gunner sat on the bed of the jeep at the left side, facing the barrel, while the loader stood outside and at the rear of the jeep, also on the left of the gun.

Mounted directly on top and at the center was a .50-caliber spotting gun. The gunner zeroed in on a target by looking into a scope containing a cross lens and making necessary adjustments by rotating two directional wheels. While the gunner did this, the loader would open the breechblock, remove a cannister form a wooden crate, and load it into the block. He'd yell, "Loaded and ready to fire!" If the target was a tank, the gunner sighted the crosshairs on it and pulled back on a knob located in the center of the directional wheels. This action would fire the .50-caliber spotting gun, which would release a tracer round and, upon striking the target, would emit a white puff of smoke, indicating that the weapon was on-target. Immediately, when the gunner saw the white smoke, he'd push in on the same knob, which sent the 106 explosive on its way. The .50-caliber saved the wasting of a 106 round and assured a direct hit every time. We took twelve practice shots and had twelve hits; that's how accurate the gun was.

Being a recoilless weapon, it was imperative that no one would be standing behind the barrel when it was fired. If not, the back blast, which was the rear releasing of pressure from the round, would kill you. It was powerful enough to knock down a wall. It was this action that allowed it to be fired from a jeep. It being on a jeep made it very mobile and easy to move around. After the round was fired, the loader would unlock the breechblock and open it; the empty cartridge would automatically eject, and the weapon would be ready to reload. The bad part about firing this weapon was that we'd have to take it back to the motor pool and spend hours cleaning the bastard. We knew how to take it apart and how each piece functioned. The bitch of all this was that after all those countless hours of training on it, we were told that the use of the 106 was discontinued in Nam due to the muddy roads and the dense jungle terrain. And because of this, our MOSs would probably be changed to 11B (infantry).

The 90mm was also fired by a two-man team. The weapon stood on a stand. The gunner would lie perpendicular to it on the left and the loader perpendicular on the right. Both made sure of staying clear from its rear for it, too, had a back blast—not quite as devastating as the 106 but enough to cause severe injury. The sight had within it a bubble that had to be leveled between a cross lens. Once the loader placed a round in the breechblock, he gave the signal of "Ready to fire." The gunner then fired the gun by just pulling a trigger. This did not have a .50-caliber spotting gun.

By now Billy and Paula had moved into their own place around back of the complex. There was a phone in our barracks, and I would call Marilyn at night if the opportunity presented itself for me to sneak out. Our place was seven miles from the fort, so as usual, she'd come and pick me up after all the sergeants and CO would leave. I'd stay until the late hours, and then she'd drop me back off by my building.

Marilyn had made an acquaintance with an attractive middle-aged woman named Regina who owned a small liquor store, which stood by itself on the main road about one mile from our apartment. It was at the pay phone outside Regina's store that I would call Marilyn every night at ten o'clock. At this time, the store was closed, and Marilyn would drive to the phone and wait for my call to make sure she was all right. She and Regina became very good friends, which I was happy about. Aside from Paula, it gave Marilyn another person to hook up with during my absence.

Regina was married to a retired Army sergeant who owned a gasoline station. They had three kids. Marilyn stayed with them or at the liquor store. I had Regina's home phone, so I was able to contact my wife most of the time to set my mind at ease. Regina had a little brown chihuahua she called Pinky. Whenever I would go into the store, Pinky would bark wildly at the sight of me with my fatigues on and run behind the counter. Marilyn grew very fond of the dog, and Regina gave him to us.

One night, I didn't have a dime to make the call, so I asked Eddie for the ten cents. In my attempt to reach Marilyn, I didn't get any response. I tried again and again, but there was still no answer. I called Regina's house. Marilyn wasn't there, and Regina said that she hadn't seen her since the afternoon.

I began to worry. I lay in my bunk staring up at the ceiling and trying to decide what to do. I tried keeping myself from thinking of the worst, but my conscience got the best of me. I couldn't rest easy not knowing for certain that Marilyn was okay. I made up my mind to go home. I figured if she was all right, I'd stay the night and she could drive me back before reveille and no one would know the difference. This was my plan.

It was after eleven o'clock, and everyone was asleep. I dubbed my bunk. I put a pillow under the sheets along with a blanket with only its corner sticking out slightly to resemble hair. I placed a pair of shoes at the foot of the bed, also under the sheets, to look like feet. After doing this, I quietly woke up Eddie and told him what I was doing and that I'd be back in the early morning. I snuck down the hall passed the CQ runner, down the stairs, and out of the building. It was late in February. The night was cold and clear with the stars shining brightly. I alternated running and walking down all the dark roads. It took me a half hour just to get off the fort. It seemed forever to go the seven miles.

I finally reached the house at about 1:15 AM. I approached the door, huffing from all the running. I could see the light on in the kitchen. I figured Marilyn would be surprised to see me. I knocked on the door. The door opened, but it wasn't Marilyn who answered it. It was Jesse, the landlord, and his jaw dropped at the sight of me standing there. I looked in and saw Paula sitting at the kitchen table smoking and holding a drink in her hand. Marilyn heard Jesse call my name; and she raced from the table to the sink, poured out a drink down the drain, and doused a cigarette. Jesse quietly left. He was more embarrassed than I was shocked. Bill's wife left abruptly and passed by me with her head down. She was such an innocent girl, and it looked as if she was partaking in an adventure that was new to her.

I had never seen that side of Marilyn before. She never drank or smoked in front of me. I couldn't help but think about what people had told me about her prior to our getting married. I had only known her six months. I simply refused to believe it when they told me she was a run-around. She swore to me she was a virgin and kept telling me not to believe any rumors that people said about her. The problem was that I was a virgin, too, and naive. I always wanted to save myself for the one special girl that I would marry. The first night of our wedding was the first time we had intercourse with each other and the first time I ever used a condom. It tore open when I attempted to put it on, so it was the last time I ever used one. The point is that I wouldn't know how to tell if she never had sex with any other man. I remember her during sex that first time telling me to push harder to break her cherry. And now that I think back, I never did see any blood. I was just excited to finally get laid.

After Jesse and Paula left, I questioned Marilyn about what was going on. She started acting sick as if she were tripping out and began breaking things. She made me believe that Jesse had spiked her drink. I was ready to go after him. She begged me not to leave her alone. I stayed with her the entire night. By morning, she was still sick. I was already AWOL (absent without official leave). I knew I was in trouble. I had never gotten caught before. I took her to the hospital on the fort. We stayed there until 10:30 AM. There was nothing wrong with her. She put on some show, probably to take my mind off what I saw. She insisted that they were just partying. I wondered what would have happened had I decided to stay in my bunk.

It was around 11:30 AM by the time Marilyn dropped me off. I knew my ass was grass. Sure enough, I was summoned to the CO's office. He threw the book at me. He didn't want to hear any excuses. According to him, I wasn't supposed to have my wife with me during training, which was no news to me. I didn't have a leg to stand on. He gave me an Article 15, which was a serious Army disciplinary action. It consisted of a fine and a bust in rank, which, aside from a pay decrease, was no big deal; also, there was a confinement to the barracks and all privileges were revoked. I was ordered to report to the CO's office every night at six o'clock sharp to clean it for two weeks. My bunk was also personally inspected every hour by a CQ (company quartermaster) runner to make sure I was there after the lights went out.

I was put on a detail in the mess hall during the daytime hours, but they made the mistake of putting me in the stockroom to take inventory. When I entered the room full of supplies, my eyes opened wide and the wheels in my devious little mind started turning. I wasn't about to let an opportunity like this go by, especially after struggling to buy groceries for the past weeks. There were plenty of empty cardboard boxes around, so I filled them with anything I could get my hands on: from meat and potatoes, canned foods, spices, and napkins to syrup. Then I sealed the boxes tightly. Then I placed them in hiding in a corner under other boxes that were empty until the time was right for me to initiate my plan of getting them out.

There was a large metal container outside by the road where the garbage was dumped. I waited for the truck to come and empty it out, which was at about three o'clock in the afternoon. Then I carried the food-filled boxes out one by one along with an empty box on top to act as a decoy. I placed them carefully in a corner of the container through a side compartment and covered them with empty cartons.

It was nearing six o'clock, and I had to report to the CO's office. I got there before any of the other punished personnel did. The CO was still there as I started to dust and sweep the floors. Then I would mop up. By now, the CO had left for the night; and when the others got there, I told them that everything was done. All they had to do was buff the floors. They were happy about that. I left and called Marilyn and told her where to pick me up. By now we knew the fort backward and forward. We drove to behind the mess hall and waited for the coast to be clear. When it was, I got out and retrieved the food-filled boxes, threw them in the car, and we took them home.

Eddie took up where Charley left off. He slept in my bunk to cover for me. He told me what happened on the morning that I got caught. He said that when they all woke up that morning, Inge, while lying in his bunk, had called everybody's name. When he got to me, he hollered, "Fratangelo, wake up." He did it three times, and when Fratangelo didn't answer, he called to Price above me to wake up Fratangelo. Price peered down and called me; and when I still didn't answer, he got down from his bunk, reached out, pulled off my covers, and then shouted, "He's gone!" We got a laugh out of that one.

Since my escapade, I was really on the shit list. One lieutenant, a pompous ass in my opinion, was a stumpy little guy with glasses named Lieutenant Frucht. He looked like a godfrey kumquat. He'd come up to me while we were all in line and put his face in mine and, while we were nose to nose, yell, "Fratangelo, you will have a haircut by this time tomorrow!" He emphasized the word *will*. I wanted to take that son of a bitch and bust him up. I'd wear my cap pushed down over my hair so as to hide most of my head. I would put off getting a haircut or shaving for as long as I could and waited for that lieutenant to bring me before the CO just to bust his balls. I knew it was a losing fight for me, but I just couldn't get used to not being my own man. I hated their stupid rules. Having short hair wasn't going to make a better soldier out of me. I also would do anything necessary to avoid saluting, especially to an asshole like Frucht. I'd bend down and fake tying my shoelace or simply walk to the other side of the road if I saw an officer approaching me.

Eddie and I went back to our rooms after we were dismissed. He told me how much he wanted to be a cop. He pulled out a stack of police magazines and showed them to me. He would get seizures on occasion. He would start to sweat and then shiver. His eyes would roll back, and he'd collapse. The episodes lasted only a few minutes, and then he'd be fine. He had made me promise not to say anything about it. He said, "If they knew about my condition, they'd probably discharge me on a medical. This would stop me from becoming a cop." Naturally, I gave him my word to help him hide it. His condition wasn't too bad. I knew what an epileptic seizure looked like from witnessing a fellow from the neighborhood. He'd just be walking on the street, and then he'd suddenly fall to the ground. He shook all over and foamed at the mouth. His eyes rolled back, and the main concern was of him hitting his head, swallowing his tongue or biting it off, or getting run over; so people would stop the oncoming traffic and place an object in his mouth to prevent that from happening. And then he was left alone until he came out of it. And when he did, he had no recognition of what had just occurred. So I knew Eddie didn't have epilepsy. I really didn't know what he had. I just was there for him whenever he needed me and so was Herbie.

We spent many hours of training on night fighting and maneuvers so we'd be able to distinguish a man from a tree or rock in the dark or tell if an object was moving or not. The shadows can play many tricks on your eyes, especially when nerves are tense in a combat situation. And with a bright full moon, there are many shadows.

To make out an object in the distance, we were taught to not look directly at it but, rather, to focus our eyes just to the right of it; and when we did, it appeared much clearer. A perfect example is to look up into the stars and pick out one and stare directly at it. It will vanish, but when you look to the side of it, the star reappears as clear as day.

To make out if an object was in motion, we'd hold up one finger steadily in the line of vision. If it was moving, it would come into view to either side of your finger. To find out if something was coming toward you or not, we'd form a circle with our thumb and pointer finger slightly larger than the object. If it was moving toward you, it would fill the circle; if away, the circle would get larger.

To fire your weapon in the dark at an attacker (and there wasn't any time to take aim), we'd hold our finger under the muzzle, point in the direction of the target, and fire.

On moonless nights, when we couldn't see inches in front of us, we were taught to walk with one hand held in front of our face to protect our head and the other hand stretched out in front, moving from left to right and not beyond the width of our shoulders. With our front arm in continuous motion, we'd place one foot in front of the other, heel to toe, and moved very slowly. This procedure would help feel for objects such as tree branches and minimize your safe space.

When in areas suspected of being booby-trapped, we'd get down on our hands and knees then crawl ever so slowly. We'd place our knees in the exact spot that our hands had been. Before we'd move again, we'd feel the ground before us very gently and slowly with one hand to feel for trip wires or booby traps. Then we'd lift one leg up and gently place it in the space that had been occupied by our hand while concentrating to hold up our lower leg and foot above the ground instead of dragging it. We did the same with the other leg. Each leg, when moved, had to be kept from touching the ground. The object was to utilize as little ground as necessary. It was a slow process and needed to be done patiently and cautiously if one wanted to live.

The final nightly lesson was to test our ability to use a compass at night. We were divided into three-man teams. The mission was to reach a designated destination. To do this, we marked a tree on one end of a wooded area by tying a ribbon around it and writing a code that only the three of us knew. We jotted down the coordinates of the tree's location. Then we traveled in the opposite direction in a zigzag motion, tracking our paces. We went ten paces to the east and then ten paces forward and then ten paces to the west, always watching the compass. Once we reached the opposite end of the wooded area, we turned and headed back to try to locate our marked tree. We knew that we moved in ten pace increments and started to the east and ended with ten to the west, and we kept count of how many times we had changed direction and how many times we went straight. And lo and behold, there before us was our tree. To locate it within ten feet in any direction was considered a successful mission. The zigzag motion was a much slower way to travel, but by moving in a nonconsistent path, the enemy would not be able to predetermine our destination and couldn't set up an ambush of high effectiveness.

That next weekend, Marilyn and I were invited to stay at Regina's home. That Saturday night, there happened to be a dance at the NCO (noncommissioned officer) club. We called Regina to let her know that we'd spend the weekend with them. She told us about the dance and asked if we wanted to go. "Sure," I told her, "but I'm not an NCO." She told us not to worry and to meet them there. I was still confined to the barracks; so as usual, I had to wait until after-hours to leave. I let Eddie and Herbie know about my plans in case they had to cover for me. They knew what to do. I always made sure to tell them that if it came to them getting in trouble to not even try to make excuses for me and to play dumb.

I knew where the club was. Marilyn brought the only suit I owned and picked me up at our usual spot. She drove. The roadway was muddy, and about one mile before the club, we skidded off the road into a ditch. We were stuck deep in the mud. I got out and tried to push, but it was hopeless. Luckily, a guy came down the road with a pickup truck. I waved him down. He saw me in my Army clothes and didn't hesitate to pull over. Fortunately, he had a rope. He got us out in no time at all. I had no money to offer him, so all I could do was to shake his hand and thank him. We continued onward, and as Marilyn drove, I changed into my suit. It was a good thing that I hadn't changed sooner or else my suit would have been covered in mud. When we got there, Regina and her husband, Jim, met us at the door; and we had no trouble getting in. I wasn't even asked for ID. Here I was, nothing but a lowly trainee, mixing it up with a bunch of E-6s and higher. I kept a low profile and still managed to have a good time. We spent that night and all Sunday at their house. It gave us the opportunity to get to know one another. We met their three kids. They were all in their teens. Jim told me how he spent thirty years in the Army and opened his gas station. He wasn't too pleased about Regina owning a liquor store. I kind of read between the lines and got the notion that they weren't happy.

On the few occasions that I went to the liquor store, I noticed that a guy named Ridley was always there. He was married. It got to the point that he and Regina would meet at our place and hang out. It was obvious that they were in love. They'd dance to love songs while embracing tightly. And you could look at them and see how much they cared for each other. They were like two teenagers. I remember that their two favorite songs were the theme from Doctor Zhivago ("Somewhere, My Love") and "This Is My Song." I told Marilyn that I wasn't happy about helping them cheat on their spouses, especially after Jim had treated us so nicely. She tried to explain to me how unhappy Regina was with her marriage and that she wanted out. Against my better judgment, I went along with it.

One day, soon after this, while I was in my quarters, I was summoned to the CO's office. The messenger told me that my wife was there and was very upset. When I got there, I looked over the captain's shoulder and saw Marilyn sitting against the far wall, crying hysterically and staring into space. I walked over to her. "What's the matter?" I said. Her voice was shattered, and she told me with shaken and broken words that she had received a telegram from her parents to call home. When she did, they told her that her aunt Ellen had been found dead. She had been run over by a train. Ellen was in her early forties and was a very attractive woman. She was married to a New York City police detective named Tom. According to eyewitnesses, she was seen kneeling on the train tracks at the Bedford Park Station in the Bronx, with her hands held together as if she was praying.

I made emergency arrangements with the airport to book her on the first available flight to New York. They scheduled her for 9:30 AM with Eastern Airlines the following morning, which was a Saturday. The company commander gave me the weekend off and lightened up on me about my being confined to the fort and didn't give me a hard time about having Marilyn down there. He didn't grant me a pass to go back to New York with her. He just told me to make sure she stayed in New York. I said, "Yes, sir." But I knew that wasn't going to happen.

In the morning, Regina picked us up and drove us to the airport. We grabbed a cup of coffee while we waited for Marilyn to board her flight. I held her and kissed her and told her that I would be missing her and to give my love and sympathy to her family.

Regina and I watched for the plane to take off; and then she drove me back to my place, and I stayed there overnight. She told me that she would come and pick me up tomorrow after she closed the store to take me back to the fort. Before leaving, she asked me if I would like to come home with her and stay until tomorrow. I told her, "Thanks, but I'd rather be alone." I asked her if she would take Pinky with her until Marilyn returned, and she gladly did. As the day grew old, I pondered over the long conversation Regina and I had about Marilyn while driving back from the airport. She told me how well she had come to know Marilyn and how fond of her she was. She knew about the problems we had as far as the relationship with the family went and how it had affected Marilyn emotionally and all about the fights we had. Regina also told me that she knew what I must have been going through, being in the middle of a family-and-wife feud. She had a similar problem with her marriage, but fortunately, it ironed itself out. I told her, "I surely hope ours smoothens out. It can't go on like this."

It had gotten so bad that the mere mention of seeing or talking to any member of my family got Marilyn into a rage. Even while riding in the car and the subject came up, she'd kick and punch the dashboard while screaming at the top of her lungs and then reach across and pull my hair and punch me. Then when I'd stop for a red light, she'd open the door and run out and start walking down the road. I had all to do to get her to quiet down and get back into the car. Do you have any idea what a girl's scream sounds like late at night on a quiet roadway? It was as if she was being murdered. As she walked, I'd follow slowly alongside and would try desperately to coax her back into the vehicle. I'd even pull over and get out and walk beside her to try to calm her down, but it would only further her tantrum. It came to the point of my getting so angry that I would be tempted to belt her one. I knew that if I did, I would hurt her badly; so to relieve the anxiety within me, I would punch the nearest lamppost or whatever object that was nearby. The last time it happened, Marilyn walked two miles to Regina's house with me following behind her in the car. If this is what marriage was all about, you could have it. It was a living nightmare.

Marilyn returned four days later. And although she drove me crazy at times, I was glad she was back. I had missed her, and I put it in my mind that I would do all I could to make the marriage work. While she was gone, I stayed in the barracks and hung out with Eddie and Herbie. I didn't have a car on the fort, and not wanting to burden Regina, I decided to put my AWOL habits on hold.

During those four days, we continued with our training. It was mostly classroom studies and learning more about the Vietcong and the North Vietnamese Regular Army and the Regular Army of South Vietnam called ARVNS, of whom we were fighting with; we also learned about how they'd been fighting for years and that the French had occupied South Vietnam for ten years and were forced to abandon the country. We were told to not take the enemy lightly and that they were excellent adversaries who had many decades of fighting experience and were well schooled on jungle warfare and that they had fought and endured in terrible conditions.

One day they took us out to a wide-open terrain. We stared out; there were scattered trees and bushes throughout, giving way for many hiding places. They lined us up overlooking a ledge and told us to turn our backs on the opened field and, when the signal was given, to turn around and try to spot the enemy. When we turned, we combed the area with our eyes. We spotted some, but we'd have been dead ducks. There, right at our feet, was the enemy and right out in broad daylight. It's common that when someone looks, he follows his eyes straight ahead. It was stressed upon us that we start our search by looking directly down at our feet and then work our way outward. I thought this was a great lesson to be learned.

Mail call was one of the high points of being in the service. When you're a soldier, there isn't much to look forward to; so getting letters from home meant a great deal. I received a letter from Tony, who was finishing his AIT at Fort Gordon. He was about to head home for his thirty-day leave before going to Nam. His letter was filled with depressing sentences. He spoke of wishing that he had done more and how sorry he was for some of the things that he did do. I knew he was referring to his refusing to be my best man. I promised myself that when I went home for my thirty-day leave, the first thing that I would do would be to make sure that I'd call him before his departure. I wanted to ease his pain about the best-man business. He went on stating in his letter of how much he missed being home and how he despised Army life. We both hated the Army and looked forward to the day we'd be out for good. There was a postscript down at the bottom of his letter. There was always a chance that we wouldn't be sent to Nam, but that didn't happen in Tony's case. He said in his ending that he'd received his orders. He was heading to Nam.

I lowered his letter to my lap, and my mind drifted back in time to when we were little kids—the one Christmas so long ago when we were seven years old. It was a time when we didn't have a care in the world or even have two cents in our pockets. We were happy, and that's all we needed. Tony helped decorate the Christmas tree, which reached up to the ceiling; it was filled with all sorts of ornaments, topped off with globs of tinsel, and brought to life with the large old-fashioned red, green, blue, and yellow bulbs. The kind of bulbs that would get so hot and would burn your fingers if you touched them. Tony, my cousin Albert Cafaro from my father's side of the family, and I snuck down the stairs early Christmas morning, before my parents were awake, to sneak a peek at the gifts; and there, standing out above all the other presents and displayed in front of the tree, was my first drum set. My eyes almost popped out of their sockets at the wonderous sight. It was a secondhand set bought by my father at a pawnshop. It only had a large bass drum with a light built into it that lit up a colorful landscape highlighted by a windmill overlooking a stream. It was a pretty scene. It also had one tom-tom drum attached to the bass drum and a cymbal with rivets all around it. There was no snare drum. But to me, it was the greatest gift ever.

AIT was nearing its end, but before graduation, it was necessary to undertake another nighttime infiltration course, similar to the one we had taken in basic. This time it was a little different. There was more than one automatic weapon in use. The bullets were fired only a few feet above us. The traces crossed one another. It resembled a psychedelic spiderweb. There were more explosives being detonated all around us, and flares were being shot into the sky, which temporarily illuminated the area. The sound was deafening. It was as real as it could get. It was a long crawl through the thick mud and puddles and under barbed wire, with us muscling our rifles in the crotch of our arms. It was a grueling trial that left us exhausted. This climaxed the seventh week of training.

I spent the weekend with Marilyn. She didn't feel too well, so we just chilled at home and didn't do much. I got to thinking about the time frame between my thirty-day leave beginning and Tony's leave ending. It was cutting it close. I didn't want to take the chance of not being able to speak to him, so I decided to call him before the weekend was over. He'd be leaving any day now. The following day, which was Sunday, I went to a pay phone and called him. His sister Teresa answered with a somber voice, and I asked her how they were all doing. She told me that it was very hard to handle and that they were all very sad. She told me, "Hold on, I'll get Tony."

The telephone conversation we had was not a lengthy one. Tony was terribly withdrawn; and as close as he and I were, I felt as if I were taking precious minutes away from the little time he had left to spend with his family. Before we hung up the phone, I said,

"Tony, you take care of yourself, you hear?" Hesitantly, I hung up the receiver. What I didn't know then was that it was to be the last time I'd ever hear his voice.

The day before graduation, Eddie, Herbie, and I were walking. Eddie suddenly stopped. I turned and asked him, "What's the matter, Eddie?" He didn't say anything. He was sweating, and he began to tremble. He was having one of his seizures. Before I was able to assist him, he passed out and fell to the ground. I told Herbie to stay with him, and I ran as fast as I could to the CO's office to get a stretcher. When they asked me what I needed it for, I told them. They weren't disturbed in the least and showed no concern. Somehow, they had found out about Eddie's condition. This was his third seizure since AIT started, and they had him pegged for a phony. I ran back with the stretcher, and by the time I got back, Eddie was coming around. He didn't remember a thing. He was one of the nicest guys I ever knew. He lost his mother when he was a little boy and was raised by his father and stepmother along with his younger sister, Mary. His dream of becoming a cop was still reachable. A medical discharge was out of the question.

The final day had come, and we readied for our graduation. Sixteen weeks of intense training came to a climax. We handed in our equipment. We didn't have to be looked down on as trainees anymore. The ceremony was brief, and at its end, we were given our orders. Every last one of us was going to Vietnam. It sounds crazy, but we cheered when we found out that we'd be going to where the action was, as if we'd have been disappointed if it were different. More importantly, I wanted to be where Tony was.

My thirty-day leave time was going by fast. Marilyn was getting sick every morning, so we went to a doctor. She was pregnant. It was the beginning of April, so she must have conceived sometime in March. In that case, the baby would be born in December. It would be over five months old when I got back from Nam.

Although we were given the good news about her pregnancy, we had our share of fights. I wanted to go back to New York and visit my folks before I left. She didn't want to. After many bickering battles, she finally consented to return to New York with me. We packed our bags and drove back to the Bronx. That New York skyline, seen from the New Jersey Turnpike, was a welcome sight. It was great to be back home.

We stayed at the apartment of Marilyn's mother. Her parents were the supers of the building. They lived on the ground floor facing the street. We were invited to my parents' house for a going-away party in my honor the following Sunday. When Sunday morning came, Marilyn didn't want anything to do with it. I phoned my mother and told her that we wouldn't be coming. I made up an excuse that Marilyn was sick. They knew that I was lying. My sister called right back and said she was coming over to talk to Marilyn. My boss, Joe, came with her. When they arrived, Joe stayed in the car. Marilyn saw them drive up and ran into the bedroom and locked herself in. She wouldn't open the door. I had to break it down. When we entered the bedroom, she had a handful of pills ready to pop in her mouth. I ran over and grabbed the pills from her hand. She was screaming at the top of her lungs for us to go away and leave her alone. She kept yelling and threw the lamp down and anything else she could get her hands on. She kicked my sister. I grabbed Marilyn and held her and told Rose to wait outside.

"No," she said, "I don't want to leave you here."

I told her, "I'll be out. Just wait outside." The bedroom was in shambles. I eventually calmed Marilyn down enough for her to listen. I told her that I was going to leave without her. She started screaming again, "Leave me alone! Get out!" I let her be and walked out. I heard things being tossed and broken. My sister was a nervous wreck. She was crying hysterically. "Let's go," I said, but before we could get into the car, Marilyn opened the apartment entrance door and stood there.

"John, where are you going?" she asked softly.

"I'm going home. I can't take you anymore."

Then she said in an even softer tone, "John, come here!"

"No," I answered.

"Please come here." I walked over to her and asked her what she wanted. "Take me with you." There had been a complete turnaround in her personality, as if nothing had happened.

"Okay," I said. She wanted a few minutes to fix herself up. We waited for her in the car. My sister and Joe couldn't believe the change in Marilyn from one minute to the next. The entire episode was one big bad scene. As horrible as the day started out, it ended up being quite nice. Everybody got along.

After the family gathering, Marilyn and I went back to her mom's place and to the mess that we had made. I apologized to her parents for the damage. I told them I would repair the door and clean up. Her mother's name was Celia, and her father's name was Ken. He was a small man with a bad temper, especially when he drank. I was the only one he would talk to. He'd call me into the kitchen while he sat in his favorite chair by the window, looking out at the street, and tell me stories of his past. He was of Native American Indian descent. He told me that in his heyday, he had been a dancer and had danced with Ginger Rogers and Fred Astaire. But one day, while he was walking in the street, a truck passed by with a chain dangling from its rear bed. It grabbed his left leg and dragged him, seriously injuring him to the point of ending his dancing career. I liked him, and we got along very well. At times, when he was quite drunk and no one wanted to go near him, I'd walk in through the front door, and he'd holler, "Who's there?" And when he saw that it was me, he'd say, "Oh, John, it's you. Come here. Sit down and talk to me."

Marilyn's mother, Celia, was the opposite. She never drank and was more subdued. Celia seemed like she was the only rational one in the family. They all drank a lot, something I wasn't used to. There was a bar around the corner on 197th Street and Webster Avenue. It was owned by a guy named Bernie, and it was the neighborhood hangout. Marilyn's sister, Donna, spent much of her time there, along with her boyfriend, Candy. She was divorced and had two girls who were split up. One of them, Laurie, lived with Celia while the other girl, Debby, lived with Donna's in-laws just up the block on the same street. Celia also took care of Marilyn's cousin Ronnie ever since he was a baby. Marilyn considered him as her younger brother. They were all fun-loving people. Candy was a character. He was Puerto Rican, and I used to have such a hard time understanding him when he spoke English. All I can say is that there was never a dull moment and that the worst was yet to come.

During my days of leave time, I kept contact with Eddie. He was getting engaged to his girl, Kathy. We were invited to Kathy's place out on Staten Island for a quiet gathering with a few of their friends on the Saturday before we were scheduled to leave for Nam.

After the party, the four of us drove back to Eddie's place in Brooklyn. We stayed there overnight. The following day, April 29, was when we had to report to Fort Dix, New Jersey. Once again, it was time for tears and goodbyes. Eddie had to bid farewell to his parents and his sixteen-year-old sister. Mary was so distraught she almost fainted. She was afraid that she would never again see her brother, who was her idol. He held her tightly in his arms and tried to comfort her and reassure her of his return. It was hard to watch that.

CHAPTER V

GOING TO NAM

W e drove Kathy home, and the three of us headed to the fort. We met Herbie and waited for the flight's schedule. It was to take off from McGuire Air Force Base, adjacent to Fort Dix, the following afternoon. We took in a movie at night. *The Reluctant Astronaut*, starring Don Knotts, was showing. After the show, I drove Eddie and Herbie to the barracks. Marilyn and I wanted to spend every possible minute together; so I drove to a desolate area on the fort and parked, and we slept in the car overnight.

The next morning, April 30, Marilyn drove me to meet up with Eddie and Herbie. They told me that the flight was delayed until the next day, so me and Eddie decided to go AWOL one more time. Herbie stayed behind to alert us of the flight's departure time. The ride from Brooklyn to the fort was about an hour, so it was possible to go ahead with our plan. We picked up Kathy and drove to Eddie's and slept over, hoping that the phone call from Herbie would never come. In a way, it was a mistake for now Eddie had to say goodbye a second time.

We all sat around waiting for the phone to ring. I called home to let my folks know what was going on. Herbie's call came at 1:00 PM, and he told us that the plane would be taking off at 4:20 PM and to get our butts there ASAP. It became a repeat of the scene from the day before. Eddie had to hold Mary and comfort her. When I hugged her, she whispered in my ear, "Please take care of Eddie for me."

"I will, don't worry."

After we dropped Kathy off in Staten Island, we hurriedly set out on our way. Staten Island was closer to the fort than Brooklyn, so it didn't take us out of our way. We got to the fort at about 3:15 PM. I gave Marilyn a kiss and said, "I'll see you in a year." Eddie, Herbie, and I grabbed our gear and fell in line with the others and got on a bus that drove us to the airfield.

We boarded the plane, which was a TWA Boeing 707. Eddie and I sat side by side, and Herbie sat directly behind us. The plane was to make three stops to refuel. The first was Oakland, California; the second, Hawaii; and the third, Okinawa. The longest nonstop flight was nine hours, which was to Vietnam. The entire trip took nineteen hours, with a distance close to thirteen thousand miles.

In a way, we were lucky to go by plane. Many troops were sent over by boat, which took nearly a month and claimed many cases of seasickness. The one good thing about going by ship was that the travel time was deducted from the year spent in Nam.

The pilot made his three refueling stops, and we were on our way. The rest of the flight was during the nighttime. It was very serene on the plane. I don't believe any of us got any sleep. Every so often, someone would make his way down the aisle to use the bathroom. I don't know what the others were tossing around in their minds, but I was wondering what lay ahead. Tony had been there close to a month and, by now, was probably getting used to the place. I remembered when we were ten and we went to see a movie called *The Vikings* with Kirk Douglas and Tony Curtis. When we got home, we got wooden sticks to use as swords and the metal garbage can covers for our shields. Naturally, inspired by the movie, we were ready to take on everyone. All those times we played Army with the gang in the neighborhood, we'd choose up sides like we did when we played baseball, ringolevio, Johnny-on-the-pony, or just plain tag. We'd use a bat and dedicate two captains—one of whom would grab the bat, and the two would go hand over hand up its barrel. If there was a little space left at the top, the guy who's turn it was would try to grab the knob, even if he had to use his fingertips. Then the other captain got three chances to kick the bat out of his opponent's hand. If he did, he got to go first and pick his team. We'd get our toy guns and take cover. "*Bang*, you're dead," someone would shout.

"No, I'm not."

"Yes, you are. I got you, man." That was a lot of fun, but now it was different. It was going to be for real.

It was about 10:00 AM on May 2, 1967, when the stewardess gave the word for us to fasten our seat belts. The plane began its descent, and we eagerly stared out the windows to get our first glimpse at the land we had heard so much about. We broke through some scattered clouds, and there it was. It seemed peaceful enough from the air with miles of rolling green hills and trees. The plane landed smoothly, and before we got off, the stewardess wished us good luck and said, "I'll see you next year." Did she also think to herself of how many of us wouldn't be making the trip back home alive? I wondered that myself.

The plane landed in a place called Bien Hoa, pronounced *ben whah*. The door of the plane swung open, and the stairway was rolled over. We stepped out with our gear swung over our shoulders and made our way down the steps. The sun was brilliant and extremely hot, hotter than I'd ever felt it before. In an instant, my lips, palms, and fingers became slimy. Eddie said, "Shit, do you feel that?" The climate was dreadful. It was so damn muggy and humid, and coming off an air-conditioned plane didn't help any. The dust being disturbed by the Boeing's engines was flying all over, making our throats even drier.

It was different from what we had expected. We thought that we'd be issued weapons and have to run for cover. On the contrary, we didn't hear a shot. Just to our left was a line of soldiers dressed in khakis facing the plane. Some of them had bandages covering their eyes or had their arms in slings. One guy had his leg in a cast and was leaning on crutches. Some may have been going on R&R (rest and relaxation), but most were going home. They gave us that look that said, "These poor guys, they don't know what they're in for." They looked at that plane like they were seeing God.

We loaded up on open-backed trucks that slowly made their way on narrow bumpy dirt roads surrounded by rundown shacks that were closely placed side by side, made from all types of scraps. Clothes were hanging everywhere. People were moving all about with large cone-shaped straw hats covering their heads, shading their faces from the hot sun. Many were on bicycles. Kids were all over the place. Girls no older than seven were seen walking while holding their younger siblings on their hips. It was my first look at the Vietnamese people and the way they lived. This was poverty at its lowest. Coming from the lifestyle we were used to, I couldn't help feeling sorry for these people. They had no running water, no bathrooms, no refrigerators or stoves. The kids didn't have any toys. We had just taken a giant step back in time. God bless America.

We were on our way to a place called the Ninetieth Replacement Center. It was an area where new recruits went to await their assignments, which usually took about two weeks or less. We hooked up with Joe Midgette after we arrived, and the four of us settled into one of the screened-in barracks.

The first night was long and lonely. It was a clear evening. The stars were out; and while lying in my bunk, staring at the sky, I listened to the pounding of bombs hitting the ground and, every so often, the sound of gunfire far off in the distance. I remember thinking that before long, I'd be out there, somewhere in the midst of it all. I started to write a letter. One thing about writing was that it took my mind off where I was and brought me back home to the other side of the world. *It's strange,* I thought, *that the family and friends back in the States are up and about due to the twelve-hour time change.* At least for them, each day, rain or shine, they lived in a land of peace and safety.

The next morning, we all assembled in the center of the compound and listened to hear if our names were among those being called for assignments. None of our names were called. There wasn't much to do during that stay aside from taking up space. But being the Army, they'd always find a way to bust our balls. That evening, Eddie and I had to do KP. We had to go to the supply room and take inventory. While in the room, I noticed a bag of chocolate morsels. My eyes lit up. My fondness for chocolate made it impossible for me to resist taking a bag. "Hey, Eddie," I said, "check this out." I grabbed a bag and opened it. The chocolate was powdery and faded due to the heat, and God only knows how long they'd been there. I ate them anyway. Eddie just ate a handful. Well, I'll tell you, talk about Montezuma's revenge. For the next five days, I couldn't move more than twenty feet from the latrine.

On the twelfth day, we were assembled as usual for roll call. Herbie's name was called. He was going to be attached to the Ninth Infantry Division located in the Mekong Delta Region of Nam. This area was very wet and swampy. Soon after, Eddie, Midgette, and I were called. The three of us were assigned to the First Infantry Division. Once again, it was goodbye time. Now it was Herbie and our close relationship that was being broken up. We never did see Herbie again. At least Midgette, Eddie, and I were headed in the same direction. We gathered our belongings and hopped on the back of a truck along with eight other guys and headed for Dion (*zee-on*), the base camp for the Big Red One.

Traveling en route to Dion, I was able to view a wider scope of the daily routines of these poverty-stricken people. There weren't any paved roads anywhere. The villages resembled the aftermath of a tornado, destroyed by its windy fury. The highest form of transportation that I witnessed was an old Army vehicle that was being used for a bus. There weren't any telephone poles, no electric wires, and no traffic lights or store-front displays.

The women, commonly called momma sans, were dressed in black-and-white silk clothing that resembled pajamas; and as I had seen before, they all had those cone-shaped straw hats with very wide brims on their heads. Some of their tasks were the washing and folding of clothes. When they did this, they assumed a squatting position. From the rear, all that was seen were those large hats that covered half their backs. Their asses were only inches above the ground. This seemed to be their most popular position. The women were much older than they appeared. I could see why. They had to deal with malnutrition and extremely hard labor their entire lives. They were small people but were able to handle the tough chores of their everyday way of life.

The men (poppa sans) were mostly thin and small and seemed to be oblivious to everything around them while working. They wore shorts and were rarely seen wearing shirts. Both sexes went about with bare feet or wore sandals. Many of them chewed on some type of gooey shit that blackened their teeth and caused them to rot. Some of the children had fungus on their feet, arms, legs, and faces. As our vehicle came close, all the kids approached us with their hands held out and begged for candy. It was sad.

After leaving the village, we passed by a rice paddy. The people were hard at work. The momma sans were standing knee-deep in mud, gathering the rice and loading it onto carts. Their infants were strapped to their backs while they did the work. A useful tool they used was a yoke. It was a curved piece of wood that lay across their shoulders. It was made up of a container on each end held to the yoke with a piece of twine. This was how they toted food or objects. They would also fill large jugs with food or water and strap them to their backs or carry them atop their heads. To aid them with their chores, they had oxen to help tote the heavier loads.

We neared Dion, and one fellow was displaying a large medallion he wore around his neck. He said, "This is my good-luck piece. You know, like in the movies, when the Bible in someone's pocket stops a bullet. Who knows? It may do the same for me some day."

I said, "Yeah, you never know."

The truck entered the entrance of the base camp. There was a large sign that read "Welcome to Dion, Home of the First Infantry Division." In the center of the billboard was a painting of the unit's insignia: a green patch with a "Big Red One" painted in the center of it. The unit's motto was written on the sign: "NO MISSION TOO GREAT. NO TASK TOO DIFFICULT."

Dion was built up and well secured. It looked like a regular Army base with wooden barracks, a PX, and an NCO club. We were assigned temporary quarters and just hung around, awaiting our next orders. One item we had to do was to exchange our greenback and any silver coins we had into Vietnam currency called piasters, which was like Monopoly paper money. Two dollars in American currency was worth two hundred piasters. Greenback was worth a lot of money in the black market, so it was forbidden to have any. One could probably get one thousand piasters for one twenty-dollar bill. But making a habit of doing that could burden our economy. At least that's what we were told. After making the exchange at one of the buildings, I pulled KP duty; but it was much different. The momma sans were hired to clean up and wash the utensils, so there wasn't much for us to do but watch them.

There was a large canopy outside the rear of the mess hall. It was there where the women washed the pots and pans—a job I had gotten stuck doing many times in basic. I hated it. I'll never forget what I saw as I sat on the edge of a table while watching them. Just to my left, lying dead on the ground, was a huge insect of some kind. I had never seen anything like it. It had been chopped in half with a machete. The thing resembled a cross between a beetle and a cockroach and had tentacles about twelve inches long and a body that had to be at least eighteen inches in length. The momma sans went about their business as if someone had just swatted a fly. They thought nothing of it. And to think I thought the roaches in New York were bad.

After spending nearly a week in Dion, we received our orders. The three of us were assigned to the 1/2nd Infantry, First Infantry Division, located in Phuoc Vinh (*fook vin*). They transported us by truck; and when we got there, we were told to wait outside an office building. There was a line of soldiers waiting alongside the wall of the place. We stood off to the rear and out of sight. The line began to move, and we were at the end of it. I was dead last. Eddie was in front of me, and Midgette was before Eddie. As we got closer, we could hear what was happening. A sergeant, sitting behind a desk, was telling each soldier what company he would be going to. It was either Alpha, Bravo, Charlie, Delta, or Echo. We approached the desk, and Midgette was assigned to the Bravo company.

When it came to me and Eddie, the sergeant paused and glanced through some papers. He looked up at us and said. "We're all filled up. There's no more room in any of the line companies. We'll have to see where to put you two guys." He hesitated, and Eddie and I glanced at each other and then turned back toward the sergeant. "Well," he said, "we'll put you in Headquarters Detachment." When we heard that, we figured we'd gotten lucky. Maybe we'd be clerks or something of that sort. But our joy was stomped on by his next words. "Yeah, we'll put you with recon. They always come back short from the field."

"Oh shit," we said, quietly. Then we walked outside. Recon! That meant scouts. And I didn't like the way he said they always came back short. It wasn't until sometime later that we found out what the term *short* meant. It was those who had little time left before going home and not short of men due to casualties.

A truck picked us up and drove us to our unit. We lucked out in the sense that we knew we'd be staying together for the rest of the tour. I saw a jeep with three men in it. But what stood out and impressed me was the fact that one of the soldiers was standing behind a machine gun mounted on a stand. I had seen something like this on television, a show called the *Rat Patrol*. It had the same setup of a squad of these gun jeeps.

We approached the guard that stood at the front gate, which separated the town of Phuoc Vinh from the base camp. The truck proceeded a little farther and screeched to a halt. The guys assigned to line companies were told to get off. Only Eddie and I remained. The driver pulled away and drove a short distance. We passed by wooden-framed barracks. They were enclosed by mesh screens and had a door on each end. The roofs were made from rows of sheet metal. The driver pulled in front of one of these buildings and stopped, and we got off. He said, "This is it," and took us to the CO's office.

In this case, the company commander was a master sergeant. Sergeant Page was his name. He was rather fat and sloppy looking. He reminded me of Mayor Peoples from the TV show *The People's Choice* with Jackie Cooper. After he learned our names, he pointed to a set of barracks next to his quarters. These two buildings were the homes of the recon platoon. He told us to go and pick out a couple of vacant bunks.

The battalion was out on an operation called Operation Junction City and were due back today. Aside from the clerk and a few sick and injured or short-timers, the place was empty and kind of peaceful. The barracks were recently built, so Eddie and I had our choice of either building and bunk. We had no sooner gotten unpacked and settled in when a convoy of deuce-and-a-halfs came roaring down the main road, carrying the battalion back from the airstrip. In a matter of minutes, the serenity was overcome by cheers and bustling. They were out in the field for weeks and were happy to be back, and they showed it.

One of the platoon sergeants came up to us and introduced himself as Dutch. He was the acting commander of recon. We met most of the other members and felt right at home. They were very friendly. Dutch told me and Eddie that he would let us know what our jobs would be as soon as everyone got settled in.

I relaxed on my bunk and started to write a letter home to Marilyn and my family to let them know how I was doing and to give them my address. Also, I wanted Tony to know where I was. I had gotten another letter from him while I was on my thirty-day leave. He was with the Twenty-Fifth Armor Division stationed at Cu Chi (*koo chee*). I was interrupted with my writing when a few guys were fooling around. They were teasing another fellow, trying to grab a stick he was carrying around. They called it "a short-timer's stick." It was symbolic of those who were about to go home. Every month, the stick would be cut shorter. This is when we learned what the term *short* meant. The short-timer got the last laugh. He held his stick up and said, "Here, all you suckers, sit on this." He was going home in two days. The lucky bastard.

Eddie and I were summoned by Dutch to meet him at the CO's office. They were enlarging the recon platoon so it would be able to be divided into two squads. Because of my size, I was made a machine gunner, and Eddie was to be my ammo bearer. This meant that the platoon would now have two gunners, one per squad, when out on patrol. Dutch told us that since the platoon was expanding, we'd be getting a new platoon leader and that we'd become the battalion recon platoon, which would consist of twenty to thirty men.

I was issued an M60 machine gun and Eddie an M16. We had very little training on these weapons. We had fired them only one time in AIT. We returned to the barracks, and Dutch introduced me to a guy named Ronnie Elza. He was the other machine gunner. "Ronnie," Dutch said, "this is John. He's going to be our other gunner. Teach him all about the weapon!"

Ronnie was a stocky Caucasian fellow a little taller than me, and he wore glasses. He was from Illinois. He showed me all there was to know about the gun: how to load and fire it and to break it down to its tiniest parts for cleaning. It fired a 7.62mm caliber bullet, just like the M14 and the AK-47 (which was a Russian-made automatic weapon used by the North Vietnamese and the Vietcong). It was belt-fed. The M60 weighed twenty-three pounds and was air-cooled and gas-operated. Attached to the front of its barrel was a bipod that could fold and open or extend to rest it on the ground at an adjustable height. It had a snap-in pouch on the left side, which could hold one hundred rounds. A tripod stand with a swivel was also used for stationary firing. To load it, the cover plate located at the top of the gun had to be lifted and the belt would be placed into a track. The plate would then be slammed down tightly. Once the bullets were loaded, the bolt located on the right side of the gun had to be pulled back and then pushed forward. This engaged the round. The safety switch located on its left side above the trigger would be disengaged, and then it would be ready to fire. When the bullet was released, the track under the cover plate along with the bolt action would recoil automatically and eject the empty shell and place another round into the track. It also had an apparatus on the rear of the buttstock that would flip up to use as a shoulder rest. The gunner's hand was protected from the hot barrel by a plastic guard. The barrel could be changed if it got too hot. An overheated barrel would cause the bullet to not travel very far. It also had an adjustable fold-down sight that would enable the gunner to take aim by aligning the sight with a raised pointer on top of the front of the barrel just behind the muzzle. It also had a handle on top to tote it and two loops, one on the front and one on the back, to hook a shoulder harness to aid in humping it in the jungles. It was a great weapon and was a tremendous asset to any squad.

Ronnie watched me take it apart and put it back together over and over until I had it down to a science. It was able to be broken down to thirty-three pieces. I noticed a notch at the bottom of the plastic guard, and I asked what it was. He told me that it was for the mount on the jeeps. "What jeeps?" I asked.

"Our jeeps," he replied and went on to explain. "When we have to go on the road for security purposes or escort a convoy, we use the gun jeeps. You and I are the main gunners who hump the bush with the M60, but there are five gun jeeps, so there are three other members of the platoon that we use as gunners whenever we use the jeeps." He went on to tell me that each jeep had a three-man team (a driver, a radio operator, and a gunner) and were assigned numbers. I thought back to that jeep I saw with the three guys on it; that impressed me. Who'da thought that I would be doing that very thing?

That first night, Eddie and I, being the two newest members, were told to pull guard duty for the entire evening. We were driven by jeep to the main gate. We didn't have weapons; but there were a pair of night-vision binoculars. We replaced the guards at 5:00 PM. There was a tiny shack off the side of the road for the men on guard duty to take shelter from the rain. It was surrounded by sandbags for further protection against any hostility.

It was still light out, so all we did was stand around and watch the Vietnamese civilians leave the camp after a day's work. They left on foot or by bicycle. They had to be out of the compound by 6:00 PM. It was at that time we had to lock the gate and the time when the children would collect the dirty laundry from the GIs or return the clothes that were already cleaned or washed. I watched as a GI told a little girl to have them back by Monday at 5:00 PM. She answered,

"Okay, Monday, five clock. No sweat." The term "no sweat," an American cliché, was an expression used by the Vietnamese children to indicate "no problem." With that, the little girl (who couldn't have been more than ten years old) took the bundle, loaded it onto her bicycle, and peddled away. One important factor that we were told to keep our eyes open for was to see that none of the people, old or young, appeared to be walking as if they were counting the paces of their steps. It was one of the sneaky ways the Vietcong had of measuring the distance of a building or ammunition-supply bunker so they would be able to zero in on them with mortars. They certainly were cunning little bastards not to be underestimated or taken for granted. Eddie and I were green, but we were learning fast.

At exactly six o'clock, we locked the gate. We were instructed to report in every hour, by two-way radio, for a position check. It was an easy task until it began to get dark. The defining sounds of the crickets gave us the jitters. Any noise we heard, we called in. The sergeant of the guard must have prepared himself for a night full of laughs. He knew that we were virgin in country and that we'd be jumping at any sound; so he paid little to no attention to our calls. He'd appease us and tell us to keep him updated.

The two guards we replaced had given us a transistor radio to use. The Army had its own broadcasting station, which recorded programs from the US and, in turn, replayed them on the air. We listened to oldies, which helped pass the time; but even with the music playing, we'd think we heard something and call in without hesitation. It was comical. One of us would turn the radio off and whisper, "Did you hear that?"

"Yeah," the other would reply. "Listen, there it is again. Do you see anything?"

Using the binoculars, one of us would answer, "I don't know. It's hard to tell." Then to aid in our suspicion, the crickets would become silent. We swore that someone was out there. We had no choice but to call in. "Post number one reporting."

The sergeant of the guard would answer, "Yes, post number one," as if to say, "What is it this time?"

Then we'd whisper, "We're sure we hear something moving out there."

His answer would be, "Okay, post number one, keep me posted."

How he must have laughed at us. Here we were, so frightened we'd barely lift our heads above the sandbags to take a peek or dare close our eyes to get some sleep. To make matters worse, the damn mosquitoes were biting the shit out of us.

"Eddie did you bring the insect repellent?"

"No."

God, that was a long-ass night.

The morning sunrise was surely a welcomed sight; and when it pushed the darkness across the horizon and diminished the singing crickets one by one, we got up and stretched our weary bodies and came to the conclusion that all the noises and shadows we'd thought we'd heard and saw had turned out to be nothing at all. I turned to Eddie and said, "Eddie, my friend, we still have a lot to learn about this place."

We were relieved from our post and were able to get some chow. The mess hall was located directly across the road from our barracks. It was furnished with wooden tables and long wooden benches. Before we got to order what we wanted to eat, we were given malaria pills. There were many cases of this disease due to the millions of mosquitoes. It wasn't a wise decision to not take them. The breakfasts were good. We were able to eat all that we wanted. The usual was pancakes and fried or scrambled eggs. Unlike in training, we had the choice of how we wanted our eggs cooked. And the scrambled eggs weren't powdered. The only catch was that you had until 6:00 AM to get there or you wouldn't eat.

After chow, we went back to our barracks and relaxed awhile. No one was bothered by the officers or sergeants. I was in the middle of writing a letter when I was disturbed by two new recruits. Their names were David C. Bender, who came from Michigan, and Craig Ver Linden from California. David C. was my height and slender and well educated, which was accentuated by his uncanny usage of the English language. He had a fantastic sense of humor. Craig was also my height, quiet, and subdued. One couldn't help but notice the large tattoos he displayed on his arms. On his left upper arm was that of a bear standing and on his left lower arm was that of Christ. His right upper arm was that of a tiger. I took notice of how neatly he placed his belongings into his locker and how meticulous he was about himself and his area. We hit it off right from the start.

After getting to know one another, I returned to my bunk and to my writing. In between thoughts, I paused and peered down at my M60, which was right alongside my bed to my right. I had it set on its tripod. It was shining from my cleaning it and the oil I had just rubbed on it. And as it stood silent, I could sense its ferociousness and its devastating ability to destroy and kill, like a silent bull before a storm. A machine gunner was also issued an Army .45 pistol. It wasn't worth a shit. Because of its kickback, it was about as accurate as a bow and arrow in a windstorm. I had it hanging over my bedpost.

On the third day, we were given special details. I was to go to the dumps with garbage and scraps leftover from the mess hall. The driver of the dump truck's name was Mike. He was a short-timer. We made our way to the dump slowly as the truck tilted and swayed from the hills and holes on the dirt roads. We bumped our heads on the roof of the cab from the sloppy ride. Just short of reaching our destination, Mike stopped the truck, and a young Vietnamese girl came running up to us and jumped onto the running board and threw her arms around Mike's neck and kissed him. They spoke for a few minutes. I was a little embarrassed watching this. I was homesick as it was, and this show of affection didn't make me feel any better. It made me miss Marilyn that much more. This was my first encounter between a GI and a Vietnamese girl. She had long straight black hair down to her waist. She was thin and plainly attractive. It was easy to see that Mike must have spent much time with her during his year in Nam. She kissed him again and went on her way. She got a few yards from the truck, turned, and stood waving. Mike shifted the throttle, and we pulled out.

We continued slowly. I saw that a bunch of kids were making their way toward the truck. Some were barely dressed, and those who were had torn clothing on. Very few had sandals on their feet. Most of them were barefoot. As Mike backed the truck up an incline and came closer to the ridge that overlooked the garbage dump, the kids were aligning themselves along on it. A familiar scene flashed through my brain of when, back home, I would drive up a similar-looking bumpy dirt road and drop off all types of debris into a landfill that would be used for a future building site; and the seagulls would be flying low, awaiting to dive into their next meal to be served.

Mike engaged the hydraulic knob that lifted the bed of the truck. It slowly made its way upward, and the garbage started to ease its way off, spreading out over the pile that existed. What I witnessed next would stay with me for the rest of my life. The seagulls diving for the food were not birds but starving children of all ages. They dove into that garbage as if it were a steak dinner. I would never had believed that had I not seen it myself; but there it was, right before my eyes—kids wallowing knee-deep in garbage, hunting in vain for food to bring back to their families. What a terrible thing, hunger. It was a pitiful sight. My father had told me of such scenes when he was in the South Pacific. Now I, too, could relate this to my children someday and hope that they realized how fortunate they were.

When we got back to the compound, I got a big laugh at the detail Eddie had to do. He had to dispose of the fecal matter and liquid waste from the latrine, which was located about one hundred feet from the barracks. It was a wooden shed that contained a bench with six potty holes. Under each potty was a fifty-five-gallon drum, which was used to catch and contain the human waste. Once they were filled, the contents had to be disposed of. To do this, the drums were dragged out from under the latrine, through a trapdoor, to a safe distance. Kerosene was poured into them and set aflame. The fire burned until it distinguished itself. It had to be repeated if necessary. For days after, we teased Eddie by saying, "Hey, Eddie, how much shit did you burn today?"

Since the battalion had recently returned from a major operation, the stay in Phuoc Vinh was extended. We were issued helmets, which we never wore but we put them to use. Each morning we'd fill them with cold water. There was no hot water. Then we'd brush our teeth, rinse off, and shave in that order. We had a bunch of five-gallon cannisters that were filled with potable water daily; therefore, water wasn't scarce. But it was good practice to form a habit of rationing it.

There was a guy named Bob who was a short-timer and had been recently shot in his foot. He found out that I had experience in plumbing and carpentry. So he asked me if I would help him build a large shower stall between the two barracks. "Sure," I said. We put in an order for the materials: a load of two-by-tens, some rolls of sheet metal, four spigots, and a pair of back-to-back fifty-five-gallon drums with the bottoms cut out and the drums welded together. We also ordered some two-by-fours to frame the stand to hold the drums and a couple of hammers and boxes of nails. We had to use handsaws to cut the wood. We built it in no time at all. It had two openings, one for each barracks. It had a divider across the middle to give some sort of privacy and was closed in by sheet-metal walls all around. A truck would come every two days to fill the drums, which were supported seven feet above our heads with a spigot tapped into each one. We just had to reach up and turn the valve of the spigot and, voilà, instant cold-water shower.

I finally got to finishing my letters to Marilyn, my family, and Tony. At least the Army made it easy for us to mail them. We didn't have to pay postage. We wrote "Free" in the corner where we'd normally put a stamp. And for the letters that were sent to other friends in Nam, we'd write "In Country" in the lower left-hand corner. This system was designed to encourage letter writing by the GIs to comfort families back home.

CHAPTER VI

JUNGLE DEVIL SCHOOL

E ddie, David C., Ver Linden, and I had to uproot ourselves and spend a week at Jungle Devil School, which was located a short distance from our newfound home but still within the company perimeter. All the newcomers were forced to attend this. We took along with us our gear and weapons. I wasn't allowed to take my machine gun, so they issued me an M16. They wouldn't let us return to our area, but we were able to eat at the mess hall whenever possible. There were forty of us, and we stayed in one large canvas tent. The school was supervised by sergeants who were short-timers. It was a good job for those who had little time left in country. They were able to use up their final days usefully and, at the same time, minimize the danger of injury or death.

There was no place to be perfectly safe in all of Vietnam. You would think that, being within your perimeter, you were fine; but all too often, one would let his guard down, as in two cases during prior classes of JD training. One fellow had walked into a booby trap and was blown to bits. Another was injured from a sniper's bullet. "Charlie" was out there and knew where we were at all times. It was wise to remember that fact. It might save your life.

This was our first taste of jungle living. We did everything in the bush. Each morning, on patrol, we'd romp through the thicket and dense jungle, wading in the mud and slush of the watery swamps. The deeper we went, the thicker it got. The only way to get through was to hack our way with machetes. At least it was cool under the trees. The monsoon season hadn't started yet, and it was terribly hot in the sun. It seemed that the sky hosted large puffy white clouds, but for some reason, they would never move in front of the sun to shield out its rays. I'd use body language to try to maneuver the clouds into position for giving us that much-needed shade, but it was no use.

Our fatigues became completely saturated with perspiration. To replace the loss of salt from our bodies, we'd take salt tablets. And I made sure I continued my daily dose of malaria pills. Those, and there were many, who faked taking them were only kidding themselves. Malaria was a serious disease that even if cured, had a tendency to resurface later on in life. I wasn't about to take that chance. There were just too many damn mosquitos around. Aside from the murky water, one of their favorite breeding grounds was around sandbags that were always moist from the morning dew. We'd use sandbags as a seat for a toilet. We'd dig a hole and then pile three to four sandbags on both sides of the pit. When someone sat on them to do his business, those pesky bastards would have a feast on your thighs or butt. I don't think there was anything on earth that I despised more than a mosquito. If I swatted one, I would put it on my knee and pound it repeatedly until it completely vanished from sight.

With each passing day, we lived less and less of the life we'd known. It was more like the life of an animal. When we ate, it didn't make any difference if dirt or bugs fell into our food or if our meals got saturated with rain. All that mattered was that we were hungry. It appeared that the entire jungle ground was covered with tiny ants. It didn't matter where we sat, ants would be crawling up on our boots and up our pants legs. The patrols were so exhausting that ants, spiders, bugs, or mud did not stop anyone from sitting or lying down, welcoming a short rest. We learned what it was to thirst and salvage the water in our canteens. I discovered my own way of not running out of water, which was to hold out for as long as I could from taking my first sip of water at the start of the day. I learned from the fact that when I would drink early in the morning, I would run out of water by noon time; and that was when the hottest time of day began.

Even if you carried more than one canteen, which most of us did, it seemed that once you took your first drink, your body craved more; and it was difficult to stop.

All during JD school, we kept little to no contact with the others back at the barracks. We went on patrol after patrol, learning more and more about the jungle and its inhabitants. One thing that bothered me was that each morning, when we started out on patrol, we'd take the same path. This, to me, didn't seem to be a wise habit to instill in us. The enemy would be able to monitor your route of travel and set up an ambush. I know that we were in training and in an area that was deemed to be safe, but it would have been better if we explored a different path each time so we'd follow that concept throughout our tour.

I received my first letter from Marilyn. I couldn't wait to open it. After all the mushy talk, she wrote that she had some bad news to tell me. She said, "Junior died of a heart attack." Her words hit me hard. Eddie and David C. saw my face drop and asked me what was wrong. I told them, "I just lost a real good friend. This fuckin' Army." I was mad that I wasn't home to be there with him. I had to swallow it up and keep focused. To help ease my sorrow, I tried to convince myself that, at least for the last year or so, he knew he had had a friend in me.

I looked all around me and said to my two friends, "Look at this shit. There's nothing but jungle and bugs and fuckin' 'Charlie' out there ready to blow us away. What the fuck are we doing here, man?" I just wanted to be alone for a while, so I walked away.

Speaking of bugs, aside from the tiny ants that could not be avoided, there were the larger red and black ants. The red ants would attack and bite the hell out of you. They caused many of the men to do a quick strip in the middle of the jungle. They occupied the branches and leaves of plants and of bushes, and when some poor unsuspecting guy walked into them, the ants were all over him in a flash. Then it was off with the clothes, and the hand slapping and dancing began.

The large black ants were not as bad as their red counterparts. They seemed to be natural enemies. When confronted against each other, you could see the red ants rear back on their hind legs and gnaw forward with their front legs and prongs in attempt to bite the enemy. The two species were forever combating one another. There were large dirt mounds, some three feet high and two-and-a-half feet wide. These were anthills and seen throughout the jungle. Oh, it gets better.

The jungle had everything in it. Monkeys, snakes, scorpions, tarantulas, leeches, bugs, and all sorts of spiders. These were the company we had to learn to live with every day and night; but still the most common and most petulant of them all was the mosquito. There was no getting away from them. We were issued insect repellent to combat the little fuckers, but that only helped to a certain degree.

Scorpions were large, six to eight inches in length, and silver in color with black streaks They had crab-like claws and long tails that they used to rear back on to attack, and they had a stinger at the end of these tails. They could mostly be seen under rocks or among damp sandbags, or they would plant themselves on the dirt walls of foxholes. Thank goodness they were not deadly, but they were able to produce enough of a sting to render a man ill.

The tarantulas were also large, approximately the size of a man's hand. They were completely covered with hair and weren't seen as frequently as scorpions. They, too, were not poisonous to humans; however, there were all sizes and species of spiders, some of which were deadly.

Large animals and reptiles such as monkeys, tigers, and snakes feared the sounds of bombs and gunfire and would vacate the areas; so they were seldom seen.

Leeches infested the rivers and streams, and if you were not properly prepared for them when wading through water, you'd find them all over you sucking your blood. If this occurred, the best way to get rid of them was to light up a cigarette and burn them off. Sometimes you would need help to get to those leeches in areas on your body that you couldn't see or reach.

Our fatigues and jungle boots were well designed for both leeches and hot temperature. They were lightweight. The shirts were long and loose and were worn outside the pants. The pants were also loose and had pull cords down by the ankles to allow tightening to keep the leeches or water snakes from going up your legs. The boots were excellent. They were made from leather and green material. They dried quickly; and if they got soaked, you'd just have to put a dry pair of socks on, and your feet would be fine. Most of us carried extra pairs of socks. It helped to aid your feet from getting jungle rot. Every third day, while out in the field, clean fatigues were flown by chopper and dropped in a pile for an exchange. All we had to do was sift through the massive mound and find a shirt and pair of pants that would fit. Once you found a set that suited you, you'd change right there and leave the dirty ones in another pile. Sometimes the fatigues that we had were in better condition than the exchange, so it was better to keep them on and wait for the next delivery. Those troops who purchased camouflaged outfits kept them rather than exchange them and washed them in a stream. Our mail was delivered to us, and I received my first of three letters from my cousin Tony. I would like to share them with you.

20 May '67

Hi John,

How are things going there in camp? You're in with a tough outfit. What type of work are you doing? Are you south of Saigon? Things here with me are fairly well. I've been in a scrap already where my truck blew up. I hit a big mine. Man, it was really something, a very strange feeling. Now I'm a scout for a while, and I drive on and off. I've been put in for spec 4 last month and this month also. I think I might make it.

John, you'll find this country a little different than what you expected, at least I think so up here. I've learned to keep my eyes open and who to trust and not to trust, and there are very few to trust. There's one town near route 1 heading north that has always given us trouble, and we destroyed it. Killed twenty VC. Captured twelve suspects and shot a twelve-year-old boy in the arm who was ready to fire an RPG-2 rocket at one of the vehicles. Our Alpha troop made the strike.

I received word that your wife is pregnant. I hope you put in for all those benefits and stuff they give for being away from your wife and things of that nature. I keep myself busy in contact with just about everyone back home and am writing often. We have a pretty good time in camp. We have beer, soda, and ice we usually put in a cooler when we go to the field. That's about it for now, John. Take care of yourself; keep your eyes open, and my regards to your wife.

Tony

That afternoon, Eddie and I were on a break. It was extremely hot, and as always, the clouds avoided the sun. We were in an open field and were sitting on two empty ammo boxes facing each other and talking. There was artillery fire in the distance. Eddie was holding a lit cigarette in the fingers of his right hand, which was draped over his right knee and hanging between his legs. Suddenly, the cigarette flew out of his hand and dropped to the ground a few feet from where we were sitting. We looked at each other, wondering how that happened. Eddie bent over and picked up the butt and examined it closely. Embedded into it was a piece of shrapnel from the artillery. They were blasting thousands of feet away from us. We didn't even have visual of their location, and the odds of a tiny piece of metal traveling that distance and getting lodged into a cigarette seemed impossible. This helped substantiate the fact that we could never be too careful or totally safe, no matter where we were.

When that break was over, they brought us back into the bush to listen to a lecture about a firefight. Although we had not yet witnessed an actual gunfight, I could only imagine the fear that would accompany one. The sergeant doing the talking was a clone to Buddy Ebsen, who played Jed Clampett from the TV show *The Beverly Hillbillies*. He made it sound as if he made a career from firefights and that it was no big deal to be a part of a shoot-out. He said, "The sooner you fire your weapons, the quicker the fear will leave you." He made us feel like there would be no way avoiding a conflict and getting shot at was inevitable.

Hearing this made me think back to when Tony and I were kids. When we walked up the block, there was an Italian restaurant on the corner of Boston Road and Bouck Avenue called Nina's. On the outside brick wall, encased in a glass enclosure, was a giant picture showing Custer's Last Stand. The two of us always stopped and stared at the colorful scene showing Custer, standing tall and dressed in his frontier outfit with his sword in his hand, surrounded by Indians. There were lots of

Custer's Last Stand.

horses and cavalry soldiers shooting back at their enemy, who outnumbered them by far. There were many casualties on both sides. It showed soldiers being scalped and some with their pants down, showing their bare butts. Being nine years old, we were so impressed by that scene. Now what we were facing was not cowboys and Indians using small-arms fire and swords and bow and arrows. This was so much more devastating. And I knew that if a battle was to happen, we'd have to put our lives in God's hands.

An important aspect that played out in just about all situations was the usage of smoke grenades. They played an important role in saving lives. They were cylinders about six inches in length and two-and-a-half inches in diameter. There was a ring connected to a cotter pin, which, when pulled, would immediately emit a colored smoke. There were a variety of colors used such as white, green, orange, and yellow. The white was solely used to designate a location for an air strike initiated by the Air Force's rocket-launching jets. Once the pilots were given the coordinates, the white smoke grenade was tossed in the general area of the enemy and would pinpoint where to fire the rockets. The other colors of smoke were used for either showing a medevac site, a supply drop, an enemy location, or to help lost troops find their way back.

One of the most important, if not *the* most important, feature in the Vietnam War was the helicopters. They were invaluable, with a numerous amount of usages. Within minutes, they would drop off supplies or hot meals or evacuate the wounded, which reduced the number of fatal casualties enormously. Their actions gave a soldier a great deal of confidence and hope that his chances of surviving were elevated. A wounded soldier could be picked up and flown to a hospital within forty-five minutes. God bless the chopper pilots and gunners. They would fly into a hot zone, taking enemy fire and putting their lives at risk, time after time.

In the jungle, there was no set time to eat. Whenever we felt hungry, we'd reach into a green sock that was tied to our shoulder strap and flung behind. It was wide and long enough to fit five K ration cans of food. The sock was an ideal place to store them because it made them easier to tote and kept them out of the way. Some guys had two socks.

The meals came in boxes of eight inches by eight inches by four inches. Each box was labeled with what was in it. Some examples were boned turkey, boned chicken, chicken noodle soup, or spaghetti and meatballs, which no Italian like me would even attempt to eat. Another of the cans contained dessert, such as pound or fruitcake, peaches, pears, applesauce, cookies, and my favorite, two pieces of chocolate wrapped in tinfoil. There was also a packet with salt, pepper, sugar, powdered milk, a pack of cocoa powder, a small roll of toilet paper, plastic utensils, and last but not least, a tiny tool to open the cans known as a P-38. There was a lot of trade-off going on among us. My personal favorites were the boned chicken and boned turkey. Anything else, to me, sucked.

Jungle devil school was nearly over, and we gained a great deal of knowledge from the one week of training there. The little hints taught to us could prove valuable when patrolling the bush. In my mind, I repeated the lessons over and over to develop an instinctive readiness. The sergeant's instructions echoed in my thoughts as I remembered him saying, "Keep a safe distance away from the man in front of you, about fifteen feet. In the event, he is to trigger a booby trap, he alone will fall victim. Avoid large gatherings or bullshit sessions. This presents a welcome target for a grenade, and in such a case, one grenade could wipe out the lot of you. Always maintain visual contact with the man ahead. It takes only seconds to lose sight of one another in the thick underbrush. Men have gotten lost, captured, or killed due to inattentiveness.

"Avoid talking and laughing. Sound travels in the quietness of the jungle, and the enemy will take advantage of this foolishness and be ready and waiting to wipe out your unsuspecting and lax asses. Always know where you and your camp are. Never leave anything behind, such as empty cans or empty shells. 'Charlie' will use this against you. Bury your garbage and human waste. 'He' is no fool. Never underestimate him. Respect him. You are fighting in his land and on his terms. He will take advantage of your mistakes. So don't make any.

"Maintain full alertness. Look into the trees as well as on the ground. Always expect the unexpected. Remember, 'Charlie' knows where you are at all times. Never return on the same path you traveled. And if you are ever captured, the best time to escape is immediately after abduction. Don't give the enemy time to take you farther away from your comrades or familiar ground. This is also the time when there is the most confusion, and chances of escape are at their best. Never touch or kick anything such as a box or can. It may turn out to be the last thing you'll ever do. Never trust any Vietnamese child or adult."

Eddie, David C., and I returned to our company area. The camp was still in its building stages. The three of us—along with two other guys, Gary and Bill—had to build two bunkers, one for each barrack, large enough to accommodate all the men of our platoon. They had to be located in the most advantageous spot, which was alongside each building, close to the door. These were designed to protect us against a mortar attack. We dug a hole four feet deep, six feet wide, and ten feet long. The bunkers had to be minimal in size; being too large would enhance the chances of a direct hit.

The dirt we took from the holes was used to fill sandbags. This was done with the aid of momma sans who assumed their usual squatting positions. The top few inches of the bags were folded, and the women would place their hands inside the bags and spread their fingers apart to hold the sacks open to allow room for the shovels to fill them with dirt. These sandbags were then set two tiers high around the perimeter of the opening. Then we'd cut four-inch round tree trunks using our machetes and lie them across the span of the pit, resting them on the top of the sandbags, side by side, until the opening was completely closed. When this was accomplished, we'd pile the sandbags on top of the tree trunks at least three high. At the end nearest to the barracks door, we'd leave an opening close to the ground, just large enough for a man to fit through. We kept our ammunition and explosives right outside the bunker, which was also surrounded and covered with sandbags. Among these were grenades, C-4 blasting material with blasting caps, claymore mines, shotgun shells, M79 rounds, and metal boxes filled with bullets. There was enough explosives and firepower in that bunker to annihilate an entire battalion.

We worked with our shirts off, and the sweat poured off our brows and down our necks and backs, which left a trail of black dirt that acted as a mini roadway to carry our beads of perspiration down behind our belt buckles and into our pants. That cold shower I helped build was a godsend after all that work.

While we were at JD school, the second platoon leader that Dutch had foretold us about had taken over the entire recon platoon. Dutch brought him over and introduced us to him. His name was Sergeant Louis Santos. He was an E-6, as was Dutch, and had been born in Peru. One look at him, and you could see that he was very militaristic. He kept his uniform neatly pleated. He wore that "Smokey the Bear" hat strapped tightly to his chin. He had a dark complexion. He seemed like a good guy. He told us that he would be assigning the jeep teams the following day.

Eddie and I still hadn't met most of the crew yet. We figured it was time to do just that. Not including the short-timers and aside from me and Eddie, their names were as follows: David C. Bender, John Deloge, Gregory "Woody" Woodhouse, Jerry "Tex" Downs, Terry "Funky" Havens, Jerry King, Abraham Rahar, Sergeant Corky "Smitty" Smith, Craig Ver Linden, Benjamin "Doc" Jimenez, Sergeant Nezat, Bill Lundsford, Arty Parker, Gus Polite, Gary, Baker, Charles House, John Sexton, Terry Schneider, Maleski, Nash, James "Baldy" Hessle, Ron Elza, "Dutch," Sergeant Santos, Mike Stark and Red.

The following day, Santos gathered all of us in one barrack and designated the five three-man crews and what jeep they would be using. My jeep was coded 2-2. I was the gunner, Deloge was the radio operator (TC operator), and Sergeant Nezat was the driver. There were five jeeps, which took fifteen of our men. The rest of the platoon rode in the rear of a one ton and a half. Eddie wanted so much to be a driver of the one ton and a half. He asked me if I would talk to Santos about it. I told him, "Don't worry, I'll take care of it."

Picture of me standing on my gun jeep with Eddie at the wheel and unknown lineman.

The jeeps were two-seaters. The gunner rode in the rear. The machine gun was mounted to an iron post and was able to swivel 360 degrees and pivot up and down. It was held on to the mount with a clasp, which could easily be released if dismounting was necessary. Attached to the left side of the mount was a metal container capable of holding two hundred rounds of ammunition weaved into a belt. We carried a dozen or so of those ammo boxes on the jeep, along with grenades and explosive materials. I rode while standing and grasping on to the gun. I used to love barreling down the dirt roads at forty to fifty miles an hour, dodging the hordes of dragonflies that would come zooming right at me. The wind from the speed of the vehicle deafened my ears. It took a little getting used to riding in an upright manner. I found that bending my knees slightly would aid in keeping my balance and being ready for any sudden turns or rough terrain. There were times when I had to hold on tightly to keep from being thrown off. Nezat and Deloge were facing forward, so they couldn't see me bouncing all over the place.

Although it was thrilling, it was also extremely dangerous. Being the possessor of the main firing power, I was the prime target: a sitting duck for a sniper's bullet. One protective piece that was placed on the front of the jeep was a long steel rod with a hook at its top. It extended high enough to reach over the gunner's head to keep him from getting his head sliced off from a cable that might be stretched across the road.

Our jeep was brand-new. The crew of the original 2-2 had run over a mine. The driver was killed. The TC operator was thrown clear from the vehicle and suffered a broken collarbone and minor cuts. The gunner lost both of his legs. The jeep was destroyed.

For protection against shrapnel, we wore flak jackets. They resembled bulletproof vests but were not able to be buttoned up. They would in no way stop a bullet. They looked good but weren't worth a shit. None of us wore helmets. They just got in the way or would fall off. Instead, we wore soft jungle hats, which were much lighter and were not a nuisance.

Later that afternoon, I was approached by Smitty. He was being transferred from the recon platoon to supplies to be the new supply sergeant. He asked me if I would help him unload crates of 105mm howitzer rounds off a truck. I said, "Sure, but there is something I have to do first." I told him that I'd be right back. I went to see Santos. I asked him to do me a favor and let Eddie be the driver of the platoon's one ton and a half. He said, "No problem." I went back to Eddie and told him that he was the driver. It brought a big smile on his face. I let him know that I was going to help Smitty with some detail and that I would see him later.

I got back to Smitty, and we went on our way. He drove a jeep to the supply area, and there were three guys waiting. One was a big Negro. His name was Henry, and he appeared to be a powerful fellow. He was about six foot six and was built to kill. All of us started to unload the trucks. Smitty saw Henry lift two crates at the same time and carry them. Smitty turned to me and said, "Go on, John, show him what you can do." So I matched Henry and lifted two crates. Each crate weighed over one hundred pounds. We had a friendly competition going, lifting two or three crates at a time. It became such a show that the other guys just stood there and watched. For all I know, they may have been taking bets to see which one of us would drop first. Henry and I unloaded three trucks in just as many hours. The sweat was pouring off us, and the respect we developed for each other was easily witnessed by all the onlookers. We became good friends for the short time we'd known each other.

Corky Smith

Smitty as chopper pilot.

117

Smitty took a special liking toward me after that performance and told me that he needed a man to work with him in the supply house and he could easily arrange for me to be that guy. He asked if I was interested. I told him that I was grateful and appreciated the offer but I wasn't interested at that time, maybe later on. Smitty ended up going to flight school and became a chopper pilot. He was shot down on October 31st 1969 and picked up on November 4th, 1969. He was alive but exhausted from the ordeal.

The next day, the entire platoon was assigned a special detail that would last the rest of the day and all through the night. Up until then, we had just used the jeeps locally. We prepared ourselves while the drivers went to retrieve the vehicles at the motor pool. I made sure my gear was in order. We heard the screeching of brakes made by the jeeps pulling up. Deloge and I tossed our equipment into the jeep and assumed our places on it. I clamped my gun on to the mount and checked the swivel and pivot then grabbed a belt of bullets from the ammo box and placed them into the holding container on the left side of the M60. I opened the cover plate of my gun and placed the first two rounds of the belt into the track; I shut it tight and pulled back on the bolt and pushed it forward to engage the round. Then I made sure it was on safety. The other crews did the same. Then we loaded up with more ammo and explosives from the ammo dump. Lastly, we grabbed a block of ice from the mess hall and set it in a cooler filled with beer and soda. This was the great thing about using the jeeps. We were able to take along cold drinks and sundries. We were all ready to go. I placed the shoulder rest of my gun atop my right shoulder, put my

Maleski, Smitty, and Woody at Phuoc Vinh, June 1967.

right hand on the trigger, and grasped the cover plate with my left. Nezat pulled out, and the forward thrust launched me rearwards, but holding the gun kept me from losing my balance.

The rainy season had started, as witnessed by the puddles along the roads and ditches of mud made by the passing of the vehicles that had gone before us. Sergeant Nezat enjoyed dodging the puddles and mudholes. He'd barrel down the road and go way ahead of the others then double back.

The first part of the assignment was to escort a convoy of trucks. One crew remained at the rear along with the one ton and a half driven by a smiling Eddie. The convoy moved slowly, so we'd go up ahead to recon the road then wait for them to catch up. We played leapfrog. Once the convoy caught up, another crew would drive forward and outpost the road, making sure it was safe, while keeping radio contact at all times.

As we were traveling down the road, I looked up ahead and saw that coming straight at us was a cloudburst. We ran smack into the rain, and in seconds, we were sopping wet. Once it passed us, I turned and could see the storm heading toward the convoy. This was typical of the rains in Nam. They came in spurts. It was so weird. When the terrain allowed and you could look all around to the horizon, the rain could be seen in the distance at intervals. A huge curtain of showers would be falling from the sky while to the right or left would be clear, then another curtain of rainstorms would be falling. You were surrounded by all this rain heading your way; you knew you were about to get drenched, and there wasn't anything you could do about it.

Now being soaked and traveling at high speeds made the wind feel like ice hitting us. This is the way it was during the monsoons. We'd get wet and dry off four to five times a day, always entering the chilly night with wet fatigues.

Escorting the convoy was a simple and somewhat enjoyable task. We met with no adversary action that day, but for us new recruits, we got a chance to get a real close-up look of the villagers and how they lived. We drove the jeeps through the yards and mini farms. Whenever we stopped, the kids would crowd around, putting out their hands in a gesture for food or candy. You just couldn't help but feel sorry for them. We'd give them candy or gum; and just as I had seen before, but closer now, were the young girls carrying their smaller siblings on their hips, never complaining. If they tired, they would simply shift the toddlers to their other hip. I'll tell you, they amazed me with their outlook and how they looked out for one another. We'd kid them and ask if they were VC. They'd reply, "No VC. Me no VC."

So innocent were their little faces, especially the girls with their large slanted brown eyes and long straight black hair; but yet I always tried to remain conscious of the stories I'd heard of their deceptiveness and heartless ability to kill. The papa sans and momma sans were quiet and reserved. They stared at us with what seemed to be that of hate and resentment. They looked to be so much older than what they were. I observed how hard they labored tending to their animals and drudging knee-deep in rice paddies. Even the children, both girls and boys, could be seen guiding the oxen-driven carts through the streets. These scenes were all new to me, and I still hadn't seen enough of what really went on here to harden my heart. All I knew then was that I was so grateful that I was born in America.

We brought the convoy to its destination; and from there, we proceeded to a place called An Loc, where we had to guard a laterite pit, which was occupied by a tribe of Montagnards. Laterite was an ore very dominant in tropical lands. It resembled red clay and was rich in iron and aluminum. To this day, I still can't figure out why we had to guard it.

Montagnards were Vietnamese natives. They were darker in complexion and were tribal. Their lifestyle was that of people out of the Stone Age. They lived in straw huts set up on bamboo stilts. The men wore nothing but a piece of cloth that covered their frontal private parts. Their butts were bare. The women walked around bare breasted and just covered their vaginas. They drank, washed, and played in the same pond, located in the center and lower part of the village. The children, both male and female, all went about completely nude. The men used spears and machetes for weapons and tools. They had a leader who we called Poppa San. The Vietcong were fearful of them. The Montagnards were like headhunters. They'd chop a VC to pieces and think nothing of it.

We took our places spread out throughout the village. Sergeant Nezat, Deloge, and I parked our jeep on a slight hill, under a tree at the furthest end of the encampment. Just to our rear was a bamboo jungle with its tall, large green leaves. All we did all day long was to sit in our jeeps and keep watch. It gave us the opportunity to see what life was like long before civilization as we know it came into existence. I mean, it was as if we traveled back in time. It was an experience that I'll never forget. I watched the women carry their little ones down to the pond and bathe them. Then they'd fill their clay pots with the same water and then return to their huts to prepare a meal. They took little to no interest of our being there. The day dragged on slowly, which was usually the way it was when you just sat idly around. We didn't think "Charlie" would be stupid enough to try any conflict against the Montagnards, especially with the firepower we had to join forces with the tribe.

The nighttime brought with it an evening of rain that lasted until dawn. I sat up all night with my poncho covering me and my gun. Nezat sat in the driver's seat, also covered up. Deloge stayed in my section of the jeep between the two of us and curled up. Disgusted with the continuous downpour, he covered himself completely with his poncho and said, "Fuck this shit," and went to sleep. It was the first long wet night that I experienced out in the open. The shivers kicked in at the wee hours of the night. There was no way to get warm. We had to grin and bear it and wait anxiously for the sun to rise. By morning, the three of us were stiff from being in the same position for all those hours. The rain had stopped, and the three of us got out of the jeep and stretched our weary bones and took a short stroll around, never veering far from our vehicle. The sun's heat felt great.

The village people came to life, and we watched them go about their daily routines. Nezat and Deloge decided to go for a walk around the village. I stayed on the jeep and sat behind my M60. My legs were stretched out when a small South Vietnamese boy came by. He looked to be about ten years old. He had on a short-sleeve shirt and wore shorts. He didn't have on any shoes. He sat at my feet and, with a stick, started to clean the red mud that was embedded in my boots. I leaned forward and motioned for him to stop, but he continued, determined to finish what he had started. I gave him a piece of chocolate. He looked at me and smiled. "What's your name?" I asked.

"Tahn," he said.

"I'm John." He spoke a fair amount of English and told me that he lived in the village just a little ways up the road. He seemed like a really nice kid and taught me some words in Vietnamese. *Sole* meant "sun." *Muir* was "rain." *Ti ti* (pronounced *tee tee*) meant "little." *Bocoo* was "much." As we conversed, I took notice of blotches on Tahn's face and legs. It looked almost like impetigo. By now, Nezat and Deloge had returned. Deloge seemed to know Than and vice versa. Deloge explained to me that he had met the kid from visiting his village. Tahn hung around most of the day. Meanwhile, Poppa San came around and, believe it or not, was selling us bottles of Coca-Cola for 50 piastres ($0.50) a bottle. The bottles were sealed and cold. The day grew very hot, and the cold sodas would be a refreshing break. We paid him two hundred piastres and bought four Cokes. It struck me funny that there, in a place like that, we could get a soda from a native.

The three of us were curious how they built their huts, so we asked Poppa San to show us how and offered to pay him 250 piastres ($2.50). He left, and in a matter of minutes, he returned with two of his tribesmen. The two went into the high bamboo thicket behind us. They came back in about fifteen minutes. One had a stack of bamboo on his shoulder, and the other had a pile of large jungle leaves across his back. They wasted no time in getting to work. We watched them intensively as one took the bamboo, one pole at a time. and pointed one of its ends using a machete. He did this to four pieces and cut the length of two of them shorter than the other two. While he was busy doing that, the other guy took bamboo poles and cut them into two-foot sections. Then he took one of them, and while holding it in one hand, he shaved strips off it with his machete. I was amazed at how thin he was able to cut the bamboo with such a crude method and how quickly he did it. Those machetes were razor-sharp.

When they finished with the prepping, one of them stood up and held one of the long, pointed pieces of bamboo poles in his hands vertically in front of him and proceeded to thrust it into the ground repeatedly until it reached the desired depth. He repeated doing this with the other three bamboo poles. He now had the two long uprights to use for the rear of the hut and two shorter ones for the front, forming the square foundation. Then he packed dirt around each riser to hold it in place. As one native held a bamboo pole horizontally across two of the upright stilts, the other guy took the bamboo strips, wrapped them around the connecting joints, and with his fingers, curled the tie strips, pulling the two poles tightly together. They did this to four bamboo cross poles on the bottom about one foot above the ground and then repeated the procedure across the top, securing them on an angle from the higher to the lower. Then they cut more pieces of bamboo a little longer than the length of the hut so that they'd overhang about six inches on both sides. They made enough of these poles to cover the roof and the floor and set them side by side, four inches apart, and secured all of them to the framing with the bamboo strips. When the structure was complete, they took the large leaves and laid layers of them across the roof, starting from the bottom and working their way up so the rain would roll off the roof, the same way we lay shingles on the roofs of our homes. The final touch was the placing of the leaves on the lower level, forming a soft cushion. They completed this task in about one hour. We checked it out and were stunned at how sturdy it was. We paid Papa San the two hundred and fifty piastres. It was another great experience that stayed with me all these years.

We headed back to Phuoc Vinh and passed by Tahn's village. We figured we'd stop for a break and pulled off the road while the others kept going. Nezat stopped the jeep at the edge of a rubber tree plantation. Rubber trees grew about fifteen feet apart and in a straight line. The locals would carve a winding groove down the trees and secure a bowl at the bottom of the groove, which would catch the liquid rubber. When I looked up, I saw something that blew my mind. In between two trees was a spiderweb. It spanned the fifteen-foot opening. And smack-dab in the middle of the web, cling-ing to it, was the largest spider I'd ever seen. It had to be eighteen inches long. It was streamlined, and it was silver with green stripes. The kids from the village ran over to us to beg for candy. Tahn was among them. He came over to me and pointed to the spider, then with two fingers, he pinched the back of his wrist and then cupped his hands and laid them on the side of his face and tilted his head and closed his eyes. He was telling me that if that son of a bitch bites you, you're dead. I was tempted to shoot the monster but figured that if it didn't bother me, then I wouldn't bother it. We handed out some goodies to the kids and went on our way.

Nezat dropped me and Deloge off and returned the jeep back to the motor pool. I took my gun apart and cleaned it thoroughly. I mounted it on the tripod and oiled it up. Mail call rolled around, and I got my second letter from Tony. After receiving my letter, he wrote the following:

Hi John,

4 June '67

Nice to hear everything's going well. It's the same with me. They're still keeping us busy with hardly a day's rest. We go outside base camp at night for security, and in the day, we get called out on reaction. And we're leaving tonight on a mission. The other day I went to Saigon to pick up a new vehicle because my first one was blown up. Boy, it sure would be good to get home out of this stinking country. It's been pretty cool here the last week or so, and they say the monsoons are due any day now.

Tell me, how is the situation down there? I hope you're not seeing too much of the VC. They're really something else. There are a lot of places and people around here we suspect of being VC, but we can't do anything unless we're fired upon. That's a lot of bull to me. There are a couple of nice girls I fool around with on the road, but it doesn't go any farther. Listen, about the R & R, let's find out when we both can go and set something up.

It's getting rough trying to keep up with everyone back home, being kept busy and all. They just give me the ass sometimes. I still haven't come to a face-to-face firefight, thank goodness for that. Things are going to be pretty good going home to a wife and child. I sure will make it a point to try and get married. That's one thing I really look forward to. Right now, I'm in my hooch listening to the radio, and the songs make me homesick. Also make me feel pretty bad about some things I did. That's about it for now, John. Take good care of yourself, and we'll see each other real soon.

Cousin Tony

After reading Tony's letter and how he mentioned missing home while listening to music, I got to thinking about the band and how

Our band, Billy Bockhold, Bob Ficarrotta, me and joe Trongone.

we got started. When I was eleven and in the sixth grade, my parents bought me a new set of drums. It was a blue mother-of-pearl Gretsch four-piece drum set and a five-piece cymbal set. There was a guitar player named Billy Bockhold who took lessons at the same music studio as me. He got my address from the owner, Mike Palumba, and came over to my house with two other guys, Bruce Bauer and Billy Beanus, to hear me audition for them. They liked the way I played and asked me to join them. The band was made up of drums, two rhythm guitars, and one bass guitar. They all had Fender Stratocasters. We got pretty good and played a bunch of gigs. Billy Beanus eventually left the group; and we got one of my cousins, Steve Marrone, who played the saxophone. Eventually, Bruce and Steve left; and that's when Joe Trongone joined us and another saxophone player named Bob Ficarrotta along with Andy, who was the singer.

Billy Bockhold was some character. We went to the same junior high school, which was John Phillip Sousa. So did Joe. Billy loved cars. His favorite was the Plymouth Sport Fury. He'd call me and tell me to look out of my window. When I did, there, parked across the street, was—you guessed it—a 1963 Plymouth. He had stolen it. His father had retired from the New York Fire Department and was an artist who painted mostly advertisement signs. So he had all sorts of colors of paint. Billy and I would remove the license plates from the car and change the numbers. We'd bang out half of an eight and turn it into a three or part of a seven and make it a one then mix the colors of the paint to match the plate. By the time we finished, you couldn't tell the difference. We'd drive to Long Island and take some girls to the beach. The one thing that always worried us was going through the tollbooths. There weren't any keys in the ignition. We finally got smart and put a dummy key in it. Another friend of ours, Marty Powers, joined us and came along for the ride. We did it three times and, luckily, never got caught. What the hell, we were sixteen and dumb (but not dumb enough to get caught). Later on, Billy played the guitar with the rock group, "The Soul Survivors".

All this thinking back to the past gave me the urge to play. I asked Eddie to come with me to the PX. There was a set of drums for anyone to use. When we got there, a few of the other guys were hanging out. I sat down and started to play. Tex walked over and asked me if I knew the song Topsy Part II by Cozy Cole. "Sure," I said to Tex, and I played it for him. I knew it well; back when I was twelve, my cousin Mike Fusco, who was a lot older than me, came over and handed me a forty-five record and asked me to learn it so that I could play a drum solo at his wedding. I must have played that solo a hundred times in my life. It felt good just to do something that had nothing to do with the Army. Tex was happy.

The following morning, after breakfast, Santos and Dutch came into the barracks. Santos spoke with an accent, and you had to concentrate on what he was saying to understand him. It was his second tour in Nam, and he was pushing for rank. He volunteered us for any shitty detail that came up. He wasn't well-liked by some members of the platoon. Sure enough, that was the reason he came to see us. He told us to get ready and that, within the hour, we had to lead a company of men on a foot patrol. Dutch chimed in and told us that in the up-and-coming days, the entire battalion was going on a full-scale operation. They were walking out when I yelled out, "Hey, Dutch, how long will the operation last?"

He answered back, "Maybe two weeks, maybe a month."

Eddie and I looked at each other and said, "Well, here we go. The fun's over."

Santos volunteered us to lead Charlie Company on patrol by sweeping the road for land mines. Eddie and I were one team, while David C. and Ver Linden were the second team. Our platoon preceded C Company, which followed behind our jeeps. We were equipped with mine detectors, which were apparatuses with long handles with a round metal disk on the ends and a set of earphones. A wire ran from the disk and connected to the headsets. It was a very slow and tedious process. The sweeper teams were on opposite sides of the road. We walked cautiously, moving the disk back and forth. I handled the sweeper, and Eddie was the prober who was positioned directly behind me. He carried C-4 and blasting caps to detonate a mine, if one was located. When a mine or any piece of metal was detected, a high shrieking sound was transmitted to the earphones. The closer to the object, the louder the sound. Once the position was pinpointed at its loudest response, the prober, with the use of a bayonet, would get down on his knees and ever so lightly jab the ground at a forty-five-degree angle to feel for the object. If a mine was present, then the dirt would be gently wiped away by hand until it was exposed. One problem, which was one big pain in the ass, was that much of the ground in Nam consisted of laterite, so there were many false alarms. We were getting all sorts of false findings; but no matter what, we still had to stay vigilant because you never know when it would be the real thing. We got about one thousand feet from the camp, and I got a signal that covered a sizable area. Eddie did his thing, and we uncovered a large antitank mine. We gave the signal for everyone to stop moving and radioed in what we discovered and told Santos that we were going to blow it. We made sure that all the vehicles and foot soldiers were far enough behind. We secured the C-4 in position on the bomb and set our blasting cap into the C-4. Then we rolled out the cable and got to a safe area before we connected the cable to the hand detonator. When this was done, we yelled, "Everyone clear?"

"Yes."

We did a quick visual and hollered out, "Fire in the hole," three times; and then we blew it.

When we finally got to the end of the road, we loaded the mine detectors on to our jeeps, grabbed our weapons, and entered the bush. The drivers took the jeeps back to Phuoc Vinh. We patrolled for the rest of the day and met no hostility. We came to a small clearing and stopped. Santos came over to tell us we were going to go back to the compound. That sounded good; we were tired from the long day. We heard the puttering sound of helicopters approaching. They landed and stood waiting. Santos said, "Come on, John, let's board the chopper."

"Why?" I said. "Are we flying back?"

Santos answered, "Why not? It beats walking." It sounded good, but Eddie and I had never flown on a helicopter before. Amazing, the things one does when there's no other choice.

Seven of us got on one of the choppers: Santos, Eddie, David C., Craig, Baldy, Schneider, and me. There was a bench that seated four. The other three sat on the floor with their backs to the bench. There were two doors that remained opened on either side of the chopper. Schneider, Eddie, Baldy, and Ver Linden sat on the bench

128

while I sat by the left-side door. David C. was in the middle, and Santos was by the right-side door. There were the pilot and copilot and two machine gunners. Once we were settled in, the pilot turned, and we gave him the thumbs-up. He gave a nod and we lifted off. It tilted back and forth slightly and leaned forward. I sat with my left leg hanging out of the door and my M60 across my lap, also hanging out of the opening. The sound was deafening. We couldn't hear ourselves talk unless we spoke very loudly.

We reached the treetops and in seconds we were high above looking down. It was fantastic. The view was beautiful. We got our first panoramic view of the country. It was like a large green blanket covering the land for miles. Everywhere we looked, we saw green trees. The higher we went, the better the view. There were the airfields, base camps, and rice paddies, which appeared to be sectioned off in grids and made up of different colors, just like on a map.

The choppers flew in groups of five in a straight line. Off to the distance were another group and another. We could see each other clearly and give a thumbs up. The ride was a thrill as well as an experience. It was the first of many to come. We approached the airstrip in Phuoc Vinh and descended. They made a complete touchdown, rather than hovering. Once the engines slowed down to an idle, we got off. The rest of the choppers landed one by one behind one another. The dust was flying all around. We kept our heads low and hung on to our hats until we cleared the area under the blades. Trucks were already there, waiting to transport all of us back to the camp.

When we got back and settled in, Dutch came by and told us that we'd be leaving in two days, on June 12, to begin what he called Operation Billings.

CHAPTER VII

OPERATION BILLINGS

T he morning of June 11 found us all getting ready for the following day. I spent seven hours cleaning my gun. I packed all the necessary essentials: poncho; shovel; air mattress; stationary; extra clothes; especially socks and underwear; and rations. I took a long green sock and stuffed five cans of K rations in it, one on top of another. It was a great way to store and carry them. The sock would get tied to the top of my shoulder strap and flung over my back. This way, they weren't a nuisance and didn't take up much room. I readied my pistol belt with a first aid kit, insect repellent, and my .45 holster. I set smoke grenades on to my shoulder strap and placed a few grenades in an ammo bag, which had a flip cover. It was a safer way to carry grenades, rather than clipping them to a shoulder strap, due to the thick brush possibly disengaging the pin. My poncho was rolled up neatly and strapped to the bottom rear of my backpack. The equipment had to be packed as neatly as possible for it was not going to be dropped off by chopper. All of us had to attach it to our bodies and hump it when we hit the LZ (landing zone). When I finished preparing all the gear, I hung it next to my bed.

The ammunition was carried in ammo pouches, which were filled with magazines, shotgun rounds, M79 rounds, and C-4 and blasting caps. My M60 ammo was in metal cannisters, which held two hundred rounds in each. We also took a spare barrel for the machine gun. I carried only the amount of ammo in the pouch attached on the side of my gun. Normally, I'd wrap a belt of bullets around my neck; but being that we had to run for our lives to the wood line, it would only be hazardous. All these extras would be given to us after we secured the LZ.

Operation Billings continued on what was the largest operation of the war, Junction City. This operation resulted in the joining forces of the First Infantry Division, the Ninth Infantry Division, the Eleventh Armored Calvary Regiment, the 196th Light Infantry Brigade, and the 173rd Airborne Division. We were supported by the Eleventh Combat Aviation Group and the Seventh Air Force Aircraft. Junction City had started early in 1967. It involved the only mass jump in the war. On February 22, 1967, seven hundred troopers from the 503rd Airborne Infantry, along with supporting elements, parachuted into a drop zone north of Tai Binh. It took twenty-three Air Force C-130 Hercules aircrafts to transport troops and their equipment. This movement helped block the enemy and released badly needed helicopters to the First and Twenty-Fifth divisions engaged in ground attacks. Within three months after it began, 2,728 enemies were killed and War Zone C was no longer a VC stronghold.

Late that afternoon, some of the guys went with Ronnie to town. It had been Ron's twentieth birthday back on May 27. He wanted to continue celebrating the big two-o. I was the only Italian in our platoon, so Baldy nicknamed me Pizza. I had just finished making a recording on a cassette tape to mail home with my latest letter to Marilyn. I was lying down on my bunk and thinking about the following day and what it would bring. I wasn't one to go in to bars and drink. I didn't like it, so I stayed back and wrote letters.

My thoughts were interrupted when the barrack's screen door swung open and Ronnie staggered in. Even with his big round-eyed glasses covering half his face, I could spot the gleam in his eyes. He was giggling as he made his way passed the empty beds toward me. He was clutching a large album in his arms. He plopped down on the bed next to mine. I sat up and faced him. Due to the fact that we were the two main gunners in the platoon, we had become very close friends.

"What's up, Ron? What did you do, trade in your M60 for a book?" I jokingly asked.

Ron, with a grin and being two sheets to the wind, answered, "No, Pizza, I want to show you something." I leaned forward as Ron proceeded to open the folder. It was filled with neatly arranged photos of his engagement party. He proudly pointed to the pictures of his fiancée, Babe, whose name he had scratched into the silver cover plate of his M60. He went on to tell me about their marriage plans. As he singled each picture out and described them, he leaned back and laughed. He felt that he could relate to me because he knew I had recently gotten married and that my wife was pregnant. As Ron flipped through the pages, the sounds of the B-52 bombers could be heard in the far-off distance dropping countless numbers of five-hundred-pound bombs that sounded more like automatic weapons being fired. The bombers were attempting to clear out our LZ somewhere in the jungles of Nam and rid the area of any enemy. At least that was the idea. When Ron got to the last page, still giddy, he closed the book. Before he got up to leave, I wished him all the luck in the world, shook his hand, and said, "They're some great pictures, and by the way, happy birthday."

He got up and said, "Good night, Pizza," and I watched him clumsily find his way out the door. He seemed to be so happy.

The early morning of June 12 came quickly; and all of us were getting ready, making last-minute checkups. I made sure I mailed my letters and cassette before leaving. I also filled two canteens with fresh water. Lastly, I checked the ammo to make sure there weren't any faulty or rusty rounds and placed them into the pouch. For some of us first-timers, it was a day of not knowing what to expect. I grabbed my gear and unhooked my gun off the tripod and, along with all the others, loaded on the back of the deuce-and-a-halfs that were waiting to transport us to the airstrip. There were choppers flying overhead all around us.

The loading was completed, and everyone stood waiting and waiting. The trucks finally started to pull out. One by one, what seemed like an endless parade of vehicles swallowed up by reddish-brown dust made their way to the chopper pad.

The choppers were lined up for as far as you could see. The props were in motion but just idling. I and the other members of the recon platoon hopped off the trucks and quickly made our way over to the first five choppers. We, being recon, had to go in first to secure the LC. We stood by, waiting to climb aboard; and the props began to rotate faster, causing the dust to billow up from the ground. I got so pissed because the dirt was getting all over my gun. I placed a towel over it to help protect it.

I, along with Eddie and David C. and four others, ducked down and got on one of the gunships. Ronnie and his crew got on a different one. The format was the same as it was when we rode on the chopper for the first time with four guys on the bench and three of us on the floor. I was on the left with my leg and gun out of the opening and my finger affixed to the trigger.

The pilots were given the "go" sign. The props geared up and rotated at full speed, drowning out any conversation we were having. The gunships started to move. They lifted off the ground, tilted to one side, and in a blink of an eye, were hundreds of feet in the air. We were on a "search and destroy" mission, which meant "kill any of the enemy and destroy anything in sight, including animals, food and suspected VC villages."

It was a hot and humid day. Everyone was already drenched from sweat. The monsoon season was in full gear, which meant we were going to get rained on multiple times a day. It had rained the entire night, so the odds were high that we'd be landing and huffing in mud. I always made it my business to recite the rosary in situations like this where a soldier wants to remind God that He's being thought of and the soldier needs the protection of His Holy Mother, Mary. It brought me comfort and hope.

The ride took about twenty-five minutes, and all of us were praying that it wouldn't be a "hot LZ" (occupied by a hostile force). The pilot turned and signaled for us to be alert. I looked below at what resembled a large blanket of green, getting closer and closer, and wondered what laid beneath it. We were going in fast and going in first, with full pack and gear strapped to our backs; and if the enemy had somehow managed to evade the bombardment the night before and were dug in, recon was dead meat. We wouldn't have a chance. We'd be like sitting ducks in a shooting gallery. All we could do was to put our lives in God's hands; after all, this was not stateside where you had a choice to not do something against your will.

The ground came within one hundred feet. The LZ, cleared from the bombs, was in plain sight amid surrounding trees and jungles. It appeared to be the size of a football field. Many trees were shattered from the B-52s. I turned to Eddie, and he looked at me. I'm not going to lie to you, but we were scared. I gave him the thumbs-up and turned back to get ready to jump. We would only have seconds to deploy, and the chopper wouldn't come to rest on the ground. It would stay hovering several feet above until we got off then return immediately to the airstrip to transport the battalion.

The chopper descended to treetop level, and suddenly we heard gunfire. It scared the shit out of us. We didn't know where it was coming from. I pulled my leg in from the open door and flicked my gun off safety and prepared to return fire. There was momentary confusion, wondering what was happening. As it turned out, it wasn't incoming at all. The two chopper gunners had opened fire to give us grazing ground coverage and sprayed the wood line with a barrage of bullets to enable us to deploy as safely as possible. We didn't know it, but that action was standard procedure to keep "Charlie" at bay.

We jumped off, and because I was at the door, I was the first one on my side to leap. I sank shin-deep into the mud. The first thing we did was to spread out. The tree line was 150 feet away. It looked like a mile. The choppers had left as soon as we were all off to head back and to avoid possibly being shot down. Humping on dry land with a machine gun and over seventy pounds of gear would have been bad enough, but running and having each step feel like it was being sucked back down into the ground was exhausting. Every ounce of effort had to be put into lifting our legs out of the mud. The tree line seemed as if it was never going to be reached. To make matters worse, we had to climb over the downed trees. I had the burden of wrestling with my gun, lifting it over the branches, and trying to keep the pouch of ammo from falling into the mud. Trying desperately to keep from tripping, I kept my eyes trained on the wood line and what might be lying behind the bushes. My heart was pounding in my chest from the constant lifting of my legs out of the mud's grasp. I was praying, "God, please, just don't let anybody be waiting for us. When am I going to reach the wood line? If I could just get to them damn trees alive." At last, I finally reached the edge, as did the others. Our prayers were answered. It was a cold LZ. The enemy wasn't waiting for us.

We deployed, and we split into two squads. Mine went to the right, and Ron was with the other and went to the left. We secured the entire perimeter. The rest of the battalion was coming in. I glanced back at them landing. The choppers were resting on the ground while the troops were calmly walking with towels around their necks and weapons slung over their shoulders. They did not have the worry of running into a dug-in VC force or huffing it to the wood line. They even gathered in groups and slowly walked in from the LZ. It looked like a church social. I nudged Eddie and David C. and laughed, saying, "Will you look at that shit." The hard part was done by our recon platoon, and we had to remain at our positions until the entire battalion landed and set up camp.

When all seemed secure, we were able to chow down. It was 10:00 AM, and the sun was getting hotter. We were hungry, so we took turns opening our rations. Two hours had gone by since we touched down. The three of us were talking about our girls back home. We were interrupted by the sound of gunshots. We grabbed our weapons and hit the ground. Everything got quiet; no more shots were heard. The only sound was that of the squelch of the radio operator's handset followed by the voice of Sergeant Santos. He hurriedly passed by our position and signaled for us to follow him. All we could make out was that one of our men had been hit. It wasn't said who, but it was bad. We rushed as fast as we could through thick bush and knee-high water to get to the location of the other squad. I was delayed because Eddie was deadly afraid of water. He had almost drowned when he was a little kid. Ever since JD school, whenever we came across water, even just a puddle, I had to hold his hand and reassure him that he'd be all right and that it was safe. We caught up to David C. and Santos and got to our objective. Santos went over to the injured man. We still didn't know who it was. Jimenez, our medic, was performing CPR. He was trying frantically to save the man's life using mouth-to-mouth restoration. "Who is it?" asked Eddie.

"I don't know, I can't see who's on the ground," I answered.

Then Baker hoisted the injured man onto his back and carried him out from the bushes. He got close to me and couldn't go any farther. I now saw that it was Ronnie. I turned to Dutch and asked, "Hey, Dutch, do you want me to carry him?"

"Do you think you can?" he answered.

"Of course," I said. I asked David C. to give me a hand to get Ronnie onto my shoulder. I laid my gun down, and together we managed to get him up. I squatted down slightly. and with a grunt, I jolted upward to reposition Ronnie. I was trying so damn hard to be careful so as to not further injure him. I told Dave to take my gun. I walked about fifty yards with David C. by my side to help keep Ronnie from falling. He started to slip off my shoulder. I told Dutch that I had to put him down. I bent over and gently set Ronnie onto the ground. Ronnie fell back, facing upward, with his hands stretched back over his head. I stared at his face and saw that Ronnie's eyes were open and had rolled back. I turned to Dutch and said, "He's dead."

"I know, I know he's dead," retorted Dutch.

I gazed into Ron's wound. It was a sunken chest wound. The bullet hit Ron's dog tags and drove them into his chest. There wasn't much blood, just a large opening in his chest cavity. I was staring down at the sight of my first dead GI who was my friend. Sergeant Santos called for a dust-off chopper, but there was nowhere for it to land in the immediate area. I just knelt there and couldn't believe what I was witnessing. Ronnie was gone. Just yesterday he and I were together, laughing and looking at his engagement pictures. Now he was just lying there, pale and lifeless—no joy, no laughter, no feeling. I knew right then and there that this was no game; we weren't playing soldier. This was for real; and that this day would put a stain in my heart that would last the rest of my life. What hurt was that the gook who shot him was never caught. He got off scot-free.

We made a stretcher from sticks and two shirts so we'd be able to carry Ron the rest of the way. Tex and I hauled Ron's body, but his arms kept falling and dragging in the mud. The weight of his body caused the shirts to stretch so that his head and shoulders also dragged in the mud and weeds. We carried him to a semi clearing and put him down. We cleared away trees and shrubs with our machetes to make way for the landing for Ronnie's body to be dusted off. I couldn't figure out why this had to happen. Why were we there? Why did we have to leave our homes to fight in some far-off land?

We heard the chopper overhead, and with that we tossed a smoke grenade to pinpoint the LZ. The chopper landed, and we carried our fallen comrade and placed him onboard. "Is he dead?" asked one fellow kneeling in the chopper while he helped put Ronnie onboard.

I looked up at him and said, "Yeah."

He shook his head and silently uttered, "Shit." Then he looked up and said to the pilot, "Okay, let's go." He slid the door closed, shutting himself and Ronnie in. I took one last glance at Ronnie and watched as the chopper rose up and left.

I turned to Tex and asked that same question that I kept asking myself, "Why, Tex, why?"

"I don't know, Pizza," he said.

By now the battalion was dug in; and none of us spoke a word as we entered the camp in single file, passing by the line companies that were scattered throughout the jungle. I could see by the deep expression of sorrow on the faces of each man we passed by that they, too, felt our loss. Today, we not only lost a comrade but we also lost a brother.

It was a long, hard, and sad day; but it was far from over. We still had to dig in. So with heavy hearts, we did so. I went to cut down some trees for the overhead cover while Eddie and David C. dug the foxhole and filled sandbags. All I had with me was a machete and my .45 pistol, so I stayed within the perimeter. Even so, I was uneasy and kept looking over my shoulder.

When we were finally able to relax, I stared down at Ron's M60 that was being held by Ron's ammo bearer, Arty Parker, and saw Babe's name scratched into the cover plate. I asked Parker what happened. He went on to explain, "Ronnie was sitting up against a tree, ready to eat breakfast. Dutch moved him twice. When Dutch was satisfied with Ron's position, he once again sat up against a tree and started to eat. He was facing a trail. A single Vietcong with an AK-47 unexpectedly walked up and spotted Ronnie. The VC lifted his weapon and, with a quick burst, shot Ron. If Dutch would have left him alone, he'd still be here."

All I could say to Parker with anger was "That son of a bitch."

It was getting dark. The three of us sat outside our hooch. Eddie spotted something on the back of my shirt. It was blood. I reached up behind my right shoulder and felt something. I grabbed it between my fingers and examined it. It was a piece of Ronnie's flesh that had stuck to the dried blood.

We grabbed a bite to eat and listened to the choppers and chinooks dropping off and lowering supplies and equipment. Santos came around to check on us and to make sure we had our foxhole and overhead cover completed. We had done a half-ass job on it by only putting a minimum number of sandbags on top of the trees spanning the foxhole. He didn't seem to notice it, or if he did, he didn't say anything. We could see in his face that he was hurting from losing one of his men. He told us that our platoon didn't have to pull guard duty that night and to get some rest because we had to go out on an early patrol; then went on his way. We inflated our air mattresses and placed them in the hooch. I slept in the middle. Eddie was on my right and David C. was to my left. We kept our weapons right beside us. None of us got much sleep due to not being able to get the loss of Ronnie out of our minds.

When morning came, we arose early. We were able to eat a hot breakfast thanks to the choppers. After chow, we led out a patrol. Woody took over Ronnie's spot and used his machine gun. We filed out in single file behind our three-point men: King, Rahar,

| Picture of me and Woody taking aim with our M-60's. (Picture taken by Terry Schneider). | With my cousins Al Cafaro, Joe Davis, Me feeding Fluffy and Timmy Davis in my back yard. | Me and Tony at age eight and my pet lamb "Fluffy" standing in the back yard of my house. |

and Schneider. Two of the line companies followed behind us. We explored deeper into the jungle, traveling very slowly, and came upon what appeared to be an abandoned VC village. As we cased the huts and looked in the trees and behind bushes, a pig came running out from one of the huts. It startled one of the men, and he shot it. The pig was wounded and yelping and screeching in pain. I hated to do it, but I raised my gun, flicked it off safety, and fired a few rounds to put the pig out of its misery. It would have had to be destroyed regardless.

I had my reasons for not wanting to kill any animal. When I was eight years old, my uncles—one of whom was Tony's father, Chi Chi—gave me a little lamb to raise. Chi Chi was the family butcher and dentist. You did not want to let him know that you had a loose tooth. If he found out you did, he'd put his fingers in your mouth and yank it out. For an entire year, I took good care of that lamb.

I walked it on a leash as if it were a dog. All the neighborhood kids would come around to pet it. It was gray and had a black face. It was so cute. I loved that lamb. One day, around Easter, Tony and I went to a movie. When we got back home, I went down the basement to see my pet. My mother had a clothesline rigged by the stairs; and when I walked down the steps, there was my little lamb's skin hanging on the clothesline. I was heartbroken. I just sat there and cried my eyes out. They had killed it to eat for Easter dinner. But as I grew older, the thing about it that bothered me mostly was that I visualized my lamb when he was grabbed and about to be slaughtered looking up and around for me and I wasn't there to save him. I can't begin to tell you what it was like to sit at that table and see people eating my little lamb. I just got up and walked away. I have never eaten lamb since.

Due to the nature of the mission, anything that could be used by the Vietcong as a weapon or food was not to be spared. There were huts all around made from twines and leaves. It resembled something from the Stone Age. There were small cages scattered about the village, similar to birdcages. As we walked past one of them, Funky motioned with his eyes and pointed his finger up into it. I bent forward slightly and peered into the upper part of the cage. There was a grenade strapped to one of its wooden prongs. I motioned to the ones behind me to be cautious and searched on.

There was a large hut in the center of the village. Standing clear of its entrance, we tossed a grenade. After the explosion and the smoke cleared, two guys entered it. It had been abandoned just like all the rest of the huts; however, there was a tunnel built underground covered by a hatch made from twigs and leaves. We opened the hatch and tossed a grenade into the tunnel; and after it blew, we sprayed the entrance with bullets. One man was sent down to investigate. He was known as a tunnel rat. He was usually one of the smallest men in the outfit. It was a dangerous job. He was going into a dark tunnel with nothing but a .45 and a flashlight, with no way of knowing if anyone was waiting to blow him away. Luckily, the tunnel was barren. It was mind-boggling the way they built their underground passageways. I was learning quickly how smart those gooks were.

We destroyed the village and moved on. The jungle was thick, and we had to chop our way through much of it. The bipods on the front of my gun kept getting hung up on the branches and pulled the extension rods out. That was most annoying. I kept having to wrestle with it to free the pods. To solve the problem, I disconnected them altogether.

Most machine gunners carried their gun on their shoulders, which helped to avoid that problem. I refused to hump my gun in that manner. I carried it on my hip without the use of a strap for two reasons. The first being that I wanted to be ready to fire as quickly as possible. If it was shouldered, the time that it took to take it down and load it could make the difference of costing a gunner his life and the lives of others. The second reason was that a person walking in the jungle could be seen from the waist up. Thus, if the enemy was monitoring a patrol, the machine gun atop one's shoulder could be spotted, making the gunner a prime target; and since he was the main firepower, he'd be the first one the enemy would want to take out. As for the strap, it limited the mobility. I wanted to have no restrictions whatsoever. The holding up of my gun was aided by the holster of my .45 pistol. It sat just right. I was able to remove my hand completely, and the gun would balance by itself. This enabled me to use my machete when needed and freed up the use of my arms.

We went deeper, always keeping one another in eyes' view but a safe distance away. Too close could put you at risk of not only having multiple men getting injured but also causing an eye or other body parts being hurt by a branch snapping back at you. I understood how easily one could get lost. It only took seconds for the man in front of you to disappear from view. All it took was to get hung up in the thick bush or to stop to check something out. When this happened, the best thing to do was to stay silent and listen for sounds or watch for moving branches.

The route of travel was always in a zigzag manner. We would travel two miles and only gain one half of a mile in a straight line. We'd stop periodically to rest, which was more than welcomed. I'd try to find a sturdy tree or a thick bush to lean against. The tiny ants were always there no matter where we sat, but by now, we didn't care; we were used to them. We'd be so fatigued; but the rest, even if we laid down, was worth more than the bugs crawling all over us.

Whenever we stopped, we'd remain apart and silent; but those damn line companies made so much noise—talking, laughing, or throwing empty cans. They were a dead giveaway all the time. We hated being attached to them. Just when our eyes became drowsy and were about to shut, we had to get up and continue onward. This stop-and-go procedure was the way it was until we returned to camp. At one point we stopped momentarily and waited silently. I heard a noise to my front left and saw branches move. I waited to see who it was. It was funky. He walked passed me without saying a word, stretched out his arm, and handed me two chocolate bars.

The rain was coming down in buckets when we started back to camp. We were drenched by the time we got there. It was chow time, and thankfully, the choppers flew in a hot meal. The chow line was long but moved along swiftly. Eddie and I grabbed two plates apiece, one to put the food in and the other to cover it. We tried to keep the rain out of our dinners, but it was no use. By the time we walked back to our tent, our food was floating in a puddle of rainwater. Our fatigues were weighted down by the mud, as were our boots. The sun never shone bright enough to dry off. We went to bed shivering. I had a way of warming up. I'd remove my shirt and submerge myself under an Army quilt with it covering my mouth and leaving my nose exposed. Then by breathing in through my nose and out of my mouth, the heat from my breath would create a cushion of warm air. That plus the heat from my body helped greatly in relieving the chill.

We awoke to the cold dampness of the morning, and those of us who slept with our shirts off did a quick dance and held our breath when we went to put them on for they were surely wet and cold. A fast hot cup of cocoa relieved the chill from our bodies and took away the shivers. We heated our food and drinks up with a small piece of C-4 rather than the heating tablets that were issued. The C-4 burned hotter and lasted longer. This was fine as long as you remembered not to stomp on it to put it out. If you did, it would explode, and you'd lose a foot.

I took a good look around at the campsite. I saw all the low-lying dark-green hooches scattered throughout and watched as the others came crawling out from their tiny enclosures. Mounds were protruding from the ground about the area, caused from the foxholes. The camp was large. It was home to five companies plus us. There was a wide, deep trench dug in the rear of the chow line to dispose of any garbage. The toilets were nothing more than a hole dug in the ground aligned with sandbags three to four high to be used as a seat. If anyone preferred, they could go into the jungle, dig a little hole, move their bowels, then bury it. We had a mail drop. Our letters required no stamps, compliments of Uncle Sam.

The next day, we went out on our own. The battalion stayed back at camp. That was the way we liked it. It enabled us to move fast and quiet and do the job we were meant to do: recon the surrounding jungles. Our point men spotted two VC. We hastened our pace and chased them deeper into the jungle. This was taking a risk. Going to many movies when I was a kid, I learned that an old Indian trick was to lure the cavalry by making them chase a few Indians and then ambush them with a larger, superior force. Luckily, it didn't happen in this case. The two VC were too quick. They evaded us, and when hopes of capturing them seemed dismal, Santos ordered an air strike. If we couldn't get them, maybe the rockets would.

Within ten minutes, the jets were flying overhead. Santos called in our coordinates, and we showed our position by tossing a few white smoke grenades. The enemy's possible location was transmitted. We took cover, and the strike began. I had never seen or heard anything like it before. It was fantastic. The sound created by the rockets was incredible. One had to imagine a lightning rod traveling on the back of a thunderbolt and hearing them crackle and crash. The jets poured it on for a good ten minutes and left. We searched in the hope of finding dead VC but came up empty-handed. There wasn't any trace of them.

We went back to camp and relaxed the rest of the day. Mail call came, and as usual, it was a welcomed time. It was one of the few things to look forward to, and without a doubt, a big letdown when there weren't any letters to read. People back home didn't know how much it lifted our spirits. I received a letter from Marilyn.

Marilyn was now in her third month of pregnancy. In her letter, she stated that her belly was starting to show. Her anxiety was growing more and more each day, and she wished that I could have been there during that time; but that was the way we planned it: her being occupied by the baby while I was away. She was due in December; therefore, the baby would be five months old by the time I got home.

Late that afternoon, Santos told us that we had to move out early in the morning. "But we just got here a few days ago," we said to him.

"I know, but we have to get going. So be ready for an early liftoff," he retorted with a smirk on his face. It was so obvious that he loved the Army with all its dangerous combat missions.

That night, once again, we heard the rapid bombing of the B-52s blasting away at our next LZ. It continued all through the night and ceased just before dawn. After a quick breakfast, we undid our hooches, caved in our foxholes, and buried all our garbage. We packed our gear and grabbed our weapons, and we were ready to go.

We lined up in a straight line facing in the direction of deployment and stayed that way until the entire battalion was ready and the word came to move out. We led them to the liftoff point, which was the same location that we had landed. Once we reached the wooded edge surrounding the LZ, we stopped and proceeded along its perimeter while the battalion sat tight and waited. We split up into two squads spanning in opposite directions. We secured the landing zone, making sure there were no VC dug in.

The gunships were on their way. We could hear the puttering of the props off in the distance getting closer. We tossed green smoke and waited. They got louder, but we still couldn't see them. Then the first of the choppers emerged from the tree line. The branches swayed from the high winds caused by the props. The first five landed, and they were our ride. We took off running, staying low and holding our hats, and hopped on. We took off and now had the new worry of hitting another LZ. I said my prayers and hoped for the best.

We were getting closer to the destination. We began to get ready for the descent. With my gun in its usual position, I focused my eyes on the trees and brush. My heart was pounding and beating more rapidly with every foot that drew us closer to the ground. When we hit treetop level, the chopper gunners opened fire at the wood line and kept it going while we jumped off. This time we knew what to expect. We ran for the wood line, staring at the jungle's edge. We huffed it for all we were worth and took cover in the bush. It was a cold LZ. By the grace of God, once again, we were lucky. We took our defensive positions and secured the LZ for the incoming battalion. We remained there until all the companies landed and were settled in.

Before joining the battalion, we patrolled the surrounding jungles. Many of the trees were uprooted and broken from the bombs. We came across a huge crater caused by one of them. We all stood around its circumference. It was at least twenty-five feet in diameter and twelve feet at its deepest part. One could only imagine the damage one of these bombs could do to a house.

Continuing on our patrol, I heard a noise coming from the ground behind a bush. I turned to see, and it was a snake. It moved quickly through the grass and disappeared into the weeds. It was unusual to see animals, reptiles, or even birds in the vicinity of a bombing. I wasn't even unnerved by the crawling nemesis. Nature's spine-chilling marauders did not faze a man who had to worry about an enemy far more dangerous and cunning.

We made no enemy contact and headed back to the perimeter. The line companies were busy digging in and setting up their defensive positions. The mortar teams were filling sandbags upon sandbags. They used two thousand sandbags every time their teams set up. That's a lot of work. Each mortar team consisted of two to three men. There were multiple teams.

The mortar was a handy and highly effective weapon. It was assembled in three parts: (1) a tube of various lengths, depending on the size of the mortar, which could be a 60mm or 81mm or a 4.2 inch; (2) a heavy disk-shaped metal base; (3) and a tripod to hold the muzzle (tube) at the proper angle, which, after the target's coordinates were confirmed, could be adjusted. The mortar shell was engaged by dropping it down the upper opening of the tube. Upon hitting the base, an explosive charge fired, and the shell was sent into flight. They had the capacity of traveling high and far and would drop straight down. Their accuracy was limited due to the short smooth barrels, but they were capable of being fired rapidly and caused much destruction and damage. When launched, the sound they emitted was that of a muffled *thump*. An aerial whistling followed, which preluded a loud, devastating explosion. Their support was called upon quite often and used by both combatants.

It started to rain when we entered the camp. The chow line was about to close, so we hurried and grabbed a dish of rain-saturated food. After drinking our dinner, we started our defensive position. The rain didn't make it any easier. We had all to do to keep from slipping in the mud as we dug our foxhole and filled sandbags. It seemed that I was the official "tree cutting down" expert, so I went to do just that. Bravo Company's medic, whose name was Antonio Ribera, came over to talk as I chopped. He was from New Mexico and was a conscientious objector. He didn't carry any weapon. He had previously told me of how he had to fight it out in court to get into the Army. He was such a great guy, a real gentleman. He was writing a book and took all sorts of pictures. He loved and admired our recon platoon and was going to devote an entire chapter about us. He was particularly fond of me and Eddie. He wanted the people back home to know about "this place," as he called it. He said, "I am really putting together quite a collection of photos for my book. I want to get more of recon. Later I'll come over and take some of you and Eddie."

"Sure, Doc," I said. "What are you going to call your book?"

He replied, "*No Sweat, GI, No Sweat.*" That expression was commonly used by the Vietnamese children. When they were asked to do something, they would answer, "No sweat."

While Doc and I were conversing, I had cut down two nice-sized trees. I put one tree on my shoulder and asked him to help me get the other one onto my other shoulder. He did, and we walked back and parted when we reached our different areas. After completing our position, Doc came over and took some more pictures of us standing by our foxhole. We told him not to forget to give us a signed copy of his book when he finished it. "Will do," he smiled and said.

After warming ourselves with a hot cup of coffee the following morning, we left on patrol without the battalion. The warmth of the sun's early morning rays felt good, and we absorbed as much of it as we could before entering the cool underbrush. We went about two hundred yards and set up a temporary ambush position. Eddie and I set up on a small hilltop. It was not a dense location; rather, there were scattered trees and bushes. Thus we had a panoramic view of the entire area. We laid side by side on our bellies, angled on the hill and gazing over the ridge. Only a few minutes had gone by when our conversation paused. Eddie had stopped talking and had started to shiver. Tears filled his eyes. His teeth began to chatter, and his lips vibrated rapidly. I attempted to ask him what was wrong. I got no response. He was having one of his seizures. I hopped to my knees quickly, removed my shirt, and covered him. "Stay still, Eddie," I said. "I'll be right back." I ran to Sergeant Santos and told him. He immediately called for a dust off. We cleared an area for the medevac chopper, which arrived in less than twenty minutes. Eddie was lifted off and taken out of the jungle. I knew it was the end of the bush for Eddie. I would miss him being with me. I saw the chopper get farther away and was torn up inside at the sight of my best friend, whom I'd gone through so much with, being taken away. I watched until it got out of sight. For the first time since I got into the country, I felt all alone. The damn war was going to be harder to face.

The following day was Sunday, and awakening without Eddie being there wasn't the same. We were going to head to a new location.

Before leaving, those of us who were Catholic attended a mass set up in camp. Prior to the service, the chaplain, Father Calter, asked if anyone wanted to receive Holy Communion and make a confession. I had never told my sins to a priest without being in a confession booth where I was hidden from view. Under the circumstances, I guessed it didn't matter. We stood side by side, facing opposite directions, and I related my confession. For the mass, we sat on empty ammo boxes and listened to a short sermon. At its end, the chaplain said a prayer asking God to keep us all safe and to bring peace soon.

We began to break down the site. I walked over to our foxhole and peered inside to make sure we hadn't left any equipment there. It was empty except that there, on the side of one of the walls, was a large scorpion. I just left it alone and went into our hooch to grab my shovel to fill in our foxhole and bury the garbage. The shovel was in its case beside my air mattress. When I pulled it out of its casing, a tarantula popped out and landed on the mattress. It was big and hairy. It moved a short distance and stopped. I grabbed my cleaning rod and struck it. I stunned it. I remembered the scorpion and thought I'd amuse myself. "How would the two creatures react if they were suddenly thrown together?" I was about to find out. I picked up the spider with the shovel and carried it outside and laid it on the ground. It was still unconscious. Then I took my rod and went over to the foxhole and pierced the scorpion with the rod. As I carried it over to mingle with the tarantula, it was moving its claws and tail. I guess it was really pissed. I grabbed a twig and pushed it onto the spider and sat back to watch the show. The scorpion grabbed the tarantula with its claws and lifted it up. The spider wrapped its legs around its opponent, and the fight began. David C. came by and watched for a moment then decided to put an end to the battle of the century and crushed them with a rock. "Damn, David C., what did you do that for?" I asked.

He just shrugged his shoulders and said, "Come on, Johnny, we gotta go."

I silently said to myself, "Man, just think, I slept right next to that tarantula for three days."

This time we'd be going on foot. Our point men were given a break, and two teams of Army dogs were attached to our platoon. They were flown out to meet us just prior to us leaving. They were two German shepherds, each with its own handler. They were large beautiful dogs and good at what they did. It was a secure feeling having them with us and leading the way. Our three point men, although spared their up-front duties, were still needed. When the dogs would alert, the point men would have to check out the vicinity. The shepherds were kept on collars and leashes. The handlers told us that if they were let loose on a Vietnamese person, they would tear them apart. They said they had all to do to hold them back, even if a gook was simply walking by or riding a bicycle anywhere near them. They would go berserk. But on patrol, you wouldn't hear a peep out of them. They'd just stop and alert at any sign or scent of the enemy.

So it would be the dogs and handlers, our point men, us, and then the battalion in that order. The dogs were a great asset, but they could be pests at times. They would stop and alert often, and we'd have do the same until the "go" sign was given. Our point men would pan off in three different directions to investigate the dog's suspicious warnings. They moved ever so quietly and precociously so as to not disturb a leaf or snap a twig.

On account of Eddie not being with me any longer, Parker joined me and David C. and became my ammo bearer. Parker was a husky black fellow from South Philadelphia. He was the heavyweight Golden Gloves boxing champion of that section of Philly.

Slowly we moved on and chopped our way through the thicket, dealing with those damn red ants. Being wet intensified their bites. The slightest shaking of a vine would cause them to shower down on us, and they'd fall ready for battle. Our most vulnerable parts for them to attack were our necks and behind our ears.

The dog teams saw us safely to our new campsite. After digging in, the three of us took it easy for the rest of the day. A clean batch of fatigues was flown in, and we were able to change from our muddy and wet clothes at last.

That night, we took turns at guard duty. We pulled one-hour shifts, sitting close by our hooch. We had to have great trust in one another. Our lives were left in the alertness of the one who kept watch. His falling asleep, which could easily occur, could cause all of us to have our throats slit. The loneliness of guard duty can only be understood by those who have ever been in that position—just sitting on a rock or on sandbags and thinking about home and how great it would be to be there. Perhaps those were the thoughts that kept a man to go on. Perhaps those were the thoughts that kept him alert and aware of his surroundings: to train his eyes to be like that of an owl so he could see what lay in the dark shadows of the jungle; to train his ears like those of an antelope to hear a leaf flutter from a tree; and to train his nose like those of a bloodhound to smell the dangers that lurked all around him.

In the morning, we led the battalion out on patrol. We lined up in two rows while our battalion commander, a full-bird colonel named Simpson, stood in the center of us. He loved our recon platoon. In camp, he wanted us to be around him and then the line companies around us.

The colonel was one to want a salute, which was odd because most officers did not want to be exposed for fear of the enemy targeting them. Whenever we filed out of camp, he'd stand in the center of the two lines, with his hands firmly on his hips in expectation of a salute from each trooper as they passed him. Well, by now, you all know that I wasn't going to oblige him. I slowly walked by him. He turned his body slightly, following my passing him by with his hands still on his hips, just waiting for me to salute him. I had my gun on my hip, which was an excellent excuse for not doing so. He looked at me, and I gazed back at him, still moving past him. I could see a hidden smirk on his face. He admired the way I handled my M60; and when I got by him, he gave a quick smile and watched me enter the wood line. Then he turned back to resume his waiting for a salute from the other soldiers. He was a great guy and leader. He did not take any chances with the lives of his command. If we got in trouble, he wouldn't hesitate a minute to call in an air strike to bail us out.

We came upon a large body of water, which had to be crossed. We secured the end of a rope to a tree, and one man was assigned to swim to the opposite end and secure the rope. With the rope in place, we followed it as a safety guide to get us to the other side. *Good thing Eddie isn't here,* I thought. *He'd have been frantic at the sight of the water.* I followed behind David C. and Parker was behind me and Tex was behind him. We got halfway across, and it got deeper. In trying to maintain my grip on the rope with one hand and holding my gun overhead to keep it dry with the other arm, my footing gave way; and I slipped and went under. David C. grabbed my gun, and Parker and Tex got hold of me and pulled me up. That was the way it was for the rest of that week: one patrol after another. Aside from the encounter we had on the first day when Ronnie was killed and the chasing of the two gooks, we hadn't run into any other resistance.

CHAPTER VIII

INCOMING

A t last, the day came for us to return to our home base. The gunships picked us up and flew us back to Phuoc Vinh. It sure felt great to be there after those weeks out in the boonies. That shower Bob and I built was a welcome sight and looked more inviting than ever.

King, Rahar, Baldy, Funky and Me in the foreground kneeling at Phuoc Vinh after operation Billings. Picture taken by Tex.

Eddie was at the barracks to greet us. We embraced each other. He told me of the fantastic job he had delivering mail to Saigon and other towns. As he was speaking, I gazed around the room at all the bunks and how great they looked covered with clean linen. "Johnny," he said, "come on, I got something for you." He took me over to his bunk and reached under it. He dragged out an entire case of K rations. While doing that he said, "I became good friends with the mess sergeant, so I can get a full case anytime I want." The best part about it was that he had filled it with nothing but boned chicken and boned turkey (my two favorites) and, better still, tropical chocolate bars.

"That's great Eddie! Thanks, man, now I don't have to worry about trading off."

The first thing I did after the good news from Eddie was to take a shower. After that pleasant experience, I put some clean, dry clothes on and laid down for a while and read some letters from home. Then I spent a couple of hours cleaning my weapon. Next, I started to write a letter to Marilyn, but I was interrupted by mail call. I received a package from home. Tex had told me how fond he was of Italian food, especially pepperoni, so I sent home for some. Outside of the barracks, I heard a yodel. It was Tex's signature. I called him in to tell him his pepperoni was here. He, Baldy, Woody, Eddie, David C., and a few of the other guys sat around and devoured the contents of the package. As for myself, even though I was Italian, I was never too fond of much of its repertoire. I indulged in the Sara Lee chocolate swirl cake and ate it as if it were a loaf of bread.

That evening, after dinner (it was, by the way, so nice to sit at a table and eat like a gentleman for a change), I went to pay a visit to a new friend I had met from Bravo Company while out in the field. His name was Harris. He was a black guy who also enjoyed bodybuilding. He was one of the top three men in the Mr. Florida contest two years earlier. He had told me that he had a set of weights in his tent. I walked the quarter mile to his place. When I got there, he introduced me to another black guy named John. The three of us worked up a sweat getting in an intense arm routine. It felt great to pump up again. I missed that invincible feeling that lifting gave me. I thanked the both of them and walked back to my area just as it was getting dark. Most of the guys had gone into town or to view an outdoor movie, which was shown every night.

That workout only enhanced my desire to relax. Gary, who was a short-timer, was going home the day after next. He was lying on his bunk. Bob had already rotated back to the States while we were out in the field. I got up and walked over to Gary. I said, "Hey, Gary, how yah doin'? Nervous?"

He said, "Yeah, a little. Counting the hours now." I asked him if he would do me a favor and get in touch with my family and my wife when he got home and to let them know that I was okay. He said, "Sure."

"Thanks, Gary." I wrote down the phone numbers and handed them to him.

Just before retiring each night, I would go out and do chin-ups on the crossbar that supported the shower's water drums. That night Bravo Company's Doc Antonio paid me and Eddie a visit. I left them and went outside. Shortly after, doc came out to talk. Eddie must have told him about Smitty's offer to work with him at supply because his first words were "John, I just found out that Smitty wants to take you with him to supply. You are going to go, aren't you?"

"Not right now, Doc. I want to put more time out on the line, at least six months."

He tried desperately to talk me into it. "But think about your wife and the baby you'll soon have. Why take the chance when you don't have to? Listen to me and go. You don't owe anyone anything or have anything to prove."

"I know," I told him and stuck with my decision.

After Doc left, a strange phenomenon occurred. I looked up at the stars and said a silent prayer, asking the Lord if I would make it back home safely and if He would somehow give me a sign. The second I asked this, a shooting star swept across the sky from one end to the other. "Thank you for that, God." I rested much easier that night.

The next day, Eddie got a package. It was a case of Kool-Aid. He had written a letter to the company telling them some sob story about the GIs in Nam going thirsty in the hot jungles. So they sent Eddie a box full of Kool-Aid. David C., being the comedian that he was, said, "Shit, I think I'll write to Cadillac. Maybe they'll have a Caddy waiting for me when I get home."

Santos came in and told us to get ready. Once again, he had volunteered us for a detail. This time we had to take our gun jeeps and escort an eight-inch cannon, which was mounted on the back of a truck. That day, the one-millionth round was being fired, and we had the honors of guarding the festivities. We escorted it to the top of a hillside overlooking a wide-open grassy field. As the truck maneuvered its way into the firing position, we took our places and outposted the area. Photographers did their thing, and after a short speech commemorating the occasion, the round was fired. We watched it travel down the small valley, hit, and explode. It was over in seconds.

When we got back, Eddie surprised us and was ready with his Kool-Aid. He had obtained two five-gallon jugs from the mess hall and jokingly wrote on them "Eddie's Kool-Aid stand, five cents a glass." We all quenched our dry mouths with Eddie's cold, tasty beverage. In the far corner of the barracks, Gary was silently packing his belongings, getting ready for the happy trip home the next day. We all raised our second round of drinks to Gary and wished him luck.

The radio was on, and a song was playing called "San Francisco" by Scott Mc Kenzie. Ver Linden hollered across from the other barracks, "Hey, John, that's the song I was telling you about." We had been previously discussing some of our favorite songs, and that was one that reminded him of home. Oddly enough, the singer ended up dedicating his song to Vietnam vets.

The day was still young, so I went over to visit Harris and get in a workout. John was there too. On my way back, I heard a gunship fly directly over our compound. A single shot fired from the chopper. It seems one of the gunners accidentally discharged a round. I didn't know where it landed, but I found out later that it pierced right through one of the barrack's roofs. Fortunately, no one was injured. I'll tell you, you were never completely safe, no matter where you were.

When I got back to the barracks, I checked my M60 mounted on the tripod, which looked good and all shined up. I hung my .45 tucked in its holster, along with my canteens next to my bed. I put a clean pair of fatigues, neatly folded on a bench. My boots were right beside my machine gun. All were within arm's reach. I wanted to make certain that I knew where all my gear was and that I would be able to grab them in a hurry. Then I put my feet up and laid down.

Eddie came over. He was feeling down. "What's the matter?" I asked him.

"I haven't gotten any mail from Kathy in almost two weeks," he answered solemnly.

"Maybe they got lost in the mail, Eddie, and you'll get a whole shitload of them all at once," I said, trying to ease his depression.

"Yeah, maybe. But I know something is wrong, and I can't do anything about it." With those words, Eddie went to his bunk, and we both called it a night. I felt sorry for Eddie. When you're so far away, being kept wondering could drive a guy nuts.

Lights went out, and I drifted off to sleep. It must have been around 11:30 PM. In my sleep, between my closed eyelids and my eyes, I saw a flash of light. They suddenly opened at a thunderous sound. We all woke up, and for an instant, we wondered what was happening; but the sound of a series of thumps that followed told us—mortars. Someone yelled, "Incoming." There were whistling sounds, flashes of light, and then one blast after another. I got up and tried to find my pants and boots in the dark. But for some reason, I couldn't. There was no time to search. No time to even grab my gun. We all made a mad dash for the bunker. The mortars were still bombarding us. We dove headfirst down into the narrow opening, barefoot and dressed only in our underwear. I felt the mud ease up through my toes as we crunched tightly together. The sirens were blasting away. The lights were turned off throughout the entire compound to eliminate their glare being targeted. The noise from the blasts was deafening. My heart was pounding in my chest. The mortars were so close that we were able to hear them hit the ground just prior to the explosions. The flashes of light were seen through the entrance of the bunker. Debris was flying all around. I kept wishing that I had my gun with me in case of a land attack after the mortars. I suddenly realized that Eddie wasn't in the bunker. "Hey, anybody see Eddie?" I hollered. After a few no's, someone said that he saw Eddie running toward the other bunker. "How about Gary, where's he?"

Before anyone could answer, Gary said calmly, "I'm right here in the corner. I was the first one in here." It was pitch-black in the bunker. There wasn't anything we could do but sit and wait and pray that we didn't catch a direct hit.

The bombing lasted about thirty minutes. When it remained silent for a while, we emerged from the bunker, knowing that there was a great possibility of a ground assault. I was relieved at the sight of Eddie running toward the barracks from the other bunker. The lights were still out when we went into the barracks. Then they suddenly came on. We dressed in a hurry, and as I was putting on my pants (which, by the way, were right where I had placed them), I saw King jump down from his bunk. He had slept right through the mortar attack. He told me that he had rolled his mattress over his body and gone back to sleep. The sirens blew, and there was word that there was movement on the line. The drivers went to get the jeeps, which were parked over in the motor pool adjacent to the airfield. Two of the jeeps had flats due to the mortar shrapnel, so they were delayed in getting to us. Smitty had gotten a piece of shrapnel in his head and was bleeding and Doc Jimenez lost no time attending to his wound, and bandaging Smitty's head.

They repaired the damage on the jeeps, and we were ready and waiting to get picked up. We hopped on, and we five gunners rapidly placed our M60s onto the mounts and snapped them in place. The rest of the platoon loaded up on the ton-and-a-half and, along with the line companies, headed to the perimeter. It was after 1:00 AM when we reached the line. We waited silently and stood our positions, anticipating an enemy attack. We remained motionless, concentrating and listening for any movement until 3:00 AM. Nothing happened. The "all clear" was given, and we headed back to our barracks, cursing those motherfuckers all the way.

We had just started to get comfortable; only, this time, most of us kept our clothes and boots on. At least, I did. Not even fifteen minutes had gone by when the sirens blew again. The word came that there was movement on the line, and we had to do it all over again. This time we stayed until sunrise. For the second time, nothing. This was "Charlie's" strategy. The VC knew when we were in from the field for some rest, and that was one of their ways of not letting us get any.

In the daylight, we got a good look at the damage. There was debris everywhere. We couldn't get any rest even if we wanted to. We had to clean up the mess. One of the company barracks took a direct hit; fortunately, no one was hurt. It took most of the day until we were able to chill.

When mail call came, Eddie finally got a letter from Kathy. I was with him and watched as he read it. His eyes filled with tears. When he was through, he handed it to me to read. Kathy stated that she was dating someone else, a doctor, and she would not be writing to him anymore. It's what was called a "Dear John" letter. "Shit, Eddie, I don't believe it." Eddie was pacing the floor. He was hurting. I didn't know what to say. The poor guy had just got engaged and had only been gone a month and a half. I was tempted to tell him that if the girl only took less than two months to dump him, then she wasn't worth it. But sometimes less said is best. I left him alone and stood by and waited for him to say something. He dried his tears and said, "Johnny, let's go to the NCO club and shoot some pool." So that's what we did.

Later that day, we had to escort another convoy down through a couple of villages. For once, I welcomed the detail. It would get Eddie's mind off Kathy's letter. Driving the one-and-a-half-ton truck made him happy. He was attached to the front of the convoy. We did our usual thing of playing leapfrog with our gun jeeps during the entire trip. There was one stretch of road that always worried me whenever we traveled through it, which was often. On both sides of it stood acres of tall thick green bushes that hugged close to the road's edge. It was impossible to see a few feet in. It was between two villages and would be an ideal spot for an ambush. A wire could easily be stretched across it, which concerned me when we took the jeeps out on our own. Escorting a convoy eliminated that danger because of the larger and higher vehicles that were in front of us. My eyes were peeled looking into and beyond that brush. I would be relieved when we got past that section.

On the trip back, we had to be extra careful. That's when "Charlie" would be more likely to set up an ambush. It would only be us. And in their way of thinking, we'd probably let our guard down, which was something we never did. We got back not having any trouble. I think the escapade helped Eddie. He seemed to be more relaxed.

Speaking of relaxing, I needed to do just that. I told Eddie that I wanted to get some shut-eye. I assumed my somber position. I thought about that mortar attack, and it reminded me of a story my father had told me about something very strange that happened to him when he was in Iwo Jima. To help you understand, I'd have to go back to when he was eighteen years old. My father had one younger brother, Joseph and five sisters, Mary, Isabella, Grace, Madeline and Lucy, who was the youngest and only six. They lived in Harlem on 113th Street and Pleasant Avenue. One morning, Lucy asked her mother if she would give her a dime to buy some candy. After a few minutes of begging, my grandmother gave it to her, and Lucy ran down the flight of stairs all excited and went into the candy store. She had a few pennies leftover, and when she left the store, one of the pennies fell from her hand and rolled into the gutter behind a delivery truck. She bent down to retrieve it; and the driver, who did not see her, backed up and ran her over. She died instantly.

Now to fast forward to 1945. My father and his platoon were in a ditch. They were told to stay put until further orders were given for them to move out. He was sitting against the dirt wall with his helmet over his eyes. He was dozing off when he saw a vision of his sister Lucy waving her arm vigorously from the opposite side of the trench. At first, he thought he was dreaming, but it happened two more times. Lucy was beckoning him to follow her. He took the omen seriously and told the members of his platoon that they had to get out of that trench ASAP. The moment they got out, a bomb hit the trench and blew it up. I thought about that scenario and realized that life is so weird. If Lucy hadn't died back then, she would not had been there to save my father and his men and I would not have been born.

Another night passed. It seems that there was always something interesting going on, which was a good thing as long as we didn't get killed. This particular incident was a fun time. That afternoon, I heard a commotion in the barracks while I was coming back from lunch. A few of the

Tex and Woody.

guys were wrestling around. King was grappling with Rahar. King was bigger than Rahar. I went over to sort of take Rahar's place and

Baldy and King.

King, Tex and Rahar.

kiddingly grabbed King off Rahar. King said, "So Pizza wants to play." We fought, being careful not to hurt each other.

Malseki was on the sidelines laughing. Baldy asked him what he was laughing at. He said, "I'm watching King get his ass kicked." I grabbed King's head and put it between my legs and wrapped my arms around his waist and lifted him up. There wasn't much he could do after that. The fun was to continue. Sexton and Tex came rushing in and said, "Hey, guys, we just got offered a challenge to a tug-of-war by Charlie Company. Are you guys in?"

"Absolutely, let's go."

We went outside, and they had filled in one of the pits caused from the mortars with water and mud. A bunch of C Company's guys were waiting for us with a thick rope. Both teams had seven men. I was the anchorman on our team. I tied a loop in the rope and placed it over my head and around my waist. This was all or nothing. The team left standing were the winners. We took our stance, and they took theirs. Someone shouted "Go!" We dug in our heels and pulled without letting up. The mud filled the soles of our boots and caused a lot of slipping and sliding, and the loss of traction caused some of us to fall. Charlie Company had to deal with the same conditions. Our team got it all together, and the other group fell one after another into the mud pit. They wanted a rematch, saying best two out of three. But they wanted one change. They insisted that I come up front to be first in line. "No problem," I told them. I walked past my guys and whispered, "Don't let me down!"

I grabbed the rope. Sexton was behind me. He said, "Don't worry, Johnny, we won't let you fall in." We got ready, and the battle was on.

I told Sexton, "There's no way I'm going into that mudhole." We all pulled for all we were worth. It felt like every muscle in my body was going to tear. I saw the edge of that pit getting closer, and I just leaned back and tugged. We put more distance between me and the edge, and down they all went. Again, victory was ours. Game over. I heard Sexton softly say to the other guys, "I'd rather get hit by a Mack truck than Pizza."

That was a lot of fun. I really enjoyed it, especially since I was spared getting doused in mud. I told my group that it reminded me of some of the rough games we played in the streets of the Bronx. "What games?" one of them asked.

"For instance, touch football, ringolevio. But," I said, "this tug of war was more like Johnny-on-the-pony."

"What the hell is Johnny-on-the-pony?"

"You're kidding," I said. "You guys never heard of Johnny-on-the-pony?" They wanted to know, so I explained that it had two teams of anywhere from four to seven guys. One guy was the pillar, and the other four were the ponies. The pillar stood against a pole. The first guy wrapped his arms around the pillar, with his head to the side, while the other team members bent over and held each other's waists—clenching their hands, tensing their bodies, and putting their heads off to the side, closing the gaps between them. The other team would send their lightest and fastest to go first so he could leap the furthest. Then, one at a time, they ran and jumped as far as they could to make room for the others to fit and came down as hard as they could onto the backs of their opponents, trying to break or cave in the chain of ponies that was formed, which was the object of the game. Naturally, the heaviest guy was last. He was in the position of doing the most damage. All the jumpers had to remain on or else they lost. If all of them managed to stay on top, the team holding them up would holler, "Johnny on the Pony, one-two-three. Repeat it three times"; and if they didn't collapse from the weight before the countdown ended, they were the winners. It could get pretty damn rough at times. But that's what growing up in the Bronx was all about.

Eddie told me that Ver Linden and Deloge wanted to go into the town and asked if I wanted to go with them. "Sure, give me a minute to get ready." We walked to town and passed by some stores and a barbershop. One of the stores was a dress shop. In the window, it displayed Asian-style kimonos. Ver Linden and I liked the white one being worn by a mannequin. We went to get a bite to eat in a small restaurant. I had some fried shrimp and french-fried potatoes and a Coke. On the way back, we stopped at that shop. Ver Linden bought the white one. I bought two multicolored ones: one for my mother and one for my sister. I asked the owner if he had another white one for Marilyn. He did, so I purchased all three. Eddie and I went back on our own. We cut through a big open area. They were setting up for a USO show. There were hundreds of chairs all lined up. Unfortunately, we never got to see the show.

We had to leave for a few days and camp outside some village. Eddie stayed at Phuoc Vinh. We took our jeeps. The area wasn't a high-alert place, so we didn't have to dig any foxholes, just hooches.

We set up our camp in the bush within walking distance from the village.

That first night, a young Vietnamese girl was snuck into our camp. She couldn't have been more than fifteen years old. I saw my buddies enter a hooch and take turns humping her. They didn't rape her. She did it willingly for the money. As much as I, too, wanted to pop my twigger, I couldn't bring myself to do it. I was trying my best to stay faithful to my wife. She came out of the tent, after they were finished with her, fixing her garments and her hair. It was very dark. I could barely make out what she looked like. She kept her head down toward the ground as if she were embarrassed. I walked by her side to see her safely out of the camp. We never spoke a word to each other.

Deloge, Nezat and funky on gun jeep with unknown USO girl.

I went back into my hooch. Deloge was there. I asked him where Nezat was. He told me that he and some of the guys were playing cards. Nezat showed up a short time after and started to count out a wad of money that he was holding in his hand. He counted about seven hundred dollars then separated one hundred dollars and told me to hold it. Then he said, "Send this money to your wife. Think of it as a gift for the baby."

"I'll do that, Serg." I thanked him. I thought that was so generous and kind of him to do that.

The next day we went on maneuvers with the gun jeeps. There was nothing doing, so we decided to get away on our own for a while. We drove away and stopped when we got to a clearing in the woods. Santos wanted us to be prepared for a surprise attack or ambush. He yelled, "Ambush," and we'd deploy off the jeeps as fast as we could. For Nezat and Deloge, it wasn't too much of a task. They just had to grab their weapons and a can of ammo for me; but I had to open the cover plate up, remove the ammo, close the plate back down, disengage my gun from the mount, leap from the jeep, and find cover. Immediately after we hit the ground, one of them would come over with my ammo and lie beside me and act as my ammo bearer and help load the belt into my gun. We practiced this exercise until we were able to do it in under ten seconds.

We spent the rest of that afternoon resting and talking about our two favorite subjects: home and women. It was the era of the Beatles and the miniskirt. We hadn't seen the shortly designed skirts yet, but we had heard about them. We could only fantasize what they were like. I had always thought of oriental girls being mysterious and beautiful with their long black hair reaching down to their hips; but after seeing them every day and witnessing their habits, I realized (and so did most of the others) that there was nothing like a big round-eyed American girl.

Talking about home created a deeper longing for being there. All of us were becoming more and more bitter as the days passed. Living in the conditions, watching friends getting killed—we couldn't understand or figure out what the hell we were doing there. The people couldn't stand us. The hate in their eyes and their contempt of us was easily observed by the way they looked at us. They didn't want us there anymore than we wanted to be there. So what were we there for? They drilled in us that it was to stop the spread of communism. South Vietnam was a small country: only 61,108 square miles; only 1,600 square miles larger than our own state of Wisconsin. With the military power that we had, it should never have lasted as long as it did.

Even a grunt like me knows that winning a war was maintaining territory. So why the fuck did they drop us off in the middle of nowhere for days or weeks at a time, lose friends in the process of securing that area, then remove us so "Charlie" could just stroll his ass right on back in again. It was a damn joke. They were using us to fatten their greedy asses. We all knew it. We were expendable, and that was all there was to it. It sucked that there wasn't anything we could do about it.

A perfect example of this ridiculous war and the point that I am trying to make was that of what was known as "Operation Apache

Snow." It took place from 10 May 1969 to 20 May 1969 at a Hill numbered 937, more commonly known as "Hamburger Hill," at the foot of the "Ap Bia Mountain," which stood alone and was heavily covered with thick forestry and unconnected to any of the surrounding ridges. It was heavily fortified with well dug in NVA enemy forces. It had little strategic value, but even so, command ordered a frontal assault by combined U.S. and ARVN forces to attempt to drive out the enemy from their strong hold overlooking the "A Shau Valley." The brave troops inched their way up the slippery, muddy slopes up the hill under intense enemy fire from a highly advantageous elevated position. They were getting chewed up but continued wave after wave for days and refused to give up until the enemy was defeated and forced to withdraw. This proved how brave our troops are and my hand goes out to my fellow comrades. However, after the loss of 70 men and 372 wounded and 639 enemy killed, the hill was abandoned five days after its capture. This to me was insane. So many casualties for nothing.

We spotted a platoon of ARVNS (Army Regulars of South Vietnam). There was a minor exchange of words, and then they were on their way. My experience with the ARVNS wasn't one of great respect. They were useless. They seemed to always be where "Charlie" wasn't. There may have been some exceptions, but I never saw it.

CHAPTER IX

BATTALION MINUS

When that three-day incursion ended, we headed back to Phuoc Vinh. When I got back, Eddie seemed to be much better. He told me that he had met a Vietnamese girl and wanted me to go into town with him to meet her. After putting my things away, I went with him. Her parents owned one of the restaurants in town. When we got there, she was standing along-side another girl. Eddie introduced us. She spoke some English. At a glance, I could see why Eddie was fond of her. She was very attractive but more so was the fact that she resembled Kathy. The other girl was slightly heavy and not as pretty. We sat down and ordered a shrimp dinner. From the table, I was able to see into the kitchen. The place was more like a shed, opened all around. The tables were covered with white cloths. The more we talked, the more I missed my wife. I was wishing she were there conversing with me instead. I just got up, gave Eddie some money, said goodbye, and left.

On my way back, I was enticed by some Vietnamese girls leaning out of a window. "GI want 'boom-boom'?"

"You number one GI."

"We give you number one 'boom-boom.'"

I ignored them and walked on by. Some kids came around and badgered me to give them some candy. At first, when I got in the country, I felt sorry for them; but now things had happened since then that changed my attitude. My heart was hardening. I told them to "Dee-dee mow," which meant "Get out of here."

I got close to my company area, and I heard someone call my name. A group of GIs were passing by on a deuce-and-a-half. Among them, sitting on the tail end of the truck, was Price, who was the guy who had slept above me in AIT. He shouted out as he went by, "Hey, Fratangelo. Brown was killed and so was Midgette." He yelled out that Herbie was hit twice but was okay.

I hollered back, "What about Inge?"

He said, "Inge is all right."

"Price, you take care of yourself, man!" I couldn't believe it. Brown, who was only eighteen years old, and Midgette, whom I knew since junior high school, were both dead.

In the barracks, I laid down on my bunk in disbelief of what I had just heard. Eddie got back, and I relayed the sad news to him. In just two months, I had lost three friends that I knew of. How many more would there be?

On the Fourth of July, we treated ourselves to our own fireworks display. We hopped in the jeeps and set out for the firing range. We were leaving the next day for the boonies, and it was a good opportunity to test our weapons. We all traded off firing one another's weapons to get a feel of them. We had a variety to shoot: the .45 pistol; shotguns; M16s; commandos; the 90-millimeter recoilless; and naturally, my favorite—the M60 machine gun. I have to say, it was fun; trouble was, now we had to clean them all.

We spent most of that afternoon cleaning them and preparing for the liftoff the following morning. Eddie wasn't around. He had gone off to visit his new girlfriend. I took a walk over to Harris to get in a workout. John came by as we got halfway through and joined in. After a nice long conversation, I left and called it a day.

As many times before, the B-52 bombers wreaked havoc on our morning's destination. The blasts echoed through the entire night, pounding away at the earth; but the more they blasted, the better the chances of us hitting the LZ without any conflict. An eerie feeling came over me every time I listened to the bombardment. I knew that in the coming morning, I would be dropped out there somewhere in the jungle right into "Charlie's" lap. The barracks seemed to be more serene on the eve of a new operation. I guess all of us shared that same eeriness. Last-minute words written on a piece of paper seemed to pacify the anxiety each of us held within. And as one hates to admit it, the thought of it possibly being the last letter home always plagued us silently in our minds.

Liftoff came right after breakfast. Woody stayed behind. He had a serious case of jungle rot on both feet. Sexton took over his machine gun. I told Eddie that I would see him when I got back. He watched as we drove farther from the barracks and waved.

We got to the chopper pad and loaded up. The rains were moving in. We knew we were going to get wet. The gunships took flight and stayed just above treetop level. Being so close to the ground was riskier. The chances of getting shot down or getting hit with a treetop claymore was greater. Aside from that, it made the turns more dangerous. My backpack was pushing me away from the bench at the back of me, and the weight of my gun and my leg hanging down caused me great concern. I thought for sure that I was going to take a deep six. I told Funky, who was sitting behind me, "You better hold on to my straps. I'm going to fall out." The pilot made a sharp turn, causing me to lean farther out. I yelled out, "Ease up on the fuckin' turns, you son of a bitch!" I wanted to shoot that bastard.

Gus Polite standing
by his gun jeep.

We landed and ran like hell to the trees. We secured one entire half of the LZ while Alpha Company took care of the other side. We transmitted the word back to the oncoming battalion, "LZ cold and secured." We stayed out there most of the day. Alpha Company pulled out and entered the camp to dig in as we hung out safeguarding the perimeter.

They called us in just as the rains came. The battalion was snug and dry in their hooches while recon, in the pouring rain, had to dig in. We took turns going for chow. David C. had gone on point. Gus Polite took his place. One of us went, and the other two dug and filled sandbags. When I went to eat, I met Cooky, whose name was James Wiltse. He was one of the cooks from the mess hall in Phuoc Vinh. "What the hell are you doing out here in the boonies?" I asked him.

"I wanted to get some time out on the front line," he replied.

"You're nuts," I told him, as if I wasn't. I went back to join Gus and Parker, and we finished our foxhole and hooch. And as so many times before, we went to bed cold and wet.

It always felt so good to feel the morning sun heat up our bodies and slowly eliminate that chill. We had to lead out on what was called a battalion minus. We would go a distance into the jungle and then stop at a suitable location and set up an ambush. The battalion would keep going deeper into the bush, and if they encountered the enemy, they would try to chase them back toward our position.

The place where we set up was thick with many low-hanging trees. The sun could barely shine its rays through the dense foliage. There was what looked like an abandoned VC trail running through it. These trails were common throughout the boonies. They were narrow paths that "Charlie" knew well and used often. The amount of grass growing on them told us if it had recently been traveled on. This one looked as if it had been idle for some time.

Mike Stark was my ammo bearer. Parker had gone with David C. and King on point. Polite went with Sexton. I set up a point position where I was able to see up the road and remain under cover. I took two claymore mines and placed two hand detonators in my pocket, along with two lengths of wire and two blasting caps. I looked up the trail and spotted a place that I felt was ideal to set up the explosives.

I placed one mine on the left side of the trail and the other on the opposite side but farther ahead. Due to the half-moon shape of the claymores, I was able to place them in a way that covered both the road and the bush. I planted the mines in the ground by extending the pointed bipods. Then I unscrewed the little adapter and put the blasting cap in its place. When this was done, I camouflaged them and the wire and returned to my position. I connected a wire to each of the hand detonators and laid them beside my gun. I set the sights of my M60 on to the trail. I positioned myself behind my gun while Mike sat, leaning against a tree, just to my right. We were sheltered by a large tree whose branches were thick and hung low.

There was a position approximately fifty feet to my right, behind some dense bushes. Santos moved that group to my rear. I saw them change location, and I figured that they were being replaced by someone else. We ate our rations and waited. Moments passed, and I looked at Mike. His eyes were closing, longing for sleep. Suddenly, the tree above me shook vigorously. I looked up and about but could not see anything. I turned to Mike, but he was in la-la land. I searched thoroughly, gazing through every branch, but there was still nothing. I knew no one would fool around and throw a rock.

Mike woke up and saw me looking up. "What's wrong?" he asked.

I told him, "Something shook that tree, and it was bugging me." I wasn't satisfied with the empty outcome. I kept searching for something in that damn tree. Mike fell back to sleep. I turned my attention to the trail and surrounding jungle.

The flowing adrenaline in my body must have speeded up my digestive system. I felt the urge to go to the bathroom. I leaned over and told Mike to keep his eyes open while I went. I had my .45, but it was so rusty I couldn't even cock it. I walked quietly to my right and passed the largest of the bushes where I thought Santos had put another position. I stopped and turned and looked down into the bush. I saw a shadow kneeling and suddenly sit back. I thought it was one of the guys. I waved my arm in gesture to signal that it was me, and I smiled. I turned and walked in a perpendicular direction from the bush. I went behind a tree to relieve myself, all the while keeping alert. I hurried to finish. It wasn't the most comfortable and safest place. Quickly, I pulled up my pants and started back the same way I went. I passed by the bush; but this time, I didn't stop. I got to my position and sat against a tree. After only a few seconds, I decided to lie down and place my finger on the trigger of my gun to see if it was still zoned in on the trail. Mike was sacked out against a tree. So much for his looking out. All of a sudden, we heard a tremendous explosion to our right. At first, I thought that someone had blown a claymore. A huge cloud of smoke emerged from the bush that I had just passed by. The debris from the blast was heard piercing the surrounding trees.

Jimenez, our medic, came running over. He was with the position that Santos moved to my rear. He said he saw me go into the bushes and didn't see me return. When he heard the explosion, he figured for sure that I had triggered a booby trap. He told me that he thought he was going to find only my body parts.

A squad of five men was chosen to search the area. It was discovered that just a few yards away from where Mike and I were set up, a grenade was lying on the ground. It was a dud. That was the mystery piece that drove me nuts, the thing that shook the tree. Fortunately, it didn't go off or we'd have been killed. We put two and two together and summed up what had happened. When the grenade failed, "Charlie" must have decided to try a claymore. The shadow I saw behind the bush was a VC setting the mine up and facing our position. When I passed him to go to the bathroom, he turned the mine in the direction I was going; and as I was on my way back, the bastard must have been on his way to detonate it. Time was on my side. Had I'd been a few seconds longer or if I'd have paused by the bush when returning, I would have been blown to kingdom come. And again, had I not had the urge to move my bowels when I did, he would have gotten both Mike and me. We were saved, and no one received as much as a scratch due to an act of fate.

We never spotted the little son of a bitch. King told me that he passed by a bush and heard a click as if a gun was flicked off safety. "I just kept on moving," he said. "I didn't even turn to look." If he did, he probably would have been shot. The gook would have been chewed to pieces by the others, but it wasn't worth the chance for him to spin and fire blindly. He was in the enemy's crosshairs. And to think, before all this happened, I had looked right at the motherfucker and smiled. It was a lucky day for all of us, even "Charlie."

We waited for Alpha Company to return, and then we went back to camp. The mail had come, and I received my third and final letter from Tony. It was dated June 29, '67. Today was July 16. Somehow, it must have gotten lost in the mail. I went into my hooch to read his letter.

29 June '67

Hi John,

Nice to hear from you again. Things are getting pretty hot down here. My squad ran into a lot of shit in the Iron Triangle. We had one guy cut in half when a recoilless and a Chinese claymore went off and another fellow got three 50 cal. bullets in him and one M16 round. Took off most of his back. I was in base camp all the time. We had quite a bit of casualties too.

Another one of my vehicles was lost out there. It was hit by an RPG-2 rocket in the gas tank. Everyone got off in time. Soon they're going to be taking about 140 guys and transferring them to different units and have the guys from the other units come here. It's because too many guys rotate in Jan., Feb., Mar., and April. They're trying to break it up. I hope I don't end up in a leg troop because this one suits me fine. We also have half a day off on Sundays from what I hear. Also, our PX is filled up with all kinds of goods: food, fans, refrigerators, radios, tape recorders, etc.

You know, the more time you have to yourself, the more you think about back home and get homesick. Well, John, until we've had a few more missions. I'll write again. Keep your eyes open.

Cousin Tony

CHAPTER X

RECON, THANK GOD

I t was now July 18, and we had the day off. Bravo Company and Charlie Company went out on patrol. Alpha Company stayed behind with us. The companies split up and went in different directions. The hours passed, and the companies were still out in the bush. There was nothing doing, so I went to see Doc Jimenez. I had gotten a large splinter in the palm of my hand, and I figured then was as good a time as any to get it removed. It would give me and Doc a chance to shoot the shit. He was in his hooch. So I went in, and both of us sat on the dirt. He was facing me. I was leaning on my left side with the weight of my body resting on my left hand. My back was tilted and low to the ground. My right hand was twisted in a position so that Jimenez would be able to dig the splinter out. He grabbed hold of my right palm and started to do his thing.

We spoke while he poked into my palm with a needle. Our conversation was quickly interrupted by the sound of a loud *pop*. Dirt came flying all over the two of us. We darted out of the low-lying tent to see what happened. Right outside the hooch was a fellow curled up on his side with his knees tucked into his chest. Both his arms were folded across his stomach. He was rocking back and forth and moaning. Our immediate thought was that he was shot, but there was no sign of a wound or any blood. We sat him up, and one of his friends gave him a lit cigarette. His hand was trembling in such a manner that he could barely hold the cigarette butt between his fingers. The poor guy wasn't hurt, but he was extremely shaken up. After Doc calmed him down, we asked his buddy what had happened.

He told us that one of his friends from Alpha Company had attempted to pick up his commando that was leaning on the entrance to Jimenez's tent. Its muzzle was facing down, and the safety button was off. He foolishly picked up the weapon by the trigger, and it fired, releasing one round; and then luckily, it jammed.

Doc and I crawled back into his hooch. I assumed my former position; but this time, when I went to place my left hand where I had it before, it dipped into a pit that wasn't there previously. We looked down and there, inches from my back, was a hole in the ground caused from the bullet that was discharged from the commando. Had it not jammed, the weapon would have risen from the firepower, and the bullets would have cut across my back and probably Doc's stomach. We just looked at each other. I saw Doc's eyes, peering through his thick eyeglasses (which made his eyes appear small), grow wide as if to say, "Holy shit." Fate had been on my side once again.

The hours passed, and it grew very hot. We laid around, taking advantage of the rare idle time. It was nearing dusk, and something was wrong. The battalions were still out there when they should have been back already. Just then Santos came running, yelling for us to get ready. Radio contact had been made with the battalion. Charlie Company was on their way in. Bravo Company had been ambushed, and they were in trouble. They had run into a large-scale enemy force on their way in and were hit bad.

Colonel Simpson had gone with them. We geared up and headed out on our rescue mission just prior to sunset, about 8:00 PM. Alpha Company stayed back on standby. We had a team of scout dogs with us along with their trainers. We went alone. Once again, it was reassuring having the dogs with us, but we knew it would be a long, slow journey. We wouldn't be able to make good time as we would like to.

As it got darker, it started to rain—not a heavy downpour but a steady trickle. During our movement, we continued to try to contact them. Santos softly kept transmitting into the radio, giving coordinates and hope to the battered troops. We didn't hear any gunfire. The rescue was slow going due to the dogs alerting and the dense jungle, which we had to hack our way through with machetes. The rain was cold and steady, and because of us having to stop every few minutes and stand perfectly still to listen, our body temperatures dropped. I developed the shakes that made my body twitch uncontrollably. The mosquito bites were intensified by the wetness of our fatigues. They were eating us alive. These were some of the subtle hazards of combat that you wouldn't know or think of unless you've lived through them.

We continually sent up flares to light up our path and to let Bravo Company know that we were coming and getting closer and to help guide their retreat in our direction. The smell of gunpowder grew stronger the closer we got. We stopped and stood at a tree line that surrounded a large muddy open field. The rain was still falling. We remained where we were, anticipating Bravo's emergence from the jungle. We waited and waited, standing like statues, looking and listening.

Due to the many casualties they had sustained, Bravo Company was unable to move quickly. We continued to fire flares. Helicopters were flying overhead, shinning spotlights onto the treetops, trying desperately to spot the weary troops.

It was 2:00 AM when we finally heard movement coming from the bushes. We waited in readiness to see who or what would emerge from the jungles. It was Bravo Company. We watched as they staggered out one by one. They were worn out from battle fatigue. Their fatigues were torn and muddied. Some had no weapons. Their faces had the look of death and expressed a state of semishock that advertised the horror that they had been through. One soldier came through the bush where I was standing and said with a sigh of relief, "Recon," and moved on.

I stood tall with my M60 on my hip and tried to give them encouragement as did my recon buddies. They appeared to be in a daze as they passed us by. Then I spotted Colonel Simpson. He was a mess. He saw me. Then this full-bird colonel, our battalion commander, stopped in front of me and fell to his knees in the mud. He reached up with his two hands and grabbed me firmly by my shirt and said, "Recon, thank God." It was as if he was staring at Jesus Christ Himself. His reaction to seeing us showed me, with no other words having to be said, of the living hell that he and Bravo Company had endured that day. I helped him to his feet and stood by him while he stayed until the very last man had exited to safety.

They were carrying their wounded and dead on makeshift stretchers. We flanked them and led them back to safety. The field acted as a dust off for the choppers to land and pick up the casualties. A few of us picked up the rear guard, looking behind to make sure no one was on our tail. We returned to camp without any further incidents. The nightmare was over for those who had survived it. Or was it?

We learned later what had happened. Bravo Company had walked into an L-shaped ambush, which was highly effective. Their M16s were jamming, so they had tossed them in anger, leaving them with minimum defense against the enemy insurgents. I had heard of the poor design of the M16s and how they would malfunction when getting wet or dirty and that the AK-47, which our enemy had, was a superior weapon to use. That was one of the reasons I liked my M60.

Once I explain to you about an L-shaped ambush, you will understand why it is so effective. To do this, foxholes were dug in two rows perpendicular to each other, creating an L. Every foxhole had two openings or ports: one on the left side and one on the right side. Then the weapons were pointed out of the ports and moved from left to right until they reached a stopping point. Any object between the two stopping points, whether it being a shrub, a small tree, or an anthill was removed. These cleaned-out sections were called firing lanes. This action left no cover or refuge for the enemy to use for protection. Each position followed suit, thus creating a devastating web of interlocking firepower for each firing lane. This area was known as the kill zone. Anyone entering it had little to no chance of survival.

Bravo Company sustained multiple WIAs and seven KIAs. An ambush of this highly successful effectiveness would have been done by a unit of North Vietnamese Regulars and not local black-pajama VC. There were multiple claymores set pointing in the same direction so if a soldier was wounded and a medic or another comrade was trying to help, he'd get blown away by a secondary claymore. The entire area was skillfully booby-trapped. If men retreated into the jungle and took cover, the clever enemy had more claymores pointed at anything that would provide such cover. Some fell victim to punji pits, which were camouflaged holes in the ground that contained bamboo poles affixed in the dirt, with pointed ends dipped in cow shit, facing upward. That made it very poisonous. If someone was left in that trap, it would be a horrible way to die.

Among the wounded that I knew was John, the fellow Harris and I worked out with. John had his leg blown off. Among the dead that I knew were my good friends Price and Doc Antonio. Doc was administering first aid to a fallen soldier and was killed by a claymore. His entire chest was blown apart. He would never be able to finish his book. Three guys came back with no heads. Harris made it out with no injury. In the weeks that followed the July 18 battle in the Tay Ninh Province of South Vietnam, Harris and I would spot each other in the field, and we'd give a thumbs-up. We never did get to work out together again.

Due to the unexpected encounter and the loss of men, the operation was brought to an end. It was extremely hot, and I went into my hooch to meditate over the loss of more of my friends. I laid down on my air mattress facing up. The top of my tent was only inches away from my face. The dark-green material of the poncho-made hooch amplified the heat from the sun and baked my face and torso. The sweat rolled off my body and down my brow into my eyes and mingled with the tears I was shedding over the loss of my comrades. And quietly, to myself, I sung the words to the songs "You'll Never Walk Alone" and "Farewell to the Mountain," with the latter having been written by an American pioneer hero, Davy Crockett. For those of you who don't know the words to these two songs, I'd like to write them down so you may absorb their meaning and know why I chose them to pay honor to my friends.

"You'll Never Walk Alone"
When you walk through a storm, hold your head up high and don't be afraid of the dark;
At the end of the storm, there's a golden sky and a sweet silver song of a lark.
Walk on through the wind, walk on through the rain, though your dreams be tossed and blown.
Walk on, walk on, with hope in your heart, and you'll never walk alone. You'll never walk alone.

"Farewell to the Mountain"
Farewell to the mountain, whose mazes to me, more beautiful far than Eden could be.
The home I redeemed from the savage and wild.
The home I have loved, as a father his child.
The wife of my bosom, farewell to y'all. In the land of the stranger, I'll rise or I'll fall.

We left the next day for Phuoc Vinh for a three-day rest period. When I got there, Eddie already knew about the bad news. He told me that he had to help to identify the bodies of Antonio and Price. He also said that it had been so hard to do and that it was something that he would never forget. It's so strange seeing and speaking with friends one day, and the next day, they're gone forever. With each passing day, our hearts grew colder and hardened as if we were slowly turning into machines, robots with no pity, no feeling, no nothing.

The few days in base camp, for the most part, turned out to be a nice rest period. Going into town was one of the pastimes. Most of the stores, restaurants, and barbershops were owned by GIs. They had themselves nice little businesses going. There were lots of ways to make money when given the opportunity, both legal and illegal. Dutch was partners with someone in one of the barbershops. If you wanted to get daring, you could sell a twenty-dollar American greenback bill for ten times the amount in piasters to the black market. But we were told that doing that was not good for our economy.

| Funky, King, Rahar and me. | Deloge, Tex and David C. | Bill Lundsforf wearing Black Scarf. |

On one of the afternoons, I was in the barracks with Parker and Woody. We were reading comic books. Woody was still recovering from his jungle rot. He and I liked the Fantastic Four. Our favorite character was Benjamin Grimm AKA the Thing, known for his expression, "It's clobberin' time."

Parker and I decided to go outside and put on the boxing gloves and spar, something he and I had done occasionally when the opportunity presented itself. "Let's Scooby Doo," we'd say, an expression he and I would say to each other. While we boxed, he'd give me some pointers he'd learned from fighting in the Golden Gloves back home in Philly. He was a good fighter.

Eddie had gone to see his girl. Santos, along with Tex, Schneider, Ver Linden, King, Baldy, Rahar, Funky, Lundsford, Deloge, and Nezat, went into town to have some beers. For some reason, which I don't recall, one of the guys from Charlie Company had it in for Santos. He didn't like him at all. This guy would always try to instigate Santos into a fight. They'd argue back and forth, but it never came to blows. I guess it took the booze to push the button. One word led to another, and the two started to tangle. Before you knew it, a fistfight broke out. It turned into a barroom brawl. Santos got the worst of it. When they returned to camp, I saw him walking with an ice pack over his nose and eye. I told Parker to hold up, and we went to see what happened. We didn't see any evidence of a fight on anybody else. Deloge came over to us and said, "We sure could have used you two guys. What a great fight we had. We were outnumbered, but we held our own. You should have seen Ver Linden holding his own against a few of them."

It never ceases to amaze me. There we were fighting together on the same side against a common enemy, and when we had a chance to relax and bond, we fought among ourselves. The human being is just so fucked up.

That evening, after chow, I went to see Santos to see how he was doing. We got along very well. He was writing a letter home. He put the paper down, and we started talking about the events that had happened thus far. I didn't mention anything about the fight. We spoke about the operations that we took part in and about the men that were lost. He mentioned things that he wouldn't say to anyone else. He told me that he received the Silver Star, which was the country's third-highest award behind the Distinguished Service Cross and the Congressional Medal of Honor.

"What did you do to get it?" I asked him.

He went on to explain how. "It was on my first tour in Nam. I was a member of a patrol, and we came across a village. No one was around. We thought it was abandoned. We searched all the huts and didn't see anything, but in one of the huts, we noticed a tunnel entrance. I volunteered to be a tunnel rat. I took out my .45 and jumped into the hole. It was very dark. I couldn't see anything. As I jumped, I saw a flash and heard shots. I fired my .45 and emptied the clip almost before I hit the ground. There were three VC in there. They missed me, but I killed all three. I tell you, Johnny, I was scared. But all I thought of was shooting, and I fired blindly in the direction of the flashes."

I asked him how it felt knowing he had killed someone. He told me that at that time, you realize it's the enemy or you and you don't even think twice. When it's all over, it bothers you at first, but you learn to get over it.

Our conversation turned to home. He said, "After that happened, I realized how close I came to never seeing my wife and two daughters again. And sometimes I think I am not going to ever see them. I get so lonely for them, and even though there are many people around, moments alone become melancholy and that thought of wondering if I will ever see home again preys on my mind."

I told him that I try not to think of never going home, although sometimes I can't help but wonder. I always try to think positive no matter what. I asked him why he volunteered for a second tour. He told me, "I am making a career out of the Army, and I want rank fast. After this tour, I am going to request to be stationed in Panama so I'll be close to my home in South America."

By the fourth week of July, we had to move out on another operation. We went by jeep, and the battalion went by convoy. We traveled with an armor division; therefore, the going was slow. We were more precautious due to the fact that the local VC may have set land mines to take out our heavy equipment. When we came across suspicious areas, we'd stop and sweep for the mines. There were Vietnamese people all around whenever we traveled by the roads, so we had to be extra careful. The bastards would talk to you in the daytime then, at night, put on a pair of black pajamas and set traps, especially knowing that you would be traveling on a particular road.

At approximately 10:00 AM, we stopped the convoy to check out a suspicious section of road. We swept the road for mines, traveling far ahead of the battalion. We had to stop many times to probe the ground. One team located an antitank mine. It was large enough and well capable of taking out a track of a tank or sending a PC carrier and its crew to the netherworld. This sized mine would not be triggered by a foot soldier or a jeep. It took much more weight to be activated. They were after the big boys. They loved putting them out of commission.

We blew the mine with a charge of C-4. We went back to meet the convoy and waited a couple of hours before we moved out. As a precautionary method, we swept the road again. Lo and behold, there in the same spot that we blew the mine earlier was another antitank mine. This was one of "Charlie's" tricks.

Another one of their tricks, when they were after a small vehicle or a foot soldier, was to dig a hole in the tire lane of a road and fill it with water then plant a mine on both sides of the puddle, figuring the driver or the man walking would avoid the water hole and drive over the bomb or walk around it. We were trained to drive or walk through the water. Although reverse psychology could be applied, and "Charlie" could plant the mine in the ditch before filling it with water. It was just a matter of luck, just like everything else was in this damn country.

CHAPTER XI

THE APPARITION

Upon reaching our destination, the armor division set up along the road and sat tight. We went into the nearby bush and set up camp, knowing that we weren't going to return to Phuoc Vinh for a few days. The rain came down hard, and as usual, we went to sleep cold and wet.

Come morning, I warmed up with a nice tasty hot cup of cocoa. I melted a tropical bar in it to give it more of a chocolate flavor. The day got hotter as the sun rose higher in the sky. Going from being cold to insane heat was a common daily hazard that we all had to get used to. The sweat poured off my bare torso. The coolness of the thick bush and overhanging trees brought some relief from the 110-degree sweltering heat. We had the day off; so to keep from getting bored, I took my M60 and broke it down to its thirty-three parts and laid them out neatly, ready to be cleaned. It was closing in on noon time, and I was finishing shining up all the parts of my "best friend." Mail call came, and I received a letter from my sister Rose. It read as follows:

> *Dear brother John;*
> *I'm afraid that this letter is bringing sad news to you. Aunt Catherine got a letter from the Army stating that Tony was missing in action. The entire family is very upset. I feel that Tony is dead. Aunt Catherine and Uncle Frank are both in a state of*

shock. You don't realize the war until it hits home. We are giving all the support we can to Uncle Frank and Aunt Catherine. We are trying to keep hope and praying that Tony will be found and return home. I don't know what we are going to do. It's such a tragedy. I have to end now, for I can't write any longer due to the tears I cannot control.

PS. Please, brother dear, be careful and come home to us.

Love,
Your sister, Rose

I did not want to believe what I was reading. "It can't be true," I kept telling myself. "Not Tony. God, please don't let it be Tony."

I put my gun back together. Santos came over to talk to me. I looked at his dark, stern Peruvian face; and then he said, "John, you may be going home."

"What do you mean? Are you kidding?" I asked. He told me that I had been chosen to be an escort. "What the hell are you talking about, an escort for what?"

He went on to explain, "There is a special detail that the Army provides when a GI gets killed. A name is selected and that person escorts the body back home and your name was picked."

"But why did they choose me?" I asked.

"I don't know. Names are chosen at random."

Santos left, and not long after, a sergeant whom I had never seen before came over to talk to me. He told me that he was sent to explain what my duty was and all about the responsibilities of an escort.

I asked him the same question that I had asked Santos, "Why was I chosen?"

"I don't know," he said. "Names are just picked. Do you have any relatives in country?"

"Yes, about four cousins. Why?"

"Sometimes a close relative is called to escort the remains back to the States. But don't worry, it's probably somebody you don't know."

"When am I going?"

"Right away. Better get your things together."

I could not help but think about the contents of my sister's letter. I loved all my relatives, but what if it was Tony? He was the closest person to me on this earth. How would I handle it? I told myself to not think of the worst; odds were it wouldn't be him. I tried to set my mind to the excitement of getting out of this hellhole for a while and being able to see my family and my wife, who was now going on five months pregnant.

I gathered all my belongings and started walking out of the base. I passed by my friends, who were ready to mount the gun jeeps and go on patrol. They all knew by now what was going on and were hollering and calling me lucky. In no time at all, a chopper was sent for me. I gave my gun and most of my gear to David C. and asked him to take care of them while I was gone. I loaded whatever things I was taking onto the chopper, said my goodbyes, and took off.

When we landed at the airstrip, there was a jeep waiting to drive me to the company headquarters. We stopped, and I got off the vehicle. The driver pointed in the direction for me to go. I thanked him and went into a small building. There was a captain standing behind a desk. We greeted each other, then he motioned for me to come closer. I hesitantly approached his desk. He was holding a piece of paper in his hand. He placed it on the table, and with the five fingers of his right hand, he slowly turned the paper to face me. He pointed to a name written on it and asked me if I knew whose name it was. I was afraid to look down. After peering into the captain's eyes, I reluctantly rolled my eyes downward to view the name. Written in script was the name "Anthony Rutigliano." My heart dropped as those letters stared up at me. I softly and solemnly answered the captain, "Yes, he's my cousin." I knew all along, deep inside, who it was going to be. I had just been in denial. From the time I read my sister's letter about the "missing in action" telegram, it was inevitable. Other than unusual circumstances, the Army knows where you are at all times.

The missing in action news was the military's way of preparing the family for the worst.

The captain then informed me that I was going on a fifteen-day TDY (temporary duty). He handed me my orders and told me that I would receive further instructions when I got stateside. He had already made arrangements to transport me back to Phuoc Vinh. After a quick handshake and a thank-you salute, I was on my way. I traveled by jeep and was dropped off right at my barracks door. I went in and started to get ready for the trip home. No one was there. I was hoping Eddie would be around so I'd have a close friend to talk to, something I truly needed at that time.

I couldn't concentrate very well on packing, so I laid down on my bunk. Now that Tony was gone, all I had were the memories we shared. I'd have to treasure them for the rest of my life. I thought back to when we were little kids romping through the woods. The two of us were the best tree climbers in our little gang, so whenever we played tag or ringolevio, no one was able to catch us for they were too afraid to climb as high as we would go.

One day after seeing a cowboy and indians movie, where the chief of Apache Indians became blood brothers with the cavalry captain by cutting their wrist and placing them together, me and Tony went home after the movie and performed the blood brother ceremony. We were brothers for life.

We had all these different-sized lots we played in. The lot directly across the street from my house was where we mostly hung out. It was the lot that we played ball in until they built a gas station that took up half of it. When they dug it up, they placed two big boulders on the part that was untouched. It was those boulders that we all flocked to. It was like our fort. We'd spend hours there just talking. It was our happy place.

My boulder from
the Bronx.

186

Then there was the time when Tony was working at the butcher shop. We were sixteen. He called me up on the phone one afternoon and said with a satisfying voice, "John, guess what? I just got laid."

"No shit," I said back, with a "happy for him but envious" voice. "You lucky bastard." Naturally, me being a guy who was still a virgin, I asked, "What was it like?"

"Johnny, it was great. You've got to try it."

I was abruptly taken out from my memory lane by a voice calling my name. It was Eddie. He had just gotten back from a mail run, and I was glad to see him. He wanted to know what I was doing there. I filled him in with what had happened and that I was getting ready to go home. He was saddened by the news and felt bad for me. "What a way to go home," he said. "When are you leaving?"

"Tomorrow."

"Maybe they'll let you stay home, being that Marilyn is pregnant."

"Maybe, but I doubt it. You know the Army."

Then Eddie asked me to do him a favor and contact his family and let them know he was okay. I assured him I would. We said our goodbyes, and I told him that I would see him in a few weeks. He left to go into town and spend the night with his girlfriend.

After Eddie's departure, I continued my packing. It was a long, dreary day for me; and the twilight hours were creeping in. By now, two other guys had returned. They were both ailing with either jungle rot or recovering from an illness. To set the scene for what happened soon after, I'd have to describe the layout of the barracks.

They were built on a concrete slab about forty feet long and fifteen feet wide. The roof was made with sheet metal similar to Q-decking. They were screened-in all around. There was a screen door at each end with an amber-colored light above each doorway. There were two rows of bunks with each row containing seven beds that bordered an aisle that ran straight through from one entrance to the other. My bunk was halfway down on the side that faced the shower area. The two ailing GIs were in the end bunks at opposite ends of the room, one of whom was on my side to my right, close to the door. He was listening to soft music playing on his transistor radio while the other fellow down the other end, across the aisle, was holding a flashlight and reading. The lights had gone out at 10:00 PM.

I was still in disbelief over the loss of Tony. I was settled under the sheets with just my undershorts on. I was still thinking of days gone by as the seconds, ticking away on the clock, were passing the night away. I gazed at both my comrades; and by the sound of their soft, steady breathing, I knew they were asleep. The music was still entertaining me. I was tired from the long day, and my eyes were weary from all the shedding of tears; but I was not sleepy. My mind was in such deep thought that it wouldn't allow me to fall into slumber.

I looked at the clock that was on Parker's bedside stand. It was nearing 1:00 AM. The only illumination was that of the amber lights over the two doorways, which were quite dim, to say the least. The one to my right partially lit up the road, which separated the barracks from the mess hall. It faded as it entered deeper into the room. As I was lying on my back, I heard footsteps outside the screen door that was to my right. I turned my head toward the entrance and saw a soldier standing outside, facing the doorway. I looked to see who it was, but I couldn't make him out. He didn't make a sound or any sort of gesture. I strained hard to try to recognize the soldier, but the dim light glaring down on him was blocked by the brim of his cap, casting a shadow that darkened his face. I leaned up onto my right elbow to try to get a better look.

Suddenly the screen door swung inward and slammed against the inside wall of the barracks. He stepped forward, and in doing so, he completely blocked out any light for now it was behind him. I was able to see that he was dressed in full khaki uniform. He began to take steady steps toward me. I leaned farther up to an almost-sitting position with both my legs still under the sheets. I took a fast glimpse at the other two soldiers in the room. They were still fast asleep. The stranger got closer, and my eyes got wider as he approached the foot of my bed. He stopped and stared down at me. I, in turn, stared back and could not believe what I was seeing. He did not say one word. I did. "Tony." He looked great. He didn't appear a ghostly figure or transparent. I couldn't see through him. He was there, standing before me in the flesh, as real as can be. Then he put his hand out, and I did likewise. He stretched his arm to meet mine, and we clasped and shook hands. He then smiled, keeping his lips closed—a slight grin that expressed his telling me not to worry and that he was on his way to a much better place. He released his grip, turned, and walked back out the door, which screeched and slammed shut behind him. I watched in awe as he left and just disappeared. When I came to my senses, I realized what had just taken place. My cousin Tony, my dearest and closest companion, with a final handshake, could not leave this world without coming to say goodbye.

CHAPTER XII

THE TRIP HOME

I don't know how I managed to get some sleep after my ghostly encounter. I woke up, and after gazing around the room and noticing my two buddies, I wondered if they had seen or heard what went on. I know they were both asleep, but the sound of that screen door slamming twice should have awakened them. I thought maybe I alone was able to see and hear due to some kind of spiritual world blockage, the same as when the Virgin Mary appeared to Bernadette in Lourdes, France. Bernadette was the only person out of thousands who was able to hear and see Mary during all her apparitions. The fact that my friends hadn't mentioned anything gave me my answer. I do know one thing for certain: I was awake. It was not a dream, and from that night on, I had no doubt whatsoever that there is another life after this. One other thing—Tony's visit helped me to heal.

I now had to concentrate on making the trip home. A jeep came to take me to Bien Hoa. I loaded up my belongings; introduced myself to the driver, whose name was Josh; and we headed out. I got my first look at Saigon on the way to the airport. Until now all I had seen of Nam were run-down villages and dense jungles. There were cars driving about and crowds of people walking and many riding bicycles to and fro. There were beautiful well-dressed girls carrying wicker-made umbrellas to shade them from the hot sun. They were wearing sheer pastel-colored apparel that covered them from the neck on down to their ankles. I observed that many of them appeared to be well educated and spoke French. There were stores and restaurants on both sides of the road. It was like being back in the real world. It was a wholesome sight to behold.

We arrived at Bien Hoa. I thanked Josh for the ride and headed for my plane. It was a TWA 747. There was a line of GIs who were rotating and waiting anxiously to board that beautiful silver angel with metal wings that would take them home. It was to be the exact opposite of when I came. There would be a nine-hour flight to Okinawa and from there to Hawaii and then to Oakland, California, where I would receive further instructions. Before we boarded, we watched the new recruits getting off. *Man, if they only knew what they were in for.* Before I knew it, I was sitting in a window seat and watching the plane take off. The pretty flight attendants were a sight for sore eyes. In a matter of seconds, Nam was nothing but a hunk of land dressed in brown and green grids. I thought of my recon buddies still below in the bush, doing the same damn shit that we did day after day. I wasn't going to miss that, but I sure as hell missed my friends already.

After refueling at the first two stops, we headed for the Golden State. They showed movies onboard, which helped pass the time for the entire trip. Then came the long-awaited words from the airline crew, "Fasten your seat belts. We are making our descent. Welcome home." Before the fastening of the seat belts, the passengers all went to the windows to see the country they loved and missed so much get closer and closer as we went lower and lower, as if the plane itself was puckering up its lips to greet the homeland with a big fat kiss of its own. The sight of that sunset beyond the California mountains was just too beautiful to put into words. The plane touched down and came to a halt. We were finally home.

When we disembarked from the plane, I don't think there was one homecoming soldier that didn't fall to his knees and kiss the American soil.

I hopped a cab ride from the airport to Oakland, where I was supposed to find out my next move. The cabbie was very inquisitive. When he heard that I was just back from Nam and the reason for me coming back, he couldn't resist giving his viewpoints of the war, "I don't know what our country is doing there. It's crazy, all those guys dying for nothing. It's crazy, I tell yah." Then he asked me how my cousin was killed and if I was with him when it happened. I told him I didn't know anything about the way Tony died and that he had been with another unit.

We came to a tollbooth approaching the Golden Gate Bridge, so I went to hand the cabbie the change to pay it. He refused the money, saying, "This one's on me."

"Thanks," I said. It was my first sight of that magnificent structure. The sun, still in its setting stage, reflected off the towering arches that held the giant cables supporting the span of the bridge. Its golden color became ever more brilliant with the sun's touch. It really was a pretty sight.

The cabbie pulled up to my Army depot and slowed the taxi to a stop. I paid the fare and tipped him, grabbed my bags, and entered the large building. I was in the dark. I didn't know where to go or who to see. I had to play it all by ear. I showed someone my orders, and after reading them, he told me the first thing that I had to do was to get fitted for a dress uniform, which was done in another building in a different area. He told me that I'd be able to hop a ride on one of the trucks going that way. He walked me out and pointed in the direction for me to go. "Thanks," I said and went on my way. I spotted a small pickup vehicle with a dozen or so GIs standing on its bed. I hopped on, hoping it was going in the right direction. It was dark out, and I stood in the rear of the truck. I couldn't help overhearing what they were saying to one another. They were talking about Nam, wondering what it was really like and telling some of the stories they had heard about it. At first, I didn't grasp the gist of their conversation, but then it dawned on me. These guys were going overseas. The truck hadn't pulled out yet, and I asked one guy where they were going. He told me that they were headed to the airport to catch a flight to Vietnam. Without any hesitation, I said, "Goodbye, pal," and I leaped off the truck. I figured it would be safer if I just walked over to the building.

When I got there, I went into a small room located to the rear of the building. Because of my unusual V-shaped body, I had to be fitted by a seamstress. I was handed a uniform, and I tried it on. It didn't fit very well. The jacket was tight around my chest. The sleeves were too long, and the bottom half of the jacket fit like a tent. The pants weren't too bad. They were just a little long and had to be taken in quite a lot at the waist. The tailor made all kinds of chalk marks, placed all sorts of pins here and there, and told me to remove the suit and wait outside. After the uniform was finally ready—which, by the way, looked really good—I was told to return to the original building. When I got there, they told me that I would have to wait until morning to catch a plane to Andrew Air Force Base in Maryland.

There were a group of pay phones lined up against the wall. I figured it was a good time to call home and give them an update of my whereabouts. I dialed my aunt Catherine's number. My uncle John Attanasio picked up the phone. I could tell in his voice the hurt everyone was feeling because of Tony's death.

He asked me how I was. After telling him I was okay, he solemnly said, "It's really bad over there, hah, John?"

What could I have said? I had to tell him the truth. "Yeah, it is."

"When will you be home?"

"Probably in a couple of days. I'm in California, and I have to get to Maryland to be briefed on what to do."

"Hold on, your sister wants to talk to you."

He handed Rose the phone. She was overjoyed to hear my voice. She started to cry and said that it was a living nightmare. "We just can't believe that this is happening."

"I know," I said, "neither can I." I tried to comfort her as best I could and assured her that I'd be home very soon. "Give my love to all and give Mom a kiss for me." I hung up the phone.

There was one other call I wanted to make before I called it a night. That was to Marilyn. I knew it was very late in New York because of the three-hour time difference, but I wanted to talk to her. I figured I'd keep it short. I was curious to find out how she was doing and if she felt the baby moving around in her stomach. When

I called, she answered the phone. It was so good to hear her voice. She told me she was doing fine and that she had help from her family and friends. "I missed you so much," I whispered. "I can't wait to see you. I love you." She told me she loved me too. The dime dropped, and the operator interrupted, asking for more money. I quickly said, "I'll see you in a couple of days." We slowly hung up the phone. I waited to hear the click on her side before I hung up. Alongside the wall stood a row of benches. And as tired as I was, they looked very inviting. I bought a cup of hot chocolate from one of the vending machines, settled onto one of the benches, and went to sleep.

In the morning, I went into the latrine, took a leak, washed my hands and face, and rinsed out my mouth. I took a cab to Travis Air Force Base where I would catch my flight to Maryland. I arrived at the base in Maryland about midday and went to get a bite to eat in the mess hall. I couldn't get over the difference between the Air Force food and that of the Army. These guys actually had a menu to choose from. Even the table settings were different. They were set up for four people instead of many. The food tasted like real food. I made friends with a couple of Air Force guys; and after we finished eating, they took me over to show me their quarters. Their rooms were only occupied by four men. "Man, you guys got the life." I bid them farewell and went on my way.

I reported to a room for a briefing along with other escorts. It was there where I learned of what to expect and what to do. They explained the funeral procedure—such as the twenty-one gun salute and the folding of the American flag, which would be handed to the parents of the deceased—and that it was customary for the escort in full dress uniform to stand beside the coffin for the duration of its display in the funeral parlor. They also informed us that we had the power of attorney to have the coffin opened in private if the parents wished to do so. In Tony's case, the casket was to remain closed during the entire wake. We were issued papers to enable us to take possession of the corps when we intercepted them at the train depot. I was to meet up with Tony's remains at the railroad station in

Philadelphia the following evening. Before we left, they handed all of us our orders.

After the briefing, I had dinner and then took a taxi to the train station. I got on a train and headed to Philly. During the ride, I had time to look over my orders. I was given fifteen days TDY, just as that captain had told me in Nam. And I had to report back to my unit on August 18.

It was late in the evening when I got there, so I booked a room at a hotel close by the train depot. It was a fourteen-story building, and I was booked a room on the eleventh floor. It was a small room with one window overlooking the main street across the station. I couldn't sleep, so I watched an entire episode of Johnny Carson's *Tonight Show*. I just wanted the time to go by so I could finally get home.

When morning came, I got ready for the day ahead. I checked out of my room and had breakfast at a luncheonette where I met a marine and another Army guy. They were both escorts and waiting to meet up with their assigned deceased bodies. To help pass the time, we went to a movie. The feature was *Hells Angels on Wheels*. It starred Peter Fonda and turned out to be a pretty good flick. There was also a short X-rated film showing a striptease skit that jump-started my nineteen-year-old hormones, making my desire to get home to Marilyn much more prominent. I kept thinking, *Just a few more hours.*

After the show, the three of us walked around for a while. We were dressed in our military uniforms. The marine was living up to the corps' reputation by acting as if he wanted to take on the entire city of South Philly. They both had to catch an early train, so we didn't have much time to see the town. We stopped in a pub to have a friendly drink; I kind of thought that we would be doing battle with the locals because of the marine's attitude. But he calmed down, and luckily, there were no incidences. We swallowed our drinks and walked over to the train station. They said goodbye and left. I still had to wait. Tony's body was due in on the 9:15 PM train.

I hung out at the station. Trains were pulling in and out. People were coming and going. The train I was waiting for was delayed. It didn't pull in to the station until 10:45 PM. I went down to the platform and showed the conductor my papers. I asked him if the coffin was on the train. He told me that three gray wooden crates had just been unloaded onto the freight platform and for me to go down the ramp to my right and that I couldn't miss them. I did what he said, and at the bottom of the ramp, I spotted them. There wasn't a living soul in sight, just me and the three bodies. I walked over to them. I didn't know which one Tony was in. I saw a tag hanging down on each of the crates. There were numbers written on the tags along with the names and destinations. I looked to see which tag number matched the one I had on my order form. I double-checked to make sure I had Tony and that it was going to New York.

A railroad employee walked up to me and asked if I needed help. I showed him the papers, and he verified which one was Tony. Up until then, it was just by word or note telling about Tony being dead. There he was. His physical presence lay at my fingertips. He was shut up tightly in a box where I couldn't see or touch him or hear his voice ever again. My God, it was for real. Tony was gone. I felt a knife being driven through my heart. I whispered, "Tony, it's me. I'm here beside you. I'm going to take you home now." That was a most traumatic point in my life.

Soon after, a crew came by and loaded the three crates onto the train to New York. I rode on the car with them, along with a porter. We got acquainted, and then he said, "John, you won't believe how many of these bodies come through here every day."

We arrived in New York's Grand Central Station somewhere between 1:00 AM and 2:00 AM. I followed the crew escorting Tony's body to the loading dock. The driver, from Ruggiero Brothers Funeral Parlor located on Arthur Avenue in the Bronx, was there waiting with the hearse. He said his name was Paul and then backed the car up to the ramp. We put the casket onto the hearse and drove up to the Bronx. Paul told me that he had known Tony from the neighborhood when Tony worked in Petrillo Brothers' Butcher Shop. He also knew Franky and Joey, Tony's two younger brothers, who started working there after Tony left for the Army. We got to the funeral parlor and unloaded the crate. I asked if I could use their phone to call my aunt to let her know that we had arrived and that I'd be there soon.

When I got off the phone, I asked Paul to give me a ride to 187th Street and Valentine Avenue, which he did. I told him to drop me off at the corner. I wanted to walk the half block to my aunt's house. I thanked him and got out of the car. I walked toward the house, and a girl came running out of the building. It was Marilyn. They were all waiting for me and saw me from the window. I picked up my pace and hurried to meet her. We put our arms around each other and held on real tight. I did not want to let go. Two of Tony's three sisters, Teresa and Laura, came running over, crying hysterically. I held them both and felt their delicate bodies trembling from sorrow. I put my arms around them, and we all went into the house. We walked up the two flights of stairs. The first one to greet me was my mother, who was also in tears. Through her tears, I could see in her eyes the joy she felt in seeing me again. My sister came running over and grabbed me. The place was filled with people.

My aunt Catherine was completely destroyed by the tragedy. The sight of me in my uniform reminded her of her lost son, and she broke down in my arms. I felt the depth of the grief she was enduring as I held her. Her heart was torn in two, and there was nothing I could say or do to help mend it. My poor uncle Frank was sitting in the corner of the room, holding a handkerchief in his hand. He was all cried out. He had no more tears left to flow from his bloodshot eyes. They were pouring into his heart, drowning him in the loss of his firstborn child.

There were no words to ever describe that night. Suddenly, something hit me. There I was standing with my mother and sister. My God, how did that make them feel, watching me hugging my mother and sister and knowing they would never be able to do the same with Tony? A sense of guilt would linger in me from that moment on. Why Tony and not me?

My cousin Tony dressed in Class A's after Basic Training.

My aunt wanted to know if I saw Tony's body. "No, the coffin was sealed," I said. Then she asked me if she could see him. I told her "Yes, but I don't think it would be a good idea. It would be better if you remember Tony as he was." She was confused on what to do. I figured I'd get off that subject and told her I was curious of how Tony was killed. So I asked her. She told me in her broken English accent that all the priest told her was that Tony was driving a truck and he ran over a mine. He was the only one killed. The rest were wounded. It happened on July 26. She said that all his personal belongings were given to her. Just his watch was missing. I told her to get some rest. Tomorrow was going to be a long, hard day.

It was the early morning of the first day of the wake. I knew the hurt I felt for Tony. But when a man hasn't seen his woman for over four months, he can't control that sexual urge that rises within him. Pregnant or not, I needed to make passionate love to my wife. I'm sure that she felt the same way. She still looked fantastic. She hadn't put on much weight, so she was carrying small. When she began to undress, her great figure had me drooling at the mouth. I needed this. If the Army feeding us saltpeter was to curb a man's sexual anxiety, it must have worn off because I had no problem stepping up to the plate. We couldn't really get into the physical foreplay that we were used to, which, for me, was the best part of our sex; but getting it on was good enough. I was built up inside like a volcano ready to erupt; and when I did climax, I could have broken chains by the climax I had. It was a long-awaiting relief that relaxed me so much that I didn't want to get up. I knew I had to get ready, and I didn't want to lie there long enough for my sweat to dry onto the sheets; so I jumped up and went into the shower, cleaned myself up, and got dressed. Then I waited for Marilyn to doll herself up.

We were staying at her mother's apartment on 197th Street and Decatur Avenue; so we were only minutes away from the funeral parlor. We got there early, before anyone else. I got my first look at the coffin outside the crate. It was closed, as I assumed it would be. It was gray in color, and the American flag was draped over it. There was a picture of Tony posing in his dress uniform with the country's flag in the background, which he had taken during AIT. It was placed on a pedestal beside the coffin. He couldn't be viewed due to the closed coffin, so at least the photograph of him gave the people something to look at. There were beautiful floral arrangements lined up throughout the room and more kept pouring in. Another cousin of mine, Frank Giannini, had just finished his tour in Vietnam. He wore his dress uniform, and the both of us stood beside Tony throughout the entire wake.

People slowly and solemnly began to enter the room. It was filled in no time. My aunt and uncle arrived, along with Tony's five siblings. They sat in the front row. Marilyn sat next to them. Franky and I stood at attention and faced them throughout the entire day. Gazing into their faces hour after hour was killing me inside. I had to be strong and hold my emotions in. I looked down at Tony's casket and wondered if he was really in there. I didn't doubt for one minute that the owners of the funeral parlor and some members of my family had their curiosity get the best of them and had opened it up to see what it held within it. I wanted so badly to see for myself. I tossed the idea around in my mind, but my better judgment ruled against it. I had had the perfect opportunity to do so the night we arrived at the funeral parlor. I did not want to open that casket and see a mangled body or a burned body or just body parts in a plastic bag or nothing at

Me and my cousin Frank Giannini at Tony's wake.

all. Just as I advised his mother, I wanted to remember Tony as I last saw him. This way, for the rest of my life, whenever I would think of him, I would visualize him as he was and not that of the remains of whatever was or wasn't in that coffin.

No matter where I looked, I saw nothing but grief-stricken people. I watched my wife stare straight ahead, almost in shock, and my aunt's tortured face from the sorrowful pain that was crushing her. People had to be revived with smelling salts as they approached the pedestal to kneel in prayer. My uncle Frank, Tony's brothers and sisters, aunts, uncles, cousins, friends, and people who had come to pay their respects were all filled with such unimaginable remorse. I did not understand how I was able to keep my composure. We were not alone. Scenes like this were happening all over the country from other losses. These were dark days.

That was how it was for three days, from 10:00 AM to 10:00 PM. Frank and I never left Tony's side—only to eat or to relieve ourselves, but we did so making sure one of us was always there. I stared at Marilyn, thinking that my stay was only temporary. Soon I would have to say goodbye and leave her once again. This time I knew what I was going back to. I didn't want to leave, especially knowing that our baby was due in a few months. I wanted so much to be there when the baby was born. Now the baby would be five months old the first time I'd see it. Just think, soon a new life would come into the world, and lying next to me was a life that had just left it. How close was the connection between life and death? Could it be that people die to save the living whenever possible in times of desperate need of intervention? If so, then did Tony's death mean life for me? Did his visit that night in the barracks and our last touching of hands mean something more than just goodbye? *Did it have anything to do with my destiny?* I wondered.

The third and final day of the wake was drawing to its end. People were still filling the seats to pay their last respects. The attendance book that people signed as they entered the room was filled with names and addresses. It was a way for the family to know who attended so they could send out thank-you cards. Twenty minutes before the parlor closed, the priest from the neighborhood parish took his place and faced the crowd. He gave a sermon to help ease the family's pain. He then asked all present to stand for the final prayers. After the prayers, he announced that the funeral procession would be leaving Ruggiero Brothers at 9:30 AM the following morning and that the funeral's mass would be held at the family parish church at 10:00 AM, followed by the burial services at Saint Raymond's Cemetery.

The next morning, the place was jam-packed with people. The priest, once again, said some prayers and everyone was told to pay their final respects by going up front and passing by the coffin. Friends were first, then the relatives, and lastly, the immediate family. Frank and I were still vigilant beside the casket. The crowd all left and made their way to their vehicles to get ready for the procession to the cemetery. Frank left the coffin's side and joined two of my uncles standing by the entrance door. Marilyn had walked out with my aunt Catherine. I was there alone, facing Tony at the center of the casket. I leaned my two fists onto the coffin, grabbing hold of the flag tightly in my grip. My head slowly lowered; and I buried my face in the red, white, and blue cloth. Silently, I vowed that I would get revenge. I crumpled the flag. My emotions, at last, let loose. I tossed the flag aside. My head got lower, and I could no longer hold back my tears. I cried out loudly and draped my body over the casket, desperately wanting to get into that coffin that held my best friend. With my arms around the top of the coffin, I shook it from side to side, calling to him, "Tony, Tony." I wanted to hold him one last time. Franky and my two uncles saw what was happening and ran over and grabbed me under my arms to pull me away before I wrecked the place. They walked me out, slowly, to calm me down.

Tony's casket.

The day wasn't over yet. We still had the burial ahead of us, which would turn out to be the most unforgettable part of the entire four days. Once again, I had to pull myself together. There was no way that I wanted Tony's family to see me that way. I let my uncles know that I was okay, but it was obvious that they were still very much concerned about my state of mind. They stayed with me until they were satisfied that I had calmed down.

We left the funeral parlor and made our way to our respective vehicles. The cars were lined up around the block—each displaying their bright lights and flashers, awaiting the hearse to lead the way. The procession made its way to the church. After parking, the crowds filed into the church and filled the pews. The coffin was in the center aisle in front of the altar. The flag that I had wrinkled up and tossed aside was back in its rightful place covering the casket. Mass was said; and the priest, after giving his sermon, blessed Tony's body while waving incense over him. The smell of the incense wormed its way through the pews and filled everyone's nostrils with a pleasant aroma while a girl with a beautiful soprano voice sang "Ave Maria", which seemed to bring a little bit of heaven

Military poll bearers at Tony's wake.

to touch the soul of everyone attending the service. People were still weeping throughout the church. The body was rolled out with the pallbearers at its side. I walked out with Marilyn, and Tony's parents walked directly behind us. The congregation followed suit as we passed by each pew. We watched them carefully load the casket into the hearse; then we all got back into our vehicles, and the procession slowly made its way through Tony's neighborhood. The police led the way on motorcycles. The streets were all blocked off. We passed by the butcher shop where Tony worked and then made one final rendezvous around the block where he lived. We stopped to pause for a moment in front of Tony's building. People were looking out of their windows and stopping on the street to offer their farewells while witnessing the final stages of the funeral. Saint Raymond's Cemetery was the next and last stop.

The caravan of vehicles entered the cemetery through a new gate that led us to a recently developed section known as Saint John's. We drove down a narrow road bordered on both sides by mausoleums and large marble tombs. Tony's final resting place was at the end of the road. We all pulled up and parked. Many car doors could be heard slamming shut as we walked toward an opened area that had a large canopy temporarily erected to cover the spot where the casket was to be set and to also offer shade for the majority of the crowd. It was a very hot day. The sky was clear and deep blue, and the sun shone brightly. A huge wall of marble squares stood before us. Each square held within it the remains of someone who once walked the earth and displayed the name and dates of birth and death of the person entombed. The wall stood thirty feet high and eighty feet wide. There was one open square located toward the right and just above eye level. This was to be Tony's final resting place.

The coffin was carried onto a rollaway stand to the center of the patio under the green canopy. The immediate family sat in chairs in the front row. A few yards from the coffin, seven military men from the burial detail formed a straight line and stood at attention with a rifle held by their sides. They were all well-dressed in khakis and wore white gloves. They stood that way for the duration of the ceremony. Once again, the priest spoke. I doubt if my aunt, sitting motionless with a black veil covering her face, heard a word he was saying. She and my uncle were both numb and just stared at the coffin that held within it their son. My uncle was still clasping on to his handkerchief.

The priest ended with a final prayer, and immediately following, a soldier played "Taps." All stood still and silent while the bugler paid tribute to a lost comrade. When he finished, the silence was broken by a voice giving the command, "Ready!" Then the sound of rifles being raised to the shoulders of the seven soldiers was heard.

The second command soon followed, "Aim!" The rifles pointed skyward.

The third command, "Fire!" was given; and the seven rifles blasted loudly. Along with the first shots fired came sighs of whimpering among the specta-tors, as if the bullets pierced through each one of them.

Twenty-one-gun salute.

"Ready! Aim! Fire!" And the second volley of shots were fired, still sur-prising those listening—most of whom never heard a gun go off before, espe-cially at such close range.

"Ready! Aim! Fire!" And the final volley of the twenty-one gun salute was completed. It took a little while for the goose bumps to settle and the chills down everyone's spine to wear off. The military personnel, including my cousin Franky and myself, came to atten-tion and saluted Tony.

Two members of the military detail took hold of the flag that was draped over the coffin and proceeded to fold it in front of my aunt and uncle. It was folded in such a way that it ended up in the shape of a triangle with the stars and blue background showing. One of the men handed the flag to Tony's mother, who reached up with her hands as if they weighed too heavy for her arms. She gently took hold of the flag and, looking up at the soldier for only a second, said in a soft, broken voice, "Thank you." When she took full possession of the flag, the soldier saluted her, turned with an about-face, and fell into formation. The soldiers lifted the coffin off the gurney and, keeping in unison, carried it ever so slowly and diligently over to the open slab. Then they gently guided it into the port and slid it in place. The marble square was set and bolted into position. Thus, Tony was put to rest, peacefully, forever. The funeral was over. The visual nightmare had come to an end. The tears we all shed were planted into the ground, and the horrible memories of those few days will never be forgotten.

As harsh as it might sound, I had to bury the events of the past week and turn my attention to my personal life and make the best of the time I had left to spend with my wife and family. Marilyn and I spent many of the precious hours in solitude in our bedroom having sex. The sexual drive was overwhelming. We couldn't get enough of each other. As soon as I was rested enough, we'd ball again. I still had eight months left in Nam, and I was making sure to try to get enough loving to carry me over.

To help build memories, we'd go to a movie or amusement park or just simply go for a ride in the car. One of the rides we took was to Brooklyn to visit Eddie's parents and his sister, Mary. I wanted to keep my promise to him about letting his family know he was all right. I knew it would mean a lot to him. I let them know that Eddie got out of the field and was doing mail runs and how he would bring me my own cases of K rations. They told me that they were so worried. All they kept seeing and hearing on the television and radio was how many of our troops were dying every day. I knew how true it was, but I also knew that I had to bring some sort of comfort to them. I had them laughing when I told them the story of how Eddie wrote to the Kool-Aid company and about his jug: "Eddie's Kool-Aid Stand, Five Cents a Glass." Their amusement was further enhanced when I told them about David C. and his Cadillac comment. I saw that my coming to see them really helped. They needed that reassurance, especially Mary. She was so close to Eddie. It broke her heart when he left for Nam. I was so glad that I stopped to see them because it wasn't that long after that Eddie's father died of a heart attack. He was only in his early fifties. Eddie's biological mother passed away when he was just a boy. The two of them were raised by his stepmother. When it was time for us to leave, Mary came over to me, crying, and put her arms around me and whispered in my ear, "Please tell Eddie to be very careful and to come home and that I miss him so much and that I love him with all my heart.

John, be careful, and please take care of my brother." I promised her I would and not to worry. With that, Marilyn and I left.

The fifteen-day TDY was flying by. It was almost mid-August. Marilyn wasn't feeling well. I called the Army detachment center in Oakland, California, to ask for an extension. I explained to the woman on the phone about my wife's condition. She told me that it would not be a problem for me to stay longer and to report to Fort Hamilton in Brooklyn when I was ready to come back. "Great, thank you," I shouted back and happily hung up the phone. I told Marilyn what she said. Then I thought, *My birthday is just two weeks away. Maybe I can stretch it out long enough to be here for my twentieth birthday.* I did just that. We took advantage of the extra time. We visited my family, took a few trips to the cemetery to see Tony, and tried to have happy times. There was a movie that I wanted to see, *The Dirty Dozen.* We took in the show. It was a great movie, reminded me of our recon platoon.

The night of my birthday, Marilyn and I were lying in bed. It was late at night. I knew that the following day was the day for me to leave. I kept staring at the ceiling in deep thought. "What's the matter?" Marilyn asked me. I told her that I was thinking of tomorrow and my buddies back in Nam. "What about them?"

"I'm worried about them. I hope they're okay." I went on to tell her how close we all were and that we'd do anything for one another, even to the point of sacrificing our lives for one another.

Then she started in, being that old bitchy person again, "You mean that if one of your friends was calling for help, you'd risk your life, knowing that you had me and a baby back home?"

"Of course. I wouldn't even hesitate," I answered her rather angrily.

"I don't believe it. You better not do anything like that," she said. I told her, getting even angrier, that there was no fuckin' way that I would ever leave a friend of mine when he needed me, no fuckin' way.

"I just cannot believe what I am hearing," she hollered back at me.

I said, "You can't believe it? I can't believe that you would expect me to punk out on my friends. What if it was reversed and I was the one that needed help? What then?" That reaction kind of made her think about it a little more, and she became more tranquil. I could see where this was heading, so I cooled down and reassured Marilyn that a situation like that would never happen. I didn't want our last night to be a disaster. I also knew that she couldn't read my mind. I was thinking that anything could happen in those jungles. She had no idea what it was like. We both calmed down and made the best of the rest of the night.

The next day, September 2, Marilyn and I drove to Fort Hamilton to report, as the woman from California told me to do. I thought I was going to receive my travel orders; but instead, because of my long overdue return, I was told to go to an Army travel bureau in Lower Manhattan to get my plane tickets. So that's what I did. It was a small two-story building. We walked in and approached a large table. Sitting behind it was a member of the military, and he asked me what he could do for me. I related my story to him, and he told me to wait. He returned with another man. I gathered that he had already told him my tale because the man said to me, "You know, you are AWOL. You're not going anywhere except to jail." I told him about the telephone conversation I had with the woman from California and what she instructed me to do. They wouldn't listen. I tried desperately to make them understand, but they were dead set on locking me up.

I was taken up to the second floor along with Marilyn to see the officer in charge. He was a captain. "Sir, this man is AWOL from a combat zone," one of them told the captain.

His reply was, "Okay, leave us alone. I'll take care of it." Then he asked me to explain.

I started from the beginning and told him my story. Then he said, "Okay, by rights, you should be locked up. But I'm going to give you a break. I'm going to send you back to your unit." I told him that I didn't have my things with me and I didn't want my wife to drive home alone due to her condition. He was very understanding and said, "I'll tell you what I'll do. I'll send you home with two MPs who will follow you to get your gear. Then they will drive you to the airport." I was very grateful to that captain and thanked him.

The MPs followed us home, and watch me they did. When we went into the apartment, one of them came in with us and waited while I gathered my belongings. I rode with them in the back seat of their vehicle. They wouldn't allow Marilyn to ride with me; so she followed behind with two friends of ours, Louie and Phoebe, an elderly couple who lived in our building. They were more than willing to agree to come along and keep Marilyn company. We drove to Kennedy Airport. The flight wouldn't be taking off for an hour, so we had time for our last lunch together. The MPs stayed with us all the while. We had barely finished our snack when a voice came over the PA system calling for all passengers to board the plane that was to begin my voyage back to hell. I said goodbye to Louie and Phoebe with a big hug and left them at the cafeteria. Marilyn and I, along with my two military police friends, walked down the corridor to the plane. We stopped just short of the runway. I turned to face Marilyn. We looked at each other, not wanting to say goodbye. We kissed and embraced. I gazed into her eyes, and tears were starting to fill her eyelids, which slowly began to flow over them and leave a thin trail of mascara down her cheeks. "I'll see you in seven months," I said. The MPs escorted me to the plane and made sure I got on. I managed to get a window seat with no one beside me, so I was able to get quite comfortable. I looked back at Marilyn, who was still standing by the runway. Louie and Phoebe were with her, which made me feel at ease knowing that she wasn't alone. I kept watching them as long as the angle of the plane allowed me to do so. It was hard for me to restrain my own tears.

It was a perfect day for flying. I psyched myself up for the trip and sat back in my seat with the earphones on and listened to music all the way. I must have heard each song play over and over at least fifty times. Two songs, till this day still stand out in my mind: "My Cup Runneth Over" sung by Jim Nabors of Gomer Pyle fame and "Silence Is Golden" sung by the Tremeloes. Whenever I hear them,

I'm right back on that plane again. As I listened to the music, I relived all the events of the past month: Tony's funeral, all the things that Marilyn and I did, almost going to jail, the movie *The Dirty Dozen* where a handful of men went out on a special mission behind enemy lines and all but three made it out alive. I couldn't help but wonder, *Will I ever come back?*

CHAPTER XIII

BACK TO NAM

The plane arrived in Vietnam the following day. When I got off the plane, I felt that familiar mugginess and slimy feeling on my lips and fingertips. It was like déjà vu. There, in a long line, were soldiers waiting to return to the States. That scene was becoming all too familiar to me. I made my way to the small terminal and waited for a ride to Phuoc Vinh, which came shortly after. Now that I was back, I was anxious to see Eddie and the others; but things turned out to be different. When I reached Phuoc Vinh and reported to my area, there were many new faces. Santos, along with Nezat and Dutch, had rotated and gone home. Doc Jimenez, Mike, Maleski, Rahar, Lundsford, and Nash, upon request, were transferred to better assignments. Baker was stricken with malaria so badly, he almost died. He was sent to Japan for treatment. Woody was still healing from his severe case of jungle rot. His feet still looked like elephant hoofs from the swelling.

Eddie was still doing his thing with the mail runs. Tex, Ver Linden, Baldy, Deloge, Schneider, Polite, Parker, House, Red, King, Sexton, Funky and David C. from the original group were still there. It goes without saying how happy we were to see one another. Eddie approached me all excited and said, "So, Johnny, how was it back home? Did you get to see my family?"

"Yeah," I answered him. "I went there and told them how good you were doing and how you had it made. I made sure to ease their worrying. Mary sends her love and says for you to hurry home. She really misses you, Eddie."

"Thanks, Johnny," he said with a big smile on his face.

"How about you guys, anything new happen here?" I asked.

He told me, "Yeah, Cookie was killed out in the field by a mortar attack."

"Really, Cookie? Man, why didn't he stay back?" It was another name to add to the KIA list that never seemed to stop growing. Eddie told me that we now had a new platoon leader, a first lieutenant named Jay Murphy. "Where's he at?" I asked.

"He's over in the next barracks."

"I'd better go over and meet him. I'll see you later, Eddie." I was wondering if the platoon leader was going to say anything about my getting back two weeks late. I went over to meet him, and I introduced myself.

"You must be Pizza. I heard a lot about you. Welcome back."

"Thanks, Lieutenant."

"Call me Murphy," he said to my surprise. He was average height, slim, and looked like he was in his late twenties. I asked him where my gun was. He told me that it had gotten damaged in the jungle and he had ordered me a new one, which was due anytime. "Just to bring you up to date, the battalion is getting ready for a major operation that will last a couple of months. We'll be leaving in two weeks." After telling me that, he left. He never even mentioned one word about my extended AWOL leave.

It felt strange. Most of the faces I knew were gone. It didn't feel the same. Instead of a reunion, like I expected, it was as if I were attending my first day in a new school. I hollered over to Eddie, who was still in the other barracks, "Hey, Eddie, let's go eat." We went into the mess hall, got our food, and sat down.

As we were eating and talking, a young Vietnamese girl caught my eye. She was bussing the tables. She was new. I had never seen her before. She was short with short black hair and very pretty. We made eye contact. Even while conversing with Eddie, I found that I couldn't take my eyes off her. "Eddie, who is she?" I asked quietly.

"I don't know, Johnny. She started working here last week." The girl finished wiping off the tables and went into the kitchen.

"I'll be right back Eddie." I got up and followed her into the kitchen.

Lt. Murphy before coming to Recon platoon in foreground with group of choppers in the background.

I didn't know what came over me to do such a thing. It wasn't like me, but there was something about her. She went outside to empty boxes into the garbage. I approached her, and we were face-to-face. "Hi, my name is John. What's yours?"

"Sahn," she replied.

"You understand English?" I asked.

Me and my M-60 showing off at Phuoc Vinh.

"Ti-ti," she answered (which meant "a little"). She grabbed hold of the empty cartons, looked at me, smiled, and then went back into the kitchen without saying anything. I figured that maybe she was one of those Vietnamese girls who were afraid of being seen getting too friendly with a GI.

I heard my name being called. "Pizza, hey, Pizza." It was Murphy. He was motioning for me to come. I went over to him.

"What's up, Murph?" I asked.

"I have something for you," he said. "Come with me!" He brought me into my barracks; and there, beside my bunk, was a brand-new M60 machine gun. "There's your baby," he said with a wink of his eye and walked out. I lost no time in picking it up and getting the feel of it. I checked all its functioning parts: the cover plate, the bolt, the safety switch, and the trigger. Then I took it apart, piece by piece, to clean any dirt that may have gotten into it and oiled it up good. I removed the front bipods. Then I filled the ammo pouch with more than the one hundred rounds of bullets that it was designed to contain. I clipped the pouch on to the side of the gun and set it on the tripod stand. It was all shined up and ready to go.

There was a ruckus going on in our other barracks, so Eddie and I went over to see what was going on. The guys had just gotten back from town. I heard that old familiar Texas yodel coming from Tex's lips, *"Ba-lay-dee-lodee, ba-lay-dee laydee, ba-lay-dee-dee."* They were half in the bag. Tex said, "Hey, Pizza, what do the miniskirts look like back home?"

"Unbelievable," was my reply. "Whenever a girl wearing one bent over, man, you could see what she ate for breakfast."

Then Tex, shockingly, said, "Hot damn, good old American broads."

Then I asked them, "You guys see any action while I was gone?"

"Not much," said Verlinden. "We saw a truck load of dead VC come into camp. That was about it. They were piled up on top of one another. Surely didn't smell too good."

It was time to get back to work. The following day, we were assigned to an armor division and had to guard a bridge on Highway 13. Before leaving, I said goodbye to Eddie. We left our jeeps behind and went by convoy. We passed through the gates of camp and went on our way. I was never to see Phuoc Vinh again or Sahn.

The steel bridge.

When we got to the bridge, we unloaded our gear and made ready our defensive positions. The bridge was about one mile outside a Vietnamese village. It spanned right in the middle of a dirt road, overlapping a small stream that flowed beneath it, which dispersed into a surrounding grassy field to the left and right of the bridge (approximately one-quarter of a mile in each direction) that met up with a rubber tree plantation on one side and jungles on the other. There was a smaller village just beyond the field's edge, hidden within the rubber trees.

The bridge was bordered on both sides by an embankment that slanted downward from the road and into the fields. The iron structure itself was just a little longer than one of our large tanks. Being that is was an open area, the first thing we did was to fill sandbags and stack them on the embankment to give us some protection. There was no room to set up hooches, so we were vulnerable to the weather.

The road was aligned with tanks and personnel carriers. Our job was to guard the bridge at night and to patrol and recon the surrounding jungle during the daytime. Attached to us once again were two teams of dogs. The villagers walked or rode by on their bikes, vehicles, or carts all day long. When the dogs were by the road, their handlers had all to do to hold them back from ripping the passersby to pieces. I mean, those dogs went berserk at the sight of the Vietnamese. They had to end up being restrained and kept off the road. It was a good thing they were because one elderly man got his oxcart stuck in the mud just prior to reaching the bridge. The more we tried to get it out, the deeper it sank. We ended up using our sandbags to solve the problem. We also got covered in mud in doing so. Man, did we curse out that son of a bitch. When I was trying to get most of the mud off my pants and boots, a one-ton-and-a-half with some troops sitting on the back of it came down the road. It was passing by an old man riding a bicycle and traveling in the same direction. What I saw next bothered me so much that even to this day, whenever I think of it, I still feel bad. As the truck passed by this man, a GI reached out and, with his hand, smacked the man in the back of his head as hard as he could. The poor guy fell off his bike and got up rubbing his head.

That had to hurt, especially when he didn't know it was coming. I knew that guys were pissed off at loosing buddies and not wanting to be there; but to me, that was downright mean.

Around midday, when the sun was at its hottest, a rickety old truck came slowly down the road. It was being driven by one elderly Vietnamese man. The rear of the truck was covered with a canvas, and in the bed of the vehicle were large blocks of ice, which were covered with straw to help prevent them from melting so quickly. We stopped the truck, and while we interrogated the driver, two of us went around back and tossed a couple of blocks of ice onto the road, which, naturally, landed in the mud. It didn't matter to us. We were used to having dirt in our food and drinks. We were eager to chop the ice into pieces to put into our canteens or to cool our sodas and beers and refresh our sun-beaten skin by rubbing the wonderfully refreshing cold ice on it. We cleaned them off with water as best we could and then placed them in our canteens and coolers. Cold water surely tasted much better. I filled my three canteens. Most of the time, I was happy just to have my canteens filled, even if the water was warm. The sun's rays penetrated the green cloth covering on them, so it didn't take long for the water to lose its coolness. I would take big swigs of water and chew on it and swish it around in my mouth before swallowing just to make it last longer.

When evening came, we closed off the road from both directions. One PC set itself on the road on one side of the bridge; then a large tank maneuvered onto the center of the bridge, taking up almost the entire span. I watched the horizontal steel structure of the bridge bend from the weight of the tank as it made its way slowly into position. A second PC took its place on the road on the other side of the bridge. We stationed ourselves around and amid the armored vehicles, trying to find some sort of comfort and protection. Some of us slept on the road while others stayed on the embankment. We took turns pulling guard duty. Believe me, nothing short of Godzilla was getting by that bridge.

It rained all night long that first night on the bridge. I stood crouched under one of the tank's tracks, holding a poncho over my head to keep from getting wet. It wasn't easy trying to sleep standing up with my arms stretched out. The minutes vapored into long hours as the rain steadily trickled down on us. The crew in the tank were playing music all night. I was enjoying listening to Johnny Mathis sing his and my favorite songs. It helped to pass the time. I became so tired and frustrated not being able to get some shut-eye and to stay dry that I went and grabbed my air mattress from the embankment, threw it in the mud between the PC and the tank, curled up on it, and covered myself with my poncho. The next thing I knew, it was morning. I awoke cold and wet. I couldn't wait to light up a piece of C-4 to heat up a cup of coffee.

We had some time to ourselves before going out on patrol. I relaxed on my air mattress, which now was back in its position on the hillside and isolated from the others. After that rough night, just taking it easy in the warm rising sun felt really good. The inflatable rubber bed cushioned me from the wet ground. I was thinking about the past. I reached into my pocket and took out my wallet. I pulled out the funeral card that had Tony's picture on it, along with a prayer. I stared at his face, visualizing days gone by when we were always together. I kept repeating over and over, "Why did you have to die?"

Peering above the card and focusing across the field, I envisioned two little boys romping through the trees, running happily and calling to each other and not having a care in the world and just enjoying life to its fullest, especially nature. The trees, the hikes, the streams, the animals, and the adventures—as small as they were—all belonged to our world, a world that Tony and I lived in together side by side. And whenever we saw a movie or read a comic book involving some hero, we'd take the character to heart and put on our own little adventure to meet his deeds. That is how it would be for as long as I remained alive: just thoughts of Tony and I and the best years of our lives.

We set out on patrol around midmorning. It was proving to be a very hot day. I went against my own rules and made the mistake of taking my first drink of water before 10:00 AM. We searched the surrounding jungles for a few hours, which gave relief from the heat; but due to my early drinking, my body kept craving water. I kept taking swigs from my canteens. The area seemed to be secure.

When we exited the bush, and near the open road, we stopped to rest. Something very peculiar happened that had nothing to do with any VC activity. I was leaning against a tree facing the road. A dragonfly came buzzing around me and landed on my boot. I sat motionless so as to not frighten it away. Then he took flight off my foot and landed on my leg. It just stayed there with its wings fluttering rapidly. It showed no fear. I sat still and watched it as it remained on my leg, almost lifeless. It was time to move out, and I hated to move and disturb it.

When I got up, it flew off. We walked farther down the road. The sun was roasting hot. We took another break. I took another drink of water. I sat, and lo and behold, the dragonfly came and landed on my leg again. I had no way of knowing if it was the same one or not; but that dining needle followed me around the rest of that day, landing and resting along with me each time I stopped. I could understand a dog following someone, but a dragonfly? I had never heard of such a thing. It had gotten so that I felt like I had found a little friend. It got braver and landed on my shoulder and stayed until I got up. Believe it or not, but that dining needle followed me for the next few days. Whenever we walked up the road and stopped, it was there.

We were heading in back toward the bridge. It was hotter than hell. The sweat was pouring off me. My fatigues were drenched from perspiration. I went to take another drink of water. All three of my canteens were empty. The rest of the platoon was way ahead of me. I spotted Parker about a quarter of a mile up the road, nearing the bridge. The armor division was lined up alongside of the road. I was dragging my ass. I passed by some of them and came to a PC with its hatch opened and heard music. I stopped and peered in. There were three guys relaxing inside. "How, you guys doin'?" I asked.

"Fine," they answered. I boldly asked, "Do you have any water you can spare?"

One of them said, "Sure, come on in." They gave me a drink of ice-cold water and filled all three of my canteens. Then, to top it off, one of them reached into a cooler and handed me a chocolate cow, which was a chocolate drink in a can. It, too, was ice-cold. Man, did that hit the spot. I could have kissed their asses in Macy's window. I related my deep gratitude and went on my way, thinking to myself, *Man, those guys got it made.*

The same scenario took place that night with the positioning of the armored vehicles. I pulled guard duty from 4:00 AM to 5:00 AM. I awoke the next man for watch, and then I went to lie on my air mattress (which was in its rightful location on the side of the embankment). It was drizzling steadily. I took my poncho and covered my gun, which was to my left. My feet longed for freedom; so I decided to remove my wet, muddy boots, something I rarely did out in the bush. I lay back down and covered myself with an Army quilt, and I must have dozed off. I was suddenly awoken by a commotion up on the road behind me. I sat up, tossing the quilt off, and heard a thumping sound followed shortly by an explosion. Still half asleep and bewildered, I looked to my rear and saw the guys making a mad dash for cover behind the tank. "What's wrong?" I shouted.

Baldy hollered back, "Incoming!" Again, I heard a thump followed by another blast that occurred beyond the tank and missing it. It wasn't a mortar attack. The explosions were not as devastating. It was more like some asshole taking potshots at us with an M79 grenade launcher. I turned and looked at Baldy. Once again, I screamed really loud, "Where the fuck are they coming from?"

Baldy, standing halfway behind the tank, pointed his finger in the direction, saying, "There, over there, the other side of the field."

I whispered to myself, "Shit. Son of a bitch, first time I take off my boots and something happens." Without any further hesitation, I threw the poncho off my M60 and picked it up. The M79 rounds were still coming in. Luckily, whoever was firing at us wasn't a good shot. I just couldn't believe that with all that firepower behind me, no one retaliated. Not a single shot was fired back to stop the bastard. I said, "Fuck this shit." I raised my gun to my hip and commenced to lay out a field of grazing fire across the edge of the marsh, allowing the rounds to skip off the edge of the field and ricochet into the edge of the jungle.

There was a better chance of hitting an unseen target that way. If I wasn't lucky enough to kill the bastard, at least I would stop him or her. In Nam, you never know who was attacking you. The instant I started shooting, the incoming rounds seized. I grabbed my boots and ran for cover while my squad followed my lead. Even the tank and PC crews got in on the action. They opened up with everything they had, which included the .50 calibers. As I was putting my boots back on, I looked up and said, "That'll be the last time I ever take my boots off."

After we administered a barrage of bullets across the fields, we noticed what appeared to be an abandoned farmhouse located a little ways in from the edge of the jungle. The bullet fever was still in us, so we took target practice at it, using an M79 grenade launcher of our own. We all took turns aiming at the rooftop and hit it many times. After doing so, we investigated and found nothing. It was a perfect location for a sniper to set up and pluck away at us. It could had very likely been the spot from where we received the incoming rounds.

As a rule, we were not supposed to fire our weapons until we were given the order to do so; but that was one rule that did not exist in my book. I'd be damned if I was going to sit back and wait to be given the okay to shoot while someone was shooting to kill me. I fired when I felt I needed to. That was what I was sent there for; and if they didn't like it, they could just send me the fuck home.

It amazed me how we regressed more and more each day from civilized human beings. For example, we dug holes along the road-side, two feet deep and one foot wide. We placed sandbags around the opening to be used as a seat. If nature called, one just sat there in view of all passersby and thought nothing of it, like dogs. We were not moved or bothered by it or anything else for that matter.

Later that afternoon, eight of us went on patrol. We were so damn disgusted with patrol after patrol. It seemed like such a waste. We came across a vacant and torn-down building with a concrete foundation. It looked like a bomb had hit it. We stopped there and rested. And it was from that spot that we patrolled. We sat our butts down, and at timely intervals, King called in our coordinates, never budging from our seats. No one ever knew the difference. We discussed what was to happen in the oncoming morning.

The major operation that Murphy had told me about was going to begin. Operation Shenandoah II, as it was to be called, was going to take place in the Binh Duong Province. The entire battalion was to be lifted off to another location and, from there, work our way toward what was known as the Black Virgin Mountain near the Iron Triangle in War Zone C.

There were rumors that the area was heavily occupied by enemy forces. We knew we were heading for rough times. It was also going to be quite different. Tex and King were not going with us. We would miss them greatly. They were part of our original recon team. We got some new replacements. One was a guy named Paul Charles who became our new squad leader, replacing Tex. Another was a Canadian named Charles Sauler who had volunteered to join the US Army to come to Nam. He had served in the Canadian Army for years. We called him Cannook. He replaced King on point. Another newcomer was a fellow whom we called Speedy. And there was a new, very

Paul Charles as a sniper outside of foxhole.

young medic who replaced our own Doc Jimenez. I don't recall his name, but I do remember that he was kind of small, wore glasses, and was only eighteen years old.

OPERATION
SHENANDOAH II

O peration Shenandoah II kicked off into full swing. As always, our platoon led the way in the first group of choppers. We touched down in a high wide-open grassy location. It was a cold LZ. We secured it for the battalion. The choppers were pouring in one group after another and kept on coming. It didn't take very long for the entire battalion to be dropped off. They started digging in. Chinooks were bringing in supplies and armor. The mortar teams were busy filling sandbags and erecting their circular protective walls with them.

By early afternoon, we were able to begin setting up our positions. While digging in, the chinooks flew low and hovered directly over our heads. The tall green grass waved in all directions. My jungle hat went flying off my head and could not be found. There, beyond the elephant grass, and all by itself above the trees stood the Black Virgin Mountain. It was large, black, and eerie. A weird mist floated over the grass and hid half of the mountain's mass. There was a strange scent in the air, enhanced by the Black Virgin's presence, as if we were invading its monumental privacy. Whether the rumors we heard about it created a psychological effect in our minds or not, I didn't know; but we felt something was closing in on us or drawing us in on it. Death was in the air like it was the day Ronnie Elza was killed. We could smell it. It's a strange thing to explain, but when you've been in combat for a long period of time, you develop a sixth sense. This area concerned me deeply. I had a bad feeling about it.

The amount of time of stay in each of our projected moves was to be short: two to four days at the most. That first night we spent setting up and pulling guard duty. We patrolled the jungles for the next two days and only came across a herd of monkeys and one snake. On the third day, we stayed in the compound. Alpha and Bravo Companies went out on patrol. They met with negative resistance.

On the fourth day, we had to make ready to move to a new location. Before we caved in our foxholes and buried our garbage, I wrote a letter home. I had to walk a short distance to place it in the mail drop. In doing so, I passed through Bravo Company's area. While walking, I heard a loud *pop*. It sounded like a gunshot, but I thought it was an explosion caused from a bottle or can that someone had tossed into a fire, which was often done and sounded like a gun round being discharged from a weapon. I didn't think much of it, so I continued on my way to mail my letter. On the way back, I noticed a commotion and a chopper hovering over a gathering of soldiers. I stopped to look. The battalion medic, Howard Gerstel, was administering first aid to a fellow, trying desperately to save the man's life.

Apparently, the wounded man's buddy in preparing for the move, was checking his weapon; and it had fired. The bullet struck his friend, who was standing by him, in the neck. He died before they were able to dust him off. I later found out his name was John Keppler.

What, I wondered, *would the Army write home to his family?* And what about the fellow who accidentally shot him? He had to not only face an involuntary manslaughter charge but he also had to live with the thought of being responsible for the death of his buddy. I would not want to be in that poor guy's shoes. I got a close look at the doctor's face. He was drawn and weary from exhaustion in his desperate attempt to keep that soldier alive. How hard would it be for him, also, to carry memories such as that around for the rest of his life? *God*, I thought, *this is like being in hell.*

Despite that unfortunate incident, plans to move out went on as scheduled. We were to lead the battalion on foot to another location, but because of the accidental shooting, an order had come down from top command (or should I say, "top asshole") that threw us for a loop. We were to proceed to our next destination, through heavily suspected enemy-occupied areas (ready for this) with unloaded weapons. David C., who was one of the point men, and I looked at each other and couldn't help but laugh. Somebody back in Washington must be getting a big kick out of this war. Whoever it was must have thought it was a big joke out here. No wonder our guys were dying like crazy. We had a bunch of pompous asses calling the shots from behind a fuckin' desk.

Murphy, who issued the order to us, winked as he announced that ridiculous order. I guess he had to cover his ass by letting us know so that he could report that the command was given. We knew that they weren't about to have us all arrested for disobeying an order. And if for any reason they did, let them. Who gave a shit?

We started out leading the way. Murphy and the captain of Charlie Company were walking beside me. They didn't seem to be too concerned about enforcing that order. They never uttered a word about it. They saw the bullets locked into place in my gun. They weren't stupid. The both of them knew how long it took to load a machine gun and that a fraction of a second delay could mean the difference between life and death.

We hacked our way through the dense jungle, pausing periodically to get our bearings. At one point, three officers and the battalion commander were standing just yards to my front, looking at maps. I put my gun down and rested, waiting for the signal to move on. When they were satisfied with their studying of the maps, we made ready to move out. I picked up my gun. They were still huddled in front of me. My gun slipped, and I lost full control of it. I felt my finger squeeze down on the trigger just as the muzzle was pointed right at them. My spontaneous thought was, *Oh my God.* The trigger depressed until it bottomed out. Good fortune was on my side, and damn good luck was with them. My safety was on and functioned properly. I would have shot all four of them. It was a horrifying split second of my life. One that, to this day, still haunts me whenever I happen to think back on it. How ironic was that after what had happened earlier that day? It would have made that bureaucratic idiot seem like he made the right call even though we all knew it wasn't. I had to clear my mind of the thought of what might have just taken place so I would be able to continue on alertly. It made me think. How many of us soldiers get killed by friendly fire?

We had to stop many times to wait for the point men to give the "all clear." The three of them—Canook, Schneider, and David C.—were good, sharp, and experienced. At times, we had to wait twenty minutes or more to allow them time to go forward and search to keep us from walking into any booby traps or an ambush. It didn't matter how exhausted or thirsty we got, we had to keep going. The shade from the trees and occasional rains helped a lot.

It was in the early evening when we broke through the jungle and came upon another large opened grassy area. The clearing was to be our next compound, but instead of the well-deserved and needed rest, it was dig-in time. The clearing was on high ground overlooking a swampy area that played host to more jungles beyond it, which were to be the domain of out next explorations. Our defensive positions were no secret to "Charlie." They knew where we were. The choppers dropping supplies constantly gave away our exact locations.

It grew dark. It was a beautiful clear night. The stars were brilliant. It was one of those evenings that would have been a "stay out till all hours of the night" evening back home, staring up at the constellations; but here we still had to finish digging in. The usual procedure had to be done. I know it sounds repetitive, but that's the way it was. Set up, break it down, move on, and do it all over again. I couldn't count how many trees I cut down with my machete and how many hundreds of sandbags we filled. We didn't have to go on any nighttime patrol; we just had to pull our own guard duty.

The rest of that evening remained quiet and peaceful. The nighttime dew was forming over the grass, and it got quite chilly. The damn mosquitos were out in full force and were biting the shit out of us. The insect repellent helped somewhat, but those little bastards knew how to work their way around it. They managed to bite us on our feet, ankles, and butt cheeks. They made life ever so much more miserable. I know, I've said this before, but it's worth repeating. I hated those little bastards so much that whenever I managed to kill one of them, I placed it on my knee and pounded it with my fist until it disappeared.

We turned in around midnight, planning to take one-hour shifts for guard duty. Whoever went first usually had company by someone who couldn't sleep. I took first watch. Parker stood up with me while Polite wanted to hit the sack. I never carried a wristwatch, but Polite did; so I asked him for his to use. It was very serene, almost as if there wasn't any war going on. The two of us sat up talking and gazing up at the picturesque night sky that was putting on a show of wonderment. We spoke about home and how the people halfway around the world in twelve hours would be sitting on their front porches, safely staring up at the same sky.

Shortly after, Parker turned in. I sat alone and continued with my watch. I was glad that it was an in-camp stay-awake rather than the usual LP or night ambush. There was a huge difference among the three. The safety factor was much higher, and if it rained, you were able to take shelter in your hooch. Guard duty was no joke. Men's lives depended on you staying awake and sharp. From all the times we stayed out there, our bodies became so alert that even when asleep, our eyes would open from the sound of a fluttering leaf falling or of the first rain drop that would break the silence of the night. A life takes only a second to get snuffed out. And we learned that no one was special. It could happen to anyone, anywhere, and at any time. And if one was smart enough to realize that fact, he'd drill it into his subconscious mind, giving himself the edge against getting caught unprepared.

After Parker went to sleep, I had some alone time. A guy has a lot of time to think at times like that. I was thinking, here I was, only twenty years old, and already so many people that I knew died. I recalled my first experience of death. Aside from my grandfather Frank dying before my fifth birthday, I had a two-year-old cousin named Maria Rubastelli. She and I were always together when our families went on a picnic at a place called Ferry Point Park, under the Whitestone Bridge. Even when we went swimming at Castle Hill Pool. She'd call for Johnny Boy to come and hold her hand, and we would walk together. We'd be wearing our colorfully designed blow-up water tubes around our waists. One day, she had to have her appendix taken out. She developed an infection after the surgery. My mother told me that Maria was calling for me and wanted to see me. She was home in bed. We went there, and I stood by her. She wanted to hold my hand as she always did. I stood next to her and grabbed her little hand. She was so happy that my mother brought me to see her. So was I. She died that night. Although our time spent together was short-lived, I never forgot her. I had another friend in elementary school. His name was Robert Verri. I remember his right eye was discolored from cataract surgery. We'd walk home from school together. The day we graduated from sixth grade, we said goodbye to each other on the corner of Boston Road and Bouck Avenue. He lived one block from me. I never saw him again. He died that summer before the age of twelve from kidney failure.

I finished my watch at 1:00 AM and woke up Polite and handed him his watch. When 3:00 AM rolled around, Parker finished his watch, and woke me up. My upper lip felt strange. It was swollen and numb. Something must have bitten me. I stood my turn. The night was very still except for the crickets serenading me. If you focused on their sounds, they could be quite deafening. I examined the nearby jungle, section by section, moving my eyes very slowly until I took in the entire perimeter. My ears were tuned in beyond the sounds of the crickets to listen for any foreign noises. Whenever I believed my eyes to be playing tricks on me, I applied the night training we received in AIT. This application proved my eyes to be seeing things that were nothing more than a tree stump, an anthill, moving weeds, or shadows from trees from the bright moonlight. Thank God for the stars. They were my comforting companions.

As if the wet boots and saturation of the lower part of my fatigues from the damp grass wasn't uncomfortable enough, now I had a fat upper lip to deal with. It felt as if there was a golf ball within it. I took my thumb and index finger and gently squeezed my lip just under my nostrils. I felt a knot and wondered what the hell it was that had bitten me. *Probably a spider,* I thought. There were so many different types of bugs in those godforsaken jungles. A soldier was at the mercy of so many hazards and afflictions. It's a wonder how any of us made it out of there.

After breakfast and stretching our weary bones, just our recon platoon was getting ready to go on patrol. Before we set out, the mortar teams launched a barrage of shells around the surrounding area. Then we humped the bush for hours, and still, everything was peaceful and quiet. Parker and I were out of water. We each filled one canteen from a spring. We dropped iodine pills into our canteens to purify the water. The water tasted much different from that of which we were accustomed to drinking; and because of this, we thought it best not to overindulge ourselves.

When we got back to the compound, one of the line companies had their turn to beat the bush. The day was still young, so it was a good opportunity to catch up on some writing and relaxation. That strange scent of danger was still haunting me. I couldn't shake that bad feeling gnawing away at my insides. My gut was telling me that something terrible was going to happen real soon. The line company returned without any trouble.

That night we had to go out on an NLP (night listening patrol). Six of us went to the perimeter's edge. We took along our air mattresses for some comfort. We took a radio with us, with its squelch set on low volume. Then we'd just lie there all night and listen for any sound or movement. As long as it didn't rain, we'd be able to hear or possibly see something. We'd call in every hour to report our status.

The LPs, were eerie, but it was comforting to know that, still being in the confines of the camp, the battalion was only a stone's throw behind us. The boredom was broken up when around 3:00 AM, we heard a humming sound coming from high above the trees. Then we saw a blinking red light. It was "puff." We had seen puff in action before, so we anxiously awaited the oncoming show. This time, we had a front-row seat. Puff was called in for an airstrike support when an enemy position was zeroed in on. It had mini guns that fired so rapidly that within a matter of seconds, thousands of bullets were projected. It sounded more like an electric ray gun. All that was heard was *bzzzt*, and every square inch of the targeted area would be completely covered with devastation. "Charlie" didn't stand a chance under its firepower. It was fun to watch. Due to the fact that light travels faster than sound, we'd first see a line of tracers streaking down from the aircraft to the poor souls at the receiving end. Seconds later, after the traces disappeared, we'd hear the sounds of the rapid-firing mini guns. It truly was something special to witness and a welcome sight for those GIs on the ground who were in trouble. Then the blinking light and the humming sound faded into the night sky. Puff had finished its mission, and only God knows how many enemy KIAs it left in its wake. We remained there until dawn, and again, there wasn't anything unusual to report. We went back for some rest.

I got some shut-eye, and after lunch, I went to see Dr. Gerstel. I was having problems with my stomach and had also developed an irritation on my penis, probably from all the patrolling. There wasn't much he could do for my nausea. I had mentioned to him that my wife was pregnant. He told me that "As strange as it may sound, sometimes a man can feel the same sickness that his pregnant wife is experiencing."

"No shit, Doc, really?"

He smiled and then he looked at my groin and told me that the soreness was from my penis rubbing against my pants while walking. At least I diagnosed that right. I was wearing my Army-issued undershorts, which were trunks and kept my groin loose. It had a large opening, and one's private part could easily pop through and rub against the zipper of his pants. I always preferred briefs. Fortunately, I had sent home for some for that very reason. I brought them with me and changed. The added support eliminated the discomfort.

That night, recon once again had to do its thing. Eight of us went out on a night ambush patrol. At least it was a clear moonlit night. We walked about a hundred yards from the compound and set up. Parker was with me. We put out our claymores and got ready for the long night ahead. There wasn't too much cover except for tall grass that we settled down in. There were scattered trees to our front. The moon was so bright that it cast distinctive shadows everywhere.

After getting comfortable, we ate some rations. I unwrapped a round piece of chocolate from its tinfoil and enjoyed my chocolate fix. Then I put the tinfoil down next to me. I kept looking in the direction of this one tree. I could have sworn there was someone in it. "Hey, Parker, look at that tree. Do you see anything?"

"Is there a guy in it, or is it my imagination?"

"Yeah, it does look like a man." We kept a steady zoom on that silhouette for rest of the night. In the meantime, I heard a noise like someone was using a P-38 to open a can.

"Parker, do you hear that?"

"Yeah, I do." I don't know, maybe we were getting combat fatigue, but between that bright moonlight casting shadows all around and that damn sound that was driving us crazy all night, I didn't know what to think. Just before dawn, I told Parker to pass the word that we were going to blow our claymores. It was taking a chance. There was nothing to take cover behind, only some scattered tree branches (which wouldn't help anyway). I was concerned about that sound. One of "Charlie's" tricks was to locate your claymores and turn them around to face you then make you think he was out there so you'd end up blowing yourself up. Everyone was on board with the idea. We sent the word back to Murphy in camp of what we were about to do. We got down as low to the ground as possible. And then I gave the "fire in the hole" signal, and we all blew the claymores. When we packed up to leave, I happened to look down to my left. There was the empty ration can and the piece of tinfoil was rocking back and forth on it, causing that sound. "I'll be a son of a bitch." I pointed it out to Parker. We looked at each other, laughed, and I said, "I won't say anything if you don't." We walked out like nothing ever happened. We never did mention it.

We had that day off. When you're out in the boonies and you have some time for yourself, there's not much to do. It's not as if you go out on the corner and hang out with the guys singing doo-wop. It's quite boring. All you can do is check out your weapon, write letters, or just sit around and bullshit. For some reason, I was thinking about my father and all the war stories he told me when I was a kid. He also told me how he got his name Johnny Legs.

Back when he was a young teenager, during Prohibition, he was a runner for the mob. They'd give him money or letters to deliver, and he would return in no time at all. One of the top mafia heads, Dutch Shultz, took him under his wing. He liked my father, so he made my father go with him to some clubs he hung out at. One night my father and Dutch Shultz were sitting at a table and in walked a few mob guys. Dutch Shultz pointed to one of them and said to my father, "Do you know who that guy is?"

"No."

"That's Legs Diamond." They walked over to the table, and Dutch Shultz introduced my father to him. "See this kid? His name is John. He's the fastest run-ner I ever seen. I think, if you don't mind using part of your name, we'll nickname him Johnny Legs. What do you think?" Legs Diamond said it was fine with him. That was my father's ID from then on. As he got older, he got to know famous people, like Sinatra and Dean Martin. He even had Jerry Vale sing the song "Mamma" to my father's mother over the phone.

One story that I'm proud to let all who read this know about was when my dad was in his late thir-ties. He was working in the scrap-iron yard in Hunts Point. A barge was about to dock to pick up scrap metal.

My father at work after saving the barge captain's life on October 8th 1942.

My father was standing by on his crane to load it. Something went wrong, and the barge crashed into the dock. It sank in minutes with the captain trapped inside. Johnny Legs jumped down off his crane and, without hesitating, dove into the mucky Bronx River. He located and freed the captain and brought him up in time. He received a medal from the City of New York for bravery and for saving the captain's life. He was on the cover of the *New York Post* newspaper. I have his medal, along with a letter from the mayor and the news article; there's also a letter from the captain thanking him. God bless and rest in peace, Dad.

Parker came over to me and said, "Guess what?"

"What?" I answered as if to say, "Now what?"

"We have to go on another ambush tonight."

"Are you fuckin' kidding me?" My stomach was acting up, and I didn't feel too good. I didn't need that news. I was so disgusted. We all were. We were constantly going out at night. Sure as shit, again, eight of us set out just before dusk. To top it off, it was raining, which was not a good thing. With our ponchos on, we worked our way through camp with just our weapons and some extra claymores.

This time we bobbed and weaved our way about two hundred meters into the jungle. We stopped at a heavily wooded area with dense jungle and overhanging trees. Darkness came sooner due to the overcast skies. Before it got too dark to see anything, we quickly set out our claymores, and each of us chose a spot to get ready for the long wet night ahead. We took notice of the whereabouts of each of us. The rain never let up. It wasn't a heavy downpour, just another one of those annoying steady-trickling showers that could be heard bouncing off the trees and bushes and our plastic ponchos all night long. The sounds of the falling rain deafened our ears to any noise that we needed to hear. The rainwater filled all the creases in our ponchos. It dripped off the rims of our jungle hats, into our eyes, down our faces, and flowed down our necks. It didn't take too long for it to get cold and the body shivers to set in.

I picked a spot and leaned against a tree. I placed my gun across my lap with the muzzle facing to my left and my right finger on the trigger. I had the claymore detonator against my right leg, so I knew exactly where it was. It was so damn dark. Just for the hell of it, I put my left hand in front of my eyes. I could not see a fuckin' thing. If I didn't have my M60 resting on my lap or the detonator where I could grab it, there would be no way that I would know where they were. I sat crouched low, leaning forward over the cover plate of my gun. My fingers were getting numb from the constant grip on the cold, wet trigger and handguard. I placed my hands beneath my poncho and held them under my armpits in an attempt to warm them. I whispered to Parker, who was sitting only a few feet to my right and whom I couldn't see, "This is nuts."

He answered softly, "Yeah, I know, man. What the fuck are we doing out here?"

There we all were, in a situation where we could neither see nor hear. I thought, *Shit, how crazy is this? Anyone could come behind us and slit our throats and we'd never know it.* It just didn't make any sense to be out there under those conditions. My bodily shivers got worse. "Man, how much more of this bullshit do we have to endure?" My stomach was getting more and more nauseous. I felt like I was going to vomit. I tried like hell to hold it in, but I leaned to my left and threw up. What a hell of a time to get sick. Parker informed Paul Charles, our squad leader, that I was ill. He, in turn, radioed back to Murphy. Murphy asked if I wanted to be lifted out. Stupidly, I said, "No, I'll wait until morning." It was already after 3:00 AM, anyway. There it was, a free ticket back for a three-day rest, and my damn foolish pride made me refuse. To top it off, we were going to move out on foot after morning chow.

Unless you've been there, you cannot imagine how long a night can last sitting motionless for hours in a pitch-black jungle with the rain pouring down and you shivering and not knowing what the next moment may bring and simply longing for the sun to rise. There's an old expression that says, "All good things must come to an end." Well, fortunately, so must all bad things. The rain, at long last, finally let up; and the sun was rising as if an angel of God was slowly lifting the shade of darkness, ushering the warmth of the sun's rays that wormed their way through the openings of the trees. What a welcome sight.

It was now the morning of October 1; and when we got ready to go back, we could barely move. All of us were so stiff from sitting in the same position in the chilled rain all night long. As soon as we entered the camp, Murphy approached me and asked me how I was feeling. I told him that I was fine. He wanted me to hop a ride on a chopper instead of walking to the next LZ. "Pizza," he said, "just make sure that our gear and equipment get there intact! This will give you a chance to rest up." I told him that I never missed any of our patrols and I wanted to be with my platoon; but he insisted that I do what he asked. I wasn't too happy about the idea, but I agreed.

I walked over to Parker and told him what Murphy wanted me to do. I handed him my M60 and asked him to take good care of it for me. So while the battalion was leaving, I waited to hitch a ride on a chinook, which was a large double-propped helicopter with rows of windows. It was used to transport heavy equipment and supplies. The chinook landed, and some of the line guys started loading their respectful companies' gear. I gathered all our stuff and made sure it was loaded onboard before I took my seat. It was my first time on a chinook. I was the only passenger. There were other choppers loading supplies and taking off.

It was late afternoon by the time we lifted off. I sat comfortably in a seat for a change. It beat the hell out of sitting on the floor of an open gunship, leading an assault on an LZ. I enjoyed the ride. The troops were long gone and well on their way to the new location.

It was close to dark by the time we landed. The line companies were already digging in. I stood close by our equipment and watched it getting unloaded. I stayed with all of it when it was dumped off the chopper. Bundle upon bundle was being dropped off by numerous other choppers. They came and went. It was like Grand Central Station. There were piles of fatigues, backpacks, extra ammo, and all kinds of shit stacked close together. What a job it was to distinguish our gear from the rest of the battalion's. My platoon members saw me and headed in my direction. Parker handed me my M60. After sorting out our things and each of us finally gaining his belongings, we spent the rest of the evening digging in. David C. was back with me and Parker. We took a break from working on our foxhole and sat and talked. It so happened that while I had spent the day packing and my buddies were humping and slicing their way through the jungle, David C., Schneider, and Canook, had taken part in a VC encounter. David C. told me what happened.

"Schneider, Canook, and I were walking point. As we neared the ending of the long hike, we walked out of the thick jungle and entered a small clearing. We stumbled onto a few gooks, who were just as surprised as we were. It became a matter of who fired first. Fortunately, we did. Without hesitating, all three of us raised our weapons and emptied our clips. We killed all three of them. Terry and Canook confiscated two of their AK-47s as a memento of their kill. I'm telling you, Johnny, it was them or us. I've heard that expression 'kill or be killed' all my life. And there we were, face-to-face, and its true—we had to kill them before they killed us. We buried one of the dead VC at the edge of the perimeter with one of his arms sticking up straight out of the ground from his elbow to his fingertips. Then we put a 'Big Red One' patch in his hand and tied one of our black scarves around his wrist."

My Black Scarf given to me by David C.

The black scarf was the token cloth of our 1/2d infantry battalion and had a bounty upon its apprehension. The scarf's origin came about in 1965 when after the 1/2nd battalion conquered a Vietcong village, rolls of black silk were found. Before destroying the material, the battalion commander suggested that scarves be made with the 1/2d insignia of different colors printed on them. There was a different color for each company, and it had to be worn around the necks of the troops. Thus, we became known as the Black Scarf Battalion.

David C. seemed to not be bothered by the incident, as did Canook, but Schneider was a bit shaken up by the ordeal. Terry was quiet and didn't speak of it. He just wandered over to his position and stayed by himself. His reaction was noticeable. We figured it would be better for us to let him be, hoping that he would get over it by morning. After another long hard day, we finished our hooches and turned in.

Morning came, and we were awoken by the sound of the others rustling about. I emerged from our hooch and looked around. I got my first good glimpse of the area. That same odd grayish mist was covering the plain of grass that stretched throughout the camp. Above the mist, not very far away, stood the Black Virgin Mountain. Once again, that feeling struck me. As I stood staring at it high above the trees, my instincts sensed a terrible presence—similar to that feeling I had just days before when I first saw it. But this time, there was something else. There was a strange, odd look to that place. I had been in many different areas of that godforsaken country, but none had ever given me such a chilling feeling. I just knew death was nearby, as if it were hiding in the mist.

I looked to my right and saw Schneider sitting alone outside his hooch. He looked pale and was shaking and appeared to be upset. I walked over toward him and sat beside him. "What's the matter, Terry?" I asked.

He said, "I didn't sleep at all last night. I can't get the face of that VC out of my head. I keep seeing him going down after I shot him. Man, John, I killed someone. I never thought it would feel this bad to shoot somebody."

"Don't let it bother you so much," I said. "It was something you had to do. It was him or you, Terry, remember that." I felt for Terry. I could see he was really hurting inside, and yet deep within me, I was wishing that I was the one who had killed that gook. I wanted so much to avenge the deaths of my friends and especially the death of my cousin Tony.

CHAPTER XV

THE HAND
OF DEATH

Picture of the Hand of Death before the
Black Scarf was tied around it.

I told Terry to come with us to get some breakfast. "Come on," I said, "it will take your mind off it." What do you say, or how do you comfort someone who feels guilty of doing something that had to be done? I gave it my best shot on easing his pain. "Listen to me, Terry, I can honestly say that I don't know how hard it must be for you to deal with this. I can see it's eating away at your insides, but you have to put it aside for now. We're going out on patrol after chow, and you're back on point again. You need to keep alert. We need you to stay sharp, okay?"

He said, "I know, John, you're right. I keep telling myself, if he would have killed me, he wouldn't have thought anything of it. I'm trying, I'm trying really hard to not let it bother me." By the time we finished breakfast and talking, he seemed to be a little better.

As we were getting ready, lining up in rows of two, the mortar teams were launching another battery of shells that were exploding beyond our perimeter. When the bombing ceased, we led the way. Bravo Company followed us. The rest stayed back.

One by one, we entered the bush, and to welcome us into the doorway to hell was the arm of the dead VC reaching up out of the ground like some dead plant waiting for us to place a ticket into its hand, allowing us entrance into its realm. I got my first good close-up view of it. The hand was tilted sideways at the wrist. The dirt-covered fingers were spread slightly apart and curled, clutching the "Red One" patch. The black scarf was tied around the wrist, covering part of the forearm. It was just as David C. had described. Each step I took gave me a closer look. I took special notice of the ants and other bugs crawling all over it. I wondered who it was that lay beneath that shallow grave. I'm sure he had a family, just as I did; maybe a wife and child who would never see him again or ever know of his whereabouts; or was he just someone's son who, like so many others, would never have the chance to grow and experience life? It was a morbid sight, a horrible reminder of the atrocities of war. It was a senseless war, but it didn't matter what we thought of that place or of the war. We had to do what we were trained for: do our job, finish our twelve-month tour, and hope we'd live to see the day that we could go home and leave it all behind.

We traveled a few kilometers, hacking our way through the dense bush in a zigzag format. There were no signs of any VC. We returned to camp in time for midday chow. The mortar teams launched more shells into the wood line, and another patrol went out. Charlie Company had their turn. They got back before dark and had nothing to report. That night, six of us went on an LP. We stayed up all night, just inside the perimeter, and listened for any enemy movement. We heard or saw nothing.

The next day, we did the same ridiculous thing all over again: the lining up in camp, the mortar bombardment, the wait to move out; and for the second day in a row, we had to pass by the hand. We stayed out patrolling most of the day, and there was still no sign of the enemy. But I was still being haunted by that strange feeling. An unknown presence kept gnawing at me. My gut was telling me that something very bad was going to take place.

That night, my team wasn't part of any detail; but even so, we had to take shifts, pulling guard duty outside our hooch. It was another one of those calm, clear, cool evenings. The night creatures were entertaining us like some weird symphony, and the stars in the moonless sky put on a display beyond description, with an occasional show of shooting stars to enhance its splendor. It was nice sleeping under such a peaceful and majestic dome for a change.

The next morning—Tuesday, October 4—started out typical of any other day. The sun hadn't risen yet to burn off the morning dew and relieve the chill. I stretched and felt the coolness of my pants and shirt touch against my skin, which caused a quick shiver of my body. I felt the dry mud stiffen my fatigues and my feet regain some of their feelings after sleeping with my boots on.

After breakfast, we began lining up into formation to head out on another patrol. My eyes roamed up and down. Standing in line were those who hadn't been with us too long. I visualized our original group: Ron, who was killed; those who had rotated back stateside; and the others who were either transferred or had to stay behind for different reasons. I missed them not being there. I closely observed those who were part of the originals: David C., Schneider, Deloge, Baldy, Sexton, Polite, Red, Parker, Verlinden, House and Funky. I took special notice of Verlinden, who was standing directly across from me on the other line. He was adjusting his gear. He squatted slightly and then jolted his right shoulder upward to reset a strap that was holding his ammo pouch, which had slid down off his shoulder. He repeated the same ritual for his left side. He looked up at me and saw me watching him as I stood there with my machine gun resting on my right hip. He said, "What, huh, what?" They were words he'd always say in jest, as if he had just done something wrong. Or he would say, "What the hell are you looking at?" Then, with a grin,

Verlinden nodded his head, gave me a thumbs-up, then turned and faced forward.

I checked my weapon, opening its cover plate to make sure the ammo was properly in place. I slammed it shut, pulled back on the bolt, shoved it forward, and put the gun on safety. I looked over my ammo pouch attached to the left side of my gun, making sure it, too, was latched and locked in place. The extra-long belt of bullets that I stuffed into the pouch was overflowing. Parker was directly behind me with two cans of ammo, each holding two hundred rounds. David C. had gone up front to walk point with Schneider and Canook. Everyone loaded and locked their magazines into their weapons. Those who carried an M79 grenade launcher cracked it open and placed a round into it then slammed it shut. The shotguns were pumped and ready; so were we. The mortar teams went silent after their steady bombardment of the outer perimeter. Lieutenant Murphy, who had gone back for some last-minute instructions, came passing by; and we started moving, leading the way. Charlie Company followed behind us.

We crossed over the edge of the compound, and just as the days prior, we had to pass by the dead man's hand. By now it had become a familiar sight, so I didn't give it much concern except for one thing: the arm was down, lying flat on the ground, and not in its usual upright position. For a split second, I thought, *That's weird.* The maggots were eating away at its flesh, so I figured it must have fallen over from decay. I pointed out its change of position to Parker. I couldn't help turning and looking back until I lost view of it. I crouched down and entered the bush just ahead of Parker. We went about fifty yards and stopped. Parker and I were standing close by each other, talking.

Only a few moments passed, and then the nightmare began. "Machine-gun fire." Arty and I hit the ground for cover along with the rest of the platoon. "Where did it come from?" I whispered to Parker.

"I don't know," he answered. We lay silent and motionless and waited. The jungle was so damned thick. We couldn't see three feet ahead of us. The adrenaline flowed, rushing through our veins, and our hearts pounded in our chests as we waited anxiously for our next move.

Everything went silent. All we could hear was the squelch from our squad leader Paul Charles's radio. He was directly ahead of me. The squelching noise cut out, and we heard Murphy trying to make contact with our three point men with no success. He then made contact with Baldy, the other squad leader, and asked for a head count. We heard Baldy's reply, "Two WIA and one KIA, Verlinden." Parker and I listened, stunned in disbelief. Craig Verlinden was dead and only minutes had gone by. "My God, Ver Linden's thumbs-up was the last I would ever see of him." Unfortunately, in combat, there was no time for remorse. There'd be time for that later; now we had to focus on our own survival.

Murphy signaled for us to keep low and to move up. I turned to Parker and said, "Well, here we go." We hugged the ground and circled to our right. Murphy headed toward Baldy's location. I followed behind Charles, who had made contact with point. He led the way toward them. We made our way out of the bush into a small clearing. We began to cross the opened area. It was a bitch trying to keep my gun and bullet belt out of the mud. The damn ammo pouch kept coming loose from the bracket. I held my machine gun in one hand and cradled the pouch and free-flowing belt of bullets between my left bicep and forearm. In trying to crawl and keep as low to the ground as possible, the bullets fell out from under my arm and dragged in the mud. I struggled across the clearing, trying to keep up with Charles. The bullets were taking on more and more dirt, trailing behind me, and that was not good; worse yet, Parker was nowhere in sight, and he was carrying all the extra ammo. Somehow, we must have gotten separated. Without him, all I had was the one-hundred-plus rounds, which now would probably cause my gun to jam.

I stopped momentarily in an attempt to gather the mud-covered ammo by pulling them toward me like I was hauling in a fish. All bunched up, I cradled them in my arms again. I commenced my crawling in hopes that Parker would follow shortly after. Luckily, there was still no exchange of gunfire. All was silent, like the calm before the storm.

I met up with Charles; and we spotted two of our point men, David C. and Schneider. Both were crouched down in a squatting position. David C. had been shot in his left arm. Schneider was okay. I asked them, "Where the hell are those bastards?"

Bender, bleeding from his left arm, replied, "Johnny, they'll kill ya. They'll kill ya dead. They got me in my arm. Canook is hurt bad and pinned down, and we can't get to him. They've got a fifty-caliber machine-gun nest right in front of us. They're just waiting for us to make a move."

The enemy was dug in and dug in well and deep with plenty of coverage all around making them practically invisible. It was the highly effective L-shaped ambush, and we had walked right into it. What was baffling was, How the fuck did those gooks manage to dig in overnight? We patrolled that area for three straight days and had LP and ambush squads at night. Not only that but they had also managed to avoid all the mortar attacks. They knew exactly where the range of apogee our mortar teams were firing and had set up inside that blasting zone. And usually, when you dig, there're piles of fresh dirt. We didn't see any. The only logical conclusion would be that after fighting for a hundred years, they already had these underground hideaways and could pop up anywhere they needed to.

We all looked up and heard Canook moaning. David C. pointed in the direction where Canook was hit and where he thought the VC were dug in. A voice came over the radio. It was Murphy calling Charles and asking about his status. Charles told him that we had gotten separated from the rest of our squad and that he and I met up with point. He told Murphy of the grim situation regarding Canook and David C. Murphy told Charles to hold on tight and that he was on his way.

Murphy met up with us along with the captain of Charlie Company, which had come to our aid. Bender headed to the rear to get dusted off. Murphy called me by my nickname and said, "Pizza, set up your gun over in that cluster of bushes," and pointed as he spoke. As I started to move, the captain stopped me and said, "Don't worry, big man, they're not going to get you." My thought was, *I hope you're right.*

I positioned my M60 in the thicket behind a log. Schneider was right next to me on my left. I placed my finger on the trigger and was ready to fire when I thought about Bender's warning of the fifty-caliber dead ahead. I knew there was nothing to take cover behind from a fifty. Its rounds could pierce a tree. I also knew that the second I fired my weapon, the fifty's sights would zoom right in my direction. Those few seconds had to be the most frightening of my life. I remembered back in jungle devil school when the sergeant told us that, during a firefight, we'd feel much better once we fired our weapons. That thought really didn't seem to make me feel any better, but I had no choice. I squeezed the trigger and started firing, anticipating the return of deadly retaliation. I prayed that it wouldn't happen and that my gun wouldn't jam. Schneider was assisting me with the feeding of the bullets. We started taking in small-arms fire. It wasn't a fifty, but it didn't matter. Having little to no protection, any size bullet could have taken us out.

Parker still hadn't shown up with my ammo. I kept shooting, moving my gun back and forth slowly, keeping the muzzle at a low angle to hover the ground, so as to try to sweep the bullets into the openings of their foxholes. I felt a tap on my shoulder; it was Parker and just in time. I was out of ammo. We loaded a fresh belt from one of the cans. I kept firing, not knowing if I was on-target. The bushes made it impossible to see through to the enemy's positions. Meanwhile, my actions made it possible for the others to deploy and commence a counterattack. Now it turned into a full-scale battle. The bullets from both sides were flying to and fro, destroying anyone or anything in their path. The shrubs were getting chewed up, and the trees between us and the enemy were splintering to pieces. Schneider left me and Parker and deployed to another position to fire his weapon.

The barrage of projectiles cleared a path of vision through the jungle, but the enemy was dug in so low that we still couldn't see them. The air soon became thickened by gun smoke and overwhelming with the smell of gunpowder. We could hear the enemy shouting, and we kept firing for all we were worth. Then, without warning, my gun malfunctioned. It jammed from a faulty piece of ammo. The barrel was as hot as hell, and we didn't have a spare. I tried ramming a cleaning rod down the barrel to clear it, but the round was lodged in too tightly and wouldn't free up. It was nerve-racking trying desperately to clear the weapon while lying in a prone position and being shot at. To give myself some bodily freedom, I took my pistol belt, holster, and shoulder straps off. Then I removed my two pouches of grenades from my shoulders. The area was still too dense to toss any grenades. Parker and I continued to try to get the gun to work, but it was hopeless. In between all the noise, Canook's moans kept taunting us to come to his aid.

In the meantime, Murphy called in an air strike. I heard the jets overhead. Their sound was like music to my ears and grew louder as they came closer and lower to launch their rockets. Man, was I glad to see them. "Bring them bombs closer," I said. "Just keep them coming." The sound of those jets firing their rockets was incredible; it was as if the sky had opened and a thunderbolt had been launched by God Himself. That air assault helped us immensely. We weren't doing battle with the usual Vietcong. These were North Vietnam Regulars, a whole battalion of them, and they were well equipped.

When the jets left, and figuring that the air assault had "Charlie" on the ropes, an attempt was made to rescue Cannok. Paul Charles and our new medic tried to reach him first. I heard a yelp. I knew he was down. He had entered the same firing lane that Canook had unexpectedly walked into. Now there were two men wounded and trapped. Everything was happening so quickly. Evidently, the VC had survived the bombing. The battle was far from over.

To the rear of the small clearing was a larger one. It was there that the medical station was set up and where the wounded could be attended to and dusted off. By now, all of Charlie Company was in position along with us. The rest of the battalion were on their way.

The casualty count was growing by the minute. With my gun out of commission, I had to try to get my hands on another weapon. I ran across the clearing to the rear station and grabbed two armfuls of ammo, which included a bag of shotgun shells, but I had no shotgun. I ran back, hoping to find one. I spotted Funky crouched down low in the brush. He had a shotgun, and he shouted to me, "Hey, Pizza, what do you have in the sacks?"

I quickly answered, "Some shotgun shells, do you need any?"

"Yeah," he replied, "I'm out." I ran over and handed him the bag of shells. Then Baldy saw me and yelled, "Pizza, I'm out of ammo." "Okay, I'll go get you some." I ran back and grabbed two bags filled with M-16 magazines, then returned and handed one sack to Baldy. Then I hurried back into the bush, toward my original position, with the remaining ammo, still with no weapon. I spotted Deloge. He was kneeling low between some bushes. I looked down at him and stretched out my arm, attempting to hand him whatever ammo I had left. He was not responsive at all. "John," I said, "here's some ammo." There was still no response from him. "Are you all right?" I asked more than once. He never acknowledged my presence. It was as if he was in some kind of trance or mild shock. He must have been thinking about seeing his good friend Verlinden gunned down, right before his eyes. Deloge had been standing right behind Verlinden when it happened. There wasn't any sign of injury on him, so I just placed the ammo at his feet. There wasn't anything I could do. I had to keep on the move. I made multiple trips for either ammo or a stretcher—anything I could grab that would be of some help.

The choppers were landing and being loaded with wounded and dead bodies. There was chaos everywhere. Seconds made the difference between life and death. No matter where I looked, someone was doing something and, all the while, dodging bullets.

I made it back to where my gun jammed. We must have made some progress in chalking up some enemy kills and casualties because we were finally able to get to Canook and Doc. House had gone in to help Paul, who was pinned down along-side of Canook and Doc and after tossing all of his grenades and emptying all of his magazines into the enemy's positions, Paul covered his two wounded comrades with his own body to shield them from further injury. Paul was wounded, but not too seriously. They dragged Doc out first. I ran over to lend a hand. Doc was still alive. He had been shot in his lower back. We laid him down, face up. I took off my shirt to cover him, and then I laid down beside him. He started talking, telling me how much it hurt. "It hurts. It hurts so much. I can't feel my legs. I'm cold."

"Take it easy. You'll be all right," I said. "Just think about going home. Do you have a girl back home?" I asked.

"Yeah," he answered with a slight grin on his face, momentarily forgetting about his pain.

I told him, "Well, just think about her and that you will be with her real soon. Keep on thinking about her. Just keep your mind on getting back to her."

I looked to my right and I saw House on his knees dragging Canook and inching his way out of the bush. He gazed up at me in exhaustion and said, "John, I need help." His cry for help triggered something inside me. From that moment on, I became oblivious to everything. I stood up, ran over, and grabbed Canook, who was lying face up. I took hold of him under his armpits, picked him up, and dragged him out. I placed him alongside of Doc. Canook, amazingly, was still alive. He had a hole in his chest that was large enough to put my hand through. He had gotten a second wound while lying mortally injured. He was shot up his face. The bullet grazed his chin, split his lip and took his nose off. He gave no response other than a soft continuous moan.

I knew I had to get them medical help and fast. I lifted Canook up into my arms. Parker came out of nowhere, saw me, ran over, and grabbed hold of Canook's legs and feet. We carried him out, and as we did, a tree branch got wedged between Canook's back and my forearm. It cut deeper into my flesh as we walked. I looked at the branch cutting my arm then at Canook's face. The bruise I was getting didn't mean anything. We carried him back to the medevac area where he was quickly attended to.

I lost no time in returning for Doc. I grabbed some more ammo, ran back to the kill zone, and handed the ammo to Sexton. Then I went to get Doc. He was still conscious. I told him that I was going to get him out of there. I picked him up onto my right shoulder and ran back across the clearing. I called for a medic and yelled, "Take care of this kid right away!" Then I shouted, "How's Canook?"

Someone answered, "He's dead." Sadly, once again, there was no time to grieve. I had to get back. I grabbed more ammo. On my return through the two clearings, the captain of Charlie Company stopped me. He put his hand on my shoulder and said, "You're doing a good job, big man, a damn good job."

"Thanks," I said and headed back into the bush. I handed the ammo to another one of my platoon members and went back for more. As I did, I saw guys from my group standing and firing wildly into the jungle. I noticed Speedy with an M60. He wasn't experienced with that weapon. I hollered to him, "Speedy, you're aiming too high! Lower your gun!" Then I continued on.

I don't know how many trips I made back and forth through those clearings under fire or what kept me from getting my head blown off. I was clearly a prime target the way I just stood up handing men ammo and carrying out the wounded. It was as if God had rendered me invisible. My guardian angel must have been on overtime.

I was exhausted, so I knelt at the edge of the clearing closest to the spot where I had picked Doc up and paused to catch my breath. The bullets were still flying all over the place. The casualties were enormous. As I was breathing in deeply to overcome my fatigue, I looked up across the clearing and the medic from Charlie Company yelled, "Man hit!" There was another soldier from his company kneeling beside him. He saw me and called out, "John, we need a stretcher." I spontaneously crawled as fast as I could across the open field to the medevac area, grabbed a stretcher, and ran it over to the medic. I laid the stretcher down beside the wounded soldier and opened it up. As I was doing that, a voice said, "Man, I never seen anybody crawl that fast. You were across that field in a flash." I didn't know who he was. And I didn't know how he knew my name. He helped me put the casualty on the stretcher.

With all the rushing and confusion, I hadn't looked to see who the wounded man was. It was Schneider. He was shot in the stomach, a very bad place to get hit. I knelt down beside my wounded comrade and looked on as the medic attempted to bandage the wound. He looked up at me and shook his head, expressing that it was hopeless. His hands were just going through the motions of trying to stop the flow of blood that was pouring out of Schneider's gut like a fountain. He was barely alive, not a sound came from his lips. He lay motionless with his eyes shut. His face was pale. I saw his Adam's apple move as he attempted to swallow. There was nothing I could do but witness another one of my good friends die before my eyes.

Schneider had to be moved to the dust-off area. I got up to take a few steps to carry the part of the stretcher where Schneider's head was. In the middle of one of my steps, it happened. *Bang!* Something hit me in my upper left thigh like a ton of bricks. I was knocked right off my feet. It was as if someone had taken a baseball bat and, with full force, swung at my left thigh. I laid down flat on my back. My entire groin area and leg felt numb and were burning as if a torch was being held to them.

Believe it or not, my first thought was to feel for my testicles. I placed my hands over my groin area and was relieved that they hadn't been shot off. Amazing, the state of mind one has in such a situation. I sat up and put my two hands on my thigh. I looked down and saw nothing but blood. I was bleeding like a pig. I couldn't move my leg at all. I hollered to the medic, "Doc, I'm hit," but he hesitated on coming over to me for fear that he, himself, would get shot by entering a firing lane as I just did. He held out his hand and told me to take it easy and to remain calm.

I kept my composure and didn't panic. I pulled myself together and lay back down on the ground. I knew I had to get out of the firing lane, so I started to roll. I heard the medic say, with his Spanish accent, "Jes, dat's it. Roll out of da way, keep rolling." I rolled and rolled toward the medical station. All I remember seeing was the green grass and then the blue sky over and over again. Lying face up, I came to a stop at the edge of the clearing, slightly astray from my intended destination. Blood was still pouring out of my wound. Another medic came running over to my aid. He took off my boots and ripped my pants right up to my crotch. I, half in a daze, asked, "Did the bullet go through?"

He answered, "Yes."

"Thank God," I said.

The wound was too high up on my thigh to apply a tourniquet. My Spanish-speaking medic friend, who couldn't come to me at first, came running over and assisted in helping me. He said, "Okay, jou gonna be oright. I goin' to gib jou a little pinch in jou ass now." He shot me up with morphine and said, "Jou a lucky man. Jou got da million-dollar one. Jou goin home, and we still be here." Meanwhile, the other medic inserted a tube into the vein in my left arm and began giving me blood plasma.

Parker came running over and knelt beside me like he was sliding into second base. He said, "Johnny Babes, how'd you go and get yourself shot?"

"Scooby Doo," I said, using the friendship phrase he and I always used when all was well.

It was getting difficult for me to breath. My chest felt heavier with each breath. I thought shock was beginning to set in. I grabbed Parker's arm and told him to stand by in case I stopped breathing. He took hold of my arm and reassured me that he'd be there. Somehow, I stayed conscious and remained calm throughout the entire ordeal. I felt life coming back with each additional drop of plasma flowing into my vein. The medics kept working on me, doing their best to stop the bleeding and bandaging my leg. God bless those medics and all medics.

They carefully placed me on a stretcher and carried me to the medevac area to be dusted off. I gave Parker the thumbs-up and waited for what seemed to be an eternity. I heard the sound of the chopper high in the air, returning to pick us up. I watched it get lower and land. I knew it was my ride out. The morphine really helped. I felt no pain. Two men came over and quickly and carefully lifted my stretcher. I felt it rock and sway as they carried me to the chopper. They handed one end of the stretcher to a crew member and then eased me onboard.

When I was strapped into place, I looked up and saw a blood-stained stretcher above me. I asked who it was. The crewman looked at the man's dog tags. It was Schneider. He was dead. The attendant asked me if I wanted a cigarette. "No, thanks," I said, "but my feet are cold." He got a blanket and covered me up.

Just prior to lifting off, two more wounded GIs hopped onboard. They were both medics. One of them had his right arm bandaged and in a sling. "Hey, how ya doin'?" he asked.

"Okay," I answered, trying to recognize who he was.

Then he said, "You don't know me, but I'm the medic who took care of you. I took a bullet in my arm just minutes after you left." I reached out my right hand and grabbed his left hand and thanked him for helping me. He saved my life, and I never got his name. Then, suddenly, the other medic jumped off the chopper. I didn't understand why.

The chopper lifted off. I turned my head to one side and looked down for a last look. The jungle below, once impregnable, was now cleared from the onslaught of bullets as if a bulldozer had just paved through it. The fighting was still going on when we took off. I later found out that Howard Gerstel, the battalion medic, while trying to help the wounded, took a bullet to the head. The medic who jumped off the chopper saw it happen and went to help Howard who unknown to him, was killed instantly. In his attempt to help, he was shot again and killed. I learned that his name was Donald Schrenk. May God rest their brave souls in peace.

Not counting the KIA's and the WIA's from the line companies; of the seventeen of us from the recon platoon, including Lt. Murphy, who went into battle that day, three were killed and eight were wounded.

Except for the horrible memories, the war was behind me now, fading farther away with each passing second. I thought back to that bad feeling and how it had played itself out. I pictured the last view I had of that hand sticking out of the ground. Was it lying flat on the ground from decay, or had it been placed in that position by his comrades vowing vengeance on us? Either way you look at it, it truly was "the hand of death."

CHAPTER XVI

THE NINETY-THIRD MEDEVAC HOSPITAL

A fter a fifteen-minute flight, the chopper landed at the Ninety-Third Medevac Hospital. The facility was set up in a huge tent, where a MASH-type unit was assembled. It was capable of handling numerous amounts of casualties. There were a multitude of doctors and nurses ready and waiting for the incoming injured. A gurney was immediately brought to my chopper, and I was placed on it. My lifesaving medic friend stayed by my side as they wheeled me over and parked me outside the operating room. He placed his hand on my chest and wished me good luck. Once again, I thanked him. I guess he realized how grateful I was for what he did for me by the way I held his hand to say goodbye. Then he went to have his own wound attended to.

I remained alone until our unit's chaplain, Father Calter, came by. He placed one hand on my chest and the other hand on my forehead and asked me how I was doing. "I'm okay, Father."

"That's good," he said. "I'm going to issue your last rights as a Christian."

"That's okay, Father, I'm not going to die."

Then he said, "I know. I know you're not going to die."

"Guess what? I'm going to have a baby."

With me saying that, he answered in surprise, "You're going to have a baby?"

"Yeah," I answered him back.

Then he retorted, "You mean you are really going to have a baby?"

Then realizing, even in my drugged state, what he was indicating, I rocked my head back and forth and said, "No, man, not me. My wife is."

"Ah, that's more like it," he said with a chuckle. Then he placed one hand back on my forehead again and administered benediction, forgave my sins, and blessed me with the sign of the cross. Seconds later, they came to take me into the operating room. Father Calter leaned down next to my ear and whispered, "Good luck with your baby."

I was rolled into a large room. I heard all sorts of commotion. There must have been four or five people working on me at the same time. I didn't know or think it at the time, but I was on the brink of life and death. They stripped my clothes off and removed the field bandages from my leg. At the same time, I felt someone doing something to my left arm. It was a pinching sensation. My veins had collapsed from the loss of so much blood. So they had to perform a cut-down, an incision made into the artery of my left arm, to enable them to insert a tube so as to administer the life-giving blood transfusion.

Another nurse was standing on my right, trying to shove a tube up my nose and down my throat and into my stomach. She kept saying, "Swallow, keep swallowing," as she continued to feed the tube up my nose. It made me gag, and I couldn't help myself from vomiting. I turned my head to the side and heaved. The tube stayed in my throat. I felt the blood entering my veins through that tube that was inserted into my artery. Miraculously, I felt life slowly coming back. I was all prepped and ready to go for x-rays.

Still under heavy sedation, I was instructed by the x-ray technician to turn onto my side, which I was not able to do. The aide had to maneuver me in all the necessary positions. When the x-rays were over with, I was brought back to the operating room. They replaced the empty pint of blood with another. I felt stronger and stronger, even my breathing had become more regular. Then, out of nowhere, a hand holding a mask came down and covered my face.

I woke up in the recovery room. I was in a great deal of pain, which caused my eyes to tear up. A thought suddenly raced through my mind, *My leg.* I moved the toes of my right foot first and then the toes of my left foot. My leg was still there. That was a huge relief.

Through the cloudiness and blurriness in my eyes caused by my tears, I saw a figure standing at the foot of my bed. When my eyes regained some focus, I saw that it was Richie, a fellow whom I had become good friends with during the last battalion operation. Richie hailed from the Bronx, so we had a lot in common. He was from one of the line companies. He told me that he had been standing there for a while, waiting for me to wake up. "How do you feel, John? You were moaning in your sleep."

"Rich, it hurts, man. It hurts like hell." I could see that he felt the pain along with me as he grabbed my hand to give me support. I paused to clear my throat and said, "Man, it's good to see you."

"Yeah, we were all worried about you. Here, I brought you these." He placed some pens and a pad along with some comic books and some chocolate bars at my side. He said, "These will help keep you occupied while you're here."

I wondered how Richie could be coming to see me so soon. After the surgery, I must have slept through the rest of the day and the night. I asked Richie, "What day is it?"

"It's Wednesday, October 5." He stayed as long as he could. I couldn't thank him enough for the visit and supplies. It's friends like him that I will never forget. The last thing I remember was Richie's goodbye. I conked out and woke up in a ward.

I looked around. There were a bunch of other wounded guys. It was a very big room. I was more awake and alert by then. I checked myself out. My left arm was in a wooden sling. The tube was still in my vein, feeding me fluids and meds. There were stitches in the crease of my left arm where the tube was. I felt my left thigh with my right hand. It was heavenly bandaged. I could not move too well.

I couldn't sit up. I had to eat, drink, go to the bathroom, and sleep lying flat on my back. I have to tell you, it wasn't easy.

There was an Asian fellow to the bed on my right. I tried communicating with him. He couldn't speak. His neck was bandaged; but with sign language, words such as *VC*, pointing our fingers to depict a gun, and pointing to our injuries, it was easy enough to figure out what each of us was trying to say. He had been shot in the neck. He was Korean and was serving with a unit from South Korea fighting against the North Vietnamese. He was a real nice guy.

I was kept heavily sedated for the rest of the day. The bandages hadn't been touched yet. I felt them to be exceptionally moist by early evening. By late evening, they had to be changed due to them being saturated with bodily fluids. A sergeant came over and told me that he was going to change my bandages. He uncovered the sheets off me and propped my leg up on two pillows to enable him to reach under it. He then carefully unraveled the blood-soaked bandages from around my thigh. My Korean friend was looking on attentively. When all the gauze was removed, all that remained was a large piece of cotton. I watched closely with deep curiosity as the sergeant removed the cotton. I got my first look at my wound. It wasn't very pretty. The wound was still wide-open. There was a four-by-eight piece of gauze lying flat inside it. The front of the wound was considerably larger than the rear due to the fact that the bullet entered the back of my thigh and exited out the front, thus bursting out and causing a large opening in the flesh. To my surprise, they hadn't sewn my leg shut. Although the bandages were soaked with blood, it wasn't bleeding. There was a long scar about sixteen inches on the inside of my thigh that was stitched up tightly. I asked him where that scar was from. He told me that it was done for exploratory reasons. The sergeant, using a pair of tweezers, gently lifted the bloody four-by-eight piece of gauze out and replaced it with a clean one. He then wrapped the leg with heavy gauze, covered me up, said good night, and left.

I lay there thinking, *How can anyone have such a large hole in his thigh and not have blood flow from it?* The wound was wide and deep. I was actually able to see down to the bone. My leg was swollen, and the flesh surrounding the wound's opening was pale and ripely. A nurse came over and gave me a shot of Demerol for pain and to relax me. She told me that I would probably be needing a shot every four hours. When she left, I took one of the comic books that Richie had given me and started to read it. In only a few minutes, the words got wavy as I read them. I held my right leg up, folded at the knee. The white sheet covering me began to resemble a cloud; and in a matter of seconds, I was off in never-never land. The injections were fantastic. They put me on cloud nine. Within minutes after they were administered, a weightless sensation would sweep over me and pleasantly, as if in slow motion, my arms would go limp and I would drift off to sleep. Man, did I look forward to those shots.

When I awoke the next morning, I felt pretty good, considering what I had gone through the last two days. My Korean neighbor was already up and in the cafeteria, having breakfast. I was hungry, but I wasn't ambulatory; so I had to wait to eat. He returned with a tray of food for me. I thought that was nice of him to do that. Thanks to him, I didn't have to wait for my breakfast. I bowed my head and said thank you. He smiled but because of his neck injury, was not able to return the gesture. The breakfast consisted of scrambled eggs made with powdered eggs. They sucked. I just couldn't get a taste for them. I ended up eating one of the chocolate bars Richie brought to me.

I was relaxing when the doctor came by with the sergeant who had dressed my leg the day before. He introduced himself to be Dr. Katz. He told me that he was the one who had operated on me. Then he asked me how I was feeling. I told him I was okay. "Let's have a look," he said. He removed the bandages and examined me. He lifted my leg high in the air to check out the back part of the wound. He lowered my leg and told the sergeant to keep the wound cleaned and dressed. He left, and the sergeant bandaged me up. The nurse came by and gave me another shot. I was entitled to one every four hours, just as she thought, which, of course, was fine by me. She was a young, very pleasant, and pretty American girl with a nice smile. She had short curly light-brown hair, hazel-colored eyes, and a nice solid figure. She looked to be in her mid—to upper twenties. I think her name was Carol.

That same routine went on for two more days. Each morning, the bandages were saturated with fluids. On October 8th, I was scheduled to be operated on again to have the front and rear wounds closed. I saw Dr. Katz. He asked if I was ready. "I'm ready," I said. I was taken to the operating room. Again, that mask was lowered down on my face, and in seconds, I was out like a light.

After recovery, I was taken back to my room. Because of the size of the opening, they had to use thick wire sutures to close up my leg. After the anesthesia wore off, the pain from the stitches was excruciating, especially the ones in the rear, which started at the crease of my butt cheek. It was a very tender area. My Korean buddy tried comforting me. He even removed my bedpan, thus saving me the embarrassment of having to call the nurse to do it.

Each morning, Dr. Katz made his rounds to examine his patients. He came to my bed along with the sergeant. They both stood at the foot of my bed. The doctor grabbed my leg by the ankle, and without warning, he raised it up high to look at the back of the thigh. Then he stretched it outward to see the inside scar. I saw the look on the sergeant's face. He squinted his eyes as he felt the pain along with me. I grabbed on to the bedrail behind me and held on for the next painful subjection. The doctor was concerned about the fluids still saturating the bandages, even with the wound now closed. He didn't say anything to me and left. Not for nothing but I was glad to see him go. The sergeant then dressed the leg with clean bandages to replace the ones that the doctor had removed.

From the time the dressings were changed that evening to the following morning, the fluids not only soaked through the gauze but also through the sheets. Dr. Katz was on his way. This time, I was ready for him. I reached behind me and took hold of the bedpost and held on tightly. Sure as shit, he performed the same exact ritual as the day before. The wire stitches felt as if they were about to rip through my skin. He showed no mercy or compassion. When he saw all the excretion oozing through the closed wound and after he was finished getting his morning exercise with my leg, he told the sergeant to remove half the sutures from the back and half from the front. The inside scar was left intact. Before the doctor left, I asked him if the tube in my left arm could be removed. He looked at it and told the sergeant to take it out.

The doctor left, and with great care and consideration, the sergeant started to remove the wire sutures. I held on in anticipation of the pain that was likely to follow. I watched as he snipped the wires and pulled them through the dry, tender skin. Each stitch had to break through the scabs that had formed around them. The front thigh was no problem. It was the tender rear that hurt like a son of a bitch. As each stitch was being removed, the wound would spread open. With every snip and tug, he glanced up at my facial expressions to see if he was causing me any further pain. He was kind enough to stop and say, "Let's rest a minute and then we'll continue." When he took all the necessary stitches out, he cleaned it. The doctor came back and asked how we were doing. The sergeant said, "Okay, sir. We're finished." Then being his inhuman self, the doctor grabbed my leg and hoisted it upward, looked closely at the opening, lowered it back down, and stared closely into the hole in the front. "That doesn't look too bad," he said. Then he told the sergeant to pack both of the openings tightly with gauze, wrap the leg well, and keep it elevated. Packing the wounds allowed them to heal from the inside out, and the packing also kept the wounds from closing on the surface only, which would leave a cavity below it. Now, because of this procedure, the leg would take a lot longer to heal.

Next came the removing of the tube from my vein. Before the sergeant started to take it out, he asked, "How long has that been in you?"

I told him, "Since day one."

He said, "Damn, that should have been taken out by now." He stood at my left side and removed the splint. Then he took off the bandages that covered the stitches that held the tube in place. I didn't know what to expect, so I anticipated more pain. He placed his fingers on the tube next to my elbow and began to pull it upward and out. He reached a certain distance and then started again. To my astonishment, it didn't hurt at all. He did this three times. The both of us couldn't believe how far the tube went into my vein. Bill, a patient to my left who was looking on, said, "I didn't think it was ever going to end." Even my Korean friend watched in awe. It must have been three feet in length. The sergeant then had to remove the few stitches from the crease of my arm. I said, "Thanks, Serg," and he left. I wish I could have remembered his name. Funny, isn't it? I remembered the name of the monster doctor but not the name of the kind and compassionate one.

I had some visitors that afternoon. I heard a yodel, which was a dead giveaway of whom one of them was—Tex. He, Doc Jimenez, Eddie, and another fellow whom I didn't recognize came walking in. They had brought me my personal belongings: pictures and my personalized bracelet that Marilyn had given me that I treasured most. They also brought the green plastic pouch that held my letters from home and Tony's three letters. The green pouch still had my blood-stains on it. I always carried the letters with me and kept them buttoned up in the lower side pocket of the right leg of my fatigues.

To my surprise, Red came walking over to my bed and joined us. I didn't know it, but he was a patient and was dressed in pajamas. I asked, "Hey, Red, what the hell are you doing here?"

He said, "Would you believe it, Pizza? The jackass that I am, I caught a back blast from the 90mm recoilless. Instead of lying to the side, I laid down behind it. Got myself third-degree burns." We all got a laugh out of that one. Red always was a clown.

What a happy reunion that was. That fellow whom I didn't know came close and introduced himself. Then I recognized him as the guy who had been kneeling next to Schneider, the same guy who had yelled for me to get a stretcher and commented on my fast crawling. He said, "Pizza, I had to come to see you and thank you."

"Thank me for what?" I asked him.

He said, "You saved my life. That bullet that got you was meant for me. That sniper had me in his sights, but when you cut across Schneider's body, you came between me and the shooter and deflected the bullet. It went through you and grazed my head and took off my helmet. Check this out." He pointed to the spot where the bullet had scarred his scalp. Then he said, "It would have gotten me right between my eyes."

"Holy shit," I said in bewilderment. "I guess both of our guardian angels were working hand in hand."

We all spoke a bit, reminiscing about the past. Tex, being his humorous self, blurted out, "Hey, Pizza, you got any pepperoni for me?"

Recalling all the Italian goody packages that I'd get from home, I told him, "I don't think you're going to find any good Italian food in this place." After a short laugh, I got serious. I knew about Ver Linden, Canook, and Schneider all being killed; but I didn't know about the outcome of our new medic. So I asked them, "What happened to Little Doc? When I left him, he was still alive." They told me that he lived but was paralyzed from the waist down. "Thank God," I said. "At least he's alive."

Then they told me about how the battalion medic, Howard, and the other medic, Donald, were killed. Then I asked, "How about the rest of the guys?" They told me that David C. was doing good and that aside from David C., Little Doc, Red, and me, four others from our platoon had been wounded: Charles, House, Speedy, and Sexton, who were all okay. As far as all the other line company's injuries, they weren't sure, but there were many. A lot of guys got hit while clearing out. We all agreed that it had been one hell of a day. They also told me that most of the guys who were wounded were going back to the field as soon as they were healed. I still wasn't sure where I was going. I kind of figured that I would be going back also. I'd watched war movies all my life, and whenever someone was shot in the arm or leg, he was up and around the very next day. I decided that I would ask Dr. Katz about my status come morning.

Doc Jimenez went on to tell me that we were credited with 250 enemy kills. How true the count was remained to be seen. I also wanted to know how Verlinden got it. I asked Doc about it. He told me that Verlinden had walked right in front of a machine-gun nest.

"He took three rounds across his chest. He never knew what hit him. He was dead before he hit the ground."

"Thanks, Doc," I said sadly; at least I had closure. "I just don't want to believe that they're dead."

Doc then said, "Yeah, John, I know. It's something we all have to live with for the rest of our lives. At least it's all over for you now, and in three more days, for me too. I probably won't be seeing you anymore, so I'll say goodbye." Jimenez and I shook hands and gave each other a hearty hug and saw each other for the last time. Maybe someday, somehow, we'd all come across one another back in the States. It was something we could hope for. Then the others, one by one, came to give me a big hug. We all said our goodbyes. I didn't want them to go. It really made me sad to see them leave. It's amazing how many times a man says goodbye to friends he's made in the Army.

I reached down into the drawer beside my bed and pulled Tony's picture out of my wallet. Once again, I stared at his picture and brought him back to life with a vision of our past. It seemed like only yesterday when we both graduated high school in 1965. He graduated from Theodore Roosevelt on Fordham Road. We drove to Orchard Beach, more commonly known to us Bronxites as Horseshit Beach. We wanted to celebrate our freedom from school days. We were happy that we were finally older. That was the day we became our own men, to do as we pleased and when we pleased. It was the beginning of a new era for the both of us, and we were ready to grab the world by the balls.

We spent the afternoon lying in the sand listening to the radio and taking an occasional dip in the ocean. Tony loved the salt water and fishing. We didn't even concern ourselves with the chicks walking by. If two happened to come our way, then all well and good; but we were just content being with each other and having our usual good times. We were two of a kind, never at a loss for words or finding something to do. There we were, ready to begin our lives as men.

I slammed the photo down into my lap. I softly said to myself, "Begin our lives as men. Tony's life was over before it ever got started." How about my life? Would it ever be the same, or for that matter, would it ever be the same for any of these other guys lying in their beds around me? I was still alive. I guess that was all that should matter. *Yeah right, I'm alive and Tony's dead. How could I possibly live with peace of mind?* I placed his picture back neatly into my wallet and filed it in the drawer.

Early the next morning, while Dr. Katz was examining me, I asked him what my situation was. For the first time since I'd known him, he sat down and spoke to me one-on-one. He told me that I would not be going back to my unit anytime soon and that he was going to transfer me to a hospital in Japan within the next few days. He also explained to me that, being that my wound was an opened one, its healing time would be prolonged and that the scars would have been much thinner if he didn't have to open them to make it heal from the inside; because of this, the scar tissue on the front and back of my leg would be thick and wide. Before he left, he showed me that he did have a human side. He placed his hand on my shoulder and said, "You know, you were very lucky. I've seen men die with the same type of wound. If that bullet would have hit your main artery that traveled down your thigh, you would have bled to death, which you came close to doing. Or had it hit the bone, it would have shattered it entirely." Then he got up and said, "I'll let you know when you'll be leaving for Japan."

All I could think of saying to this man, who probably saved my life, was "Thanks, Doc." I've got to say, as rough as he was, he was one hell of a physician and surgeon.

That afternoon, I was visited by a captain. He was holding a small box. He opened it, and inside was a medal. It was a Purple Heart, awarded to those who shed blood in combat. It was a purple medallion trimmed in gold with a profile of the head of George Washington, also gold-plated, in its center. The officer took it out of the box and pinned it on me. He congratulated me and saluted. He shook my hand and left.

It was now eight days since I had been wounded. My folks back home still knew nothing about it. The Army acknowledged my request of not letting my family know that I was injured unless mortally wounded. That was my choice when I filled out the forms that first night at Fort Jackson. I wrote to only two people, telling them the truth: my father and my cousin Tony Giannini. I addressed my father's letter to his place of business so my mother wouldn't see it. He had a laundromat on Archer Street in "the Bronx." I kept writing home regularly so my mother wouldn't suspect anything. I used my usual return address.

Dr. Katz's news of me going to Japan was music to my ears, but he never mentioned when or if, I would be going home. I had heard that many men who were seriously injured were sent to Japan to recover and then sent back to Nam to finish their tour. I didn't want that to be my case. I wanted to get home as fast as possible. The baby was due soon, and I wanted to be there to witness my first child being born.

Two days later, on October 14, Dr. Katz told me that I was scheduled to leave for Japan the day after next. My anxiety grew with each passing minute; but on the next day, October 15, I had a problem. I broke out in a high fever, which was the sign of an infection. Carol told me that I wouldn't be allowed to be moved as long as I was running a temperature. "We'll have to pack you in ice," she said, "and hope the fever breaks." She placed a bag of ice under each of my armpits and another one under my crotch. I stayed packed in ice all day and all night and all of the following morning, October 16, which was supposed to be the day of my departure. At first it was very cold and uncomfortable, but I got used to it; besides, I knew it would get me to Japan.

By the time late morning came, the fever broke, and I was able to leave as scheduled. To wait any longer would have driven me crazy. When waiting to leave Nam, minutes seemed like hours. *Charlie, don't you mortar us now. Damn, what if we were to get mortared. Most of us are lying here helpless. Just a few more hours. A few more hours, and I'll be on the plane and on my way.* My stomach was full of butterflies from the anxiety of waiting to go. Now I knew how Gary felt the night before he left.

Shortly after lunch, the sergeant came with a gurney to get me. "Ya ready, John?" An answer from me was not necessary. He knew how ready I was. He positioned the rolling stretcher alongside my bed, carefully slid me over onto it, put a pillow under my leg, and covered me with a sheet. I turned to my bedside companion Bill, whom I had come to know very well in the two weeks, and shook his hand and then switched over and gave a warm and grateful hug to my Korean friend. I knew I would never see them ever again and that I would never forget their kindness and friendship and how they helped me get through those two weeks. It was one of those bittersweet moments.

I was wheeled to a corridor and left somewhere off to one side. I waited and waited, hoping that I wouldn't be forgotten. Finally, someone came and wheeled me over to a large vestibule. I heard the engines of a plane just outside. I raised my head and saw through the swinging glass doors. The sun was shining, the sky was bright blue, and the plane was getting ready to take off. The glass doors were held open. Through them I was pushed and then up the ramp at the rear of the plane. It was a C-130: a huge camouflaged Army-propped aircraft used to carry heavy equipment and troops. I felt like Jonah being swallowed into the belly of the great whale. We had flown on them a few times while being transferred from one place to another along with our gun jeeps. There were no windows, and it was dark and tremendously loud; we'd be standing on the ramp, crammed shoulder to shoulder, not knowing where we were going and anxiously waiting for the ramp doors to open so we could get the hell out of that sardine can.

Today, in this case, it was to be carrying a load of stretcher cases to Japan. There weren't any seats. Its interior was large and spacious. I don't recall seeing any windows. It was illuminated by a few dim lights. There were many men on stretchers with nurses and doctors to care for us. As I described before, the engines were extremely loud, and their humming buzzed in my ears. The plane swerved and started to move. The sounds of the engines grew more intense. A nurse came over and checked my stretcher to make sure I was strapped in securely and that the gurney was braced. She gave me a shot of Demerol. The plane took off, and we were on our way. "Goodbye, Vietnam."

The heavy sedative allowed me to sleep for most of the trip. The voyage was long, loud, and tiring. We arrived at Johnson Air Force Base in Japan late that evening where I was to be hospitalized for God knows how long.

CHAPTER XVII

JOHNSON AIR FORCE BASE

Once again, I was taken off a plane and rolled into a medical facility. They placed me in a ward similar to the one in Nam but much larger. There were many patients lined up on both sides of the room. It wasn't long before a nurse came to check on me. She was middle-aged and of Japanese descent. She proceeded to change my bandages. They hadn't been touched since early that morning. The dressings were completely saturated with yellowish-green fluids. She unraveled the messy gauze and did very little to clean the inside. She just wiped around the outside and wrapped the leg with clean bandages. Then she gave me my shot and left.

I overheard the ambulatory patients speaking about heading into town to spend the night. We weren't far from Tokyo; and from what they were saying, I gathered that it was the next best thing to New York. The long day and the recent injection made it very easy for me to fall asleep and stay that way for the rest of the night.

In the morning, that same nurse came by to clean my wound. She slowly took off the gauze, which was again soaked with disgusting-looking fluids. I was lying flat on my back, and after taking off all the bandages, she placed her hand under the back of my thigh and applied slight pressure. Fluid came gushing out of the opening in the front of my leg. She didn't say anything. She just looked up at me and then repeated what she had just done. Again, ugly liquid came oozing out. She wrapped me back up, covered me, and went away, leaving me wondering.

A short time later, she returned with a doctor. He removed the bandages and examined my leg. He took an eight-inch Q-tip and placed it down into my wound. The wound was filled with that green-and-yellow stuff. He kept dipping the Q-tip in and out, as if he were mixing a bowl of porridge. He raised the cue tip up close to his nose and smelled it. Then he bent over and put his nose close to the wound and took a whiff, as if he was trying to make a diagnosis from the odor it was emitting. Neither he nor the nurse said anything to me as I lay there wondering what was going on. The doctor put the Q-tip into a container and left. The nurse stayed to bandage my leg.

The doctor returned and stood at the foot of my bed. He leaned forward and rested his hands on the footrail, and then he said, "I have some bad news for you."

Oh shit, I thought with all kinds of ideas quickly running through my brain; but before I had enough time to worry, he set me at ease when he said, "Oh, you're not going to lose your leg or anything."

I wanted to tell him, "Then why the fuck would you even say that, you stupid bastard?" But I kept my mouth shut. I wasn't too concerned about what he was going to tell me next after that.

He went on to say that I had a serious staph infection, which was highly contagious and very common, and that I would have to be moved to another ward and placed in isolation until the infection cleared. He left, and I was placed in a room that I would be occupying all by myself. It even had its own private bathroom. The packing in my leg was not touched for the rest of that day or night.

That next morning was one I'd never forget. A Navy corpsman came in to change the dressing, unaware that he was not supposed to do so. He said his name was Robert. I told him my name. He stood at the foot of my bed and put sterile rubber gloves on his hands. He laid out all the necessary supplies that were needed to clean the wound. As he was unraveling the outer layer of bandages encircling my thigh, he told me that he was from Texas and had been stationed in Japan for eight months. He put those wrappings in a pail and was ready for step two.

The packing in my wound was compacted very tightly. The coloring of the fluid that was soaked into the gauze was bad. I was simply lying down. By now I was sort of used to the procedure, so I was relaxed. He made his first attempt at removing the packing. With just two fingers, he pinched and gripped the top portion of the packing. Then, ever so delicately, he went to remove it. He had barely raised his hand a fraction of an inch when I jolted my entire body and let out a loud yelp. I felt a pain that I'd never experienced in my entire life. It shot through me from my head to my toes. It was so intense that my whole body began to tremble. I grabbed the bedpost behind me and held on. It caught me off guard. My upper body was shaking. The male nurse was shaken as well. He never expected such a reaction.

A Negro doctor must have heard my cry of pain and came running in. He asked the corpsman what had happened. Robert told him. Then the doctor said rather sternly, "You weren't supposed to touch that packing. The doctors are coming tomorrow to remove it all." Then he came over to me and asked how I was. I was still shaking from that jolting pain. He quickly called for a nurse to give me a shot to calm me down. Robert came over by my side and placed his hand on my shoulder and told me how sorry he was. I felt bad for the poor guy. I told him not to worry about it. The injection the nurse gave me was helping to relax me, and I started to calm down.

The male nurse sat next to me for a while. He wanted to make sure I was okay. We talked about our families, and naturally, I told him about the baby soon to be born. I asked him what he thought of my chances that I'd be sent back to Nam. He said that he was not in the position to let me know that, but he whispered and told me not to worry. There was no way that I'd be going back. I told him, "Thanks for letting me know that, Rob."

He said, "The least I could do for you, after what happened. I'll see you later, John."

He left my room, and I let the Demerol do its job. I was drifting off when, suddenly, a thought struck me. *Shit, if a mere finger's touch caused me that much pain, how much more anguish would I have to go through when the doctors come to take it all out tomorrow?* I didn't rest easy that entire night, anticipating what I was in for. I knew then what it must have been like for Jesus when He went to pray alone in the Garden of Gethsemane knowing that he was going to be crucified the next day. It's no wonder why He sweat blood.

In the early morning of October 28th, two doctors came in to see me. They both had white gloves on their hands. One of them was the same doctor that told me I had staph. He stood at the foot of my bed while the other doctor sat beside me to my right. They were getting ready to remove the packing. I grabbed hold of the doctor's wrist to my right and told him what had happened the day before. He said, "I know, we heard all about it. Don't worry, we're going to give you a good fix right into your vein."

"Good," I answered. He stretched out my right arm, wiped my vein with alcohol, then injected a needle directly into my vein. He slowly pushed in on the plunger, and the medicine began to flow into me. In a matter of seconds, I felt light-headed. As soon as he finished the dose and took the needle out, the thought of yesterday's pain repeating itself had me grabbing on to the bedrails; in spite of the injection, I wasn't taking any chances.

The doctor at the foot of my bed started to slowly and very cautiously ease out the packing inch by inch. The other doctor stayed by my side with one hand on my chest and the other clasping my right wrist. The packing-extracting doctor's hand rose in the air, pulling out the green gauze. His arm dropped, and taking another fingertip hold of the gauze, he lifted his arm again. I couldn't believe how much packing was stuffed into my wound. He did that repeatedly; and when he saw that he was reaching the end, he slowed down. His eyes peered up at me each time he tugged at the packing. Up to that point, all was fine. I still remained tense with anticipation. The gauze was all out except for the tail end. A final tug and, once again, that pain soared through my body. Even the heavy dose of novocaine didn't help. The end of the packing must have attached itself to a nerve. Both doctors held me to try to calm me down. My whole body trembled from the intense pain. It was over, but it took a little time for my body to calm down. They both stayed with me until I was at ease and then left.

The wound looked bad and ugly. The infection had taken its toll. The muscle tissue was too far gone to heal. I needed an operation. The infected tissue had to be cut out. The surgery was scheduled for the following morning.

I laid down and thought about the folks back home. I started to write them a letter. I still wanted to keep my situation hidden from them, especially Marilyn, who was now going into her eighth month. In the letter, I told them that I was transferred to Japan because they needed a maintenance man to work in a hospital. And being that I had written down in my paperwork when I entered the service that I was a plumber, I was selected for the position. I figured by letting them know that, they wouldn't get curious and I'd be able to use my new address; and by me writing, they wouldn't think anything was wrong.

While I was writing, a fellow came rolling in, sitting in a wheelchair. "How yah doin'?" he said. "My name's Randy." He wheeled himself closer, and as we shook hands, I told him my name. We became well acquainted. His full name was Randy Brown. He was from Vera Cruz, California, and had spent much of his time on the beaches until the Army called him. He was a slender good-looking guy with wavy light-brown hair and hazel-colored eyes.

We spoke of each other's experiences and how we were wounded. Randy was with the Ninth Infantry Division; and while on an operation, his platoon was ambushed. He had gotten separated from his unit; and while crawling, trying to make his way back to them, he was shot in the back by a sniper in a tree. He attempted to move and was shot two more times. He lay still and played dead for two days until reinforcements came and were able to evacuate the wounded and the dead. He told me, "John, I thought it was all over. For the two days, all I did was pray." When help finally did come for him, he was unconscious and barely alive. They thought he was dead. He awoke in the hospital. They had to cut him open and operate through his stomach. He had a large scar running down the center of his gut. The three wounds in his back were left open to drain. And like me, because of a staph infection, he had to be in isolation.

Randy had a great sense of humor and joked around quite often. He was always grabbing his stomach to try to hold back his laughter. It hurt like hell every time he would laugh. His insides must have been so sore. When he spoke, he had to say a few words at a time and take breaths in between syllables. He had to stretch his neck up to aid in his getting the words out of his mouth.

Randy came by a few times a day to spend time with me. He helped the days go by. There really wasn't much to look forward to except for a movie that was shown every other evening and was often canceled, which was a grave disappointment. To see a movie, I had to be helped onto a wheelchair with a long board stretched out to hold up my leg. We all set up in the main room to view the show. The only movie I remember was *Gambit*, starring Michael Caine and Shirley MacLaine. It was a good flick. In that main room, there was also a TV, but all that was on were Japanese-speaking programs. To my surprise, there were many musical shows, which were entertaining. After all, music is the universal language.

In the interim of talking to Randy and resting, another GI kept walking back and forth in the hallway outside my room. He walked slowly. It appeared that he was going through some kind of exercise routine. Each time he'd pass, he'd look in. It was done often enough until, finally, we said hi to each other as if we had already been good buddies. His room was across from mine.

His name was Mike La Bate, and he reared from Brooklyn, New York. I took notice of a plastic bag he had attached to the right side of his abdomen. In it was what looked like a piece of raw meat. I asked him what that was. He told me that it was a part of his colon and that it was called a colostomy and that it sucked. He said, "Man, I can't control my bowl movements or gas."

"Shit," I said, "that's got to be so embarrassing." I told him that it was the first time I had ever heard of or seen one. I was curious about how he had been wounded. He went on to tell me his story.

"I was attached to an armor division and assigned to a tank crew. My unit was out posting a road and was attacked by the VC. I was on foot, near the tank, firing at the enemy. A friend of mine drew his .45 pistol, fired it, and accidentally shot me in the back. I turned to him and yelled, "You dumb motherfucker," and then I fell to the ground. Because of the nature of my wound, I had to have a colostomy, but the good thing is that it's only temporary. And once my insides heal, they're going to put it back in me. And you're right, it is embarrassing. I ended up getting an infection, and here I am with you guys."

Seeing Mike's colostomy made me realize how amazing those doctors were. They could actually take you apart and put you back together again. Knowing of their skills reassured me, and my mind was put at ease for the following morning's surgery. All three of us had to have surgery of some kind. I was the first to go under the knife. Randy and Mike were to be scheduled within the next few days. That was to be my third operation. All this just because of one bullet. Fast, easy, and painless recoveries only happen in Hollywood, and don't ever think differently.

My mail was forwarded to me, and I read a letter from my good friend Mike Cotter. In the letter, he told me of some sad news. Marty Powers had been killed in Nam, another victim to that senseless war. Remember, he was the fellow who went with me and Billy Bockhold on our stolen car excursions. He and I also worked the "Kill the Cat" tent in the neighborhood bazaar. Every year our neighborhood parish church, Saints Phillip and James, held a fund-raising carnival in the parking lot. It was also the Catholic school where Mike Cotter and Marty attended their elementary classes. We were sixteen the year we helped at the bazaar. The best thing about working there was checking out all the girls, and even more enjoyable was seeing them checking us out. Marty and I would look at each other every time a good-looking chick walked by and rated them. Damn, he was a great guy. And now he was gone—another friend I would never see again. According to the information in the letter, Marty had joined the Marines. He was with A Company, Ninth Engineer Battalion, First Marine Division in the Quang Tin Province of South Vietnam and had been working on some pole and died as the result of an accident. They called it an accidental homicide. Now, that sucks. Rest in peace, my friend.

I stayed awake most of that night. Every time I got bad news, it would send my brain into overdrive. For the past year now, since I was inducted into "this man's Army," I'd had to live with the loss of so many friends and my cousin. I just kept thinking, *How many more will there be?* How many of the friends I'd known in my past that were lost didn't I know about? It was only by a miracle and divine intervention that I was still around—the grenade that turned out to be a dud, the claymore that was turned around, the commando that jammed, running back and forth under fire time after time. And for the life of me, I couldn't figure out how a bullet of substantial size could pierce through the center of my thigh and not hit the bone or sever the artery. I had so much to be thankful for, but it's hard to be so grateful when so many I had known made the ultimate sacrifice. Their names scrolled through my head like a roll call sent from heaven: my cousin Tony, Ron Elsa, Craig Verlinden, Charles "Canook" Sauler, Terry Schneider, Howard "Doc" Gerstel, Donald "Doc" Shrenk, Walter Brown, Price, Joe Midgette, James "Cookie" Wiltse, Marty Powers, Antonio "Doc" Ribera, Max Batchelor, John Keppler.

Martin Powers   Anthony Rutigliano   James "Cookie" Wiltse

Craig Verlinden | Terence Schneider | Charles "Canook" Sauler

Howard "Doc" Gerstel | John Keppler | Antonio "Doc" Ribera

Max Batchelor | Joe Midgette | Donald "Doc" Schrenk

Ronald Elza   Walter Brown

I must have dozed off late in the night because I was awoken by a nurse prepping my right arm for an injection to relax me. Then she placed an IV into my arm. I wasn't able to eat anything prior to surgery. After placing me on a gurney, they rolled me out of my room and down the corridor where I passed by Mike, Randy, and the others, who all gave me a thumbs-up. I was taken to the prep room where a male nurse sat beside me and told me that I wasn't going to get ether or an injection to put me under. I was going to have the anesthesia administered through the IV. He asked me if I was ready. I said "yes," and then he told me to count to ten. He put a needle into the tube, and I started counting. One, two, and the next thing I knew, I was waking up in the recovery room. I slept the rest of that day. Randy and Mike came to see me, but I was too groggy to hold a conversation with them.

The doctor came by and told me that everything had gone well and that my wound was still wide-open. He told me that they were going to continue with the same process they'd been doing; it was going to be kept packed with gauze and allowed to heal from the inside out, and the scrubbings would be done three times per day, which wouldn't begin for at least twenty-four hours.

Robert was the male nurse who started my scrubbings. I raised myself onto my elbows and watched him unravel the bandages. It was interesting to observe. The hole in my leg was still large but cleaner. The ugly fluid was gone. I was able to see right down to

273

the bone. I was amazed that a hole in one's leg so large and deep could exist without blood gushing out. Every item had to be sterile. He wore plastic gloves and touched any gauze with tweezers, rather than his hands. He poured peroxide directly from the bottle into the wound and then scrubbed harshly with a sterile pad and a long Q-tip. His hand went right down into my leg. He rubbed his fingers from side to side. This action kept the wound from getting infected. Just for the hell of it, he showed me how deep it was by placing an eight-inch Q-tip into it. The Q-tip was completely buried. There was no pain at all during the entire cleansing.

The surgery did not aid in the mobility of my leg. I still had to remain flat on my back during sleep. I couldn't turn onto my side. One young male nurse would try to get me to move my leg by tickling my toes. "Come on, let me see you move that leg. Come on, you can do it," he'd say. But my leg just couldn't move. Only my foot and toes would dance, trying to escape his wiggling fingers.

I was not used to being idle for such a long period of time. I felt sluggish. I'd lost quite a bit of weight and strength. I asked the nurse if there was any type of exercise equipment available. She told me that there was, and so she brought me a pair of dumbbells. They were nothing compared to what I was used to, but they would have to do. Because of their light weight, I concentrated on each movement and did them very slowly and strictly.

Messing around with those weights must have done something. When I went to sleep that night, I was able to turn onto my side for the first time in weeks. It was like heaven to finally be able to sleep in a different position. Between the sleeping pills and the comfort, I fell into a deep sleep. I was awoken in the middle of the night by my bed shaking. I thought the nurse had come in to check up on me. The bed trembled slightly but rapidly. It was a weird sensation. My tiredness made me think nothing of it. I was barely awake and ignored it and drifted back off to sleep. I found out the next morning that Japan had undergone a mild earthquake. I had never witnessed one. It was a very odd feeling, to say the least.

In the oncoming days, Mike and Randy had their surgeries. Mike's colon was reinserted with no problems. Randy's gunshot holes were sewn up and healing, and he was getting around much better. I was finally able to maneuver myself in and out of my wheelchair using a wooden board rest to support my leg. I still couldn't bend or move it. I managed to use the bathroom without any help. It was the end of the bedpan and urinal. My wound was healing. The flesh in my thigh got better each day. It went from ugly to a clean reddish color, like a medium-rare steak. The hole was closing, but very slowly. It was still being scrubbed three times a day and kept packed with gauze.

The doctors sent for me to be examined. I was wheeled to their examination room. They helped me onto a table and told me to try to stand up. I said, "I don't think I can." I knew my leg wouldn't support my weight.

"Try," they said. I slowly lowered my feet to the floor, holding my weight up with my arms and right leg. "Let go and stand," one of them said. I let go and tried putting my weight on both my legs, and down I went. They both caught me before I hit the floor. My left leg was still very weak due to the fact that, when they operated, they had to remove a large portion of muscle tissue from my lower thigh also. They saw that I was not able to walk yet and set me back in my wheelchair. They told me not to be too concerned about not being able to stand yet and that I was doing fine but the healing process still had a ways to go. One of them repeated what Dr. Katz had told me in Nam—that he had seen patients die from similar wounds and I was very lucky.

I went back to my room and was frantic about the weight I had lost, so I started using the dumbbells more frequently. The more my leg healed, the stronger it got; and before long I was able to stand on my own and walk very slowly. Mike and I had Randy take a picture of us standing side by side. He used a Polaroid camera that he had. I looked at the photo and said, "Man, Mike, look how thin I got."

"What? Are you kidding?" he said. "You make me look like I ain't even there." He made me laugh, but it didn't help with the fact that I had lost forty pounds since my injury. I had worked so hard for the past seven years to put weight on, and losing it like that did not make me very happy. In my mind, I was comparing it to a couple of pictures that had been taken of me two months prior to my seven-

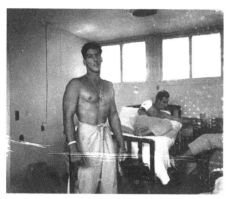

Me, finally able to stand and 40 pounds lighter.

teenth birthday. I was walking on Boston Road, and a stranger walked up to me who said his name was Willie. He had a French accent, and he asked me if I would let him take some pictures of me. I told him I didn't mind. So he came home with me, and he took two shots of me posing in my backyard: one with no shirt on and one with me wearing an undershirt. I didn't think it was weird. I had people and kids walk up to me every day and ask me questions. Kids would follow me. Some called me a freak, but I ignored them. Back then, I had a fifty-two-inch chest and a twenty-six-inch waist, which was very rare. I looked like an hourglass with feet. This guy Willy would come to visit me on occasion. He gave me the pictures. They came out pretty good. Now with my present condition, I wondered if I would ever be able to work out hard and heavy again.

The recuperation and the regaining of strength made me more and more anxious about going home. The time for the baby to come was getting closer. My hopes of being there in time were growing. I received mail from home. Somehow, they had found out about me. My little ploy about being a janitor was blown.

Me before my 17th birthday taken by Willie in the back yard of my house.

276

In one of the letters, my sister wanted to take a trip to Japan and visit me. I decided that I would put the question to the doctors the next time they came to see me. I was still concerned about going back to Nam. Some of the guys were healed up and sent back to their units to finish their tour.

When the doctors did come, I asked them if I was going to be sent back to Vietnam. "No. You're finished with Nam," one of them said.

"Doc, my wife is due to have a baby any day. Do you think that I could get to go home soon?"

To my surprise, he answered, "You want to go home? Sure, I'll send you right home." At first, I thought he was pulling my leg, but then he said, "I'll make the arrangements." Talk about good news. Man, that was the ultimate. I was finally going home to stay.

In my excitement, I wanted to let Marilyn know about the good news. I asked for a phone to be brought to me. They granted my request, and I called my mother-in-law's number collect, hoping that Marilyn would answer. She didn't. My mother-in-law did, and being the penny-pinching person that she was, she refused the call. Well, I have to tell you, I was pissed. I wrote a letter to Marilyn, and in it, I called her mother just about any name I could think of. I probably should have waited until I calmed down, but I didn't. It really was a nasty letter. It was, by far, out of character. I did like my mother-in-law; she was a good person, and she didn't deserve that treatment. It just goes to show you that anger and spur-of-the-moment actions can really bring out the evil in someone and cause unwarranted hurt.

Before I gave back the phone, I called my sister and told her it wasn't necessary for her to make the trip and that I would be home soon. I also wanted to know how my two nephews (Anthony, who was four, and Jon, who was two) were doing. She told me they were doing great, as was my brother-in-law, Jack.

The following days filled me with the anxiety of going home. Representatives from the Red Cross and the Salvation Army helped pass the time. They sat with me and played cards or just talked. I was also visited by an Army liaisons officer who asked me to sign forms concerning my disability case for when I got out of the service. He told me that it would make the processing of paperwork much easier if I did it now while I was still in service. Some of the GIs said, "Fuck it, I just want out." They were making a big mistake. They were missing out on something that they had earned and deserved: a disability pension for the rest of their lives. My mother didn't raise no fool. I wasn't about to be stupid. I was happy to cooperate. He also asked me what Army fort was closest to my home. I told him, "Fort Dix, New Jersey."

CHAPTER XVIII

GOING HOME

The big day came: November 16, exactly one year from the day I entered the service and my mother's birthday. What better gift could a mother ask for? I was still not ambulatory and couldn't hang my leg over a chair to sit. I would have to remain on a stretcher for the trip home. Now came the downer of the good news of leaving. I had to say goodbye to Randy and Mike. The two of them had turned out to be true friends. They really helped me get through my ordeal. I was going to miss them dearly.

I was going back to the States on another C-130 being used for a medevac cargo plane, which carried a multitude of stretcher patients. It was like a replay of my trip from Nam to Japan. The engines roared; the plane lifted off; and I knew, at last, that it was all behind me. From then on, Vietnam and all its horrific experiences that I and countless others had to endure would just be a memory.

So many thoughts ran through my mind on the long journey home. It was constantly dark and noisy inside the monster plane, so all one could do if not sleep was to think. I thought about the night Marilyn and I had that argument about me going to help friends if they needed me and how mad she had gotten when I told her I wouldn't hesitate to risk my life for theirs. Who would have thought of that scenario actually becoming a reality? How weird was that?

On a lighter side, I remembered when Tony and I were on our way to a party near Fordham. He was driving his car; and when we got to the corner of Webster and Fordham, I saw a girl I knew named

Pat standing at the bus stop. She was with another girl, who looked hot. I told Tony, "Pull over. I know that girl." I got out and greeted Pat, then I asked them if they would like to go to a party with us. They said, "Sure."

Pat said, "John, this is my sister, Marie."

"Hi, Marie. As you already heard, I'm John." Then I grabbed Marie by her hand and said, "Come on, you're with me." She was a pretty girl. She filled out the jeans she had on that said, "Come and get me," so I went and got her. We got in the car, and the four of us spent the night together. The point of the story is that when we were at the party, Marie and I were making out in the stairwell of the apartment building. I put my hands on her breasts, and she let me do it. It was the first time I ever felt a girl's teats. We left the party and drove them home. It was a nice and memorable experience for me. Thank you, Marie, wherever you are.

The plane arrived in Boston, Massachusetts, the following day in the early evening. It was dark, and when I was rolled off the plane into a building, a camera and spotlight were aimed directly down on me and followed me until I got through the doors. They did the same with the others. Some TV news program was doing a special on wounded GIs evacuated from Nam. I never did get to see it.

I stayed in Boston overnight. The next day, I flew on a small private plane with a nurse and three other patients, all on stretchers. The flight was nauseating. I tried to stay on my side to keep from throwing up. I glanced out the window, and there it was: the New York skyline. What a sight to behold.

We landed at Kennedy Airport, and I was taken by ambulance to Saint Alban's Naval Hospital in Queens. It turned out to be better. I thought that Fort Dix was the closest to my home. I had never heard of Saint Alban's. Somebody had done me a favor. Queens was only a hop, skip, and jump from my place in the Bronx.

They placed me in a large ward filled with Nam evacuees. The fellow on my right had one leg missing all the way to his hip. The guy two beds down to my left had both legs missing to the hip. He was amazingly high spirited and must have been there quite a while. He was able to get around rather well in a wheelchair. It appeared that he had come to grips with his loss of both legs for the time being. Who knows? Maybe the dead were the lucky ones. They didn't come back half a man or lie with the mental and physical anguish of the loss of body parts many had to live with.

I called home as soon as I could. It didn't take long for Marilyn and my family to get there. Marilyn came with Cliff, a friend of ours, who lived in our building. Joe Trongone drove my father. My mother and sister stayed at home. It was just so great to see them and to see Marilyn's stomach puffed out, which I never thought that I'd get to do. They wanted to see my leg. I warned them that it wasn't very pretty. I'll never forget the look on my father's face when he saw the wound. He didn't say anything and turned and walked over to the opposite bed, but I knew what he and the other visitors were thinking after gazing at my injury and looking around the room and seeing all the young soldiers missing limbs. I also knew what Marilyn was thinking by the look on her face and her attitude. She didn't greet me like I was expecting her to. Instead of that happy and "it's so great to have you home" reception, she was cold and barely put her arms around me. I thought to myself, *Oh. Here we go. She's pissed about the letter I sent, cursing out her mother.*

They stayed and visited for a while, and after they left, Cliff told Marilyn that he would wait out in the car. She pulled out the letter from her bag; and before she went off, I told her, "Look, I know what you're going to say. But before we get into an argument, I just want to apologize for what I wrote. I was so mad, and I shouldn't have said all those nasty things about your mother. It was bad what I wrote. Tell her I'm sorry for it. And when I get home, I'll tell her myself."

She calmed down and capped off the conversation with "Okay, but don't ever say anything like that about my mother again!"

"No, don't worry, I won't." With all that was said, at least she left on a happier note than when she came.

I made friends with a guy to my left. His name was Bruce. I was able to walk, so he and I would go to the physical therapy room together and use their equipment. The next time I spoke to Marilyn, I asked her to get ahold of Mike Cotter to bring in my dumbbells from home so I could work out in bed. I was regaining my strength rapidly, and within two and a half weeks, I had put twenty pounds back on.

One morning, while I was walking down the long corridor to the cafeteria, I was nudged from behind. To my surprise, it was Mike Labate. "Holy shit, Mike, when did you get here?"

"Last night."

"What about Randy? What happened to him?"

"He's okay. They sent him close to his home in Cal."

"Damn, it's good to see you, Mikey. Did they tell you when you'd be going home?"

"Yeah, in two days."

Mike got his medical discharge and went home two days later. For the second time, I said goodbye to him. I never saw him again. But I think about him and all the other good friends I made during my stay in the Army, hoping that someday we will meet up to rehash our friendships and talk about those days when all we had was one another.

After three weeks of therapy and recuperation, I was walking much better with the use of a cane. At my request, I was granted my thirty-day convalescent leave. I went home on December 9, the day before Marilyn gave birth. I squared away with my mother-in-law, and all was fine. In fact, it went even better that I thought it would.

We all enjoyed playing cards, especially poker. That night, we were playing. I sat out, sitting behind Marilyn and watching. The game was five-card draw. Celia (my mother-in-law), Aggie (Marilyn's aunt), and Cliff's mother (Madeline) and her boyfriend (Pete) were the other participants. They dealt the five cards, and Marilyn picked up her hand, and unlike an experienced poker player who would squeeze out their hand, she sloppily picked up her five cards and quickly separated them in her hand. I sat up, and my eyes opened widely at what I saw. Four aces. I know it was just a friendly nickel-and-dime game, but you normally wouldn't expect that to happen. It was comical the way it happened.

During the game, at around 11:00 PM, Marilyn started getting stomach pains. She was due anytime. The pains got worse, so she went to lie down. I went with her. We called her pediatrician, Dr. Slutsky, and told him what was going on. He told us to time the pains and, if they got five minutes apart, to get her to the hospital. They only lasted a short time, and then she felt better. It was a false alarm.

December 10 proved to be a different scenario. That night, around 9:00 PM, again during a card game, the labor pains started, and they got worse rapidly. In less than an hour, Marilyn's water broke, and I rushed her to Park Chester General Hospital on Zerega Avenue, which was only fifteen minutes away. They called Dr. Slutsky, and he met me there. It was 10:30 PM. The staff took her right in, and he went in to do his thing. I paced the floor with my cane. The place was empty. I was the only one there. The doctor came out in less than a half an hour wearing his green operating robe and head covering. He undid the elastic straps around his ears that held his mouth mask in place and removed it. He was sweating when he came over to shake my hand and congratulate me on the birth of my healthy six-pound-five-ounce baby girl. He told me everything went great and that Marilyn was doing fine. I thanked him and asked if I could see them. He said, "Sure." I went in to see the baby. The nurse brought her to the glass window so I could get a good close-up look and, with her fingers, gently pulled the wrappings from the baby's face. She was so tiny and so cute. I'd always heard that people check to see if their newborn babies have all their fingers and toes. So I found myself counting them. They were all present and accounted for. Then I went to check up on Marilyn. She was half asleep, so I didn't want to disturb her.

Marilyn and I had agreed that if it was a boy, we'd name him John. If it was a girl, we'd name her Dawn Marie. So that night, December 10, 1967, at 11:12 PM, little Dawn Marie Fratangelo was

Me holding my daughter
Dawn Marie while
on convalescent leave.
December, 1967.

born; and the bullet wound I received in Nam got me home in the nick of time to see it happen.

Marilyn and the baby came home three days later. My leg was still very weak and needed nursing. The hole in it was not completely closed and had to be cleaned and have fresh packing inserted. I had shown Marilyn how to clean it with peroxide and the correct way of packing it and bandaging it. I taught her all that, and she taught me how to change the baby's diapers.

We both were lucky. Little Dawn was such a good baby. She took regular naps and slept through the night. She was also a very quiet baby. She hardly ever cried. This was good because we were staying in the back bedroom of her mother's apartment, and it was quite crowded. For the first two weeks, I rarely came out. Marilyn even brought me my breakfast, lunch, and dinner into the room. I don't know why, but I was almost like a hermit. Maybe I had to get used to family living again. Celia used to tell Marilyn to tell me to come out and join them. One morning, I made up my mind to act human again and mingle with my in-laws.

One afternoon, I was surprised by an unexpected visitor. It was Richie, the fellow who came to see me after my first surgery in Nam, the one who brought me comic books and writing materials. I had given him Marilyn's address. I introduced him to Marilyn. We sat at the kitchen table and talked. He told me that he re-upped and volunteered to go back to Nam as a chopper gunner. "Why the hell do you want to do that?" I asked, shaking my head in disbelief.

He said, "John, I just gotta go back. I lost too many friends."

"Richie, are you sure? Man, think about what you are doing. What about your family, what did they say?"

"I know, I had it out with them. But it's something that I need to do. That day, when I saw you laid up in pain, was when I made up my mind."

I tried my best to talk him out of it, but he was fixed on getting revenge. He stayed for about an hour and got up to leave. He told me that he didn't want to go back without seeing me and telling me what he was going to do. There was nothing I could say or do but wish him luck and say goodbye. Before he left, he wanted to see the baby. Marilyn brought Dawn out, and Richie gave the baby a kiss. I put my arms around him and whispered in his ear, "Richie, you take care of yourself, my good friend!" I never saw or heard from him again. I can only pray that he made it back alive. I wish I could remember his last name. I'd be able to know closure.

After my thirty-day leave, I returned to Saint Albans and was put back on duty. I commuted back and forth daily, in civilian clothes, and worked in the hospital cleaning test tubes that had been used for blood tests. I'd get up at six o'clock every morning to the sound of the radio alarm playing the song "Light My Fire" by the Doors. I'd give Marilyn and the baby a kiss; and after a quick cup of instant coffee and a piece of cake, I'd drive to Queens. I worked from 8:00 AM to 3:00 PM. It was like having a civilian job. The drive was long enough to give me a chance to wake up and listen to music. It was like clockwork. Every morning, the same songs would come on at the same time. One favorite was a song that had the lyrics "Woman, have you got cheating on your mind" ("Woman, Woman") sung by Gary Puckett and the Union Gap. How the words to that song would come to play out big-time in my life.

CHAPTER XIX

FORT DIX

I did this for a whole month; and then in March of '68, I received my orders to report to Fort Dix, New Jersey, to finish out my nine months of active service. Unlike Mike, I was not eligible for a medical discharge. Fortunately, I was able to obtain Army quarters on the base. It was an attached private brick home. It had two stories. The fort was sectioned off in nicely developed neighborhoods. My area was known as Sheridanville. We moved in and familiarized ourselves with the neighborhood.

I reported to the Second Brigade Headquarters Detachment and was told to bring all my medical records to the records building. I hand-carried them there and gave them to the clerk. I watched him file them and left.

I guess there wasn't much that they could do with me. I couldn't be used for training because of my leg, so they made me a mail clerk along with three other Vietnam returnees: Simone, Anthony (Augie), and Charley. The sergeant in charge was Sergeant Garcia. At first glance, I could see that Garcia and I weren't going to hit it off by the way he looked at me. I had grown my hair long, and he wasn't liking it.

The four of us got to know one another well. Simone was from New Jersey and was a dance instructor. He was also about to get out of the Army in a matter of days. Augie was from Long Island and wanted to open a women's clothing store and was going to call it Femme Fatales. I don't recall anything personal about Charley.

Our job was to go to the main post office on the fort and pick up the sacks of mail and packages, twice a day. It was for the entire brigade, which included six battalions with five companies per battalion. That's a lot of mail. The morning run was the worst. There were multiple canvas sacks filled to the brim with letters. We'd do the loading and unloading.

In the mail room there was a wooden rack divided into thirty compartments labeled from A-1 to A-5 all the way to F-1 to F-5. The rack was on top of a bench, where we'd dump out the sacks of mail one at a time. Then two of us would stand and sort the letters to their corresponding cubicles. This took hours; and as soon as we got through, we'd have to go for the afternoon run. At least that didn't have anywhere near the amount of mail as the morning run. We literally sorted thousands of letters every day. It got so we were able to do it without looking. I swore I'd never look at another letter for as long as I lived.

Now the packages were a little different. There were five rows of racks with six large canvas sacks hung on hooks in the open position and labeled just like the letter rack. One of us dumped out a bunch of packages onto a table facing the rows of racks. Then we'd get to practice our two-point shots by tossing them into the sacks. If the package was marked fragile, we'd hand-carry it and place it carefully into the sack; or if it was too big to toss, we'd carry it over and fit it in manually.

Augie and I got to talking; and after me telling him about my platoon getting ambushed, he told me what happened to him. Here's his story: "We were out at night, and we came under fire. We were pinned down, and the VC played a message over a loudspeaker. They told us to give up. They said, 'Hey, you, Joe. You surrender or you die.' And kept repeating it over and over. I got so pissed that I stood up and shouted out, 'Fuck you.' I no sooner finished cursing them out when I got shot in the back."

"Holy shit, Augie," I said, "that's like a scene out of a movie I saw, *Bataan*. The same exact thing happened. You were lucky. The guy in the movie wasn't."

We'd work until five o'clock, and then I would go home. We started to get to know our neighbors. To our left was a young couple from Rochester, New York: Bob and Charlotte; they had a little dog named Patches. Charlotte was pregnant. Bob was an E-5. Two houses down to our left lived a staff sergeant, Tom, who was married to a Japanese woman named Petee. That woman shined her floors to the point of seeing yourself in it as clear as day. She was immaculate. To our right was another staff sergeant, Jim, and his wife, Maggie.

It didn't take long from that point in time for my marital nightmare to pick up where it left off. Marilyn started with her jealous tantrums. If I was watching television and female dancers happened to come on, she'd get up and stand in front of the TV to block my view. Then she'd say, "We don't need to look at this," and she'd change the channel. If we happened to go out for dinner and there was an attractive waitress, I couldn't look up at the waitress to order my dinner. God forbid if I did, she'd make a scene; so rather than go through the embarrassment and the risk of arguing for the entire evening, I'd order with my face staring in the menu. She'd constantly keep her eye on me to see if I gazed up at any girl, no matter where we were. If we were walking and a girl passed by, she'd turn toward me and start any old stupid conversation just to make sure I didn't turn my head. She was bad. It was like being in prison when I was with her. I was not a happy camper. She made me wish that I was back in Nam.

Between working in that damn mail room, I had to attend physical therapy three times a week at the fort's Walson Army Hospital. I had no more need for my cane. My leg was getting stronger and was almost completely healed. I just walked with a slight limp. Part of my therapy was to sit on a machine with my leg hanging. The attendant hooked up some wires attached to a rubber mat. He would place the mat over my knee and thigh and then set the machine for a certain amount of voltage. It worked on a timing basis. Every so many seconds, an electrical charge was transmitted from the machine to the muscles of my thigh. This caused the contraction of my thigh muscle, which lifted my leg. It felt like a bunch of pins and needles. When the charge finished, my leg relaxed. The machine's power dial went from 0 to 10. It had the capability of breaking a bone if set too high. My leg was so weak that the attendant set it almost to its highest setting. There was no way a person could fake having a weak leg while on that machine. You had no control. This, along with exercise, was very instrumental in strengthening my leg.

One afternoon, I was driving on my road back to my quarters. I spotted a familiar face just up ahead of me. He was washing his car. I got closer, and sure enough, it was Sergeant Santos. I stopped the car right in the middle of the road, got out, and greeted him with open arms. I couldn't believe it. Talk about a small world. He told me that he was temporarily stationed at Fort Dix. We were so happy to see each other.

We got together the very next day. He and his wife and two girls came over to my place. Naturally, we spoke of our time back in Nam. He asked me if I had ever received the medal he put me in for. It was the first I heard of it. "No, what medal? For what?" I asked. He told me that he recommended me for the Bronze Star with a V cluster for my actions on the day Ronnie was killed. He said that the paperwork had been approved and that I should have gotten it. I said, "All I did was carry him a short distance. How does that warrant a medal?"

He said, "You and Baker both took a risk with the enemy near, and I felt it deserved a medal."

I told him, "I don't know about Baker, but I never got it."

It may sound crazy, but as we spoke, we mentioned how much we missed the platoon and the closeness we all had and felt for one another. I asked him what his future plans were. He told me that after twelve years, he was getting ready to leave the service and go back to Peru. He was leaving in a few days. He loved the Army. He didn't want out, but it had taken its toll on his wife, leading her to multiple attempts on her life. I guess he didn't have any choice.

This may be hard for you to believe, but it's true. The very next day, I was once again on my way home, and who do I see walking up the road dressed in his class As? Woody. "This can't be happening," I said as if someone was in the car with me. I jammed on the brakes and hopped out of the car. We both looked at each other in disbelief. "Woody," I shouted, "is that you?"

He yelled back, "Pizza, I don't believe it. Man, how the fuck are you?"

"I'm fine. Holy shit, I don't believe this." I told him to get in the car and that there was someone I wanted him to see. I drove him down the road to Santos's place. Talk about a reunion. That was amazing. When Santos saw Woody, he couldn't believe his eyes. Right before him stood his two machine gunners. He told Woody, "You were a real good soldier, but you had a bad attitude. Did you change, or are you still as wild and crazy?"

Woody said, "Yeah, man, I'm still that crazy bastard you knew and loved."

Woody filled us in on why he was there. He rotated out from Nam at the end of April and was assigned to the Third BCT Brigade at Fort Dix and was going to NCO school to become a drill sergeant. I invited them over for dinner. Santos had plans, but Woody was able to come. I drove him to his quarters to get changed, and then we went back to my place. I introduced him to Marilyn and Dawn. She made dinner, and we sat around talking over old times. He told me that his feet had finally healed from that jungle rot. He ended up staying in Dix for six months and then was transferred to Fort Carson in Colorado.

That short reunion, which happened by chance and coincidence, gave three old friends the opportunity to get together and rehash some memorable times and to say goodbye, probably for the last time. I knew I'd never see Santos again; but I was hoping that I would run into Woody now and then. I have to say, they were damn good soldiers and even better friends.

The meeting up with Santos and Woody got me thinking about the guys back in Nam. I wrote a letter to Eddie. I wanted to know how everyone was doing. I gave him my address, hoping that he'd write back. I updated him on my situation about the baby and all and told him about my uncanny run in with Santos and Woody.

Back in the mail room, it was time for Simone to leave. There was another goodbye to be said. The three of us wished him the best of luck. A funny thing about saying goodbye to someone who wasn't in the thick of things together with you than to those who were was that it didn't have that special touching, sentimental feeling. Augie took over as head honcho of the mail room. His attitude changed when he became in charge. He was more spit shine and polish. It was as if he thought who the hell he was. He kind of reminded me of Gomer back in basic but not quite as bad. The difference was that we were not trainees. We were experienced combat vets, and a combat vet won't stand for being talked down to.

A couple of weeks passed, and Sergeant Garcia came down to inspect the mail room, along with some colonel. That's one part of the Army we didn't have to worry about in my recon platoon. Inspections didn't exist. I was sitting in my usual place in the back of the room. The colonel looked at me and, moving his head in my direction, asked Garcia, "Who's that guy back there with the long hair? I want him out of here." Garcia never had any love for me anyway because of my hairstyle, so it was a pleasant task for him to arrange for my transfer. After the colonel finished his stupid inspection and left, Garcia walked over to me and told me that he'd be getting rid of me real soon. As if I really gave a shit.

When I got home that night, Marilyn was upset. I asked her what was wrong. She said that she didn't want to tell me, but it was bothering her. "Well," I said, "tell me already."

She went on to explain, "Our neighbor Tom came over and was making advances on me."

"Are you serious? He doesn't seem like the type of guy that would do that, especially with his wife two doors down. What did he do?" I asked her in anticipation of her answer.

Then she said, "I'd rather not say, but you better go and have a talk with him." So I went over to his place and knocked on the door. He answered, and I told him that I needed to talk to him. He invited me in, and I went right to the point. I told him what Marilyn had said. He denied it and got somewhat defensive. I raised my voice and told him to stay the fuck away from my wife. He pointed to the door and told me to get out of his house. I went back and told Marilyn that he wouldn't be bothering her anymore. I just hoped that I didn't falsely accuse him of something that Marilyn made up. After that inci-

291

dent, Tom must have put in for a transfer because, shortly after that incident, he and Petee ended up moving out. Another married couple moved into their place, a black sergeant and a white German girl.

It was mid-May when something happened in the mail room. I was sitting in my spot, listening to the radio. Garcia showed up by the doorway with a piece of paper in his hand. He handed the paper to Charley and Augie to read. I was thinking that it was my transfer papers that he was so eager to get. As they were reading it, they glanced up at me and then continued reading. Now, by seeing that, I thought for sure it was about me leaving.

After they all finished reading it, Garcia called me over to him and handed the paper to me, saying, "I'm not supposed to show you this." I read what was written and then gave it back. It was special orders that I was to receive the Silver Star. The citation explaining the basis of the medal accompanied the order. Garcia asked me, "Is this true?"

I simply said, "Yes," as if it was no big deal and returned to my seat. It was placed in the Fort Dix Army Post newspaper. The citation read as follows:

Award of the Silver Star
4 October 1967
Republic of Vietnam

For gallantry in action against a hostile force: On this date, during Operation Shenandoah II, Specialist Fratangelo was serving as a machine gunner on a search-and-destroy mission in War Zone C. The battalion established a night defensive position and sent out a reconnaissance patrol to clear the area surrounding the perimeter. Specialist Fratangelo was a member of the patrol. It had moved approximately three hundred meters through the dense jungle area when it was suddenly engaged by a numerical superior Vietcong force. During the initial barrage, the unit sustained numerous casualties and requested reinforcements. Specialist Fratangelo immediately moved to a forward position from which he directed a devastating volume of automatic weapons fire upon the advancing insurgents. His actions enabled the remainder of his patrol to redeploy and move on line. He continued firing upon the enemy until his machine gun suddenly malfunctioned and could not be repaired. With complete disregard for his personal safety, he ran throughout the Vietcong kill zone searching for and evacuating casualties. He made five trips from the kill zone to the rear area, carrying wounded men on his back. As he was carrying his sixth man from the kill zone, he was wounded and was evacuated. His bold initiative and exemplary courage significantly contributed to the redeployment of his unit into the most advantageous firing positions and to the saving of numerous lives. Specialist Four Fratangelo's unquestionable valor while engaged in military operations involving conflict with an insurgent force is in keeping with the finest traditions of the military service and reflects great credit upon himself, the 1st Infantry Division, and the United States Army.

By direction of the president, as established by an Act of Congress, 9 July 1918, and USARV Message 16695, dated 1 July 1966.

For the Commander:
Frederick C. Krause
Official: Colonel, GS
Chief of Staff
S. F. Tomasek
Captain, AGC
Assistant Adjutant General

When I got home, I told Marilyn about the news and that they were going to have the presentation on Armed Forces Day just a week and a half away. I said, "I'm going to call my folks and tell them to come."

She said, "No, I don't want them here."

"What the hell do you mean you don't want them here?" One word led into another, and we had an all-out battle. She was screaming at the top of her lungs. "If they come, I won't go!" Marilyn had a way of getting me to the breaking point. I had to control my temper. So much was built up inside me. Once again, to keep the peace and to shut her up without busting her jaw and for Dawn's sake, I gave in and agreed that I wouldn't tell my family.

Me receiving the silver Star from General Kenneth W. Collins on May 28th 1968.

Me, second from left after receiving the Silver Star.

On May 21, 1968, Armed Forces Day, I was awarded the Silver Star. There were two others who also received the medal, and an award of Sergeant of the Year was presented to a staff sergeant. It was the most thrilling day of my life. It was a cool, breezy, overcast day. The entire fort honored the four of us. At first, they lined us up in front of the grandstand, facing out toward the open field. The general noticed my limp and came up to me and asked if I was all right to walk to the center of the stadium. I told him that I was fine.

Marilyn was in the stands with the baby. I would have at least liked Woody to be there, but he had gone home for the long holiday weekend. It really bothered me that no one from my family was there to witness that great day. It was something that Marilyn made me do that I was sorry for, for the rest of my life. I knew my father, being an ex-Marine, would have been so proud.

The ceremony started with the four of us walking to the middle of the field and doing an about-face to look toward the crowd. We were dressed in our class A uniforms. I was standing in the center of us three Silver Star recipients. The sergeant of the year was on the end to our left. The color guard was behind us in a straight line, side by side, also facing the stands and holding all types of flags. They were dressed in khakis and wore white gloves. The military personnel, along with the armor division and motorized vehicles, were all lined up. The band was off to the side in front of the spectators. They opened with the playing of the national anthem.

At the conclusion of the opening song, the general came forward with a sergeant and a girl who was Ms. Fort Dix. He placed a medal on the chest of the sergeant of the year and saluted him as the MC read a letter of accomplishments to honor him. Then the general came and stood in front of each of us; and as he pinned the medal on our chests and saluted, the MC recited our award citations. After that presentation of the medals, we marched to the front of the stands and turned around to face the color guard. The band played a marching song while the entire procession, troops, armored vehicles, and jeeps all paraded in front of us and did an "Eyes, right" and saluted us. We stood at attention until they all passed us by with the flags waving high and proud, honoring us. How ironic was that. There I was, the one guy who had refused and hated to salute, was being saluted by every trooper and officer on that field.

From that day forth, the American flag took on a whole new meaning for me, and I get the chills whenever I see one for I know that the red drops of blood my comrades and I spilt on the battlefield helped color its stripes and kept its glory waving high and proud.

By early June, we got a replacement for Simone in the mail room. His name was Mack. He hailed from Baltimore. We became good friends. He often came over and spent time with me and Marilyn. Marilyn developed a friendship with our neighbor, Charlotte, who was in her fourth month of pregnancy. She and her husband, Bob, were having minor marital problems. His re-upping for the $3,000 bonus didn't help their relationship. Mac took a liking to her, but nothing became of it. He told me that he had feelings for Charlotte and that if their marriage were to break up, he'd be there for her. The more he came around, the stronger his feelings grew. When he saw there was no hope for a relationship, he was hurt and he stopped coming around. We just kept our friendship confined to the mail room.

In late June, Charlotte was rushed to the hospital. She went into labor, and she gave birth to a baby girl who everyone referred to as the "miracle baby." She was born one pound and three ounces. I believe she was the tiniest baby on record at that time. They named her Hope. She had to be incubated for quite some time. It was touch and go, but the precious little bundle from heaven pulled through. It was a joyous occasion when they brought Hope home. I couldn't believe how tiny she was. It truly was a miracle. I think she was the Band-Aid that healed the wound in their marriage. The both of them seemed to be much happier.

The first Monday in July, when I went into work, Sergeant Garcia handed me my transfer papers. The maintenance crew needed a plumber so that's where they sent me. It was the best thing that they could have done for me. I was placed with a bunch of short-timers who were all Vietnam veterans. Maintaining the plumbing on fort beat the hell out of sorting thousands of letters every day.

The following Saturday, my sister, Rose, called me and said that she was going to come and visit us on Sunday. I told her, "Great, I want to show you the medal I got."

She said, "We didn't know you got a medal."

I said, "Yeah, they gave it to me on Armed Forces Day."

Then, naturally, she asked me why I hadn't let them know so they could have been there. I told her that it happened so fast. They told me at the last-minute, and there was no time to call. She wasn't stupid. I knew she knew it was all Marilyn's doing.

When I told Marilyn about Rose coming, she started in with me. And as usual, we had a huge fight. She just hated my sister with a passion. I knew what I was in for come the next day. My sister showed up around noon time with a lady named Agnes. She was the mother of a guy, Jimmy, who was a cop in the Forty-Seventh Precinct in the Bronx and who my sister was dating since her separation from Jack. Agnes owned the Log Cabin Inn in Pelham Bay, where Rose worked as a waitress and hostess.

When they walked in the door, they had bags of groceries with them. That's the way my sister was. She had a heart of gold and would help anybody in need. I thought nothing of it but her wanting to help us out. But Marilyn? Forget about it; she went berserk, screaming and carrying on like a lunatic. She told them to get out. Rather than stand there and argue, they left; but before my sister got out of the door, she turned and yelled back at Marilyn, who had run up the stairs and locked herself in the bathroom, "He'll be my brother longer than he'll be your husband." I just stood there, and I didn't know what to do. I felt bad for them; but I had taken those damn vows, and now I had to live with them.

I checked on Dawn to make sure she was all right. She was in her rocker, dozing off. I thought it best to let Marilyn alone and give her time to calm down. Pinky was curled up in the corner behind a chair and shaking. I picked her up and held her in my lap. I knew Marilyn would come down shortly and act as if nothing had happened. She had gotten her way, and that was all that mattered. She didn't give two shits about what I felt. I was starting to think that she was schizophrenic; she had split personalities. It was inevitable that sooner or later, I was going to have to get her some psychiatric help.

To help keep my sanity, every now and then, I would take out Tony's letters and a letter that I got from David C. back in April and go off by myself and read them. You've all read Tony's letters, but I didn't share David C.'s with you. The following were his words.

April 6, 1968

Johnny—

I read the letter you sent Eddie the other day, and he gave me the envelope so I'd have your address.

I was happy to hear you're doing well and super happy to hear the Mrs. and young Dawn are well too.

We're all getting short now, Johnny. I've got only twenty-five more days here. I'm going to Fort Riley. I hope your leg is all shaped up by now. I hardly even notice the hole in my arm anymore. That was some day, wasn't it? Thank God we didn't get any more killed and wounded than we did. Tex, Funky, Deloge, Nash, Maleski, well, you know—all of them except the ones who came with us are home.

The one's who came with us—Schneider and Craig killed, you and I and Sexton wounded. Eddie and Lundsford had something go wrong with their health, and Rahar got out of the field. Not a perfect record but one I'll always be proud of, I think.

I'm over at jungle devil school now, where we started this whole mess. I do a little teaching, and I'm a company clerk in between times. It makes the time go fast.

My love to your wife and family, Johnny, and my best to you. I hope I'll see you sometime in the States. I'll buy you a turkey loaf dinner with a dozen tropical Hershey bars for dessert.

I understand you live about a block from Sergeant Santos. Tell him 21 Tango says hello. Good old 29er. There aren't many soldiers I've ever known to compare with him—or with you either.

Good luck—
David C., 21 Tango, out

It was just as I said. Marilyn came out from behind closed doors and acted like nothing was wrong. That night when we went up to bed, I got a little hungry; so I went down to get a bite to eat. When I turned on the light in the kitchen, I heard the pitter-patter of the night crawlers that the housing developments were infested with. They were big black water bugs that would race across the room as soon as the light went on. They scrambled across the floor in every which way to get to safety. You could actually hear them climb out of the garbage bag, and in seconds, they would be gone. The Army knew all about that infestation and would send the exterminators over to spray both the outside and inside. I got so used to them that I paid them no mind and just went about my business. Besides, after the bugs I saw in Nam, these weren't anything to be concerned about.

When I went back to bed, I had the most amazing dream I'd ever had in my life. It had to do with Tony. Just to refresh your memory, Tony's death was caused by his PC being blown up by a mine. The dream went as follows:

Tony and I were in a jeep. He was driving, and I was in the passenger side. We were going across an open grassy field and talking. I happened to look to my right, and I saw a lady standing on a slope. She was dressed all in white. I turned to Tony and said, "Tony, stop the jeep!"

"What?" he asked me.

"Stop the jeep. Didn't you see that lady?"

"Where?"

"Over there on the hillside. Stop the jeep. It's Our Lady. It's the Blessed Mother. Stop the jeep!" And as soon as I said that, we ran over a mine and the jeep blew up. We both went flying in the air. Tony went to the left and I went to the right and I landed at the feet of the lady. I tried to look at her face to see who she was, but the light surrounding her was too brilliant and blinded me.

I said, "Who are you? I can't see your face. The light is too bright."

Then the lady told me in a beautiful voice, "Don't look at my face. I want you to turn and look at your cousin Tony!" And when I did, I saw Tony lying on a green hill, face up, with his eyes closed and a peaceful smile on his face.

I guess Our Lady was trying to tell me not to worry about Tony and that he was safe and happy and in good hands. What a dream that was. It was so real, and it helped greatly to ease the pain of his loss. I woke up that morning feeling very good. Who wouldn't after such a blessed encounter?

The following Saturday evening, I had to do CQ duty at the company commander's office. It was the weekend, so all the officers were off. I took Marilyn and Dawn with me to spend the night. We took along some blankets and pillows. I set them up in a chair in the back room. All I had to do was answer the phone in the event someone called. There I was, breaking the rules again. It was quiet; there were no calls. Then at around 11:00 PM, I heard the door open and the sound of two voices—something I never expected to happen. I told Marilyn to keep the baby quiet, and I quickly hustled to the main room, closing the door behind me. It was the company commander and the colonel. I greeted them. They knew me and said, "Fratangelo, everything all right?"

I said, "Yes, sir. No calls, all is quiet." All the while, I was hoping that they didn't venture into the back room. Thank god, Dawn was a quiet baby and never made a peep. They stayed close to an hour. I stayed with them until they left. I don't know if they would have said anything if they had walked in on my family, but I was surely glad that I didn't have to find out.

The base was undergoing reconstruction of the bathrooms in the housing developments. When they got to ours, the workers, who were all retired military, noticed my medals hanging on the wall. They read the citation; and one of them, Louie "What a Set" (that was his nickname), told Marilyn that he seen guys get the Medal of Honor for less. He asked what I did for a living. She told them that I was a plumber. Louie said, "Ask your husband if he wants a job when he gets out. I'll introduce him to our boss, John, who is a contractor."

When I got home, Marilyn relayed the news to me. The following day, I came home for lunch to meet them. They eventually took us to the contractor's home and introduced me. He told me that he'd tell his plumber about me. To make a long story short, I met the plumber, and he told me that when I got out of the Army, to come and see him. He'd have a job for me, and he'd start me out at $4.65 an hour. To me that sounded like a fortune after earning a lousy $125.00 a month in the service. I told him that I was definitely interested and that I'd be there. Now, with that offer in my mind, the time couldn't go by fast enough.

The reconstruction of our bathroom took a couple of weeks, and I remained in contact with all of them. We were invited over to John's house for dinner. He had a Japanese wife named Dee who ran his business for him. They lived in a beautiful ninety-foot red-brick ranch-style home, all on one level. It looked like a king's mansion to us. John had a bad heart, and I could see that the stress of his work was taking its toll. He was only in his late forties and had already had one major heart attack. Dee told us that she was very worried about him and that if he didn't slow down, it would kill him.

One night toward the end of August, our neighbors Bob and Charlotte asked us to go out with them for some drinks at the post's

NCO club. They had gotten a babysitter to watch Hope. I told them that I'd rather stay in with Dawn and told Marilyn to go. So they left at about 7:00 PM. It must have been around 10:00 PM when Charlotte drove home by herself and knocked on my door. She told me that something was wrong with Marilyn. She must have had too much to drink or something. She was out in the street, down the road, tripping out. I grabbed Dawn from her swing, and I placed her on the back seat of my car. I followed Charlette to the spot where Marilyn was. Charlotte had to leave to get back home because the babysitter had to go home. Her husband, Bob and some friend of his were there in the road, trying to get Marilyn to come out of her trance. I got out of the car and approached her. She was looking up at the sky and pointing, saying, "Look at the clowns. Can you see the funny clowns?" Other people were also there trying to help. I told one woman to watch my daughter while I grabbed ahold of Marilyn and took her to the hospital's emergency room. The woman gave me her address and phone number. She assured me that Dawn would be well taken care of until morning and for me not to worry. She knew Bob and Charlotte and where they lived, so I felt comfortable with her watching Dawn.

I drove to the hospital, and they took Marilyn right in. They told me that she must have been given some drug that had caused her to hallucinate. They gave her some kind of sedative to relax her, and we stayed about two hours. I was worried about the fact that I had to leave Dawn with a complete stranger, but I didn't have much choice. I didn't trust Bob or the guy he was with. They were high on something too. And I figured they were the ones that had spiked Marilyn's drink. I knew Charlotte had nothing to do with it.

By the time we got home, it was too late for me to go and pick up Dawn. I called the woman and asked how my daughter was. She told me Dawn was fine and asleep. I asked her if it would be all right with her if I'd come and get Dawn in the morning. She said, "Of course. Don't worry, she will be fine." The next morning, I went to get Dawn. I couldn't thank that lady enough. When I got home,

I told Marilyn, "Now you know why I don't like bars or excessive drinking. And because of it, I had to leave Dawn with a stranger."

I never thought Bob would take part in something like that. I didn't know him that well, and I was able to see why he and Charlotte were having problems. I never trusted him again. I couldn't get angry at Marilyn that time. It wasn't her fault that her drink was tampered with. Regardless of innocence of that incident, I told her that it was time that she got professional help. Whenever she drank, she would get very nasty and impossible to live with. It was always "Just one more drink and we'll go." One more ended up being ten more, and the night would always turn into a nightmare. It was the main reason why I avoided going out. To my surprise, she agreed to go for help. I started to take her to a psychiatrist located in the city of Trenton. We went once a week at $40 a pop.

One week after my twenty-first birthday, my new company sergeant put me in for a promotion. I wanted to make E-5 so when it came time to leave the Army, they would move us and pay the expenses, even if we wanted to move to California.

I stood before a board of five officers. They asked me questions. One of them asked me about routing a specific type of letter and who would be the one to sign it. I stood there with my thumb up my ass and couldn't give them an answer. I saw that they had my records on the table and would peer down at them. They looked at one another when I was unable to respond to their stupid question. Then one of them looked at me and asked, "What position is the bolt in on the M60 machine gun?" Well, that was more like it.

Without hesitation, I said, while gesturing with my hands, "You pull the bolt back and then push it forward." That was the last question they asked me, and they granted me my promotion. I was glad that one of those board members was smart enough to look at my paperwork and realize what my specialty was. I was now a sergeant E-5.

That weekend we went to look for a place to live in Brownsville, not far from the fort, and it was close to where the plumbing contractor had his business. We found a nice brand-new duplex apartment on the second floor. The rent was $95 per month. We moved in on the first of October, and because of my rank, the Army moved us for free.

Halloween rolled around, and we got Dawn her first pumpkin. It was a large round one, almost as big as the baby. I carved it and removed all the guts then scraped it clean. I placed a candle in it. She sat on the table and watched the entire process. I fired up a match, and her eyes followed the path of the flame down into the open head of the pumpkin and on to the wick of the candle. I told Marilyn to turn off the light to enhance the glow. Dawn seemed to be enchanted by the smell and the flickering of the lit candle. It was a pleasant memory.

CHAPTER XX

GETTING DISCHARGED

The first chance I had, I went to see the plumbing contractor about the job he'd said he'd have for me. I told him that I'd be getting out of the Army on November 15 and I could start any day after that. Then he lowered the boom on me. He told me that business was slow and that he wouldn't be able to hire me right now. "Maybe after the winter," he said. I had gone there all hyped up about making a decent salary. Talk about a slap in the face after I had the Army move me and we had settled in an apartment. Now I had no job. I walked away very depressed and thinking, *How could anyone make a promise like that and then not keep it?*

I went home and gave Marilyn the bad news. I told her we'd have to go back to the Bronx. "Call your mother, and ask her if there's an apartment available in her building." She did and there wasn't. I said, "We're not in any position to look around for a place, being so far away. So there's only one thing left for us to do. We could go and live at my mother's for the time being. She has the apartment in the basement we could stay at, and it wouldn't cost us anything." I stressed the fact that we'd have our own private entrance so Marilyn wouldn't have to confront my mother so often and we wouldn't have to worry about looking for a spot to park the car. She thought about it and agreed to make the move. I told her, "We'll stay here until the end of the month, and I'll rent a U-Haul." I called my mother to let her know about our plans, and she was thrilled. So far, so good.

The day of my discharge, I had to report to headquarters to get my papers and sign some forms. I was told to go and pick up my medical records. When I went to retrieve them, the clerk came out from the records room and told me that they weren't there. "What do you mean they're not there? I personally brought them and handed them to you."

Then he said, "I don't know what happened to them, but I can't find them." I left there really pissed off. *All my medical records conveniently misplaced. This Army fucks everybody any chance they get.* The thought of me getting out in a matter of minutes helped me to keep calm. Back at the office, they handed me my discharge papers and some severance pay, and I was out of there. November 15, 1968, the day I waited for, for two years, had come at last.

As much as I despised the Army and lost all trust in our government, run by lying bureaucratic politicians that fatten their pockets at our expense, I have to admit; I learned a lot about life during that time. I learned to appreciate living and the little everyday things that make life pleasurable. To value life, no matter who or what and to be grateful to be alive and thankful for all I have. I saw things and places I will never forget. I made good friends and lost good friends I will never forget. I learned the horrors of war and how it affects men and women in different ways. I'd seen people young and old, who were poverty stricken, beaten down by war. I found out what closeness of men was, regardless of race, color or creed. That everyone bleeds red and I thank All-Mighty God for all He's given me and done for me and for allowing me to be born in America, the greatest country on the face of the earth. But the greatest lesson I learned is the value of true friendship; how the guy next to you would sacrifice his own life to save yours without thinking twice about it.

And never a day shall pass that I will not silently, in my thoughts, return to be with those whom I'd known and loved, whom I laughed and cried with, those whom I had fought with, and those whom I had lost, especially my cousin Tony. Their faces, their voices, their laughter, and their memory will be branded in my mind and heart; and I will carry them with me to my grave. During my lifetime, I can't begin to count how many times I had to say goodbye; and someday, the time will come when I'll have to bid my wife and children ***"THE LAST GOODBYE"***.

The End

The dramatic sequence of events that followed
is another story for another time.

Present day get together after 45 years. David
C., Me, Tex, Deloge and Woody.

ABOUT THE AUTHOR

The author was born, John Joseph Fratangelo on September 1st, 1947 in The South East section of the Bronx, New York. He is of Italian descent, of Catholic religion and is a firm believer in putting God and Jesus first and foremost above all others. He has one sibling, a sister named Rose. At the age of four, he began playing the drums and went on to play professionally by the age of thirteen until the age of nineteen when he was drafted into the United states Army. He indulged in hobbies that consisted of playing baseball, body building, puzzle making and enjoyed building things. He attended De Witt Clinton High School and graduated in 1965. He got married to his first wife, Marilyn at nineteen while in the army and had two children, Dawn Marie and John. After being refused a N.Y. city job for the Department of Sanitation, due to gunshot wounds received in Vietnam, he went through five years of apprenticeship school and became a plumber in local #2 in N.Y.C. He moved to Rockland County while married to his second wife, Dolores and had his third child, Nicole Bernadette and raised two stepchildren, Joe-Joe and Jeannie. He worked at General Motors in Tarrytown N.Y. as a pipefitter leader until they shut down. He now resides in Mahopac, N.Y. Where he lives with and is happily married to his third wife, Judith, and raised two more stepchildren, David and Michael. He is an avid celebrator of Christmas and loves animals, especially dogs of which he treasures his three West Highland terriers, Cody, Marty and Sofia. He invented a talking religious statue of "Moses and the Burning Bush", which lights up and recites "The Ten Commandments" and he created three table top games. And being a highly sentimental person, he personally went to get the three ton boulder that he and his cousin Tony played on as kids in the Bronx and brought it to his home in Rockland and took it with him when he moved to Mahopac, New York and he proudly displays it on his lawn. He wrote this book forty-two years ago, which he never completed the final draft until now.

Lightning Source UK Ltd.
Milton Keynes UK
UKHW021247140720
366520UK00008B/1272